THE ACCIDENTAL STRIKE TEAM

ANDREW NELSON

Published in Australia by Sid Harta Books & Print Pty Ltd,
ABN: 34632585293
23 Stirling Crescent, Glen Waverley, Victoria 3150 Australia
Telephone: +61 3 9560 9920, Facsimile: +61 3 9545 1742
E-mail: author@sidharta.com.au

First published in Australia 2023
This edition published 2023
Copyright © Andrew Nelson 2023

Cover design, typesetting: WorkingType (www.workingtype.com.au)

Andrew Nelson
The Accidental Strike Team
ISBN: 978-1-922958-31-0

*Dedicated to my wife, Maria, whose encouragement
motivated this project from start to finish.*

ABOUT THE AUTHOR

Andrew Nelson wishes he could be cool like Joe Burnett. Unfortunately, Andrew is considerably older and way more pedestrian then Joe. After a successful career as a contract accountant, Andrew left Sydney for the shores of Lake Macquarie with his wife, Maria and their dog Bear.

A rookie with the local RFS brigade and a keen small boat sailor, Andrew found time to write this, his first novel, a dream he had cherished for decades. He hopes you enjoy it!

ACKNOWLEDGEMENT

Special thanks to Sid Harta Publishers
and Kirsty Arnold, editor.

ACKNOWLEDGEMENTS

During the writing of this book, I spoke to many people about details and ideas. I asked odd questions out of the blue. I would like to thank the many friends, acquaintances and professional people who cheerfully engaged with my questions and, without realising, helped me clarify my thoughts.

My thanks also go to my editor, who patiently dealt with my inexperience in the publishing field.

CONTENTS

PROLOGUE

The Foreman watched the two shipping containers being loaded onto the semi-trailer. The driver operated the self-loading cranes with care. He had been advised that he was transporting live chickens. With the worst fire season in Australia's history darkening the sky to the west, he needed no more explanation.

The driver climbed into the truck's cab and started the engine. The Foreman was already on his way down to open the front gate. The truck left the property and started its journey to Newcastle harbour. The regional harbour was closer and more suited to their requirements.

'That's most of the stock gone. The two containers will be loaded onto a supply ship which will take them to the offshore processer outside territorial waters.' The four men looked blankly back at the Foreman. No one had thought they were worth an education. They had been born, raised and were now the property of the facility for life. They were the Foreman's labour force and enforcers.

'OK, ten left. The drugged food should keep them quiet for at least another day. It was easier to drug the lot and separate them while unconscious than prepare two separate meals.' He consulted a clipboard. 'Put number 221, the blond boy, in the van first thing in the morning as I need to take him down to Sydney for the Boss's entertainment. Meanwhile, shitheads, clean this place up.'

He closed the gate and jumped in a 4WD pick-up truck and returned to the house in the centre of a dozen long, galvanised iron sheds set up in two rows marching up the foot of the ridge to the north. The four men turned and began walking up the slope from the gate to the facility. They hadn't expected a lift.

CHAPTER 1

Dangling 70 metres above a burning forest from a helicopter on a top-secret mission. Twenty kilograms of gear swinging on a rope, a metre below his feet.

Joe tried to pretend it was just another day fighting the Gospers Mountain wildfire. The Wollemi pines were older than the dinosaurs and existed only in one secret gorge in the Blue Mountains, west of Sydney, Australia. Joe had been selected as part of the special squad of Rural Fire Service (RFS) and National Parks firefighters chosen to save the two hundred pines left.

Their mission: build an irrigation system within the forest to slow and cool down the advancing fire front. Their destination was a closely guarded secret known only to a select few, but unlike in *Mission Impossible* it was not the message that would burn but the whole forest. Hotter and quicker than ever before in the sixty-million-year history of the trees

Lowered down through a gap in the canopy, the helicopters were struggling to hold station in the swirling conditions created by the fires. The team bounced from one tree to another as they landed in a controlled crash on the forest floor. One moment it was quiet and the air clear, the next swirling smoke still hot from the fires blasted through the forest.

'No injuries from the landing?' the crew leader's voice squawked the radio.

'Number off!'

'One,'

'Two,'

'Three,'

'Four,'

'OK, meet me at the creek above the falls as per the briefing. Bring the gear. Lucky the spring supplying this creek has survived the drought.'

The group gathered round the officer-in-charge beside a spring-fed pool sustaining a small waterfall, before running off as a creek through the floor of the gorge.

'A quick recap. The strainer and intake go in here; we lead the hose down the falls and across the west side of the gorge. Every two metres there is a sprinkler head. We should be able to get a gravity-fed water supply from here down the pipe to the sprinklers. The sprinklers should then moisten the ground and air ahead of the fire front making the fire survivable for the trees.'

'Boss, who thinks this crap up?'

As a landscape irrigation exercise, it wasn't that hard. Of course, the remoteness and the approaching fire front added an extra dimension.

Two hours later the helicopters lowered their harnesses and winched the firefighters to safety. Seated in the helicopter, intercom attached, Fred leaned over to Joe, 'That ascent, with the fire front breathing down our necks, was like riding a manic pendulum on a cranky grandfather clock.' Joe grinned; he always appreciated Fred's commentary.

'At least we didn't have to worry about giving away the secret location. The smoke is so thick from the fire it's like looking through dirty cotton wool out there,' replied Joe pointing out the front of the helicopter. 'Hope the pilot knows where he is going!'

Two hours later, back at their temporary base, 'Well that was one for the books.' Joe sat with Fred, sore, hot and bothered while waiting their turn for a shower.

'Just hope it works. Wouldn't have wanted to go through all that shit just to have the whole lot go up in flames.'

'Fred, no point stressing about it. No one will be able to recce the area for at least another couple of weeks even if we do get rain. Any idea what's next?'

'Mate, it's the RFS, like a combat unit till this shitfight ends. You know, hurry up and wait, then hit the panic button leading to a few hours of craziness, so we can move to another place and wait.'

'And you'd know, wouldn't you Fred?'

'Ha, remember Joe, I tell you about my past I'll have to kill you.'

'Yeah, right, Fred 005'.

'There is supposed to be a briefing at 1800 hours.'

'Good, I'll see you at 6 pm then. Once I am showered, I am going to catch a nap in case we move again straight away.'

Someone was beating a drum. Joe struggled to break through to the surface of consciousness.

'Briefing ten minutes. Everyone to the common room now please.'

Still in a daze, Joe followed the drift of firefighters into the common room.

A map had been tacked to the wall, and the executive types were sitting in chairs across the front of it, facing the room. Joe scoped them out. They were all experienced firefighters. *At least they are letting people lead this clusterfuck who have actually fought fires in the past*, thought Joe. Every firefighter knew and dreaded the politicians and bureaucrats taking command.

'OK, pay attention.'

'This map shows the ridge from Mount White through Mangrove Mountain, across to the Wollombi Valley. The road generally follows the crest of the ridge running 60 km north south. To the west the Macdonald River valley, and to the east of the ridge we have the populated areas of the coastal plain. This is the local government area of the Central Coast and the road gives us our last opportunity to stop this fire before it reaches these areas.

'There are townships and villages scattered along this road where we will commence property protection measures. Where there is open bush, we will be building firebreaks through back-burning and ground clearing. Each truck or unit will be part of a sector. Each sector will have a sector leader who will report back to a divisional commander, who will in return report to us at this command centre. The latest weather information has been pushed through to your firefighter app and will be updated as more comes to hand. We have a weather window to stop this beast. It is small, so it's critical we build a containment line while we can back-burn. One day to back-burn and remove the fuel before the fire front arrives. After that the heat and wind return and back-burning won't be possible.

'A list of units and shifts is posted on the board. Sector leaders please arrange communications with your crew leaders for each truck. Crew leaders please ensure your trucks are fuelled, water tanks are full, that all your crew are operational, and you have adequate welfare supplies.'

*

Joe and Fred scanned the crowd and found their captain. As members of the elite response group they prepared themselves for a detailed briefing of their roles. 'OK, guys, you are back on the bikes. Our job is to act as an advanced lookout and reconnaissance.

'Aerial reconnaissance is struggling to see through the smoke, so it is hoped that you blokes on your trail bikes can help paint a better picture of the fire front. Also, keep a look out for any signs of habitation as there are quite a few off-gridders, old hippies and the like out there.

'We will be supporting the southern half of the line, Upper Hunter the north. Each pair will be posted to a sector, so you will also liaise with the sector leader as well as back to me here at base.

Download your sector to your Firestorm app on your phones. This will give real-time data transfer.

'OK, risk assessment and strategy. We will run through an overall risk assessment and strategy, then I will do a run through by sector to isolate any individual issues requiring attention.'

'Bike team Bravo?' a voice yelled across the room.

'Here,' yelled the captain.

'We just received word a vehicle has been found off the St Albans to Wollombi road. Police have chased up the ownership and it appears we have a pair of hikers on the ground east of the Macdonald River. We need that area cleared immediately so we can start a back-burn. We only have a twenty-four-hour weather window,' an assistant commissioner bawled out at them.

If they couldn't account for the hikers, they couldn't back-burn. No back-burn, no containment line.

'Stupid fucking morons doesn't really cover it, does it?' Joe asked no one in particular.

'We have two hours of daylight, try and make a start. Plan to bivouac at Buckettey Fire Station. I'll have welfare ready for you at 2000 hours. Go, ride, find them,' responded the captain, making a decision on the fly.

'Channel 37, radio in when you are in the area. We should have a search area assigned to you by then.'

Joe and Fred dashed to their bikes. The bikes were fuelled, water was stored and other essential gear packed on the completion of the last assignment. Gear on and a sprint down the B-road across the ridge line. The trail bikes were safe to about 80 km/h on the blacktop. They didn't really come into their own until they entered the bush.

Fifteen minutes later they were at the head of the Rugby fire trail on the ridge to the east of the Macdonald River. Joe radioed in using the intercom in his helmet.

'Bike team Bravo, take the area between the top of the fire trail and west of Mangrove Dam.'

'Map on Firestorm the tracks you cover. We can then coordinate the data with the other teams, live. Weather team estimates you have an hour of light. As discussed, bivouac will be at Bucketty's Fire Station so you are on site first thing in the morning.'

No one found the hikers that evening. Still tired from the Wollemi Pines rescue that morning, bike team Bravo accepted a meal from the catering team. The locals at Bucketty Fire Station took their hospitality duties seriously. A few beers were found in the fridge and a few yarns where told, each one taller than the last. Finally, after Fred fell asleep in his chair, the locals declared the night over and let the boys climb into their cots for a few hours' sleep.

Support was there before the firefighters awoke. Bacon and eggs cooking on the BBQ. The bikes refuelled and the coffee hot. By dawn Fred and Joe were back in the search area. The day dragged on riding one track after another at Control's direction. Visibility was poor to non-existent. The smoke irritated the eyes and throat. By 3 pm the heat was back up and the westerly had started to blow again.

'Targets found and evacuated. Bike team Bravo stand down and return to Mangrove Mountain Base.'

'Reckon they'll get the back-burn in, Joe?'

'Reckon that ship has sailed. We just moved from a SNAFU to a full-on clusterfuck.'

'SNAFU?'

'Yeah, Fred, it's an accounting term, Situation Normal All Fucked Up.'

'It's been nearly two weeks, now I am really over this shit,' grumbled Fred.

'There's some great coffee at Tommy's Café, the biker's café on the way back.'

'Mate, it feels like we're the only ones available, everyone else has gone home.'

'Fred, the whole fucking eastern side of the fucking state is on fire. That's about a 2000 kilometre-long fire front. No one's getting a chance to bloody well tie their boot laces never mind going home and getting a good night's sleep. All hands on fucking deck. And then we have entitled arseholes like these two hikers, who wouldn't lift a finger to help anyone else, fuck-up our only real chance of stopping this monster.'

Fred knew there was no point arguing with Joe. Especially since he agreed with him. It was frustration and exhaustion speaking. 'That café you mentioned, would it still be open?'

'Yeah, it's only fifteen minutes back towards Mangrove Mountain.'

'Well at least there is only one road through, the rest are just tracks. Even you couldn't get lost.'

Joe knew his mate was teasing him to pull him out of the mental doldrums the seemingly endless fight against the monster fire triggered. He pulled out into the road and headed back towards the base. Halfway back, Tommy's café appeared through the gloom. The old service station still sold fuel, but its main business was keeping the bikers and car clubbers who cruised the back road fuelled with caffeine and pastries.

The café was called Tommy's so everyone called the owner, cook and chief dishwasher, Tommy, even though it was common knowledge he had bought the business and kept the former name.

Tommy was arguing with a couple of young men in bespoke hiking gear. 'Leave, you're not welcome here, we will not serve you.'

'Fuck off you old refo,' replied one of the men leaning menacingly over Tommy.

'Hey what's going on here?' yelled Joe.

'This upstart won't serve us.'

'Don't worry, his coffee's probably shit anyway,' added the second man. 'Let's get back, I want to put in a complaint about those arseholes who kicked us out of the park.'

'Who kicked you out of where?' asked Joe, his interest piqued.

'Some of your RFS mates. We wanted to get some selfies with the fire in the background, but they forced us to leave. We are going to sue them. Fuck them.'

'You know, you arseholes stopped us from back-burning. It was our only chance of stopping the fire. No wonder Tommy won't serve you.'

'Mate, your incompetence is not my problem, if you blokes did your jobs, the whole thing would be over now. Fuck off.'

'I suggest you leave,' said Fred politely. In his mind he could hear a whistle blowing; it was the steam blowing out of Joe's ears.

Joe stepped forward, one of the men pushed him back, Joe pretended to trip and flung his arm out to stop his fall. It was the arm he was holding his helmet with, it swung round as he windmilled and smashed into the side window of the men's top-of-the-line Porsche SUV. The window shattered.

'What the fuck,' shrieked the man who had been yelling at Tommy. 'You gunna pay for that, arsehole.'

'Sorry, mate, he pushed me,' said Joe, pointing at the second man. 'Take it up with him.'

Fred was still wearing his helmet. He tapped the small cylinder on top. 'Got it all here on film. Reckon we have you guys for assault.'

'You better get yourselves a bloody good lawyer,' retaliated the first man, climbing into the driver's seat of the Porsche. His mate looked around, Fred tapped his helmet attachment again and the second protagonist climbed into the passenger seat. The Porsche roared off.

'Fred and his magic torch. When did it become a camera?' asked Joe.

'Since it needed to be,' replied Fred, deadpan.

'I feel better for that,' sighed Joe. 'Hope that doesn't make me a bad person?'

Tommy answered for Fred, 'No, it makes you a pair of dudes with a free lunch.'

The two riders relaxed with an Australian late lunch: pies, chips and coffee. Both men had eyed off the beers in the fridge but realised this was not the time or place, especially as they were still in uniform. Even if those uniforms looked and smelt a bit the worse for wear.

Time to head back to base for a debrief and hopefully a stand-down order so they could sleep in their own beds that night.

CHAPTER 3

'You have to be out of your mind. You could get killed, or worse.'

'That's bullshit coming from you. I have seen you sniffing round The Cross pretending to be a Salvo,' Sara Jane responded.

Jessica took a deep breath. *That's the trouble with little sisters – they grow up*, she thought.

'But wait, was I that obvious?'

'I'm your bloody sister, I have been watching you for twenty-six years. But, it's good to see you cops are starting to take an interest in these disappearances.'

It was no coincidence that Jessica was stalking the streets of Sydney's Kings Cross. As an investigative, independent journalist, her sister, Sara Jane, had hit home with her article questioning the disappearance of invisible people, those that no one misses when they disappear. As an undercover cop it was Jessica's job to verify and stop whatever was happening.

The Cross, as it was affectionately known, had been sanitised and gentrified as opposed to its heady days of the mid-twentieth century. However, there was still a lot happening and a lot of opportunity for the greedy and sleezy to make a quick buck.

'The disappearances I spoke about in that article are only the tip of the iceberg. These people are targeting all the invisibles: tourists who have outstayed their visas; international students attending shonky private colleges, especially from countries where the locals don't trust the authorities; runaways whose families have written them off as druggies; and worse. The organisation is also selective harvesting, taking a few people from here, a couple from there, and one from somewhere else, making the pattern hard to follow.'

'The strangest thing,' Sara Jane continued,' is that some of them return ten to twelve months later not knowing where they have been or what they have done. The ones that return, that I have tracked down, have all been female. They have all come back physically healthy but mentally broken.

'Actually, I wouldn't say broken so much as cowed. You know, timid or intimated, subservient maybe subdued? But definitely not themselves.'

'Any medicals done on these returnees?' queried Jessica on a hunch.

'Not yet, that's my next step. But these girls are scared, so I haven't had any luck gaining their confidence. And I know what you're thinking.'

'Baby farming? Human trafficking of babies that have never existed in the system?'

'That's my guess, Jess. To make it work these people must have some heavy-duty protection and a facility somewhere out of the way, but not too far from Sydney.'

Jessica was undercover, but she didn't want to let Sara Jane know just how far off the books this investigation was. As Sara Jane had surmised, there was some seriously heavy political protection behind this gang. So much so that Jessica no longer worked for the New South Wales state police but had been seconded to a clandestine group outside the chain-of-command. This operation had to be undercover not only on the street but invisible at the highest levels of law enforcement and government in the country.

'It doesn't help that we also have these wildfires to the north, west and south of Sydney. The heat, wind and smoke are making everyone a bit troppo.'

'Yeah, makes you wonder if this gang's facility is going to be impacted. Might make them less vigilant if they are worried about getting their arses fried,' Jessica responded.

'Let's grab a coffee and share what we have,' Sara Jane suggested.

'OK, but out in suburbia away from any unwanted attention. Dee Why beachfront? Tomorrow? We have been standing here together for too long as it is.'

CHAPTER 4

The black van was lurking down the street from the hostel. The young Asian woman left the hostel and walked along the street to the takeaway where she worked. Studying English at a nearby private college, she had not been in the country long. She kept to herself, slept, studied and endured her shift serving soft serves to an indifferent clientele.

Inside the van two dark shadows watched. Twilight came. The van merged with the evening, parked in the dark space between two streetlights. The young woman's shift ended. She exited through the side door of the takeaway and walked back towards the hostel. As she walked past the van, its side door ajar, an arm reached out to grab her as a dark form caught her from behind. They had done it before and they would do it again. She was bundled into the van without a sound, the door slid shut and the van left the curb and disappeared into the night.

In the hostel her bed was stripped and her belongings removed. A tingle of anticipation went through the housekeeper's body as she anticipated slotting the cash burning a hole through her pocket into the pokie machines. The bursar at the college would pocket his bundle of cash and the young woman's records would disappear. The young woman had no friends out here and no one in her home country would report her missing. They were conditioned not to trust the authorities. She was officially a non-person, and now she had disappeared.

The black van entered through the roller door into the factory unit garage and reversed into the corner of the warehouse. Strapped to a stretcher the now-drugged victim was transferred into a ride-on mower box attached to a wooden pallet.

Completing a three-point turn the black van exited and began a sweep of The Cross picking up a load of homeless people to be fed and showered in the facility that fronted the warehouse. By bussing the less fortunate to a free shower and dinner, the black van and the transfer centre seemed legitimate.

The same bland warehouse building, in an industrial area just south of Sydney. The Foreman was seated at a conference table fiddling with his phone. Of slim build, he leans back in his chair, jean-clad legs crossed at the ankles stretched straight out in front of him. His flannelette shirt is at odds with the hot weather. His face is weather- and man-beaten, brown and leathery from the sun. A child can be heard whimpering in the next room, separated by a thin gyprock wall; the Foreman is unaffected by the child's distress and the noises that had preceded it. In fact, he looks pleased with himself as he saves and closes the video on his phone.

A second man enters the room. He is tall at more than two metres, and his once-athletic body has gone to fat, which even his tailored clothes cannot hide.

'That's one shit disguise. From the crappy wig, shades and Dr Who scarf I suppose no one could ID you. Much as I would expect from your kind; great at giving orders, crap at getting your poncy hands dirty. Have fun next door? Hope you didn't damage the stock too much,' grunted the Foreman, not bothering to get to his feet.

'Shut the fuck up and let's get down to business. That's just a perk of my position,' was the reply. 'There are a few things we need to cover off and a couple of new stock items.

'Firstly the fires and the facility. The excess stock have been moved offshore as you know. They will now be processed in the offshore facility. We will keep stock levels at a minimum until the fires have passed. Then we will ramp up again. The Bureau of Meteorology are predicting the fires will impact you. We expect you to keep the facility secure and secret. Be prepared for visitors, and don't draw any attention to yourself or the operation.'

'Don't worry, any dickhead that comes snooping around here will disappear.'

'What part of "don't attract attention" don't you understand? You start wasting fucking fireys we will have the whole fucking state down on us.'

'Your type never has the balls to deal with a matter decisively. Just issue orders and make excuses 'cause you can't stomach what it takes.'

The man in disguise, who obviously considered himself the superior being, expelled a long breath. 'I'm not sure where you got the idea that this is a discussion. I am delivering your orders; you will execute those orders.

'Secondly, that reporter. The one writing the online news blog. She is getting too close. I am seeing requests for action crossing my desk. It needs to be closed down. There is only so much I can do to block an investigation. She needs to be silenced. The crew here have orders to take her and transfer her to you. If we have to dispose of a problem, we might as well make a profit on it.'

'Hang on, first you say keep a low profile, then you want to light a firecracker by kidnapping Marlowe?'

'The boys overseas will lay a false trail. The world will think she disappeared up the back of Tibet somewhere.

'Also, there's a package in the garage being transferred to your van. It was picked up last night. Take it and the kid back this afternoon.'

'OK, anything else?'

'No, just wanted a face-to-face so you get the message that we are watching you. At the moment, we hold the evidence that would put you away for the rest of your life. Just toe the fucking line or we will drop it on a cop's desk or we will make you part of the product line. Some of the boys are fed up with your attitude, and fuck-ups.'

'Just what I would expect from a bunch of wankers like your lot.

Do you really think I haven't organised some sort of insurance policy? Just remember, fuckwits like you have further to fall than me.'

'Discussion over. I am out of here. Stay in this room for ten minutes after I leave.' The disguised man pushes his chair back, stands, turns and exits the room. He can be heard ordering a bodyguard to follow him.

*

The Foreman waited. Despite his bombast, he knew the precariousness of his position and his future if he crossed "the Boss" as the tall man liked to be called. His role was as the Foreman; he had his orders. He was expected to follow them and not step outside the box. He might not have had the education, but he had enough street and bush smarts to put a few escape hatches in the box.

He spent the time reviewing the conversation. Upmost in his mind was the significance of being dragged down here to their city facility, away from the processing facility he ran. Normally he would receive his instructions over the phone. This meeting was supposed to intimidate him. It made him wary, figuring the pressure was being passed down from up high. The other man's disguise neutered the intimidation; it told the Foreman that like any bully the Boss was a coward, but because of his privileged upbringing he was too arrogant to recognise his own shortcomings.

He had deliberately provoked the Boss. His strategy was to keep him on the back foot. He sensed the Boss was more than a little afraid of him. He knew the Boss had a bodyguard stand just outside the door during the conversation. He still had not discovered the Boss's identity, but the video recorded in the next room would help him narrow the field, and he'd gleaned two other clues from their meeting. The Foreman now knew the Boss was exceptionally tall and spoke with a "holier than thou" attitude. Once back at the facility he would spend some time surfing the internet, dissecting Sydney's upper crust. He was pretty certain he would have a short list of tall gents quite quickly.

Time to move. The Foreman stood, and entered the room next door. The naked child was bleeding and bruised, lying in a pool of his own filth on a rubber sheet. The Foreman unwound a hose from the floor, connected it to a tap on the wall and hosed down the child, the bed and the floor. The effluent was washed down a drain. The room had been furnished like a bedroom but built like a bathroom so it could be cleaned, and the evidence flushed. Luckily the drugs had reduced the kid to a semi-conscious state. The Foreman decided to inject a booster; he wanted a quiet trip home. He picked up the kid's limp body and descended a flight of stairs attached to an unadorned cement slab wall. The stairs ended on a small landing with a single door. He pushed open the door into a garage containing two vehicles: a black people-mover and an ex-ambulance Mercedes van. Opening the rear doors of the van, the Foreman laid the kid on a makeshift stretcher and strapped him down. Over the top of the stretcher he dropped a plywood box with no bottom. It had contained a ride-on mower and covered the inert form and the stretcher perfectly. A similar box was already resting on a pallet in the van, as promised.

The turbo diesel engine turned over easily, and by pressing a button on a fob attached to the key ring, the garage door flipped open. The heat, the smouldering red-brown sky and bushfire-tainted air ripped at his eyes and nose. The air-conditioning blasted from the vents still set to maximum from the trip down that morning. No point hanging around waiting for it to cool. There were a couple of tunnels between him and the north side of the harbour. They would shield him from the sun long enough for the air-conditioning to cool the van.

He turned on the radio. He had known there was a risk this

morning that he could be cut off by the fires this afternoon on his return to the facility. The roads were still clear. *No point hanging around*, he thought, aggressively pushing the van through the traffic.

Forty-five minutes later he was on the motorway heading north across the Hawkesbury River – Sydney's northern-most boundary. He contemplated the day. All over he considered it a win. He had video of the Boss raping and bashing a child, and he had enough clues to start assembling a profile of the Boss. Hopefully this would lead him to discover his identity. The Foreman believed he would then be the one issuing the orders and the Boss would be obsolete in the eyes of the Syndicate.

CHAPTER 6

*A*ustralians *do love to flock to the coast*, Jessica thought while trying to find a car park near the beach.

'The Gospers fire has now linked to the Wollombi fire and is moving steadily eastward towards the Central Coast, north of Sydney. The weather bureau doesn't see any significant rain for at least another week. In the meantime, all firefighters can hope to do is minimise loss of life and property,' blasted the radio announcer before Jessica could turn off the engine.

Don't really have to be told that, just look at the sky, smell the smoke and feel the heat, mused Jessica. Car parked, now to walk to the beach and try to find a private place to chat with Sara Jane. Jessica wanted the information Sara Jane had, but on the other hand she did not want her sister hurt. They were still looking for their last undercover agent. No one expected to see her alive again.

Dee Why beach is about halfway along the strip of beaches that run from the north side of Sydney Harbour to the world famous and exclusive Palm Beach, about 40 km to the north. The strip opposite the beachfront park held several cafés and surf shops, and although it was crowded today, Jessica hoped to be able to walk along the beach for some privacy. Although she was miles from the epicentre of the disappearances, she was still wary of being overheard and betrayed.

Jessica's phone rang. Sara Jane's name showed on the screen. 'I just ordered a couple of coffees to go. I'll grab them and start walking to the north along the sand.'

'No worries, SJ, I'll see you about 300 m north of the surf club. Don't spill the coffee.'

'One flat white, delivered,' said Sara Jane handing over Jessica's coffee. 'Glad you took the time to lose the Salvos uniform.'

'Yeah, every and any disconnect – it appears the only way to stay safe. You sure you were not followed?'

'Yes, I have been doing this for a while you know,' Sara Jane responded.

'OK, so what do we have besides our suspicions?'

'Not much. It all appears to be pretty normal at the moment. There does seem to be a bit more fear among the homeless. They know members of their tribe are disappearing. They just don't know how. All the same players, no obvious newcomers, no one has seen anyone being grabbed or forced into vehicles.'

'What vehicles would these people usually enter that wouldn't attract attention?'

'Charities, homeless shelters and occasionally police,' responded Sara Jane. 'But there is no pattern of people entering a certain vehicle belonging to a certain organisation and disappearing. The only thing I can think of is that they are using some kind of front.'

'What about the victims, is there a profile there? I mean if what we suspect is true then the victims would need to be young, mostly female and in relatively good health. I have The Cross and Bondi as areas where I am hearing of disappearances.'

'But, Jessica, I have nothing concrete, not even circumstantial – just rumours and innuendo. These are people who were already under the radar. So basically, we are trying to prove that someone who doesn't exist has disappeared. I need to get inside.'

'Shit, Sara Jane, don't even think about it. It's a one-way ticket. Get yourself picked up, then what are you going to do? If you can't communicate or escape, they will just disappear you. Worse still it would be pointless, because if no one knows where you went, no one would be able to rescue you, or more likely, retrieve your corpse.'

Jessica continued, 'OK, let's try some old-fashioned police work.

At least now we can do most of it in an air-conditioned office reviewing CCTV. It's a darn sight quicker and a hell of a lot more discrete. I'll get the boss to load some footage up onto the cloud from cameras around The Cross and Bondi.'

'Split up now and meet me at my place in half an hour.'

'What, doesn't your boss let you use the office?' Sara quipped.

'Yep, I am that far undercover. The air-conditioned office is my spare bedroom.'

*

Back in the lounge room of her apartment, Jessica showed Sara Jane how to log on to the cloud account where the CCTV footage had been loaded. 'What are we looking for?'

'Anything that doesn't belong, or if it does belong, acting out of character. Concentrate on any vehicles picking people off the streets. First run-through we make a short list. Cut the section of video using this app here and copy it to this directory. Once we have all the suspect pieces together, we will do a second run-through. We will write the details of each vehicle on this whiteboard, and a brief description of its operations.'

A few hours later and a lot of coffee. 'OK, we have a list of vehicles. Wayside Chapel, Mission Australia, Second Harvest and a couple of smaller outfits in unmarked vehicles,' said Jessica looking at the whiteboard. 'Let's study each pick-up. We are looking for surprise and a reluctance to enter the van.'

Another run-through. It was heading towards midnight. 'OK, the regulars were obvious. The charities and service providers, as expected, all vanilla. Same people each day for most of them. Let's put those ones to one side for the moment.' The short list was shortened again.

More hours of poor-quality security video seared their eyes.

Hours later, 'Who is the Church of the Holy Redeemer?' Jessica asked.

'Yeah, we see them around. Black van that regularly picks up the homeless and gives them a shower and a meal.'

'So, we could expect them to be cruising The Cross, but here they are in Bondi last night. They seem to be staking out that hostel. The patrons of the hostel already have somewhere to stay. I think there is something here. We need to watch it frame by frame, then google them to see who they are.'

In the poor-quality video taken from a traffic light CCTV, the van was seen parked on the side of the road on the side of the frame. As they clicked through the frame, night fell and the van merged into the background. A person was seen walking down the street. The light was bad, the video worse; the sisters could not even tell if the figure was male or female. Jessica was processing one frame at a time. She moved her mouse to the right of the frame where the next streetlight provided a cone of light adjacent to the doorway of the hostel. She moved forward frame by frame, concentrating on the cone of light. The figure did not reappear. The tail-lights of the van flared in the next frame, then jerking from frame to frame it pulled out into the road and disappeared. Jessica and Sara Jane searched the next frame for the person walking down the street. They were not there.

'Shit. We know something happened. But it doesn't show. Shit, shit, SHIT,' Jessica stood up and threw a stapler that had been innocently sitting on her desk across the room.

Sara Jane leaned back in her chair. 'We have the Church of the Holy Redeemer, and we have the hostel.'

Sara Jane ran them past Google. 'The Church of the Holy Redeemer is a private charity providing shelter and meals to the homeless, according to their webpage. Could this be a case of hiding in plain sight?'

'Any link to the hostel?' asked Jessica, opening a browser and starting her own searches.

'Very little background on who either the Redeemers or the hostel are. Let's try searching the corporate, charities and associations database. A connection between the two would be a bonus,' suggested Jessica.

'Hmm, not much here. Not much substance. Strange for a charity not to want to be found.'

'The hostel is owned by a corporation that specialises in this sort of accommodation. Also a dead end. The owners probably have no idea what's happening at the hostel as long as the numbers are OK. Maybe a cleaner or manager is fingering the victims?' mused Jessica.

'I think I will have a poke around there tomorrow,' said Sara Jane. 'Sorry, I meant later today. Can I borrow your spare room? I have a change of clothes in the car and don't want to waste time going home, when I can grab some sleep here.'

'Yeah no problems. Reckon we are onto something?' asked Jessica.

'Smells like a duck, quacks like a duck, waddles like a duck, probably not a chicken.'

'Ha,' scoffed Jessica, 'that's mixing a metaphor with a bad joke, that has to be illegal. You channelling Dad now?'

CHAPTER 7

Jessica's mobile rang.

'Hi, Mum.'

'Hello, Jessica, I just got a postcard from India saying what a lovely time Sara Jane was having and that she would be out of touch for a while as she was taking a break from work and going trekking. Did you know? You could have told us. We know Sara Jane can be a bit impetuous, but she would have a least told you.'

'Sorry, Mum, breathe, it was so sudden I am still processing it. I will call you back. I am in the middle of something for work.' Jessica flung her laptop open and scanned through for traces of Sara Jane. Sara Jane didn't do postcards; she was a digital girl. If what Jessica suspected was true, this would have been posted to placate her mother and others by parties unknown. They needed to go along with the ploy. Sara Jane's continued existence depended on everyone believing she was in India.

'India? there is no way that Sara Jane is in India. Fuck that,' Jessica huffed at her laptop, checking Sara Jane's Facebook account, which had been inactive for months, but was now full of selfies of Sara Jane in front of the Taj Mahal. Only a day had passed. Had Sara Jane followed up the Mission of the Holy Redeemer? And been caught? Was someone impersonating her on Facebook and laying a false trail that will see her disappear fifteen thousand miles away?

'Lots of questions, girl, let's get grounded. What do we know versus what do we suspect?'

Sara Jane kept notes on her stories. Her professionalism demanded it. Sara Jane was paranoid enough that her notes were kept in a cloud account. Sara Jane had shown Jessica how to access it. The note file was in a hidden folder among the online photo albums the family shared.

Jessica opened the browser and navigated to the family albums on the shared account. Opening one of the folders, finding the correct photo, she clicked on the left eye of a mongrel dog sitting between the two sisters on a beach. A hidden folder appeared on the screen and a password box opened.

Typing in the random password, Jessica accessed the files. Searching by date she found the latest.

'Fuck, fuck, FUCK.' The notes detailed Sara Jane's plan to go start surveillance of the Redeemers' soup kitchen. Her notes detailed the coming and going of the black van and the details of a Mercedes ex-ambulance seen in the same garage. She had recorded the rego number of the van. Hopefully a break. That was two days ago. Nothing since except a postcard from India. Jessica contemplated the timing. So, Sara Jane had been onto the Redeemers before her discussion with Jessica. She had let Jessica discover them for herself, probably to verify her own theories.

*

Checking the registration of the Mercedes van led nowhere. The van was registered to the factory unit address the Redeemers were using. Check the Police Traffic database, maybe something will show up. A parking ticket in Wyong and a speed camera infringement at Peats Ridge. A sizeable town and a hamlet, both within an hour of the northern fringes of Sydney. Time to take this to the boss.

Jessica organised a video conference with her commander Ms Bowman. 'You know we are putting all our resources into this one lead?'

'Yes,' replied Jessica, 'but we have no other leads, no other avenues of active inquiry. I believe the risk that we are wrong is smaller than the risk that something fatal will happen to SJ. We owe her because she has unearthed the only viable lead in this case.'

'What's your plan?'

Jessica detailed her thought process. 'There is no gain from raiding the Redeemers' soup kitchen in town. We have searched all the databases public and non-public that we can access and there appear no real anomalies except the Mercedes van picking up a load of ride-on mowers and disappearing. They must be moving the victims in the same way.

'In Sara Jane's notes I found a link to a miniature camera she set up across the road. I can see when the van leaves and we know it heads north. I can therefore pick it up near the Hawkesbury bridge on the northern border of the Sydney metro area. I'll use a plain Jane rental so I should be invisible if they are looking for a tail.'

After a few minutes consideration, Ms Bowman agreed. 'OK, go ahead, unearth some intel, but do not engage. Also be aware of the fires and firefighting operations in that area. It could make things tricky.'

Authorisation was a bonus even though the timings may have to be fudged in her action report.

*

Jessica had already rented a white Corolla and had it parked outside her apartment on Sydney's Northern Beaches. She was thirty minutes closer to the motorway, leaving Sydney to the north, than the Redeemers' soup kitchen. Watching the feed from Sara Jane's hidden camera on her mobile phone, Jessica saw the roller door of the Redeemers' warehouse open. The Mercedes had been parked in the loading bay. As she stared at the screen, the van pulled out onto the street.

Time to move.

Thirty minutes later, parked in a layby on the motorway just north of Sydney, Jessica knew she was making many assumptions. She was hoping the Mercedes would follow a pattern and she would be able to intercept it, following it to the facility she guessed was hidden somewhere north of Sydney. No one had been able to get close enough to hide a tracker in the van or cargo, nor did they have the resources to be able to track its route with multiple vehicles. It seemed like the van should have passed minutes ago but when Jessica looked her watch she saw it would take at least another fifteen minutes to pass the rest area where she was stopped. Impatience could wreck this operation.

A news broadcast came over the radio:

'Fire control has just released details of a daring top-secret mission to save the last copse of Wollemi Pines, a sixty-million-year-old tree species found only in one gorge worldwide. Meanwhile, plans are being drawn up to halt the Gospers mega blaze before it can impact the Central Coast.'

No wonder visibility was shit, thought Jessica. *Luckily it's a van and not an ordinary car I am trying to find in this smog.*

And there it was. Jessica let a few cars pass, the high vehicle was easy to see and the limited exits on the motorway meant she didn't have to stay too close. Even though it was only 4 pm on a summer's afternoon, the higher they climbed from the Hawkesbury River onto the sandstone ranges, the thicker the smoke was. The sky was a dirty brown orange and the sun an orange disc so weak you could look straight at it.

The van took an exit about forty minutes north and continued along the two-lane B-road. Through villages and hamlets, nothing big enough to be called a town, they travelled. Luckily the road was clogged with firefighting vehicles, support vehicles and locals either leaving or attempting to get to their properties. Combined with the limited visibility, Jessica felt anonymous enough to continue the tail. Speed was down and twenty minutes later, when the van signalled a left turn onto a local road, Jessica pulled over after passing the intersection and had a look at her GPS. The road was a dead end with several unsealed roads winding into the valleys of the spurs on either side of it. An ancient creek bed that for millennia had produced a fissured valley of fertile farmlands ran beside the road.

Jessica U-turned and went right up the spur road. She was confident that given the visibility, she would not be noticed by the van driver. She drove up the spur road at a leisurely pace. She was looking to see which of the dirt tracks leading off the spur the van had taken. Finally she saw what she was looking for: a cloud of dust blowing across a tree-studded rise to the right of the spur road. Following further would be too obvious. Jessica drove past, pulled over and waited for thirty minutes. If someone was watching the road, she wanted the opposition to think she had an appointment at one of the properties further up the creek valley. Any misdirection helped.

*

The nearest town of any size was Wyong, once a centre for the agriculture in the area but now a dormitory town for Sydney. But at least it would have a motel. Jessica wanted to stay close by while she did some research.

It would be charitable to award the room three stars, but she couldn't imagine that there was much of a tourist trade through Wyong. The courtesy folder did promote the Watagans National Park to the northwest and Lake Macquarie to the north. She was a suburban girl, definitely out of her element. A bit of dirt bike riding with her dad and Sara Jane years ago was her limit.

Jessica had packed enough clothes and bathroom essentials to survive a night or two away from home. She had been at this caper long enough to know that when following a lead, office hours and returning to her own bed were not always an option. Opening her laptop, she brough up Google maps and switched it to satellite view. Beside the laptop she compared the GPS tracking from her phone. Following the GPS trail on the larger screen she was able to see the trail where the van had disappeared.

The trail crested a small, wooded rise then wound through a cleared valley terminating after about five kilometres in what looked like an industrial-scale chicken farm. Rows of single-storey sheds clustered around a homestead and a barn. It was the only viable facility. All other structures in the valley looked derelict and the pastures overgrown. Behind the chicken farm the bushland rose up the side of the valley. She switched back to map view. There they were. Several fire trails showed up on the ridge behind the farm. It was a risk as she couldn't date the imagery, and things on the ground may have changed, but it was a starting point for some on-the-ground reconnaissance.

*

So, what approach should she use? Brazen or covert? She could hire an SUV, have some farm and station agent cards printed, and knock on their front door. Probably not a realistic approach with these fires. Lost mountain biker, dirt bike rider? Maybe she just needed to scope the place out without been seen? Keep it simple; hide the car in the layby she had turned around in, hike down the road before dawn, observe and come out after dark. Probably the best option. OK, prepare dark clothes, food and water for the morning. Set the alarm for 3 am. Get a feed and get to bed.

CHAPTER 8

'You need to get in and out quick. Once this fire tops that ridge it will suck itself through that valley turning anything in its path to toast.'

If that wasn't an instruction to ride hard, Joe thought, *I'll never hear one.*

Over the roar of the fire, the thumping of the truck and pump engines, and the yelling of firefighters, it was nearly impossible to hear yourself think. Exhaustion after two weeks of fighting this wildfire didn't help. Joe shrugged. At least the smoke and dust hid the smell of a twelve-hour shift in forty-plus degree heat.

Two weeks since the smoke was first spotted in the valleys northwest of Sydney. Two weeks since their world had compressed into riding sorties, clearing civilians out of harm's way, gathering intelligence on the soulless enemy so the experts could determine a way of stopping the beast. Two weeks since their existence was measured in twelve hours on and twelve hours off. Two weeks since the largest fire from a single source ever recorded erupted, and now it was coming out of the bush into the towns and villages on the coastal plain.

They were on a spur road up a valley between two ridges east of the fire front. The firestorm of the previous evening had jumped the containment line raining embers down onto the dense tinder-dry forest of the ridge to the west of the valley. The heat, smoke and wind created a weather engine that dragged the fire relentlessly to the east.

The valleys, eroded out of the sandstone, drained ancient creeks out of the hills leaving fertile valleys dotted with pastures, country estates and farms. Drones and manned aircraft had done as much surveillance as they could; now it was up to ground crews to evacuate the last stubborn landowners.

Joe and Fred were tasked with reconnoitring a valley hidden behind a small, wooded rise. The drones had identified a factory farm set up at the head of the valley that appeared inhabited. Fire crews had set up a forward base in a layby just up from the track.

Joe looked around. 'Come on Fred, get your shit together.'

'Yeah, yeah, don't get your knickers in a knot.'

'No choice, we go now, or we don't go at all.'

'One last thing. I just want to make sure someone is aware of the unattended white rental car. Probably some blogger wanting to get some action shots to boost their page.'

Joe and Fred mounted their Yamaha dirt bikes and started their engines.

'Radio check, fire com mand , this is bike team Bravo about to clear Hidden Valley of civilians. Please acknowledge.'

'Bike team Bravo you are good to go. Please switch to channel 37.'

'Roger Control. Also note we suspect there may be a civilian on foot in the area as we have an unattended vehicle on site.'

'Noted and all units will be updated to look for a civilian on foot in the area.'

Following the dirt road, cresting the wooded rise that hid the valley, third gear, tap the rear brake, let the rear start to drift then on the throttle, the two riders drifted through the first dog leg and began their descent into the valley.

Speed was of the essence, but visibility was poor because of the smoke; the faster they went the more they would have to concentrate on the road, and the less they would be able to observe around them. They would be hastening cautiously.

Two weeks non-stop firefighting was too much for Fred's

machine; the rear tyre was shredding. Fred shuddered to a halt. Joe pulled up beside him.

'You will never make it back through that gap unless you limp back now,' Joe yelled into the intercom over their idling engines.

'Rules state we must travel as a pair. What about that chicken farm at the head of the valley? Flyovers showed it as inhabited.'

'Fuck the rules, get your arse back over that ridge. Tell them I have gone on when you get there. Better to apologise after the event, rather than disobey a "stop" order up front.'

'Your funeral, make that cremation. Look at that ridge, the way the smoke appears to be black and blowing over the top of us. This shithole is going to explode as soon as the first embers start raining down, you already need a knife to cut the air.'

Fred gingerly shuffled his bike through a five-point turn, the shredded rear tyre handicapping his manoeuvrability. Joe watched over his shoulder as his mate worked his way back up through the tree line. The smoke was reducing visibility to an orangey-brown gloom, and without a mask breathing would have been painful.

This valley doesn't make sense, thought Joe. *This close to Sydney anything like this is snapped up and gentrified.* Joe considered the overgrown pastures, rotted and incomplete fences, and boarded-up farmhouses and outbuildings. Joe shrugged. None of it would be standing in the morning.

Twisting his throttle, Joe badgers himself forward. *C'mon on, hit it you stupid bastard. The quicker you get your arse to the end of the trail the quicker you can get out of this death-trap.*

CHAPTER 9

Even to a city girl, the farm did not look right. The quiet, the surrounding electric fence, the surveillance cameras pointed inwards towards the compound. Maybe it was her suspicions that were colouring her observations, but it looked more like a prison than a working chicken farm.

At dawn Jessica had found herself a small blackberry bush to wriggle into, clearing a nest protected by the thorny shrubbery. She was peering slightly up hill into the compound, restricting her view. With the light dimmed by the smoke, she was considering her exit strategy. The fires were starting to make her nervous, but she could not let herself be spotted from the compound in front of her. She really wanted to move around, behind and uphill of the target to improve her surveillance. The fires however crossed that option off the list.

It was very quiet for a chicken farm. She had seen a couple of men walking about the property, however, they seemed more like guards on patrol than farmhands going from one chore to the next. She could see the rear of the Mercedes van poking out of an open-faced shed, parked next to a ute and a tractor. There was a typical weatherboard farmhouse in the centre of the compound, facing the driveway, and to its right an industrial-looking shed with some heavy-duty refrigeration units on the outside. These were surrounded by several long, low corrugated-iron sheds. She was wondering if they had shut down operations during the fire emergency. If they had, she was going to have nothing to report and no justification to force her way inside.

There was a large dam, noticeably full, especially given the drought, to the left of the facility. From a shed on the bank a diesel engine cranked to life, blowing a cloud of black smoke then settling down to a steady rhythm. Sprinkler heads across the grounds and roof caps of the building started to push a fine mist of water into the air.

So, they are going to stay and fight, thought Jessica. *No choice, they can't risk anyone coming in or moving the prisoners out.*

From close behind she heard the drone of a four-stroke dirt bike. A figure in yellow was approaching the gate, almost certainly from the Rural Fire Service. He dismounted. From the shed the 4WD ute trundled down to meet him. Two men exited the ute and strutted to the gate, the passenger grabbing a rifle from the rear seat.

The meeting did not go well. She saw the firefighter point to the west where smoke blotted out the sky, and to the south where the track came through the valley. The only exit. She saw the two men shake their heads in a negative. The firefighter tried again. The driver pointed back out of the valley. The rifle was now pointing at the firefighter's feet. He put up his hands, shrugged his shoulders, remounted his bike, turned and started back down the track. The guard with the rifle raised it, sighted down the barrel and looked like he was about to take a shot at the retreating firefighter. The driver saw and batted the barrel towards the ground. The shot went wide. The rider appeared not to have noticed. The whole pantomime lasted no more than two minutes.

The driver and passenger re-entered the ute, made a three-point turn and headed back into the compound.

Jessica seized her moment and leaped from behind the bush onto the track just in time to stop the rider. She leaped on the bike screaming 'Go, go, go, go'. He responded and Jessica felt her head whipped back as he accelerated down the track.

This guy can ride, was her first impression. Two fast corners and they were out of sight of the compound. The bike stopped behind a hillock. The rider pulled of his full-face helmet. It was not a standard helmet, with a built-in radio and air filters. A face appeared stubbled and sooty. Blue eyes rimmed with red and brown hair shot through with grey streaks momentarily distracted Jessica, her eyes and nose telling her the rider had been on the frontline for weeks. *Bet he scrubs up OK though*, nudged her subconscious.

'What the fuck was that about? Who the fuck are they and who the fuck are you?' were his first words.

Jessica needed a moment to think. 'You know they took a shot at you?'

'Yeah, this round thing on the handlebars is called a mirror. I saw his mate swat the barrel away. Nice redirection, but back to my original questions.'

Jessica decided on a variation of the truth.

'My name is Sara Jane Marlowe, I run my own digital newspaper. I was following a tip-off about that farm.'

'You the white Corolla parked on the spur road?'

'Yeah, I walked in this morning before dawn.'

'OK, I need to radio in and get us out of here. The rest doesn't really matter.'

'Control, this is Joe, bike team Bravo.'

'Fuck, Joe, what are you doing? You are in the shit this time. If you survive the fire the captain'll kill you. The fire has blocked the rise; we have had to withdraw to the main road. Get under cover and prepare for an overrun. We have ordered in the chopper to water bomb the creek bed where the sandy bed is on the sat. photo. It will be a blind shot so good luck. We will send help as soon as we can.'

'Hold on.' Joe pulled his helmet back on, gunned the bike. Jessica held tight around his waist. Joe held the bike on the edge of traction. Handling on the dirt was seriously compromised as, with a pillion,

Joe could not stand on the foot pegs and the weight distribution was out of kilter. He found the creek bed, left the road using the bank as a ramp down to the dry sandy bottom. The front wheel bogged down in the sand, Joe twisted the throttle full round in an attempt to pop the front wheel, but the weight was just too much. The front wheel caught in the sand, twisted hard left, and threw the bike down on its right side. The dry creek bed was sand so the fall was survivable. The fire would not be.

Joe dragged a woollen fire blanket out of his kit bag, ran ten metres down the sandy creek bed, and started digging with his gloved hands in the sand. 'We need to dig in here. Hopefully the fire will jump the banks and leave us singed but not barbequed. Dig as much sand as you can. We will try to burrow down and cover up. I can hear the chopper but it's going to be a lucky shot. The deeper we can get the more chance the sand might still be a bit damp.'

As Joe had hoped, the sand became damper as they dug deeper. The heat was now so intense, the air unbreathable, the roar deafening, that Joe knew the fire was upon them. He threw Jessica full length into the ditch they had dug, lay down on top of her, pulled the blanket over his back while trying to scoop sand over as much of them as he could.

Out of the sky a torrent of water dropped on them. The helicopter had honed in on Joe's GPS and scored a direct hit. He owed that pilot a beer or three.

Joe held Jessica down for another ten minutes before cautiously raising his head. As the creek was in the middle of an overgrown pasture the fire had passed through quickly and blasted across the valley floor, being dragged by its own wind. Ten metres back up the creek bed the bike had not been so lucky. Leaking petrol after the tumble had reached flash point. It was still burning.

'Let's get out of here before we get anymore unwanted attention.'

'Can't we wait for help from your mates?' Jessica asked.

'I want to put some distance between us and the farm in case they come looking for us. The smoke will hide us. You not hurt, are you?'

'Bruised, battered, scraped and still choking on sand. Just a normal bloody Tuesday.'

'I think it's a Friday.'

'Well that fucking explains it then.'

'So, let's get away from that bike in case they come to investigate. What is it, a dope farm?'

'Yeah that's it. Pretty heavy-duty dealers.' Jessica lied but did not want to involve this stranger anymore.

*

'Control code red. This is bike team Bravo requesting pick up for two. We are walking towards the spur road about two k's down the track.'

'Two?'

'Yeah, found the journo that left the rental back on the spur road.'

'Yeah, well let her know she will not be getting her deposit back.'

'Here comes our lift.' Joe sighed as the 4WD LandCruiser rumbled into sight. 'That's not one of our trucks.'

'Taxi service for Mr Joe Burnett,' yelled Fred out of the rear seat. 'Fucked another bike I see.'

'Meet Ms Bowman, Joe. Your journo mate's boss,' continued Fred.

'For a journo you sure have some juice,' continued Fred. 'She turns up, makes a couple of calls and suddenly we're getting all sorts of commands coming down from on high.'

Joe scrambled up into the back seat of the LandCruiser, Jessica took the front next to her boss. The truck bumped over the still smouldering verge in a three-point turn and proceeded out of the valley. Whoever Ms Bowman was, she could drive. They were too busy holding on as the big V8 pushed the boundaries of physics to attempt conversation. Joe was debating whether he wanted to know more. He had the feeling that knowing more was not necessarily a good thing for his future wellbeing.

Once back on the bitumen, Joe could not contain his curiosity any longer.

'What about the farm at the end?' Joe queried.

'That was one of the orders. We are to leave it alone,' replied Fred.

'I can live with that.' Joe was quite happy to delegate that particular matter to the "someone else's problem" basket. He still had to explain the destroyed bike.

'Here is my ID.' Ms Bowman passed a wallet over to the back seat. 'You two gentleman are to keep your mouths shut about what you saw today. National security.'

'Federal police? Fuck that,' Joe turned to Jessica, 'I thought you were a journo.'

'That's a cover story. You talk about this people will die.'

'OK, OK, we get it, drop us back at the command centre.'

'Your captain knows enough not to dig too deep. Just do a normal debrief and don't mention what happened at the farm,' Ms Bowman instructed as she dropped them at the community hall the RFS was using as a command centre.

'Let's do the debrief, get showered, changed, and then I am going home. I have had enough of this shit for one day. I am going to sit in my sunroom and down a couple of cold recuperating ales.'

The captain didn't look happy.

'Evening, chief, had a good day?'

'It's Captain not chief, Joe. Who the fuck do you think you are: Maxwell Smart, James Bond, destroying another bike on Her Majesty's secret service? Then fucking "M" turns up in her LandCruiser from hell, picks up Fred without a by-your-leave and mounts a rescue. This is so screwed up I don't know what we can debrief and what we can't. You two are off-duty until further notice. Just get the fuck out of my sight.'

Joe and Fred walked out to the parking lot. 'Captain mustn't be spy-thriller fan. Sorry about dragging you into this, Fred.'

'You mean the trouble with the Captain? I wouldn't worry about it. He's scared shitless someone's going to get killed on his watch. Everyone will have forgotten about this little sideshow tomorrow. As for the rest of it, I am just a spectator. I leave the action up to you players.'

'If I'm a player how come I have no bloody idea what's going on. Lucky fluke LandCruiser lady knew to pick you up though, wasn't it?'

Hearing was the first sense to return. Someone was talking to her. The words appeared to be whispered; the tone kind and concerned. She felt something cool and damp on her forehead. She had a hangover; she just couldn't remember the party. The place stank, she stank, her new friend stank. Something was not right. Sara Jane decided to keep her eyes closed and her body still waiting for her brain to kickstart and provide some perspective.

Memory returned and it was not good. She had planted the digital camera in a tree across from the Redeemers' warehouse. It had its own SIM card, so she was able to view it remotely using her mobile phone. She had not been seen, she was sure. So, what had happened?

She was here because of her story, because someone had decided she needed to be silenced. She took a deep breath and tried to focus on a course of events that made sense.

'I know you are in there, but I don't blame you for pretending to be out of it,' whispered her new friend.

It had been night. She had gone down the street to the local Thai for a takeaway dinner. A grab from behind, a glimpse of a van, then nothing until now. She was going to have to open her eyes if she wanted answers.

Sara Jane was in a dark room partitioned-off from a large, corrugated-iron shed. A young Asian woman with a bruised and dirty face was rinsing SJ's face with a wet rag. It was hot, smoky and stifling. They must be closer to the bushfires.

'I am hoping we can help each other,' she whispered, 'They think I only speak a little English. I was working to expose them but things moved too quickly. Now I have no back-up.'

The door slammed open. 'Have you woken the bitch up yet, slant?' bellowed a coarse, male voice from across the room.

'No, Two, I do best I can. She no wake.'

'Give us the fucking bucket.'

A torrent of warm dirty warm water slammed SJ's head back onto the boards she was lying on. The shock made her involuntarily jerk upright and open her eyes. A slap from a rough hand smashed her head back down again. 'You fucking awake now? Welcome to your new home. We own you, and we don't give a fuck whether you live or die.'

Boots thumped across the room. The door slammed. They were alone again. 'I am Lui Chin, you are Sara Jane Marlowe. The people I work for followed your blog. They sent me to discover what happened to a couple of girls who came to Sydney, to study, from small towns in the Philippines. Unfortunately, things happened a bit too quick and I was taken before I had back-up in place. I only woke up a day or so ago.

'Sara Jane, they took you because you were getting too close. The fires have slowed them down, I am not sure what they are planning, but I have been told I will have to wait to be "tested and graded" whatever that means. I think it has bought us a day or so.'

Outside a commanding male voice could be heard, 'One and Two: take the ute, go to the front gate and tell the firey standing out there to fuck off. Tell him we will manage our own defences. Report to me as soon as you are back.' A diesel engine starts and the sound recedes into the distance. Nothing but silence as Sara Jane and Lui Chin listen intently. Both women are aware the owner of the voice could be just the other side of the wall.

A shot rings out across the silence. 'For fuck's sake, what are those morons doing?' proving the owner of the voice was only the other side of the wall. They hear footsteps quickly receding.

Lui Chin drops her mouth down beside Sara Jane's ear. 'That guy is some sort of manager, One and Two are like trustees. There are five of them altogether from what I can gather.'

The ute returned, the Foreman yelled out the window, 'Get Three and Four here now.'

Another two minutes of silence, the two women imagined him scanning the valley. 'We have about fifteen minutes before the fire hits us. Remember the drills. One gets the pump started. Two, walk round the building, make sure all the sprinklers are working. You other two check the sheds are locked and make sure the stock cannot escape. Shoot any that try to make a run for it.

'As soon as you can, One and Two report back to me and give me a hand getting the firefighting trailer on the back of the ute.'

The air became thicker, darker. It burnt the insides of their noses when they took a breath. The silence was being overwhelmed by a white noise that was slowly growing in depth and intensity. Now it was a roar; the fire had arrived.

The two women hit the floor. The wet cloth was where it dropped. They took turns breathing through it. Total sensory overload. Time lost all meaning. It was eternity and it was over in an instant, simultaneously.

It was over. Like the Doppler Effect of a fast-approaching car disappearing into the distance the roar was gone. Not so the heat and smoke. Then silence, then children screaming and crying.

Water could be seen flowing off the roof of the shed. The smoke haze was clearing. 'They must have a sprinkler system on the roof of the shed. I remember being shown one when I was doing a story on bushfire survival,' said Sara Jane.

'Well now we know it works! All you have to do is survive this, escape, and you can do a follow-up.'

They heard the diesel ute pull up outside again. 'Right, you four inspect the grounds. Look for any damage. If you see any spot fires come back immediately so we can deal with them. Double-check the fences and the cameras.

'We will have to suspend operations for a couple of days until the Doc can make it out here again and we can get the secure internet up and running. Soon as you have checked the grounds check the sheds, make sure none of the stock is missing or damaged. If you need me, I will be in the office on the satellite phone to the powers-that-be, letting them know we still exist but will not be uploading anything for a couple of days.'

SJ and Lui Chin heard the door to their shed open. Footsteps sounded along the floor, receding down the centre of the shed. A far door opened and closed. Then there was silence. The air was still, hot and acrid. They looked at each other, stood carefully and made their way to the first door. It was locked. The walls of the shed did not quite reach to the roof leaving a gap to allow air to pass from one side to the other. They pulled the table SJ had been lying on over to the airway and peered through the gap. They appeared to be in the centre of a row of long narrow sheds made of corrugated iron. 'This reminds me of a factory chicken farm,' observed Sara Jane. 'I can see down the valley. It is all burnt and black, but there is a dam beside us that must have provided the water for the sprinkler system. Let's see what we can see from the other side.'

They carried the table across the breadth of the shed. Again, they peered through the gap. Looking sideways, they could see another row of similar sheds and a house with a couple of demountable-looking factory sheds behind it.

Twilight fell quickly. It didn't have far to fall as the air had yet to clear. Thunder could be heard in the distance. The night was dark, the smoke blocked any light from the moon, stars or neighbouring towns from seeping through its veil. A puff of wind, lightning, a tense wait, then thunder. There was a drumming on the roof, tentative at first then more insistent, rising in a deafening crescendo as the storm burst across the valley. The weather had turned. Sara Jane and Lui Chin fell asleep on the floor as the rain settled to an even rhythm on the tin roof.

CHAPTER 12

The rain had passed by daybreak, in places the ground was steaming and still smouldering.

The three men stood in the gully looking down at the burnt-out remains of the RFS motorcycle.

Ten metres away was a depression in the sand and a RFS fire blanket.

Outside the eroded creek bed, the valley was ash and charcoal, the only green was the facility and the track of bushland behind it. The sprinkler system had worked. The fire had stopped at the fence.

'Leave it. I expect they will come back for it in a day or so. Let's not have another dickhead banging on the gate looking for the motorcycle. You morons overplayed our hand already. Hopefully the Boss can find out who he is and we can take him out.'

'There are two sets of footprints leaving here, see there and there.'

'He must have needed help. You sure you missed him? You will be in all kinds of pain if they find your bullet in him.'

'Definitely missed him.'

'OK let's continue. We need our security back in place like yesterday. This is just another fuck-up.'

The Foreman took a photo of the bike's number plate, the characters punched into the metal still visible even if the paint was gone. The Foreman returned to the driver's seat of the white ute. One of his henchmen jumped in the passenger side, the other in the back seat of the dual cab. He was the Foreman not because of his hard work and diligence, but because he was ruthless and totally immoral. He grabbed his mobile, checked the reception, marvelled that the fires hadn't destroyed all the towers, and hit a speed dial.

'Boss, Foreman here, all clear, no damage to the facility or the stock, we have also escaped any scrutiny. We should be able to start getting back into production tomorrow.'

'No fuckwit, you will be confirming that you are back in production tomorrow,' replied the Boss, attempting to dominate the conversation. 'Nothing has passed over my desk, so you are all clear. Confirm the package arrived, last report you were cut off.'

'Yes, she is still out of it. You need to make sure we are not going to be disturbed.'

'Listen shit-for-brains, I don't need garbage like you giving me instructions. That has already been taken care of.' With that the Boss was gone. The Foreman was holding a dead phone to his ear.

'Not going to tell him about the firey?' asked one of the henchmen.

'Why the fuck would I? I'm paid to deal with stuff on the local level. We will go through everything this evening. While we are out here, let's do a reccy, make sure we aren't going to get any more surprises. I'll drive, you two stand in the back, hold the rack and search for anything that ain't right.'

'What should we be looking for? And how can we see in this crap?'

'Fucking anything that ain't right. If I knew what the fuck it was, I wouldn't need you arseholes to find it for me. If you miss something you will get it in the neck.'

The two men climbed into the rear tray of the ute, the Foreman did a three-point turn and just above walking speed drove back to the facility.

*

The organisation had purchased all the properties in the valley as a security zone around the facility. While the rest of the area was going up market at a rate of knots, they had let their valley run down. The fire had cleansed the remnants. The valley was clear from east to west and north to south. Just a steaming, smouldering, black wasteland. The few stands of trees along the creek bed were skeletal. Strangely enough the screen of trees at the foot of the valley where it met the spur road were all in one piece, whether this was through good planning, hard work or just plain luck no one would ever know. The screen did, however, provide some privacy to the facility. Although it now stood out like the proverbial green thumb.

The denuding of the valley floor gave the three men a clear view of their domain. All the scrap and ruins that had previously been hidden were now exposed. Old homesteads were now nothing but a pile of scorched iron roofing with the odd brick chimney remaining. Junk that had previously been hidden by blackberry bushes was now revealed, including the occasional old truck or tractor.

*

The ute left the track and crossed open country to pass the facility on its left-hand side. It passed a corner of the electric fence and continued across the top of the dam. 'We need to check the whole fence line. Including across the top. The Boss is going to want us back up to speed ASAP,' yelled the Foreman over the idle of the diesel engine. 'Watch for any damage to the fence and any trees or branches still smouldering.'

As the facility backed onto the side of a hill, with woods behind it, the fire had left a stripe of unburnt timber stretching to the ridge line behind the facility. Strangely enough the fire had not joined up behind the facility. The Foreman assumed that this was the result of the sprinkler system that had saved the facility by producing a misting spray which had been drawn up the hill by the flames. The country on the far side of the dam had been scorched, but once they were further up, the forest was still intact. This brought the ute to a stop.

'You two morons continue across the top fence on foot. I will go back down and around and meet you on the far side.' The two men dismounted from the tray of the ute and began tramping across the top of the property. No words were spoken between them. They were tramping along a cleared space about one metre wide on the uphill side of the property. On one side of the cleared path was the uppermost boundary fence; on the other was virgin bush. The fence line paid no respect to the terrain but cut a straight line across the contour of the hill. Granite and sandstone boulders were either exploded or had been built into the fence line. This left the two scrambling, and occasionally climbing, over the terrain.

The only break was a gate about a third of the way along. The gate was robust and padlocked. A well-tended dirt road exited through the gate and followed a depression in the slope to the left. It provided an opportunity for a rest and a look around as the road broke the tree cover for a metre or two. A drift of drizzle penetrated the gap, a natural break from the humidity, heat and flies that were trapped by the forest canopy along the rest of the route.

The henchmen tramped and scrambled onwards. Dressed in boots, socks, shorts and T-shirts they were soon covered in scratches and grazes on their exposed legs and arms. Sweat would then mix with the drizzle and drip into these areas of raw flesh, stinging and drawing the flies. The five-hundred metre trek was becoming a torture. The two men were distracted and continued their scramble, now focused only on completing their assignment and regaining the air-conditioned comfort of the ute.

The king brown snake was not happy. Even on a good day these are aggressive, venomous snakes. Today had not been a good day. The fire had driven him hard and only luck had saved him. He had been close to the side fence of the facility and as he raced up the hill to escape the inferno, he was able to break left across the top of the facility where he now rested on top of a large boulder. The noise and the smell of the diesel engine upwind of his position garnered his full attention. Thus, he did not notice the two men approaching him from the other side of the boulder on which he was lying.

The leading man placed his left hand on the top of the boulder and prepared to push off the ground with his right foot. The boulder stood just over his head. As he pushed up, he extended his right arm and searched for a hand hold. His hand closed around the first lump it passed over. The lump was the king brown's back. The snake immediately snapped round and sank its fangs into the man's forearm. The fangs pierced the naked arm and injected a full load of venom.

'I've been fucken bitten'.

'Keep moving, the ute's only on the other side of the boulder. Foreman will fix you.'

'Bullshit, I need Doc.'

'Well, you'd better hope he can get through.'

Unable to use his right arm, the injured man scrambled onto the top of the boulder, his companion pushing him from behind. He staggered to his feet, all but fell down the other side and stumbled to the ute. His companion pushed up behind him, opened the rear passenger door and shoved him across the back seat.'

'What's wrong with that moron?'

'Snakebite.'

'Fuck, can't you idiots do anything without screwing it up?'

The exertion of climbing the rock and staggering to the ute, along with the adrenaline his body had pushed out as a consequence of the shock of the snakebite, had pushed the poison through the man's system. He was not in a good way. Emitting sounds alternating between a whimper and a muffled scream, sweat was pouring off him. The Foreman took one look at him and reached a decision. He turned the ute back down the hill and followed the fence which crossed the front of the property.

'Open the gate,' he ordered the man in the passenger seat. The gate was opened, the ute passed through. 'Now close the fucking thing.'

The ute passed across the front of the facility and followed the path to a brick building with a chimney on the far side of the fenced-off area.

'Give me a hand,' the Foreman said, as he parked next to a square steel portal in the front of the building.

'What are you doing boss?'

'Throwing him in the fucking incinerator.'

'But he is not even dead.'

'Yeah well, he will be when I light the gas. Now shove him in.'

The stricken man went through the portal headfirst — not even able to protect himself with his hands as he landed on the steel grate inside. His whimpering grew louder and more intense until it was shut off by the slamming of the hatch and the turning of the handle, dogging the door down tight.

'Open the flu while I light the gas.'

The Foreman waited for the whoosh of the furnace igniting and returned to the ute. He did not offer the survivor a lift. 'Tell the rest of your mates they will need to work harder to cover Three's load. It will be a while before he can be replaced. Tomorrow, shovel out the ashes and spread them across the corn paddock.' With that he drove off, leaving the survivor to walk back to the trustees' compound. The death of his companion meant nothing. He had helped a good many people into the furnace before and knew he would be cremating a few more in the future. His only concern being to remain the helper, not the helped.

CHAPTER 13

The trustees had known no other life. They were born into the facility, removed from their mothers immediately and raised with the other infant stock. A smattering of stock managed to survive until adolescence: the males as trustees and studs, the females as breeding stock. Both male and female stock starred in the productions filmed in the studios hidden behind the main house.

*

'Up slut, Boss wants to see ya,' accompanied the toe of a boot into Sara Jane's side. She jerked up totally disorientated, then came to her senses as memories of the previous day crashed through her consciousness.

The owner of the boot stood over her. Dressed in filthy, second-hand clothes, the face peering down at her had never seen a razor, nor a dentist, and only had a passing acquaintance with clean water. He seemed to be in his early twenties, slightly above average height, with a body that suggested hard work and not quite enough food. He stank.

'I need to go to the loo first,' replied SJ.

'Youse can take a piss when I say so.' He dropped his hand down, grabbed a handful of her hair and dragged her to her feet. She gritted her teeth, rose to her feet and willed herself to relax. She wasn't going to learn anything by getting knocked about at this point. Behind her back she gave Lui Chin the thumbs up, she would only learn more by seeing the Boss.

57

She was dragged across the shed and through the door. The door was shut and bolted from the outside. Then she was dragged by the hair across to a farmhouse, up the half dozen stairs, across the verandah and into the front room which was now an office. The floorboards were bare, and a metal desk stood facing the doorway with the light of the window behind it. An old wooden chair stood in front of the desk. Sara Jane was half-dragged across the floor and deposited in the chair.

Thinning brown hair, faded blue eyes, coarse skin and a couple of days of beard growth. More human than the animal who had dragged her across from the shed but one look was enough, this was not a person you wanted to meet.

'Sara Jane Marlowe, legendary journalist in her own lunchtime. You've fucked with the wrong people this time. I am the Foreman here, the bloke behind you and his two mates are my deputies. You see, the boys were born here, raised here, this is all they know. You belong to me; I decide whether you eat, sleep or live.'

'People will miss me, they will search, they know what I was working on,' replied SJ.

'Bullshit,' the Foreman turned around his computer, opened to a Facebook page.

'Here you are enjoying the sights of India, about to embark on a trek into the unknown. Unfortunately, you and your new boyfriend will disappear here at the base of the Himalayas.'

'That will not fool anyone. What a crock of shit.'

'Don't worry we are about to send those that matter a more direct warning. You see one of the sidelines we have here is movie-making. A certain type of movie, and one that Four enjoys making. You are about to become a star.

'We'll send out the finished product through a server in India as a further misdirection.

'This movie will have a happy ending. This time, you'll still be alive at the end of it.'

The thug behind her gripped her by the hair again. Sara Jane was dragged from the office, out the front door, and round the back of the house into one of the demountable buildings behind it. The door slammed shut. It was a film studio, several cameras fixed to the walls on swivel mounts. There was a bed and no other furniture, the sheets were plastic.

A hidden speaker came alive. 'Shakespeare wrote *The Taming of the Shrew*. Today we will make a little improv movie called *Taming of the Slut* starring Sara Jane Marlowe,' the Foreman's voice intoned.

'And rolling.'

The thug known as Four was actually drooling. Sara Jane assessed the situation. He stood a good twelve inches taller than she did. He was depending on weight, height and fear to overpower his prey. They had underestimated her so entirely they hadn't even confiscated her high-sided sneakers. The ones with the composite carbon fibre caps. Lighter and stronger than steel.

Sara Jane took a couple of steps backwards. Reinforcing the image of a helpless, frightened victim, she avoided his eyes, hunched her shoulders, and forced a whimper out between her lips. He strode towards her; she retreated. They picked up speed towards the rear wall. She skipped backwards, he was almost on her. Out of her peripheral vision she saw she was nearly backed up against the wall. She whimpered and shuffled backwards, arms held out in front of her, palms forward, elbows bent, her whole body language one of fear and panic. He charged, she stepped forward and to her left, grabbed his outstretched arm, spun and using his momentum slammed him into the wall. She continued her spin, twirling around behind him in the same movement. Focusing her momentum through her lifted arm, she rammed her open palm into the back of his head, slamming his face into the wall. All in one fluid movement.

There was a moment's silence, shock and awe, that Sara Jane

used to slam her toe into his knee, smashing it sideways. It hurt him but did not damage him. He was beyond reason, six-foot-four of unfettered fury as she danced back across the room, dodging the bed, back to the wall by the door they had entered. He charged again, this time she looked him in the face and raised her hands as though she was going to use her fists. He came at her, she sidestepped and kicked the same knee again. This time there was a pop and the leg collapsed beneath him. He stumbled and fell.

He was down on all fours in front of her his legs slightly spread and she aimed her kick between them. Her foot felt the squish as his genitals were crushed against his pubic bone, she put a second kick into the same place for good measure. He collapsed onto his side. She walked round to his face and placed a kick into each of his eye sockets and his nose.

CHAPTER 14

The phone rings. Not the one on the desk, the one in the drawer.

The Foreman answers the phone, 'Foreman here.'

'Report. Update from yesterday.'

'We are hoping to return to normal production very soon.'

'Anyone show any interest in the facility?'

'As mentioned, one firey came to the gate and advised us to evacuate. I told him we were OK and he left.'

'You don't think they will be back again to check? You don't want me to drop a message down the line to have them tick you off as OK? I would rather they stayed away from the facility.'

'Yeah, do that.'

'I want that place to have a profile seriously less than low.'

'Agreed,' returned the Foreman.

'OK, so we have a backlog of orders and we are down on stock. You have two new females. They are to be kept as breeders. See if you can add to them. It is going to take a few years to be back to full stock, so breeding females are a premium. Have the doc run comparisons between our order book and stock, let's make sure we achieve maximum utilisiation from each kill. Also have him put the females on fertility drugs; let's see if we can push through some multiple births.

'The movies are still turning over a steady income, but there also we need some fresh material. Let's make sure the next one is as good as the last one. Making the lovey-dovey one first, then the snuff flick gives us a two-for-one. But tell your clowns to stretch it out. Longer flicks are exponentially more profitable. A longer snuff flick even more so.'

The Foreman, thought on this for a second, 'You sure you want to keep the reporter woman around? She could be dangerous.'

'Let me worry about that, just make sure you keep her alive and relatively undamaged until we decide what to do with her. I have mentioned her to the Syndicate and they have promised to discuss her at their next meeting. I believe they have plans for her.'

The Foreman's eyes looked up at the security monitor on his wall. The bottom left quarter showed the studio. Four had just entered the room and was stalking Sara Jane.

A light sweat formed on the Foreman's top lip. He needed to end this call and intervene before Sara Jane was toast. 'We're all good with that. I will give you a ping to signal the next call when I have the results from Doc.'

The Foreman terminated the call and jumped up from his desk sending his chair flying. He needed to get to the studio before Four damaged the reporter. From the sounds of the Boss's orders, the Syndicate would be wanting Sara Jane for their own private stock. He rushed out without looking up again.

The door slammed open and the other two thugs rushed in; she knew she couldn't beat three at once but hoped that their anger would make her end quick.

The Foreman was crashing through the door screaming, 'Don't damage the fucking goods, don't damage the fucking goods. Bring the slut to me.'

'Fuck, fuck, fuck.' He slapped her face while the thugs held her. 'I'd let them kill you right now, right fucking here, but I am under fucking orders to keep you alive and undamaged. But if I had my way you'd take a long, painful time getting fucking dead.'

CHAPTER 15

A light rain was falling.

It had been pushed across the Australian continent by a cyclone off the northwest coast of Western Australia, then back up the coast as a "southerly buster". The fires north of Sydney were now last week's news. South of Sydney was a different story.

Joe was just finishing his first day back at work after nearly a month fighting the fires. Having left behind his corporate job in Sydney two years ago, Joe was settling into the rhythm of the lakeside community he had bought into. Semi-retired he supposed was the correct definition. Not bad for thirty-two. Now it was time to discover life outside the office!

The house had been a blank canvas, left empty for a couple of years, the middle-aged children of the elderly owner had taken their time deciding what to do with the place. Being left in limbo for that time, the house was almost derelict when Joe discovered it on the shores of Lake Macquarie, an hour-and-a-half north of Sydney. Joe was quickly discovering the old house was a demanding mistress. Every time he thought his head was above water a whole lot of new challenges appeared and he was sucked back under again.

Still, after all that time fighting fires, even the small amount of corporate work he did now for pocket money was behind schedule. The first day back had been a short one. It was hard to adjust to sitting in front of a computer. Luckily his office was in the spare bedroom so it was a short commute to the kitchen.

His dog, whom he had hardly seen since the fires started, kept to his side in case he disappeared again. It was time he gave his best mate some attention. Joe looked outside; it was only drizzling. Time to take the dog for a walk.

Keys, lead, poo baggies and umbrella. The mid-sized labradoodle pranced round excitedly. Joe lassoed him into his harness and stepped out, locking the door behind him. It was definitely drizzling. That steady, boring dampness that was not quite rain but still left you saturated. It did not take long for Joe to decide it was not that pleasant after all, and he now had a wet dog to dry, so he turned for home.

Letting himself back in, he found Jessica sitting at the kitchen table. The dog ran up to say hello. *Traitor* thought Joe, *you've never met her before.* Joe took off his shoes, walked through into the bathroom, pulled a towel off the rack and dried his hair. He then went into his room and changed into a dry T-shirt and shorts. 'Well that could have been interesting. Usually I dump my wet stuff in the garage and do a nudie walk into the bedroom,' he said. 'Lucky for you I have been on so many strike teams lately, I haven't got used to been on my lonesome again.

'Sara Jane, what brings an urban sophisticate like yourself to a rustic setting such as this?' continued Joe, channelling " the Kid" from *Blazing Saddles.*

'Actually, it's Jessica, Sara Jane's my sister.'

'Identical twins?'

'No, I was using Sara Jane's name.'

'So, Jessica, not Sara Jane, who entered my house through a locked door, and whose boss can order the whole Rural Fire Service around on a whim. I don't know whether to be intrigued or pissed off? Luckily I am still on the fence, otherwise I might call the cops.'

'I am the cops, but this is a personal matter.'

'Spill.'

'Aren't you going to offer me a coffee or a drink?'

'Depends which side of the fence I come down on!'

'OK, Sara Jane's my sister, she actually is a journalist, and is missing. She believes, and has convinced me, that she is on the trail of a human trafficking and baby-farming operation. That property I was watching was one of their bases of operation.

'I was recruited out of the NSW police into a Federal Police special unit tasked with routing out organised crime, concentrating on connections within the government. Basically, her work and my work started to overlap.

'Now she has disappeared and I believe she is being held at the facility in that valley. I would appreciate your help with accessing the property.'

'Why me?'

'Simple. You already know and suspect something is wrong with the property. We have to keep this tight. The lives of the people at that facility depend on it. The protection they are getting means any attempts we make through normal channels will be fed straight back to the facility and the captives will disappear, permanently.'

'I am sort of falling onto the "bullshit" side of the fence. Sounds a bit over-the-top. Anyway, I have had enough for tonight. It is Friday night and I am going to enjoy a steak and a bottle of wine. There's the door, please use it.'

'No.'

Joe relented. He had to admit to himself he was a little bit intrigued by the whole thing. 'OK, well I am going up the shops, grabbing a steak, some spuds and a bottle of red. I am not going to talk about this until I have had a decent feed. You can join me or not.'

Jessica's stomach came alive. Ignored since the Thai the night before and some energy bars in the field, it let her know that steak and chips would be really appreciated. 'OK, I'm in.'

'Back in fifteen minutes. Keep the dog entertained.'

Joe wanted the time to himself. He had to admit that Jessica had turned his head. He was a different man now that he had left the city and the long working hours with hardly any breaks. The internet company his team put together had listed, and at thirty Joe had cashed in his stock, sold his place in Sydney's wealthy eastern suburbs, and landed on the shores of Lake Macquarie, ninety minutes to the north. There had been women, usually taken home after a few drinks after work, but with the business all-encompassing they never stayed round for more than a couple of weeks.

He didn't think there was a future between himself and Jessica. He saw himself in her, a few years ago, with only room in her life for her commitment to the job. Still, if anyone was going to break into his house at least she would be easy to describe to the police. Hazel eyes, brown hair with highlights, a fit, lean body just over average height. She also seemed brave and determined, but given the circumstances probably unattainable. And she might shoot him if he tried. *Must be getting broody*, thought Joe, realising he was appraising Jessica as a life partner not a night's entertainment.

Chopping up some carrot, potato, onion and pumpkin, adding a bit of olive oil and some seasoning, Joe loaded his air fryer. Definitely the bachelor's best friend. He let the veggies cook for a few minutes while the steaks marinated, he threw on the steaks and set the timer on his phone for twelve minutes, poured two glasses of red and joined Jessica.

'I lived off takeaway and restaurant food for years, then spent hours in the gym sweating it back out of my system. Now I take a little bit more care.'

Joe looked at Jessica, he could see she was about to lose patience with this veneer of normality. 'I don't really give a crap, but I do need the food.'

Jessica pushed her laptop over to Joe. 'Read this. It is Sara Jane's last article.' The article was tight and well-written, listing the facts Sara Jane had discovered, then leading on to her assumptions, clearly stated, and her conclusion. It explained the reception he had received at the chicken farm.

Jessica changed screens. Joe was now looking at a Facebook page. 'This is Sara Jane. See how there is nothing for months and now we are seeing selfies in front of the Taj Mahal? Sara Jane doesn't do selfies.' Joe had a look at the images. He could see they were sisters. He looked closer.

'This is the same picture of your sister in each shot, pasted over different backgrounds.'

'Yes, and look at the last entry.'

'"Going off-grid, going to do some trekking with new friends. Might even be some romance with an Englishman and a gentleman",' Jessica read.

'My guess is she won't survive the trek, but the focus will be on the Himalayas not back of fucking Wyong Creek.

'Also, anyone who knows Sara Jane knows this is a fake. SJ prefers girls.'

'Not much of her,' observed Joe. He could see Sara Jane was probably a couple of inches under Jessica's height, but like Jessica, she did look strong and fit, not gym fit, athlete fit.

'While I spent time down the surf club, did netball and a bit of dirt bike riding, SJ went her own way and became a martial arts fanatic. She was the smart kid and always seemed to have this sense of injustice but was petite and often bullied. When she came out, determined to let the world know she was gay, she was thirteen and it got worse. By then SJ, and I am not sure of the correct expression, was a multiple danned black belt. Two arseholes, a couple of years older than her, decided that they would "convince her to bat for the right side". Needless to say, Mum and Dad were not happy when the arseholes' parents wanted us to pay their medical bills. SJ initiated a social media campaign and the arseholes nearly ended up in jail.

'SJ doesn't take a backward step. Previously she has always got herself out of these predicaments. But this time I think she is in way over her head. Without help she is dead.'

The air fryer pinged and Joe plated the food. He went to pour Jessica another glass of wine, but she covered her glass with her hand. 'Driving,' she said. They ate in silence, Joe poured himself another glass of wine or three.

*

'OK, OK, OK, I need time to process this. First, I am an accountant not a superhero. Second, I am knackered from the last couple of months and third, I need to think about this with a clear head. But I think I do have the seeds of a plan.

'Can you please open Google maps and enlarge the area behind the farm,' he instructed Jessica. 'After a fire it is customary for the Rural Fire Service to survey the fire trails for damage and access. We can hire a couple of trail bikes, wear my RFS bike gear – luckily I have two sets – and have a good look at the place. Once we know what we are dealing with, we can plan a course of action.

'With the Watagan Mountains behind us being a popular riding spot, the local bike shop has some bikes we can rent.'

Joe focused on the map. 'We are only about fifteen kilometres from this road here, we follow it up into the Watagan Mountains National Park and turn left at this junction, follow it along the ridge line, turn left again and follow this fire trail which should take us behind the facility. That area did not burn so we should have decent cover, and as an RFS "survey team" we have a believable excuse for being in the area.'

Joe sipped the last of the wine. 'Be here at 7 am tomorrow.'

'I will need authority from my team leader to do this,' replied Jessica.

'No deal. No one knows until after the event. I don't want to ride into an ambush.'

'You can trust her,' bristled Jessica.

'Yeah, but then it has to go through channels, and for an organisation such as this, these guys must be connected. Otherwise they couldn't survive. So, while you trust your boss, I don't trust the system.'

'Be here at 7 am tomorrow. No good doing any more planning now. Anything I do after a bottle of red is usually a screw-up. You are welcome to stay here if you wish. We will deal with this tomorrow.'

'I have a place for tonight. I will be here at seven tomorrow morning. Just make sure you are in a fit state to do the job.' With that Jessica stood up and walked out the kitchen door. Joe heard her car start and accelerate into the night.

He had slept like a log. *Probably sounded like a lumberjack with a chainsaw*, was Joe's first thought on waking. At 6 am Joe climbed out of bed, disturbing his dog.

'Come on, get up, ya bludger.'

The dog, realising breakfast was on the agenda, sprung out of bed and escorted Joe to the kitchen. A bowl full of kibble and a top-up of his water bowl and all was right in his world.

Joe knocked himself up a bowl of cereal and fruit. He started a checklist of supplies to pack for the day. He packed only what he could carry in his pockets, the first of his criteria for ensuring they could make a quick exit. His previous experience and Jessica's briefing had convinced him he was dealing with some nasty characters.

He assembled his two RFS riding outfits and the supplies he thought they would need. The bike shop would not be open until eight, giving him time to work through the equipment and plan with Jessica.

The Rural Fire Service did not like to waste money, so the motorcycle teams mostly wore one-size-fits-all protective clothing in the familiar yellow-gold colours. Joe had his own helmets which he had fitted with an intercom set. Jessica and he would be able to talk to each other while they rode.

At 6:45 Jessica was at his door. Joe let her into the kitchen and took her through the equipment and supplies he had laid out on the dining-room table. Together they test fitted and adjusted the gear Jessica was to wear. Luckily, she had brought her own steel-capped boots. She added a pair of high-definition cameras to the pile. 'We can strap these to some trees, they have their own SIM cards so we can access them remotely,' she explained.

At 8:15 Joe rang the bike shop. He quickly arranged the hire of two Yamaha DR 450s. Perfect for the fire trails they would be covering. Everything was in his car ten minutes later.

Joe and Jessica rode the bikes out of the bike shop and into a quiet corner of the industrial estate where Joe had parked his car. They hadn't wanted to draw attention to themselves by wearing the RFS disguises in front of the shop staff. Once changed, Joe locked his car and they rode out of the industrial estate taking the B-road across the Sydney-Newcastle motorway and into the rich farmland at the foot of the Watagan Mountains.

The rain and drizzle from the last few days was becoming more sporadic. While cloudy, the still air was becoming hot. The resultant humidity resulted in some patches of fog and mist. Joe and Jessica kept the revs down and used the torque of the single-cylinder engines to keep their exhaust noise muted. They left the B-road and took the well-tended gravel road into the national park. With every turn they took towards their destination the road deteriorated, and by the time they reached the trail above the facility, it was reduced to a pair of tyre tracks through the scrub. Much of the way had been burnt out by the fires, but as they closed in on their target they found the forest had mostly survived thanks to the effectiveness of the farm's sprinkler system stopping the fire.

They left the bikes in a patch of scrub bordered by lantana bushes that provided plenty of cover from three sides. The bikes were parked facing the fourth, cleared side in case the pair needed to make a quick exit. They were standing in the bush on the ridge one hundred metres behind their target. Joe and Jessica kept their helmets on so they could communicate using the intercom.

Finding places for the cameras was their next task. Joe and Jessica cut across the ridge and down to towards the corner boundary of the property. Joe found a tree which looked diagonally across the property, taking in the fence line and the rear of the target. He attached the camera with a pair of cable ties and switched it on. Checking his mobile, he confirmed the clarity of the signal and showed his screen to Jessica for her approval. Before mounting the second camera they retreated to the bikes to decide the best placement, based on what they had seen of the farm. Jessica drew a square representing the property in a patch of dirt. She showed the first camera's coverage as a set of dotted lines fanning out across the rear fence and behind the buildings. There was about one hundred metres of cleared land between the two. Next, she poked a hole in the ground with her stick representing a position about three-quarters of the way across the rear fence and further up the slope. The fan lines she drew penetrated down the passageway between the corrugated sheds and into the courtyard further down the slope.

Joe scanned the forest. He spied a tree just below their position. 'That tree there, we could use the second fork?'

'Yep,' confirmed Jessica.

They descended to the tree. Joe was able to climb up and verify the sightline was clear. He strapped the camera quickly round the branch with cable ties and slithered back down to the ground. He had felt a bit exposed sitting up there above the scrub. He quickly checked he was receiving the transmission from the second camera. This time when they returned to the bikes, they jumped straight on, started the motors, and as quietly as they could rode back to the intersecting track.

Once they had ridden two or so kilometres the adrenaline could no longer be denied. They picked up speed and pushed the bikes harder. Coming wide into a gravel corner, weight forward and inside leg stretched out, foot sliding across the gravel, Joe goosed the throttle and let the rear wheel slide, tightening his line through the corner. He could hear Jessica's laughter in his ear through the intercom as she followed his tracks. Seconds later they were staring down the bullbar of a LandCruiser belonging to a family sightseeing the destruction wrought by the fires. They both braked, blocking the track, and forcing the LandCruiser to stop as well. Apologies all round, and they continued on their way. As they were still in disguise, Joe wondering if the near miss would be reported back to the RFS.

They parked the bikes at a picnic ground in the national park. Each linked to one of the cameras with their mobile phones. 'Lucky we have coverage out here,' commented Jessica.

'Yeah, saves going all the way back into town. Fuck, would you look at that!' replied Joe.

Sara Jane was shoved back into the pen she had awoken in earlier. Lui Chin guided her to the bench. Sara Jane, panting like a cornered wild animal, paced their cage, staring at the bolted door. She closed her eyes, took deep slow breaths through her nose and released them slowly through her mouth. Her heart rate began to subside.

'Shit, what did you do? Those two thugs were scared shitless of you. They couldn't off-load you fast enough.'

'I doubt I'll get away with that again. I got one of the bastards, took him out. We need to get the fuck out of here NOW. Once they regroup, they won't give me a second chance.'

They searched the pen. The walls were corrugated iron bolted to the upright posts supporting the roof. The gap between the top of the corrugated iron and the roof was fortified with chicken wire. The door hinged inward and appeared to be chained and padlocked on the outside. They searched for tools. Lui Chin examined the hinges holding the back of the door to one of the upright posts. By wriggling the door backwards and forwards she saw the hinges were only bolted through the corrugated iron of the door not to a frame or backing plate. She reached up stretching her arms and, on her toes, she grabbed the rear edge of the door where it met the chicken wire across its top edge. She swung her weight of the top. The metal around the hinges deformed.

'I know we are a pair of short-arses but if we swing the top of this door in and out, I reckon these hinges will rip free of the metal.'

Sara Jane took two steps and leaped, curling her hands over

the top of the door next to Lui Chin. Together they pulled the door an inch or two into the pen. When it reached its limit, they pushed it out into the corridor outside the room. Kneeling down, Sara Jane took hold of the bottom of the door, now protruding into their pen, and lifted. The metal stretched again. Together they set a rhythm with the door moving more each cycle. It was going to take a while, especially as they had to be stealthy, sacrificing speed for silence.

The metal surrounding the top hinge let go. It had taken them all night. The door was still suspended by the latch and padlock and the bottom hinge, but they were able to pivot it far enough to clamber over the top. They propped the door back into position and shimmied along the wall away from the end of the building Sara Jane had been dragged through on her way to the studio.

They could see a floor-to-roof gate at the end of the corridor, and the distant view of a dam. The ground rose outside from left to right. The storm front had pushed through and the last hot spots from the fire were still steaming. The gate was unlocked. The security depended on the prisoners being subdued by fear and the drugs in their food. Sara Jane and Lui Chin hadn't eaten and had not been in the facility long enough to be drugged. They undid the latch and exited the building. The only surviving bush was uphill. They could faintly hear two dirt bikes.

'We have to go uphill into the bush. It's the only cover. Those bikes are on tracks, our only chance is to follow them and hope they lead somewhere.'

Darting from the rear of one shed to another they made their way up the hill. 'See that ditch, it goes under the fence. Looks like a wombat has opened up the creek bed. Since the fires, this place must be one of the only places with decent feed. Don't touch that single wire across the top. It looks electrified.'

They managed to get though the fence and into the scrub. It was as far as they could go; their abductions, lack of food and water and flagging adrenaline had sapped their strength.

A gloved arm attached to a yellow sleeve reached down and clutched Sara Jane's hand. A similar hand had latched onto Lui Chin's right arm. The two escapees were dragged up the slope and into a clearing sheltered by lantana. Two trail bikes were idling in the clearing. 'Come with us if you want to live,' uttered one of the figures in a poor imitation of an Austrian-American accent.

'Don't mind him, just get on the fucking bikes so we can get the fuck out of here.'

'Jessica,' yelled Sara Jane.

'Yep, here to get you out of the shit again.'

'Who's that?'

'Meet Joe.'

The facility had remained ominously quiet. Joe straddled his bike and clutched hold of Lui Chin's sleeve and pulled. She resisted for a second, then jumped on the rear of the bike. Lifted her legs onto the pegs and wrapped her arms round Joe's waist in a death grip. Joe clunked the bike into first, released the clutch and opened the throttle. Jessica, with Sara Jane pillion, followed.

It wasn't a comfortable ride, with both bikes were overloaded and going as hard as they could. The rear suspension constantly bottoming out, hitting the stops. At each intersection the track improved until they were on the well-graded road of the Watagan National Park. The bikes descended from the forest and were soon on the black top. With two passengers each they could only maintain a wobbly seventy kilometres an hour. For Joe this was the most nerve-racking time. They had to stay on this road but could easily be run down by any pursuing vehicle from the facility hunting the escapees.

Joe rode straight through the industrial area, through town and out to the lake. He stopped long enough on his driveway to zap open the garage door and ride straight in. Jessica followed and he zapped the door closed. They were out of sight. Whether or not any one had noticed them remained to be seen.

*

'How the fuck did you manage that?' demanded Sara Jane.

Joe and Jessica took off their helmets. 'Basically, we just got lucky,' replied Joe.

'By the way I am Joe Burnett, and you are?' asked Joe turning towards Lui Chin. He had recognised Sara Jane straight away.

'Me Lui Chin, hello Joe,' replied Lui Chin in her best Filipino accent.

'Ha, the missing global Task Force operative. How are you going, Tracey?' replied Jessica.

'How am I supposed to be undercover when the whole fucking world seems to know who I am?'

'OK, let's can the meet-and-greet for a minute. Jessica, let's return these bikes. But first we need to change into normal riding gear. We will back in about twenty minutes.'

Joe and Jessica shucked out of the RFS uniforms and into some old motorcycling gear Joe had lying around. He wanted to pour cold water on their trail as much as possible. The ride back to the bike shop was an anticlimax after the run through the forest. Joe and Jessica were soon back in Joe's house with his car in the garage.

'Well, I am going to have a coffee. I also have tea. It's out of a jar, I can't be bothered with a coffee machine,' commented Joe on the way to the kitchen. 'Dunny's through that door there if you need it. Shower is the next one along.'

Ten minutes later they were sitting round the kitchen table drinking strong coffee with extra sugar. The dog was beside himself with all these new people to meet.

'So how did you pull that off?' asked Sara Jane.

'We snuck in this morning and placed two cameras watching the back of the place for intel so we could work out how to rescue you. That we rescued Tracey is a bonus,' answered Jessica. 'Once we had placed the cameras, we scootered back to a picnic spot in the centre of the Watagans and were able to connect to a camera each with our phones. And what do you know, but out pop you two.'

'There are at least another ten prisoners there, mostly kids,' replied Tracey. 'I could hear them while Sara Jane was out from the drugs. My sources believe they ran the numbers down because of the fires. We will need to free those remaining.'

'I'll contact my boss, and we'll take it from here,' said Jessica.

'Be very careful, we believe there is a leak in your organisation,' cautioned Tracey.

'Yes, we have suspected that, but our team is only small, and we are operating outside the chain-of-command.'

Tracey thought this over momentarily, 'OK, no worries Jessica. By the way how does Joe fit in?'

'He doesn't, he was just wrong place right time.'

'Twice,' added Joe.

Joe decided it was the right time to take the dog for a walk. He had no interest in becoming more involved. He could see it was about to become official, and with that, jurisdictions and politics came into play. 'See yah in about an hour, make yourselves at home,' he said to no one in particular as he exited the room with the dog on his heels.

Joe and Jessica's cameras where not the only ones in the forest behind the facility. The Foreman sat at his desk staring at the computer. He watched as the two Rural Fire Fighters assisted Sara Jane and Lui Chin up the hill. Time to make some enquiries into the RFS bike squad. If that's who they were; two visits in three days was too much interest for it to be a coincidence.

He opened the CCTV footage from the incident down at the front gate three days ago. There was a good chance, he thought, a representative of the RFS asking people to abandon their properties would be wearing an official identification badge. He zoomed in and there it was. Front left label of the guy's riding jacket, "Joe Burnett, Headland Rural Fire Service". Bingo.

'Let's have a look at you, Mr Burnett.' The Foreman moved the freeze pane of Joe onto his second screen. On the primary computer screen, he enlarged a still from the morning's escape. The name badge was missing, but looking at the two stills together, the helmets were the same. Closer inspection showed the same scorch marks on the jacket from previous fire fights. Confirmed.

'Got you, dirt bag. So who is Joe Burnett when he's at home?'

Joe was an open book. He'd never had a reason to hide. A quick search of Facebook and the Foreman had all he needed.

What to do with the information? He really did not want to get the Boss involved. With the clues attained at their last meeting and some time trawling through the society pages, the Foreman was ninety per cent certain he had detected the Boss's real identity.

He had no doubt the Boss would set him up as the sacrificial lamb should anything go wrong. The escape of the women and discovery of the facility by Burnett were as about as wrong as it could go. The Syndicate's early retirement plan was fatal.

It was time to disappear. Not only disappear but offer the Syndicate and the authorities a juicier target. The Boss. He needed to assume he only had a matter of hours. His protagonists would be back to rescue the rest of the stock. All the pieces were in place. Since he'd commenced as Foreman of the facility, he knew his exit plan was his most challenging task.

There would be one additional task. This one was personal, more a retirement gift to himself. Joe Burnett must die.

He opened the Syndicate's VPN and the TOR browser. Time for a trawl through the dark web for some specialised services. The nature of dark websites and the encryption levels built into TOR made searches considerably slower than a normal web search. While he was waiting, the Foreman lit a cigarette and contemplated his future.

His computer beeped. A list appeared on the screen. The Foremen clicked on one of the links. Some cryptic emails were exchanged. Joe's details were forwarded and a fee agreed upon.

He had his own bitcoin account. But for the first time he used the Syndicate's bitcoin account. He had obtained the public and private keys to the Syndicate's bitcoin wallet previously but had never used them. It had been easy. Many people assumed that because Bitcoin was clandestine, it was also secure. Long ago he had broken into the office of the Syndicate's local Bookkeeper and installed a key logger on his computer. The Bookkeeper accessed the bitcoin account to transfer the funds into a local credit card account which he then used to pay local bills such as electricity and council rates.

From watching the transactions, the Foreman knew the Syndicate processed all its revenue through this wallet, which it cleared daily into a second wallet for security. The Foreman paid the agreed-upon fee for killing Joe. He then changed the destination of the clearing account to his own. He knew it would be discovered but even two or three days income of an international crime organisation like the Syndicate would keep him in luxury for several lifetimes.

Next, he created a single-use Gmail account. He addressed an email to the anonymous Crime Stoppers police intelligence gathering unit and attached the video of the Boss and the boy from the Alexandria warehouse. He included some stills showing a scar on the man's hands and a picture from a society magazine showing a prominent Sydney identity with the same scar. Using Photoshop he cut and pasted a picture of the Boss's head and face over the top of the hood in the video. A bit of colouring and shading and the result looked half-reasonable. This he posted on a dark web child pornography site. He copied the link and once it was activated, would email it to a state politician with a reputation for pursuing paedophiles for his own glorification.

Now the diversions were in place, time to implement his escape and obliterate the evidence. In the shed behind the homestead he opened the rear barn doors of the old ambulance. Peeling back a dusty tarpaulin in the rear of the garage he exposed a midrange motorcycle, it's side and rear paniers prepacked for a quick exit. He wheeled the bike into the rear of the ambulance and strapped it down to the floor. He would drive out as per normal, park in the local industrial area, wait until nightfall and roll the bike down the ramp, to ride off into the night a new man, the Foreman's identity left behind in the van.

A timer was attached to the wall. It was set for three hours. Scattered around the facility were barrels of fertiliser mixed with diesel fuel. The wires from the timer led to detonators located inside these barrels of homemade ANFO explosives. The explosives had been designed and placed to cause fires less suspicious than blowing the place to smithereens. He started the timer, climbed into the old ambulance, started its engine and motored out of the facility for the last time.

82

Joe walked past the boat ramp, through the park then up his driveway and in through the kitchen door.

'Joe, this is my boss Ms Bowman,' said Jessica before Joe could ask who the newcomer was. Joe recognised her as the driver of the LandCruiser that had rescued them a couple of days ago. She was dressed in what looked like combat fatigues, with muted colours and multiple pockets, an expensive bob haircut, manicured hands and muted but tasteful make-up. Joe was not quite sure how best to react.

'Good morning, you got here quickly,' he held out his hand. Ms Bowman stood and shook it. She had a firm and dry handshake. Joe estimated she was mid-fifties, fit, and about average height.

'I brought a team up first thing this morning, we were on standby about ten minutes away.'

'Well, I hope those two black SUVs over in the boat ramp carpark are yours, otherwise I am afraid the bad guys might have found us.'

'Yes, that's my team.'

'They can park round the side and come in if you want.'

'No, we are mounting up and going in to rescue the rest of the hostages,' Ms Bowman said. 'I have just received Jessica's report. Sara Jane and Tracey have added what they know.

'We need your help. I have a team of four plus Jessica. Sara Jane and Tracey need rest. They would probably slow us down, and you know the tracks and fire trails. So we are asking if could assist us.

'We leave now. You ride with Jessica and myself. I will brief you on the way.'

Joe turned towards Sara Jane and Tracey, 'Can you please mind the dog till we get back?' Joe asked, wanting to appear in control of something, no matter how small. Sara Jane and Tracey nodded their agreement. Joe took a second look at them. 'You can use the beds in my room and the spare room. You two look like death warmed up.'

'Fuck off,' snarled Sara Jane. Joe realised being left behind had made her angry. Personally, he agreed with the decision. Sara Jane and Tracey would be a liability, they were just too exhausted to help. It didn't mean they had to like it.

'Looks quiet there at the moment,' commented Jessica connecting her mobile phone to the cameras still mounted in the trees behind the facility. 'Strange, I would expect to see some activity. Surely they know Sara Jane and Tracey have escaped.'

'Yeah, according to Sara Jane there are two trustees and the Foreman still fit and active. Is this only "live" or is it recorded as well?' asked Ms Bowman.

Joe handed over his phone. 'It's recorded to the cloud. Here is the site address.'

'Jessica, view it in the car. We need to get going. Joe, you are navigating with me in the lead vehicle,' instructed Ms Bowman as she led the way out of the room. 'Make sure you are dressed for some low-profile bush bashing.'

Ms Bowman opened her mobile phone and hit a stored number. 'Everyone clear vehicle one, I will drive it with Burnett navigating. Officer J will be with us. Remember the target probably has CCTV and booby traps. This will be a dark mission. Remember to use your hoods.'

Joe and Jessica jogged to keep up as Ms Bowman left the house, strode across the road and approached the vehicles in the boat ramp carpark. The vehicle on the left had both front doors open. 'Joe, you drive, I want to brief the troops.'

The car was a generic heavy-duty 4WD. Seven seats. All badges had been removed and the vehicle painted a flat charcoal grey with lighter waves through it. Camouflaged but still threatening.

The keys were in the ignition. The diesel V8 rumbled into life. 'Not very stealthy,' commented Joe.

From the passenger seat Ms Bowman replied, 'The blue button switches it to electric mode. Good for about ten kilometres at about twenty kilometres per hour max speed. Stealth mode. We will use it for the final approach. Jessica, keep an eye on the live feed.'

For the second time that day, Joe approached the Watagan Mountains. Once on the gravel he engaged 4WD high range. 'Switch to electric mode when we reach the last intersection. Plan A: all teams follow us to the clearing marked on the map. We will turn the vehicles around there for a quick exit. Team Beta, your task will be to guard the trucks. Everyone use your tasers. No gunfire unless absolutely unavoidable. Burnett will lead team Alpha down to the fence; team A lpha will breech the fence ensuring the electric fence remains intact to avoid tripping any alarm. Burnett will then return to the vehicle and remain with team Beta.'

'Plan B: plan B comes into play should Jess detect activity at the target. In which case we will leave the vehicles on the main fire trail, turned around, engines running for a quick exit. We will infiltrate on foot. We will use the tranquiliser gun on any opposition from the clearing above here, then revert to the second half of plan A. We may call team Beta to bring in a vehicle if we need to make a quick exit.'

Jessica was studying the camera feed. 'The two trustees appear to be looking for someone. I am guessing it's the Foreman. No urgency or concern. In fact, they looked relieved that they can't find him. They just opened the shed behind the house and seem to be confirming a vehicle is missing. Judging by their body language, this is normal. Now they have moved to a silo with some buckets. I guess the kibble for the prisoners' daily meal, as mentioned by Tracey.'

'OK, plan A is "go". Two unarmed hostiles, no leader. Channel 13 on your radios.'

Where the track left the fire trail, Joe hit the blue button, and instantly the exhaust note died. He moved the transfer case to 4WD low-range for extra grip. First to the clearing, he performed a five-point turn and forced the vehicle into the undergrowth to let the following vehicles turn around.

Everyone disembarked. Joe left the vehicle in "park" with the electric motor still running in case they needed to make a hasty retreat. There were eight of them including Jessica, Joe and Ms Bowman. The other five looked like the undercover Special Forces team that Joe assumed they were. One glance told him asking questions about their origins was not an option.

Joe led the way down the path they had made that morning. Once they reached the fence they could see where Sara Jane and Tracey had crawled through the wombat's hole under the fence. Two men with wire cutters extended the hole up to the electric security wire, then widened it for easy access. They then attached a bridging wire on two points of the electric wire and cut it between the bridging connections, putting a metre of slack in the wire which they lifted with a couple of sticks. There was now an open gate into the facility. Ms Bowmen led the way followed by Jessica and the commandos.

He had no intention of returning to the vehicles without doing some scouting. As an accountant, he knew that at the heart of any operation there had to be a data-management system. Even criminal businesses needed to be organised. It would be on a computer. The obvious place for it was in the house. The rest of the team would be tied up with the hostages. He made for the farmhouse. It was pretty dank inside, but his guess was right. The lounge room, the first room he entered, was the office. On the desk in the centre was a computer with two screens. It was still turned on and open. Joe logged onto his cloud storage account and instructed the computer to upload a full back-up of its hard disk, all the files, programs and databases. While this was happening, he searched the desk. Pocketing anything he thought would provide insight into the operation of the business. Riffling through the bottom drawer of the desk, he found a piece of paper taped to the underside of the drawer above it. Gently he removed it, unfolded it and found he was looking at a password list. He was not surprised, no one could remember all the passwords required in the digital world.

Jessica was still watching the feed from the cameras. She had seen the two trustees enter the top right shed with the now empty bucket of kibble. They had been in there for ten minutes. Tapping Ms Bowman on the shoulder she showed her the feed. Using hand signals, Ms Bowman left two commandos between the fence and the long shed. Able to see the gap in the fence and the length of the building, their job was to keep the exit route secure. Ms Bowman had the rest of the team take up position either side of the door on the far end where the centre corridor of the building opened into the grounds. They could hear the two trustees approaching, oblivious to the insurgents and making no effort to be quiet. As the trustees exited the building, twin wires shot out from each side of the doorway; the taser's prongs completing a circuit and ten thousand volts shocking their systems. They collapsed, shuddering, to the ground.

The team members with the tasers reloaded their barbs and stood guard over the two trustees while the rest of the team entered the building. The building had several rooms, or pens, usually used for the chickens, leading off the central corridor. Four of these pens were locked from the outside with a chain and padlock. They had come prepared, and bolt cutters made short work of the padlocks. In the four rooms they found ten prisoners aged from about four to late-teens. They looked like the survivors from a disaster movie. The prisoners were dead silent. They were beyond feeling; the brutality and the drugs having reduced them to a near-catatonic state. The team herded them out of the rooms along the corridor and out of the building, through the fence and up to the vehicles. A couple of the younger ones had to be carried.

One door was unlocked and inside they found the injured trustee. He didn't need tasering. It took two team members to drag him to the vehicles. By the door the two tasered trustees had been forced to their feet, their arms cuffed behind them with cable ties and led away to the vehicles.

Joe heard a ping. The sort of ping a digital device makes letting you know it is operating. It came from the top drawer on the other side of the desk. He noticed smoke coming from the drawer. He ran.

'Where's Burnett?' demanded Ms Bowman, having crammed everyone into the waiting vehicles.

'Facility is booby trapped; let's get out of here,' squawked all the radios at once, surprising everyone as they had been silent the whole operation. The explosions were muffled but the flames spread quickly. Joe burst into the clearing, leaned forward with his hands on his knees, and caught his breath.

He saw the rescued hostages, the team members and the trustees. Everyone seemed to be accounted for and unharmed except for one trustee. 'Whoa, fuck that was close,' Joe exclaimed, grinning with the buzz of success.

'You work with me, you follow orders,' responded Ms Bowman.

'Hey, I'm a consultant not an employee, different rules,' retaliated Joe.

'Mount up. Let's get the fuck out of here,' ordered Ms Bowman, deciding to ignore Joe's attempt at humour.

Joe led the convoy. They retraced their tracks and were soon dropping down out of the Watagan Mountains. As their wheels touched the blacktop, a uniformed policeman walked out from in front of a small bus and signalled for them to pull over to the side of the road. In front of the bus, a luxury European sedan was parked. Joe pulled over behind the bus, the other three vehicles pulling into line behind him. Joe hit the button and his window dropped into the door.

The policeman ignored Joe and looked into the rear of the vehicle. 'Ms Bowman, please come with me,' he said in a quiet voice.

'What's going on?' demanded Joe.

'Nothing, I recognise this man,' she said, turning to the policeman, 'your chief in the car?'

'Yes, he would like a word,' replied the uniformed policeman.

Ms Bowman entered the back seat of the car. Ten minutes later she was back. Joe could see she was furious. In a quiet, controlled voice, she spoke into her radio, 'Please assist the hostages onto the bus. There are community services officers waiting to help them. All of them including the trustees.'

She watched her team shepherd the rescued hostages and trustees into the bus. The policeman opened the driver's door of the sedan and climbed in. The car indicated then pulled out into the road and left, the bus followed.

An awkward silence fell over the parked vehicles. The silence was broken by the siren of a fire truck heading into the Watagans. 'OK what was that about?' asked Joe.

'We have been stood down. The operation now belongs with a special division of the state police,' answered Ms Bowman in a monotone.

'Well, I am going home. Seems a good result to me.'

'Something stinks. This will all disappear. We may have saved some kids but we didn't slay the dragon,' murmured Ms Bowman as Joe drove.

A few hours' rest, a shower and then Joe knocked together a quick dinner. He poured five glasses of red wine and passed them round the table. 'It's just a spag bol. One of my favourites after a day in the field,' explained Joe, pretending the day had been just another ordinary day. 'Hope it doesn't offend anyone's dietary preferences.'

'I'm a vegan,' replied Ms Bowman straight-faced.

'I'm, ah, sorry, let's see what I can do.'

'Actually Joe, she only eats raw meat,' responded Jessica. It nearly got a laugh. Everyone was still flat after the highs and lows of the raid and their dismissal.

Joe's mobile rang. Joe recognised the caller. 'Hi, Fred mate, how you doing?'

Joe listened for a minute. 'Hang on, I'll just put you on speaker, I have my hands full.'

Fred's voice came over the speaker. 'That weird chicken farm that wouldn't evacuate, it went up in flames today. And the weirdness continues. Apart from there being no chickens, we thought the fire was a bit suss and then all these plain clothes coppers turned up and told us to leave before we could have a good sniff around.'

'Fred, tell the boys to have beer and forget about it.'

'Yeah, we have enough on as it is, not our problem. See you Joe, catch-up soon.'

The call ended.

'And are you going to forget about it, Joe?' asked Jessica.

Joe thought about the data sitting in his cloud account, the notebook and password list he had stashed in his office. He looked around at his dinner guests, 'No, probably not'.

CHAPTER 20

Joe woke, made coffee and sat down to watch the first rays of sun hit the water. The rain overnight had rinsed much of the smoke out of the air. Joe had assumed he would be taking it easy today. Now he realised there was no way he would be able to change gears that quickly. His consciousness was still in battle-mode. He was going to have to do something active to transition back to his normal routines. Jessica, Sara Jane and Tracey were still asleep in the spare room. Ms Bowman had left after dinner the previous night.

Joe had been stood down from his firefighting duties. Fire command was using the break provided by the weather change to rest as many crews as possible. Fatigue could be as dangerous as the fires. Joe doubted they had anticipated how he would spend his downtime. New outbreaks in the mountains south of Sydney had erupted from lightning strikes generated by the change. Most of the moisture had been dropped on the coast, but as the cold front pushed the clouds over the Great Dividing Range, they were forced to dump most of their load. A whole new fire catastrophe was about to erupt around the nation's capital, Canberra, and burn down to the coast.

Like many of the volunteers, for Joe, the combination of the last two months firefighting and the knowledge that there was a whole new battlefront opening up down south, added to the activities of the last day and a half, had cancelled any chance of relaxing. Joe needed to do something. He hadn't ridden his bike for weeks. The Triumph Explorer 1200 wasn't new and carried a couple of well-earned battle scars. He would head to Tommy's, the biker café he had visited with Fred up on the Mangrove Mountain road. Then on to Wollombi to check out how the containment was going. Not that he had any real reason, he just could not let go after such an intense campaign.

The bike had not been ridden for a while, so there were some checks Joe would need to make. Starting from the ground up, he first checked the tyre pressure and used the hand pump to add a couple of PSI to the pressure front and back. Check the levels of brake, clutch and engine oil through the peep holes, and then the big one, did the battery have enough juice to bring the big triple-cylinder to life? No point getting his gear on until he knew the beast was going to start.

Ignition on, and the tell-tale lights lit up on the instrument binnacle, Joe compressed the starter button with his right thumb. At first reluctantly, the starter motor cranked the engine over a couple of times before the first cylinder caught, followed nearly instantaneously by the other two. The engine settled down to a steady idle. Joe let it idle for three minutes before shutting it down and returning to the house to climb into his bike gear.

Jessica awoke and stumbled into the kitchen as Joe was pulling his gear out of the cupboard. 'I need to blow some cobwebs out of my brain,' he explained. 'I'll do a lap or two of the peninsula then hit the open road. I will be back by lunchtime. We can have a chat then.'

'Yeah, right, whatever,' replied Jessica, more interested in finding the makings of a cup of coffee than anything else.

Fully armoured in his riding kit, Joe returned to the garage, flipped the button on the remote opener, mounted the bike and rode out to meet the day. Before hitting the open road, Joe meandered around the local back streets. Doubling back across the front of his own house, he performed some brake tests to sharpen his muscle memory and to check the braking systems. Joe clicked up the gears with his left foot, letting the bike run along at low revs for a while to check for any misses in the engine. Not one for loud exhausts, he was able to cruise the neighbourhood, lapping the peninsula he lived on twice without disturbing anyone's lie-in. Satisfied, he wound his way out of the suburbs, hugging the shores of Lake Macquarie. Within minutes the road wound through paddocks and bushland.

As Jessica watched Joe disappear, a white pick-up truck, tricked out in gangsta punk started up from across the road and drove off in the direction Joe had taken. When Joe rode past from the opposite direction, Jessica noticed the pick-up was still trailing him. She picked up her phone and called Ms Bowman, then woke her sister and Tracey.

The fifty kilometres to the café had a bit of everything. Flat farmland, forested ridges, a scenic valley and then a winding road up the mountain spur to the road along the ridge. The same ridge road that Joe and Fred had ridden only days before was still busy with firefighters. Joe noted temporary speed limits had been posted to allow the lumbering fire trucks a degree of operational safety as this road was still the containment line for the Gospers mega-fire. Pockets were still burning and despite the rain over the previous night, there was genuine concern that fire could reignite. It would be nearly a month before the fire could be declared completely extinguished.

*

Joe sipped his coffee while waiting for his bacon and eggs. The café had always been a favourite of the biker crowd and now was also a favourite of the firefighters patrolling the ridge road. Joe could not decide whether he should feel guilty or not, sitting back enjoying the day while other volunteers were still battling the beast. Again, he recognised the symptoms. Fred, as a family doctor, was familiar with mental illness and had briefed the brigade on the early signs of PTSD: the inability to relax and the anxiety of not been on the frontline were tickling around the back of Joe's mind. He decided to flush them out by concentrating on the day.

'Can't keep away?' asked the waitress laying his bacon and eggs in front of him. 'I saw you coming and going a few times over the last couple of days. On the RFS bike. Some of the staff are still recovering from your mate's bad jokes.'

'Yeah, he is usually only allowed to expose his kids to those. It's why we have to ride bikes; they won't let him in the truck.'

'Ha, you're just as bad I see. Riding far today?'

'Along to Wollombi then back across to the lake, only about a hundred and sixty kilometres all up.'

'Well take it carefully along the road. Still a lot of action happening as they try to put it out before the hot weather starts again.'

Joe looked around. 'How you guys coping?' he asked.

'Not too bad. Tommy stayed open as long as he could. Figuring your lot would need as much caffeine as possible. But then we were evacuated as the fire came up out of the valley. They stopped on the fence line of those hobby farms across the road. The fire arrived with the southerly change and they were able to hold the fire until the rain came a couple of hours later.

'It's pretty busy with a lot of riders turning up to support us and the fireys passing through. The only downer is there are some weirdos turning up. Not sure if they are lookie-loos or looters. Some of them are definitely suspect.'

'I can see there are more cars than normal.'

'Take a gander at that one over there.' The waitress pointed with her eyes to a white ute parked in the corner of the yard. 'No one has got out. I can't see through the tint very clearly, but it looks like there are four of them in there. They arrived slightly after you did.'

*

Joe had been aware of the ute for a while. Dual-cab utes or pick-ups were the most common vehicle on the road. Especially outside of the city. This one, however, definitely looked more urban gangsta than desert explorer. Although a 4WD, its suspension had been lowered; it had twenty-inch rims fitted with low-profile tyres. But what had really pipped Joe's interest was his suspicion that he had seen this vehicle before, in fact he was suspicious that it had been following him. *Jessica's doing no doubt*, he thought, *only a city slicker would think a heap of shit like that would blend in outside of the ghetto.*

Joe started to ponder some alternative routes home, which could be a little user unfriendly for the crew in the ute. He smiled ruefully to himself. His thoughts were interrupted by the muscular burble of a V8 engine. Joe looked around expecting the arrival of a muscle car. The beige LandCruiser that rescued them two days previously pulled into the parking area beside the café. The plain beige exterior of the LandCruiser was contradicted by the burble of the ground-shaking V8 engine. *Now that's what I call a Q-ship*, thought Joe, referring to the old naval trick of disguising a war ship as a harmless merchant man, *and Ms Bowman's mob also like their privacy judging by the almost illegally dark window tint.*

A middle-aged woman alighted from the driver's seat. Idly Joe assessed her. *Not a bad disguise*, Joe concluded, taking into account her worn jodhpurs, boots, sunglasses and baseball hat. Joe suspected a few of the horsey crowd would be attempting to retrieve their precious mounts, some worth north of a million dollars, and move them to safety now that the road had been reopened by emergency services. As she came closer Joe determined she was pretending not to know him. He played along.

She seemed to be taking an interest in the bikes, in Joe's specifically. Since Joe was only sitting at a table half a metre from where his bike leaned onto its side-stand, Joe nodded to her in acknowledgement.

'Your Explorer?' Ms Bowman asked. 'My husband is trying to decide between one of these and a Beemer GS.'

'Well, the GS is the standard, the Triumph is more for those who prefer to be a bit different. It is a personal thing; he would want to ride both and see which he likes best.'

'I do like the lamb's wool seat cover,' she said, running her hand over the pillion seat.

'Yeah, some mob in Brisbane make them and they do the GS as well. They have a website but I cannot remember its name off the top of my head.'

'Thanks, I am sure mister Google will find it for me, now I know such a thing is possible.'

'Thanks and enjoy your day.'

With that she continued into the café's interior.

Joe decided to check his phone. He noticed he had received a message from Fred.

He opened it. Bored, back at work on a Saturday morning, Joe read. He chuckled to himself. He knew how dedicated Fred was to his work. It drove Fred's wife to distraction. He worried so much about his patients he often forgot to look after himself.

Yeah, just remember to hold your breath. You spend the day curing the little buggers then you come around my place, bludge a cold one, and release all the bugs in my living room, Joe typed, still blaming Fred for a cold he caught last winter.

An image of a raised middle finger extending from a closed fist landed on Joe's screen seconds later.

A new message arrived. You are being followed, it said. Joe did not recognise the number.

I know, by Bowman and you, he typed, assuming it was Jessica.

No, the white ute, we followed it. We picked it up heading out of town after you'd done a couple of laps of the peninsula.

Joe looked up from his phone just in time to see Ms Bowman

open the left-hand door of the LandCruiser and hand in a tray of four takeaway coffees. She returned to the driver's door, saw Joe watching and gave him a little wave. She left the door cracked open and Joe could see her sipping her coffee between carrying on a conversation with the other occupants of the vehicle. Joe pretended to lose interest.

Idly he returned his attention to the white ute. *It must be getting hot in there,* Joe thought. As if reading his mind, he heard the motor start. *Would have been more efficient to open the door than run the air-con.*

A door opened and a man stepped on to the concrete apron. Least Joe thought it was a man. The head and face were buried deep in the top of the hoodie, atop thin-legged poo-catcher jeans with strategic and expensive tears at the knees. Three inches of designer underwear was visible above the drooping waistline of the jeans though it was the bright red sneakers that really caught your attention. The passenger sauntered around the corner to the bathrooms. Joe suspected he was the first. The rest would be following shortly for their own relief.

The passenger returned to the ute. The driver was the next to visit the amenities. As he turned the corner Joe stood and prepared to leave. The moment he stood, the LandCruiser fired up its engine and returned to the highway, turned right and accelerated out of sight.

The ute driver had still not returned, but now two others had exited the ute, awaiting their own turns to use the toilet. Joe remained seated while donning his bike gear and surreptitiously watching the ute. Once fully dressed, he stood and stepped quickly over to his bike, threw his leg over and hit the start button. As a member of the emergency services, Joe had learnt long ago to always park your vehicle back into the curb so you can leave immediately. He kicked up the stand, released the clutch, and turned right to follow the ridge to Wollombi. As he left, he saw frantic activity round the ute as the driver ran back and the two waiting to use the toilet jumped back into the cab.

Joe held is speed down to 60 km/h, about 20 km/h below the speed limit. He chuckled to himself imagining the discomfort the two gangbangers in the back of the ute must be feeling. A full bladder and a cramped back seat. Rounding a corner, he rode down a hill and up the other side before rounding another corner. He watched his mirrors. The ute was around two hundred metres behind him and gaining. Ms Bowman and the LandCruiser where ahead of him out of sight. Joe let his speed climb to a smidgen above the speed limit. The ute was still gaining.

The bike was cruising the tacho showing a lazy 2000 RPM in top gear. The redline was at 10 500, the big triple begging to be set free. Joe eased back to the speed limit. He had seen the tail of the LandCruiser disappearing around a corner at the end of the last straight section of road. By Joe's calculations, Ms Bowman was trundling along slow enough for Joe to catch her in about thirty seconds. Joe knew the road ahead would descend into a valley, alternating between ever-tightening right- and left-hand bends until it reached the valley floor.

Joe let the bike catch the LandCruiser as the ute was closing on his rear. The procession of three vehicles rounded one of the last corners of the plateau where there would be a straight before the descent into the valley. Joe closed up on the LandCruiser. Halfway around the corner he let the bike drift wide so it was positioned off the LandCruiser's rear taillight, just inside the centre line of the road. The ute had closed in even further. Joe changed down two gears but held the clutch in with his left hand. As the LandCruiser entered the final straight he flicked the bike out into the oncoming lane, twisted the throttle, gripped with his knees and moved his upper body over the petrol tank. He released the clutch. The bike leaped forward and around the LandCruiser in seconds. The ute attempted to follow. A car was coming the other way.

The ute was on the wrong side of the road and the oncoming car had punched its brakes, but even with anti-lock brakes , smoke was coming from the front wheels as the driver attempted to slow. The ute kept trying to pass Ms Bowman. She slammed on the LandCruiser's brakes and swerved to the side of the road, two wheels on the broken verge. The ute shot the gap and fishtailed back into its own lane, allowing the oncoming car to squeak through the gap. The LandCruiser bobbled, its left wheels in the verge, attempting to pull the big 4WD off the road completely. Ms Bowman gingerly finessed the LandCruiser back onto the road, straightened up, swore, then stomped the accelerator to the floor. The LandCruiser's burbling V8 engine bellowed, the automatic transmission dropped down to a lower gear, the rear squatted on the suspension, shooting them forward in pursuit of Joe and the ute.

Joe imagined the road ahead in his mind: a series of rolling switchbacks dropping slightly downhill as the road angled down a spur in the ridge, then a hard right-hander. No barrier, no warning. Exit the switchback and there it was. It was called Lemmings Leap. It had a reputation. The cliff dropped two hundred feet, gum trees tenaciously gripping any purchase they could find, waiting to pulverise any fool misjudging the corner.

He glanced in his mirror. He had been watching the ute, letting it gain on him through the switchback. The ute was no longer trying to be discreet. It was coming for Joe. He let them move closer, they were now inches from his taillight. The downhill gradient of the road had increased. The ute was on the outer limit of its roadholding. What looked good in the ghetto was no match for a mountain road.

Lemmings Leap suddenly appeared around the last flowing bend. Joe edged his bike to the outside of the road away from the corner. He was going to be on the edge of his ability to negotiate the corner, but luckily well within the capabilities of his bike and tyres.

He pulled in the clutch, dropped down two gears. He desperately wanted to use his brakes, but didn't want to alert the ute. He let go of the clutch, the slipper clutch doing its job and controlling the deceleration. The ute nearly hit his rear end, a goose of the throttle just keeping it clear. The ute driver instinctively hit the brakes with everything he had. The wheels locked up. It was now a lead-pointed arrow. Unfortunately, Joe was still between the drop-off and the careening ute. He threw his weight into the turn, twisting the throttle as he did. The big bike started to lean and accelerated, the acceleration trying to straighten it up, Joe leaned harder, inside foot peg-scraping. The big bike shot across the front of the ute with nothing to spare, the rear tyre breaking traction slightly as it shot through the turn. Joe, still accelerating, righted the bike and looked in his mirror. The ute had taken the leap. He could hear metal crumpling against the gum trees as it bounced its way to the bottom of the cliff.

Joe slowed down to a crawl, he U-turned, his whole body shaking. Slowly he returned up the hill to the corner; a set of skid marks leading straight off the cliff were the only clue on the road. Steam and smoke were rising from the valley.

The LandCruiser had stopped at the preceding bend. Joe wondered how much they had seen. He made his way to the side of the road, tugged his helmet over his head, dropped it on the ground, put his hands on his knees and threw up his breakfast.

Ms Bowman knew she only had seconds before they had company. She jogged down with Jessica, Sara Jane and Tracey.

'Push the bike off the cliff.'

'What the fuck, no fucking way,' responded Joe.

'They won't give up until you are dead. You have to disappear.'

Numb, Joe returned to his bike. He saw the sense in her order. He didn't like it, it seemed like sacrilege after the bike had just saved him. He was still shaking. It took four of them, with Ms Bowman supervising, to turn the bike round and push it off the cliff. Joe turned away, the sound of the bike bouncing off the trees was too much.

'Quick, get in the truck,' she ordered him. She had heard other vehicles approaching. They all ran and scrambled in, the LandCruiser moving off before all the doors were closed. 'There is a fire trail across the bottom of this cliff,' Ms Bowman said, pointing to the navigation screen on the dash. 'We will gain access to the crash site and see what needs to be done.'

Joe suddenly realised that he was in too deep and wasn't wearing a life jacket. His ego and bravado had really dropped him in the proverbial this time. Not only had he wiped out his future, his present and past looked like they were about to disappear as well. He mentally kicked himself. If he had just stayed at Tommy's and drunk coffee. Sooner or later one of the police Highway Patrol cars the bikers attract would have turned up, and he could have taken refuge with the officer.

Joe's ponderings were interrupted as he was thrown about the rear seat between Sara Jane and Tracey as Ms Bowman hit the fire trail. Changing to 4WD on the fly, Ms Bowman was bent slightly forward attempting to avoid the worst of the track. Jessica was riding shotgun, her phone in one hand open on a mapping application, looking for more detail than the vehicle's navigation system showed. The LandCruiser charged along the valley floor, bouncing along the track at an incredible speed.

Joe managed to fasten his seatbelt and braced his hands against the roof. 'Here, here, here, turn right,' Jessica directed, pointing across a field. On the far edge of the field, smoke could be seen gathering round the bottom of the tree line. The LandCruiser launched across the field, slamming to a halt adjacent to the tree line. Everyone jumped out.

Joe ran to the tree line. He looked back up the cliff. The ute had come to rest about twenty metres up the slope. He led the way, his motorcycle gear the best choice for forcing a way through the undergrowth. He saw the crumpled ute lying on its side, its cabin roof crushed by the trunk of the gum tree supporting it. Jammed against another tree ten or so metres above the carcass of the ute, he could see his bike, the front wheel buckled under the frame, lights and plastic fairings missing, He bent down and glanced in the cabin of the ute. The driver's body was still trapped behind the wheel, one of the rear passengers appeared to be hanging by his seatbelt. Both dead. He looked around, one of the other two was squashed under the ute, the last between the bike and the ute. All dead. Thrown slightly further down the slope was a mobile phone. Joe pocketed it.

The others were standing slightly downhill from him. Joe looked at them and shook his head.

Joe looked around. It always amazed him how a fire as gigantic as the Gospers mega-blaze still left patches of unburnt bush. The timing of the rain and location of this little patch had saved it. The rain had passed some days ago and the bush had dried out again. As Joe descended, he noticed the petrol and other liquids seeping down from the ute. He could see the ruptured tank of his bike. He turned back around to see Ms Bowman standing there with a cigarette lighter. He was aghast at her intentions.

'This lot has to go,' she said. 'Nothing we can do for them; we must cover our trail.'

'Jessica, there is a spare phone in the centre console, it is untraceable. Call the fire brigade, report the fire.'

'What fire?' asked Joe still in shock, his mind a bit slow.

'This one. Get in the truck.' Ms Bowman knelt down and touched her lighter to the tinder covering the ground. The flame crept up the slope. It didn't look very dangerous, as though it would die from lack of enthusiasm at any moment. Then it sniffed the fuel from the crashed ute. There was a pause of a second or so, then, whoosh, the whole cliff face was alight.

They scrambled back in to the LandCruiser. Jessica was yelling into the phone. 'We tried to get to them but it's caught fire. Hurry, hurry!' she screamed hysterically into the phone. 'We have to leave, we are about to be cut off by the fire.' Calmly she hung up, removed the SIM card from the phone and crushed it.

The LandCruiser retraced its way to the blacktop. Once on the road, Ms Bowman turned away from the smoke, accelerated to the speed limit and drove.

Calmly she turned in her seat and said to Joe, 'Joe, you are now officially dead. Welcome to the team.'

Joe pondered his position. He was in a new warehouse unit in the local regional industrial park. He could not go home. He could not contact his friends or family. He could not be seen in public.

He was dead. He had killed.

In a week his life had spun out of control and vanished. He didn't know how to move forward. He did not know how he should feel or react. He was on the sideline and the game of life was moving on without him.

Jessica, Ms Bowman, Sara Jane and Tracey had all been in and out of the unit. They also did not seem to know what to do with Joe.

He sat at a desk in front of a computer. It had two screens and an internet connection. Joe turned it on, not because he had a purpose but to avoid dealing with his new reality. He surfed through a couple of news sites. The reports of the crash on Lemmings Leap were vague. Four dead plus a motorcyclist. Because of the fire it had been impossible to investigate the crash site. There was a pad and pen on the desk. Joe jotted down a note to discuss this with Ms Bowman. He had a feeling his to-do list was going to grow quickly. He could have used the PC but for thinking outside the box, he liked to start with ink and paper. He chuckled to himself and mumbled, 'Sunshine, you are a long way out of any box you have ever known.'

He pushed the pad and pen aside and opened a word-processing program. He typed a title across the top of the first page, Resources. Under that he typed I am alive and uninjured. Joe felt he needed a positive message to jump start his brain. He turned around and seeing his bike jacket hanging on a hook on the wall, he walked over to it and went through the pockets. The usual pocket debris plus the list he had found under the Foreman's desk and phone he had picked up from the crash site.

To his resources list he added, Team: Jessica, Sara Jane, Tracey and Ms Bowman.

Next line, List of passwords.

Next line, Gangbanger's phone.

Next line, Upload of facilities computer.

As a warm-up exercise he decided to have a browse through the files he had uploaded. Maybe if he knew what he was up against he might be able to plan a way through. Joe typed in the login and password to his cloud account. The files were there and judging by the size, Joe thought he would be busy for the next day or so deciding what data was valid information and what was of no use.

The data appeared to be split in two, part pertaining to the management of the facility and part the Foreman's personal files. A quick browse through the folders in each helped Joe to decide to have a look through the Foreman's personal files. The folder headings indicated the Foreman may have intended these files to be his safeguard against reprisals from the mysterious Syndicate.

Joe scrolled down to the next page on his Word document. Goals, he typed across the top of the page. Next line down, Get life back. He leaned back in his chair and stared at the last line. Would he be able to return to his old life? Would he be able, and would he want to? Joe had a feeling the events of the last week or so had changed him forever. Would he be able to go back to cruising through life as he had been? Or was he after more?

He backspaced, deleting the heading he had just typed. He typed a new line in capitals DECIDE LIFE DIRECTION.

He saved the document to his cloud account not knowing when or where he would have access again. Joe leaned back in his chair and stared at the far wall. Plain unadorned concrete slab. No answers there.

Joe stood and walked to the staircase leading to the mezzanine level of the warehouse unit. The original fit-out included offices, bathrooms, a kitchen and common area. Maybe a cup of coffee would get his brain moving. The offices had been furnished as bedrooms; Joe was not the only resident, all the team were staying there until Ms Bowman could determine their safety. Ironically, Joe had the accountant's office.

Sara Jane and Tracey exited the office marked "Operations". They were smiling at each other and holding hands. Joe added extra water to the kettle. 'Cuppa?' he asked.

'Yes please,' they both replied, still holding hands and smiling at Joe. He suspected they were waiting for him to say something, so he smiled back. 'Coming up, how do you have it?'

Both women relaxed. Joe was happy for them. That they could commence a relationship after the trauma they had both been through pleased him, not only for their sake but for his own. Maybe a return to normality was possible.

Joe put three mugs, the jar of coffee, sugar and milk on the table and returned to the bench to wait for the kettle to boil. Sara Jane and Tracey sat at the table and waited for Joe to bring the kettle over and pour. The three of them went through the production of making coffee. Joe sat at the table with them.

The slower pace after the last few days appeared to affect everyone. It felt like living in slow motion. They sat silently and sipped their coffee.

'Sorry about your bike,' said Sara Jane, breaking the silence and the ice.

'It was insured,' responded Joe without thinking. He paused. 'Not that I can claim as I'm dead. I suppose my brothers will receive the claim. It hurts more not been able to contact them. Letting them think I am dead is shitting me. I can find a new bike in a couple of hours on the net. I think it's going to take more than a few hours to explain becoming "undead" to my family and friends.'

'I thought all you bikers idolised your bikes?' queried Sara Jane.

'I saw a sentiment a couple of years ago, "Love people use things". I thought, shit this bloke's onto something.' So since then I have tried to apply that thinking. It does free your mind. However, it does help to have the cash in the bank not to have to worry about stuff.'

'Well, that's fucking Zen,' piped up Tracey.

'Yeah, suddenly we are living the dream now! A Buddhist monk has more than I do now, at least he keeps his fucking identity! Anyway, how long they keeping you two here?'

'Ms Bowman isn't sure,' replied Sara Jane. 'She is trying to figure out the fallout from everything that has gone down. We may have busted up their facility, but that's not the end of it. In fact, I think all we have done is piss them off. She requested we stay here until she and Jessica return from Sydney. They hope to have some idea about repercussions then.'

'You make it sound like we are the bad guys hiding out from the sheriff,' said Joe.

'Mate, this Syndicate is huge, unimaginably wealthy and like a virus, corrupting everything and everyone. The people behind it are among the richest in the world. They are so accustomed to getting their own way they see anyone who stands up against them as nothing more than a bug to be fucking squashed. That facility we found and destroyed – nothing, a backwater in their global operation. I have been chipping away at this for months. They are so powerful they don't even bother to hide their operations that well. They just buy protection from the top down. Bowman and Jessica will be lucky not to be arrested or disappeared. You should accept you are on your fucking own, Joe. We are all basically non-people now; we are fucking invisible. You are kidding yourself if you think this is all going to be fixed and you can go back to your old fucking life. Remember Jeffrey Epstein hanged himself in a New York lock-up and no one noticed until it was too late? It needed like three coincidences and two incompetents to interact for it to be fucking possible.'

Sara Jane realised she was now standing, thumping the table and shouting at Joe. Tracey calmed Sara Jane down and wiped at the spilled coffee. Joe wasn't surprised, he too felt his emotions just below the surface ready to explode without provocation.

He picked up what she had said. Turned it around and looked at it from several angles. He had to admit he was new to this and had been reacting to events. Sara Jane had been studying the organisation he now thought of as the enemy before she had been dragged into the action. However, the implications to his perceptions of the world and to his own future were a slap in the face. Unfortunately, events appeared to favour Sara Jane's perspective better than his local, and seemingly naïve, view. The future just grew dimmer.

Joe was staring at the wall again, 'So what the fuck do we do?'

'The way I see it we have two choices, we fight back, or we run and hide. If you choose to run and hide you will be doing it for the rest of your life, and most likely they will find you in the end and kill you,' replied Tracey. 'Sara Jane and myself have discussed this. We are going to fight back. You will need to decide for yourself, Mr Fireman.'

'Well, I am actually an accountant. More a corporate manager than a fireman. The firefighting is just a volunteer thing.'

'Well, you got us out of the shit, so you are of some use. Thanks, by the way!' Sara Jane added.

Joe paused, 'Just hope those other victims we rescued are going to be OK.'

'Yeah, it's a worry. Hopefully Ms Bowman will know if they are safe from the Syndicate.'

Joe kept his mouth shut. He still remembered how the other escapees were herded onto the bus, and Ms Bowman and her team were pushed aside.

'Do you know how to fight, Joe?'

'What, with a computer or with my fists or a gun?' Joe replied.

'OK, before we can do anything I admit we need research, but we need to prepare ourselves to fight. I had Ms Bowman organise some gym equipment. It is still packed up downstairs. Let's start with assembling it. IKEA 101. We need to blow off some steam anyway.'

The three of them trouped back downstairs. The ground level of the warehouse was an open space with a small office under the stairs. A large roller door, large enough to swallow a full-size truck, took up most of the front wall. Light came from skylights in the roof. The mezzanine level was suspended around two sides. In a normal warehouse, the space below the mezzanine floor would be used for the storage of the company's product. In the corner of this space was a stack of carboard boxes.

'Looks like our first session will be assembling our gym. Then we will see how ready you are, Joe.'

Sara Jane strode over to the packaged equipment. Tracey glanced at Joe with a nervous grin and followed. Joe decided to hunt round the warehouse for a knife and some tools. Luckily whoever had provisioned the space had left a rudimentary tool kit on the bench.

The afternoon wore on towards evening. Since arriving at the warehouse none of them had been outside. Joe was glad he had set his digital watch to the 24-hour clock. Otherwise he would be having difficulty keeping track of the days and whether it was day or night in the outside world.

By 4 pm or 1600 hours by Joe's watch, the equipment was unpacked and assembled. A couple of rowing machines, some free weights, a couple of exercise bikes, and a punching bag and boxing gloves. Luckily, they had found some padded mats for the concrete floor as well.

'Put on the gloves and hit the bag,' said Sara Jane.

Joe chose the largest gloves, walked up to the punching bag, and landed a couple of roundhouse punches. He was quite pleased with his effort.

'Fucking great for a boxersize class at some swanky Eastern Suburbs gym, totally fucking useless in the real world,' scoffed Sara Jane embracing the role of the personal trainer from hell.

CHAPTER 24

'Quentin Brightly QC has examined the evidence and found that on the balance of probability the facility you liberated was a stand-alone operation. He has found the grandiose claims of a global conspiracy the ramblings of an ambitious, self-promoting, pseudo-journalist who has since disappeared overseas for a jaunt with her boyfriend,' the Federal Attorney-General proclaimed.

'On his advice we are terminating any further examination of this matter. Federal and state police have been alerted and a manhunt has been organised for the man referred to as the Foreman. We wish to thank Ms Bowman and her team for their efforts in destroying this child pornography ring.

'Thank you all for attending this meeting. The meeting is hereby closed.'

Under the table Ms Bowman was holding tightly onto Jessica's wrist. Jessica took this as a signal to keep her mouth shut. 'Thank you for your time, your excellencies,' said Ms Bowman standing and pulling Jessica up with her. 'Please excuse my associate and myself as we have some pressing business to attend to on another matter.' Without further comment Ms Bowman and Jessica left the conference room.

Jessica was about to explode. As soon as they were outside, Ms Bowman turned to Jessica and touched her chin. This was their prearranged signal requesting Jessica keep her mouth shut. She realised Ms Bowman suspected that they may be overheard.

Jessica had travelled down on the train. She had left the warehouse they were calling the "office" just after dawn to reach the centre of Sydney by 9 am using an indirect route. Ms Bowman had met her at a table on the footpath outside one of Central Station's many coffee shops. It was there Ms Bowman briefed Jessica on the upcoming meeting. It seemed to Jessica that Ms Bowman was out of uniform. Gone were usual impeccable make-up, stylish suit and understated bob haircut. Instead she was dressed in jeans, boots, and a flannelette shirt, with no make-up and her hair held back behind her ears. If she had not grabbed Jessica's elbow as she walked towards the table, Jessica would have ignored her completely. At Ms Bowman's feet were two large shopping bags from the local, upmarket department store.

'Go back into the station and change into the outfit in this bag,' said Ms Bowman, passing one of the shopping bags to Jessica. 'There are some lockers in the bathroom in the Grand Concourse where the regional trains terminate. Place the clothes you are wearing in a locker; we will change back later. The keys are available from a vending machine so you can use coins, not your credit card. At 1pm today we are attending a hearing about the facility we destroyed and the allegations of an international crime Syndicate. The hearing will decide that there is no evidence to support such a Syndicate. I have made it easy for them by holding back some of the facts. If we are wrong and the Syndicate does not exist, the hearing will be correct. If we are right, pushing the matter will only expose us and what we know. A Syndicate like this cannot exist without support from the highest levels. As I see it the only way to fight the Syndicate is in stealth mode.'

Jessica remembered Ms Bowman's briefing from the morning. She slowed her breathing. Deep breaths in through the nose and exhaled slowly through her mouth. She wanted to appear as relaxed as Ms Bowman beside her. The conference room had appeared to be rented just for that meeting. They were on the tenth floor and waiting for a lift. Jessica assumed the building must be a co-working, temporary office facility. It was that generic. The lift pinged and they entered along with a random selection of office workers, generic as the offices they were leaving. Jessica and Ms Bowman were both jostled on the ride down to the ground floor.

They walked the five hundred metres to Central Station. At the station, before they separated, Ms Bowman turned to Jessica, leaned towards her and passed her a piece of paper. She must have written it while pretending to take notes in the meeting. *Check for any surveillance but I am pretty sure we were bugged at some point. When we enter the station take some anti-tail manoeuvres and make your way to the toilets where we left our clothes. Change back into your travelling gear in a toilet cubicle to avoid surveillance cameras and search your new suit for any trackers or bugs before dumping it in the locker. Throw the key in the bin. Take any trackers and place them on one of the regional trains. Afterwards, meet me out here on the concourse. Sit on that seat and pretend to be looking at your phone.*

Following Ms Bowman's instructions took the best part of half an hour. She had found a tracker and placed it on a train travelling west across the Blue Mountains. Briefly she thought of Joe and his adventures saving the Wollemi Pines. He was appearing in her thoughts too often. Peak hour was starting, which worked for and against them. The crowds hid them but also hid anyone following them. Jessica sat on the bench. A strange man approached her. It took a moment or two before she realised it was Ms Bowman in a beard. Jessica managed not to laugh. Ms Bowman produced a map of Manly, and pointing to the iconic Steyne Hotel said, 'Where is this place? I have to meet someone there in two hours.' Jessica pointed to the exit to the underground city trains. 'Sir, take the train to Circular Quay, then the ferry across the harbour to Manly. Walk through Manly to the ocean beach.' The bearded Ms Bowman left in the direction Jessica had indicated. Jessica now knew their next meeting point.

Instead of following, Jessica decided to take a different route to Manly. As it was peak hour there would be plenty of buses heading around Sydney Harbour. She would catch one halfway, disembark and catch a different bus for the second part of the trip. It seemed obsessive, but being overly cautious was the only way to guarantee their safety. That they were on the Syndicate's radar was the assumption until proven wrong, if they wanted to stay alive.

Jessica dawdled her commute long enough to allow evening to descend. Alighting from the bus in the seaside suburb of Manly, Jessica pretended to look in a couple of the many local real estate agents as though looking for a property. She used the windows to check behind her and to force anyone following her to walk on past her position. Entering the hotel, Jessica was emotionally jolted by the crowd. It took her a moment to realise the crowded bar was a sanctuary not a threat. *Paranoia is only real if someone is out to get you*, she thought to herself.

She found Ms Bowman nursing a middy of beer in the corner of the beer garden. 'I preferred you with the beard,' quipped Jessica.

'Bloody thing itched, binned it when I got here. Let's get out of here. I am coming with you back to the "office". I need to be take myself off the radar if we are going to move this forward.

'I left the LandCruiser parked on the side of the street a couple of suburbs over. We can catch a bus to it and return to the office.'

'Won't they know the car?'

'No, it is completely off the books. And, we won't be taking it all the way. The federal database that recorded its confiscation is not linked to the state numberplate recognition system. However, we will take the train for part of the trip.'

Jessica was about to argue but sensing Ms Bowman was not about to change her mind, relented. They retrieved the LandCruiser, taking time to inspect it and ensure Ms Bowman's tell-tales had not been disturbed. It had been a long day and Jessica sighed as she settled into the leather upholstery. The V8 engine rumbled to life. Ms Bowman adjusted the customised suspension to allow the LandCruiser to settle slightly into road mode.

It took about forty minutes to traverse the northern suburbs of Sydney to the start of the M1 motorway heading north. 'So how are you finding the Lake Macquarie area?' asked Ms Bowman.

Jessica paused for a moment, 'Well, according to Joe, it's great. He enjoys the lake and the countryside, doesn't miss Sydney at all. It's only a couple of hours away and forty minutes to Newcastle. Me, I wouldn't know, we don't leave the office in the Morisset industrial estate, unless absolutely necessary.'

*

In a darkened office a man was staring at a computer screen. Under instruction he had linked his computer to the federal listing of confiscated vehicles, those used by criminals, confiscated and auctioned off to the public. However, not all of them were auctioned, a few being held back by the Federal Police as undercover vehicles. They were assuming Ms Bowman was using such a vehicle. The hack had not been that hard as the voice issuing his instructions had provided enough access codes to ease the way. He cross-referenced with the state vehicle registrations database.

He picked up the phone, dialled, was answered immediately and spoke, 'We have a beige LandCruiser confiscated a couple of months ago re-registered in NSW and no record of it being auctioned. It has just been spotted travelling towards the M1. Current NSW rego BCE 24T'.

The phone went dead. The computer continued its search cross-referencing the two databases.

*

'The M1 starts soon,' Jessica said more for something to say than assisting Ms Bowman. Minutes later they rolled down the ramp onto the motorway.

Ms Bowman eased the big 4WD into the centre lane and set the cruise control to the speed limit. The traffic had lightened but the road was still busy. After a couple of kilometres she disconnected the cruise control and drifted into the left lane behind a large two-trailer truck letting the traffic behind speed past.

'Shit.'

Jessica jumped; she had never before heard Ms Bowman swear.

'Programmable ECU, let's try sports mode,' said Ms Bowman moving a circular dial on the centre consul. 'It changes the settings on the car's computer to a more aggressive mode. The guy who had it before did not want to get caught. I think we have acquired a cling-on.'

Ms Bowman feathered her left foot on the brake pedal while pressing the accelerator and watching her driver's side mirror. Jessica could feel the load in the transmission. Foot off the brake, she pulled out into a gap; the big V8 roared and the truck leaped forward. Jessica was staring between the two front seats through the back window. She narrowly avoided whiplash. Then the car behind, nearly invisible driving under parking lights only, also pulled out and went with them, switching to high beam, blinding Jessica.

The rear window turned into a spider's web. Then it shattered. Jessica felt a punch in her shoulder. It went numb. Ms Bowman mashed the brake pedal into the floor. The sports mode stiffening the suspension still allowed the front to dip and the rear to lift, the pursuing vehicle, also now crash braking, submarined under the LandCruiser's towbar. The solid metal fitting destroyed the front end and radiator of the perusing car. Ms Bowman accelerated again. The Landcruiser ripped itself loose of the pursuing car and roared forward. The pursuers lost control spearing off the road into a copse of young trees.

Jessica's shoulder was no longer numb. It was in torment. 'Fuck, I've been shot,' she gasped.

'Press something into the wound to stop the bleeding. We can't stop.' Jessica wadded up her jumper and pressed it into the wound, wrapping the sleeves around herself in an attempt to hold it in place.

'Give me the remote for the door to the office, I am going straight in. Treating your injury is the priority. About thirty minutes. No time for subterfuge now.'

Jessica handed over the fob. The LandCruiser did not appear to be damaged in any vital way. It was hammering up the highway. It took a minute for Jessica to comprehend, but the blue and red flashes reflected off the road were coming from their car. She hoped it was enough to keep the real police away.

*

Minutes passed, in silence. Ms Bowman took the exit, tyres squealing, bounced over two roundabouts and blasted into the industrial estate. All lights extinguished, she hit the fob.

The roller door fronting the "office" began to rise. The LandCruiser hit the forecourt and Ms Bowman slammed on the brakes slowing enough for the LandCruiser to slip under the raising door. Inside, shuddering to a stop, its ABS barely holding back a skid, it nudged the punching bag Sara Jane and Joe had been using earlier in the evening.

Joe hit the button closing the roller door.

'Quick, move, Jessica's been shot,' commanded Ms Bowman as she scrambled out of the vehicle.

Tracey took charge. Between them they withdrew Jessica from the LandCruiser. She was in pain and her right upper arm was bloody. Together they laid her on one of the gym mats they had been training on earlier in the day. Untying the jumper she had wrapped around her shoulders, they saw the wound was still seeping blood.

'Scissors,' ordered Tracey. Sara Jane raced upstairs; she had seen a pair in the kitchen. She snatched the first aid kit down from the shelf while she was there. She leaped back down the stairs. Tracey was looking at Jessica's shirt trying to determine the best way to remove it without doing any damage to the traumatised tissue underneath. She grabbed the scissors and cut first up the right sleeve and then across the top of Jessica's shoulder from the collar. When the two cuts met, she peeled the two sides away from Jessica's right arm and shoulder, pulling the wrecked shirt down Jessica's left arm and chucking it onto the sweater. 'Warm water and Dettol,' Tracey instructed to the room.

It was Joe's turn to sprint up to the kitchen and pour warm water and a dash of antiseptic into a saucepan and rush back down again. Tracey wadded up some cloth bandage from the first aid kit and began to wash down Jessica's arm and shoulder looking for the wound. She found the entry wound and felt around for the bullet. She found it just under the skin on the outside top of Jessica's arm. Jessica screamed, vomited on the floor and fainted.

'We need a doctor, I trained with the medics but this is going to need surgery. Lucky it didn't go in very far, a flesh wound as they say in the movies, but still deadly if it gets infected and debilitating if we leave it there,' Tracey surmised.

'I know a doc we can trust. Local too,' replied Joe.

'We have no choice. Call him on a burner and then dump the phone,' ordered Ms Bowman.

Navigating through the Rural Fire Brigade's private application, Joe was able to track down Fred's number. He called. As soon as the call was picked up Joe started talking. 'Medic needed, Red, Medic needed Red,' Joe said, using the Rural Fire Brigade's urgent medical assistance radio code. 'Don't mention my name,' Joe continued as Fred started to speak. 'Take the dog for a walk and I'll meet you at the beer o'clock bench. Be aware you may be being watched.'

The LandCruiser was too obvious, so Joe opted for his plain Jane Subaru Tracey had picked up earlier. He figured he was only known to the Foreman, so details like his car's description were probably not circulated. He couldn't be sure but couldn't see a way round it.

Joe and Fred had often had a sundowner sharing a bench at the local dog-walking park. Joe drove down there and parked around the corner. Leaving the car, he found a spot in the shadows of some elderly gums and waited for Fred to appear. Fred wandered out of the light of the streetlight leading his dog and Joe's. Bear, Joe's dog, immediately started pulling frantically on his lead dragging Fred over to Joe's position.

Bear went crazy jumping up and desperately trying to lick his owner to death. 'I think he may have missed you,' said Fred, pretending meetings like this were part of his normal routine.

'Come with me, we need your help. By the way don't tell anyone you saw me,' replied Joe.

'No worries, been a few years since I have had to worry about the cloak-and-dagger routine, but my lips are sealed. Now, give me a brief on the patient.'

'Female, fit, about thirty years old, gunshot wound,' summed up

Joe, driving back through town to the industrial park.

'OK, first stop, in town, I will need to pick up my medical bag and some bits and pieces.'

Joe drove down the back street behind the medical centre, turned off his lights and entered the rear carpark. Fred jumped out, walked across to the back door and entered his key-code into the staff entrance. Joe noticed no lights coming on in the centre and was thankful Fred had thought to use his phone to light his passage. Minutes later Fred was back.

'So, Joe Bond 008, what gives?'

'Shit just got real,' replied Joe. 'It all started with that chicken farm up the back of Wyong Valley. It's been going to shit in a handbasket ever since.'

'Situation normal all fucked up or the full clusterfuck?'

'Mate, we blasted through SNAFU, jumped CF and now we are in uncharted territory,' replied Joe. 'By the way, why are you so unfazed? I'm having all sorts of trouble dealing with this.'

'That's a story for another day and a few beers. Your shout of course.'

As they entered the industrial park, 'Pretend to be learner driver,' said Fred adjusting the wing mirror so he could keep a look out for anyone following them. Joe did two laps round the block stopping, reverse parking and U-turning like a learner driver practising. There were at least two other cars doing the same thing as it was a popular spot for training young drivers even this late at night. It also reassured Joe he was not being followed.

He drove onto the forecourt of the office and the roller door rose. He drove inside and door rolled down again. Fred and Joe exited the car.

'Major,' said Fred.

'It's Ms Bowman now, Sergeant Shan,' replied Ms Bowman.

'Fuck,' said Joe to no one in particular.

Fred placed his bag next to Jessica's head and knelt next to her head facing the injury. He dug in his bag, loaded a syringe with local anaesthetic and injected it into her arm above the wound.

'Hope she isn't allergic. We will need to give this a couple of minutes; then we can go after the slug.'

Joe looked around for a seat. Finding none he walked over to the Subaru and sat in the passenger seat, feet on the warehouse floor. His dog jumped over from the rear seat to sit on his lap. He was so far out of his depth. His life as a corporate wheeler-dealer gave him no point of reference. Even Fred appeared to be part of this world he had stumbled into.

Within minutes Fred had extracted the bullet and was stitching up Jessica's shoulder. He pulled off his disposable gloves and walked over to the LandCruiser with Ms Bowman. Joe stood and followed.

'Confiscated vehicle, was supposed to have bullet-proof glass,' said Ms Bowman.

'Bullet-resistant glass would be a better description. But it no doubt saved her life. First bullet damaged the glass, second penetrated but went through the rear seat then her seat before hitting her in the shoulder. That's why it is so misshapen and why it only did so little damage. One lucky girl,' Fred explained.

'Fuck off, lucky to get fucking shot, bullshit,' spluttered Jessica.

'Who the fuck are you?' Joe asked Fred.

'I was SAS. We put Sergeant Shan though his medical degree. You are probably in so deep now Fred can tell you his story,' replied Ms Bowman for Fred.

'I'll come back in a couple of days. Take these antibiotics.' Fred handed a plastic bottle of pills to Jessica. 'Joe, you want to take me home? You better leave Bear with me until we sort this out. Don't want any questions.'

Joe stood his ground. 'What are the chances of a doc I know being known to you lot?' he asked.

'How many doctors do you know in the RFS? Not many? Generally, people from a military background end up in organisations like the fireys as it bridges the emotional gap between civilian and military. So, it follows that any doc in the RFS is most likely ex-military,' explained Ms Bowman. Joe thought the explanation was a bit shaky but left it alone. He was not confident he would like the answer if he dug deeper.

He drove Fred back to the lakefront and let him and the two dogs out. 'Won't your wife notice your bag?' asked Joe.

'No, I'll leave it in my car on the way in. And, no, before you ask, she knows when not to ask questions. She's like me, a Tamil refugee. One day I will tell you the whole story. Then I will have to kill you.' Fred burst into laughter at the expression on Joe's face.

'That's a joke, son. You are on the fucking inside now whether you like it or not, Joe 008.'

CHAPTER 26

It wasn't rocket science.

The orders to attack Ms Bowman and Jessica had to have originated from someone connected to the meeting they had attended, and that same someone must have some serious connections to arrange the ambush.

Conclusion: trust no one, be self-sufficient.

Question: How?

Reverse up a bit.

Joe stood and went to the whiteboard. He wrote in large letters across the top of the board, Self-Sufficient Resources.

Down the side of the board he started a list:

Funding

Premises

Vehicles

IT, internet, communications

People

'What are you doing Joe?' He spun around to see Jessica had wandered into the corner of the warehouse Joe was using as an office.

'Get any sleep last night?' asked Joe. Seeing Jessica's arm in a sling and the dark circles round her eyes.

'Yeah, not too bad. Fred's painkillers and the local helped. I think Ms Bowman is more shook up than I am. She has always believed the establishment has her back. The idea that her arse was hanging out of her finely tailored suit is not sitting well. She's ex-military and the chain-of-command is taken for granted; it all goes to crap when the higher-ups are suddenly the enemy.'

'That's my worry. How compromised are we? How long before this place is raided?'

'Yesterday morning, I would have said we were safe as houses here. Now I think we need to post a lookout and keep our guns close,' replied Jessica.

'How many guns do we have?' Joe had not thought of weapons.

'Two handguns and about twenty rounds of ammo.'

'Hmm, about all they would be good for is blowing our own fucking brains out before they captured any of us.'

'That's about right, Joe. I'll round up the others; we all need to get onto this.'

While Jessica rounded up the troops, Joe rehearsed his opening lines. His corporate experience mixed with the diversity of the team caused Joe to assume a predisposition towards endless discussion if he didn't open the session strongly and provide direction.

'It seems to me that we need to disconnect and go dark. Last night's attack makes it clear to me that this Syndicate has corrupted the highest levels and left us isolated up shit creek in the barbed wire boat,' explained Joe.

'The list down the left side of the board shows the areas I believe we need to master so we can disappear off any grid or chain-of-command. We will need to be self-sufficient in all these areas. Can anyone think of any others?'

'Guns and weapons,' added Jessica.

'Training,' piped Sara Jane, 'unless you're going to beat someone to death with your calculator.'

Joe wrote the two extra line items down, ignoring Sara Jane's attempt at humour.

'We need to get out of here. Immediately. Everything else can wait. Last night showed how compromised we are,' interjected Ms Bowman. 'I have a clean credit card and driver's licence in a different name I set up years ago. Unfortunately, in my game disappearing sometimes becomes necessary.'

'OK, but we can't use the LandCruiser and the Subaru is too small,' added Joe.

'I saw a hire place down the road. I'll grab a moving truck or small bus. Joe, find us an Airbnb or such like. Say around Cessnock, in the wineries area. Something big enough for all of us, with some privacy.' Ms Bowman didn't wait around for questions and the rest of the team were happy to have someone take the lead.

By the time Ms Bowman returned with a small self-move truck, Joe had picked out two likely properties. Both were in the wine country about a hundred kilometres away, catered for groups and had private grounds. Ms Bowman handed over the credit card and Joe booked his favourite for two weeks under a company name belonging to a dormant company owned by one of his clients. As the credit card was not linked to the company, he doubted anyone would join the dots.

'If last night taught us one thing, it's complacency kills. From now on at least one team member is on lookout duty. Jessica put a roster together of one-hour shifts, night and day. When it's your shift it is all you do. Drop everything else and watch over the team. My mistake last night was nearly fatal. Worse than that the LandCruiser is now compromised. Sara Jane, Tracey and Joe start loading everything into the truck. Jessica, lookout duties, rest your shoulder. Once everything is loaded, we need to scrub this place. They might be onto Jessica and myself, but we need to keep Sara Jane, Tracey and Joe off their radar if we can. So, wipe down everything and vacuum the floor. We will take the vacuum and used wipes with us. Hit it people.'

Joe looked at his list on the whiteboard. He had to agree with the priorities even if the solutions were only temporary. *It bought them some breathing space, well, some keep-breathing space,* thought Joe, savouring the pun. He decided to keep it to himself, rubbing the bruises from where Sara Jane had belted him in training yesterday.

Nothing motivates like the threat of imminent discovery and death. The only item left behind was the shot-up LandCruiser. Ms Bowman and Jessica left first in the moving van. Joe locked the warehouse and followed in the Subaru with Sara Jane and Tracey. As agreed, Joe dropped back for a while and about halfway there, overtook the moving van. He then stopped at a highway rest area and let the van pass again. In this fashion they leap-frogged their way to the Airbnb, one vehicle checking the other for tails at every pass.

Ms Bowman returned the van with Tracey driving her back to the Airbnb in the Subaru. While they were gone, she had Jessica place an order for groceries to be delivered that afternoon, and Sara Jane and Joe walking the boundary. Their assignment was to find a second exit in case they needed to make a speedy retreat. Joe had examined the property using Google Maps and knew there was a road running along the rear boundary towards the Watagan Mountains, providing an escape route taking them in the opposite direction to town. They found the rear fence was accessible and after some fine tuning with some tools they found in the shed, the old rusty padlock on the rear gate had its hasp snapped. Joe and Sara Jane double-checked the old gate could swing open and the track to the road was passable.

They gathered on the balcony. The house was a pseudo-colonial with wrap-around balconies and manicured gardens. There were spectacular views from all sides, plenty of rooms, and even a pool. *Oh well, if we are going to be on the run, we might as well do it in style,* thought Joe.

Joe had placed his whiteboard in the lounge room. He could see no way out of their situation in the short term. Therefore, the items he listed previously would need to be solved in the medium to long term. They had bought themselves some space but hadn't solved their problems.

He set up his computer on a desk in the media room. He thought about using the complimentary wi-fi but opted for using one of the burner phones Ms Bowman had issued earlier as a modem. The more anonymous he was, the safer he felt. He had an hour before his turn as lookout so he opened the browser and connected to his cloud account. He began to examine the files he had uploaded from the Foreman's computer. An idea had evolved from his browse through the files the previous day. He confirmed his suspicions with a few clicks and reference to the password list he had liberated from the Foreman's desk.

He logged onto a bitcoin exchange and using the first two series of numbers on the list, entered a public and private key. The account opened and he noted the transactions. He opened a new browser tab, searched through the Foreman's files until he found his credit card statements. The amounts withdrawn from the bitcoin account matched the payments into the Foreman's personal credit card account.

Joe created his own bitcoin account. Since he had the Foreman's public and private keys, he was able to transfer the Foreman's balance into his own account. Scanning the Foreman's account, Joe deducted that the Foreman had recently created an automatic daily clearing transfer from one of the other accounts on the list Joe had found. Joe did the same, clearing the Foreman's account into his own on a daily basis. He then changed the Foreman's private key or password. Now the account was under Joe's control and the Foreman's access was blocked. Another new tab and he created a Cayman Islands private company, then a bank account for that company. He transferred the balance of his new bitcoin account through the exchange and into the new Cayman Islands account. The Foreman's bitcoin account was now empty, and an untraceable Cayman Islands Corporation was now sitting on two million USD. It was a good start.

Joe was on lookout duty. In the distance he could hear a car approaching the property. It was not the first of his watch and probably would not be the last. They all drove past. It was easy just to ignore them. This one slowed down as it neared the driveway. He heard its tyres roll over the grid at the entrance to the property. He could see the car now. He had never seen it before.

'We have visitors,' he said into the portable radio he was holding. The others should be dropping everything and hurrying to their designated defensive positions.

Joe walked forward into the parking space fronting the house, conscious of the unseen guns at his back. His orders were to drop like a stone at the first sight of anything untoward, clearing the firing range for the team hidden behind the curtains of the front windows.

The car pulled up in front of Joe, the car was a rental Toyota Camry in white, basically invisible in the tourist infested area they were hiding in. He recognised the single occupant sitting in the driver's seat. Joe smiled. He knew being seen in such a humble vehicle would be acutely embarrassing for Fred.

Fred opened the door and extradited himself from the Camry. He grabbed his medical bag from the back seat. 'Joe, there's some supplies in the boot, could you grab them and bring them in? Where's Jessica?' Fred wandered off towards the house, while Joe popped the boot latch, picked up the supplies and followed.

Joe had given up being surprised. By the time he had lowered the clinking bags onto the kitchen counter Fred was unwrapping the dressings on Jessica's shoulder using the antique dining table as a work bench. Joe hustled back outside. He realised he needed to be double vigilant in case Fred had acquired a tail. Ms Bowman had Tracey and Sara Jane examining the car. Joe assumed they were checking for any tracking devices. He decided a walk down the winding drive to the road wouldn't be a bad idea. He could check up and down for any parked cars. He would then do the same out the back. Anyone with Google Maps could find the rear entrance.

'While the medic's here, can you pull a double shift?' Ms Bowman's voice came over the radio.

'No probs, I am just checking the outer perimeter, seeing if there were any Klingons.'

'Klingons?'

Joe heard Fred's voice in the background, 'It's a bad pun, bad guys from Star Trek or something stuck to my bum.'

'OK, be careful. Over.' The radio went dead.

It was evening by the time Joe returned to the house. In fact, it was a beautiful, summer's evening, a sea breeze having sprung up to take the heat out of the day. Joe surprised himself even registering such an ambience, he suspected he may be accepting his current circumstances as a new normal. Ms Bowman had warned them to be alert for drones. It was still and quiet, a good time to check. Joe stood still, closed his eyes and listened. He could hear nothing.

Joe returned to the house and found the others seated around the dining-room table. 'I didn't see anything, nor could I hear anything. It all seems clear,' he reported to the room.

'My shift,' replied Tracey standing and leaving the room.

'OK, Joe you just pulled a double so that's ten hours to your next shift,' said Ms Bowman. 'I think it's time you and Fred had a catch-up.'

The two empty beer bottles in front of Fred spoke for themselves;

Fred was staying the night. 'Grab yourself a beer and one for me, old mate,' said Fred.

Joe ambled over to the fridge and extracted two beers. Everyone else seemed to be already nursing a drink so he ambled back over to the table and sat opposite Fred.

'What's your story then?'

Fred sipped his beer. 'You know I am an ethnic Tamil originally from Sri Lanka, and so is my wife. Relatives bought each of us out here after our families were massacred by the government of that country. We were fostered out to different Australian families but kept in touch. When I graduated high school, I joined the Army on a university scholarship program. My wife and I started seeing each other socially and we realised our life experiences meant we needed to be together for life. We married and she became an Army wife. I graduated uni and by that time I had become a medic in the SAS where I came into contact with the Major. Eventually I left the Army as it was time to settle down to concentrate on raising the family. I built the practice from a one-man operation into four medical centres. These days I only work as a GP, the wife and kids run the centres, especially now the kids have finished uni. All in all I have it bloody easy these days, which gives me time to bail you out from messes like this.' Fred took a sip of his beer. Joe knew he was hearing the edited version. Even so, reading between the lines, he knew there was one hell of a story there.

'The outcome of our experience surviving what was basically a genocide, and growing up in Australia, is that both my wife and myself know we have an obligation to fight shit. Be it state-sponsored or criminal gangs. That's why I am here, good buddy. With the wife's and kids' approval, though your dog's pretty pissed off about the whole thing,' finished Fred clinking beers with Joe.

'I knew it was serious when I saw you in a Camry,' quipped Joe.

'Somehow a bright purple 1970s muscle car is not stealth material.

Go figure,' said Fred referring to his daily drive. Joe knew Fred had given him the short version. He didn't push for more details. It was obvious Fred didn't want to go into details, most of it was too painful.

Joe had always known there was one hell of a back story to Fred's quiet lifestyle with his wife and kids on the shores of Lake Macquarie. Outwardly there was nothing remarkable about him. He looked like a local GP approaching middle-age, happy with his lot in life. Not as tall as Joe, his dark hair was starting to show a few grey strands, especially in his neat beard. However, Joe had been on enough fire calls with him to know that man could go and go. He had seen Fred in the shower, the well-defined muscles and the unexplained scars. There had always been something about Fred's quiet competence under physical and mental pressure that challenged his laidback outer shell. The SAS connection explained a lot.

Joe was relaxing. A couple of beers down and he was opening a bottle of red wine. He realised he was hungry and therefore most likely so was everyone else. 'Spag bol, everyone?' he asked.

There was relief all round. Joe had become the unofficial team cook. Ms Bowman just expected it to happen, Jessica only had one working arm, and everyone was still shell-shocked by something involving chicken, Tracey's love of chilli and Sara Jane's complete lack of patience with food preparation.

He knocked it up casually while sipping wine and gossiping with Fred about members of the brigade. A little bitter-sweet for Joe, as, no matter how much he tried to relax he couldn't see a way back to his old life. He dished up leaving enough in the pots for Sara Jane. Tracey ate half of hers then contacted Sara Jane swapping lookout duty for half the meal with her partner. Sara Jane reported nothing out of the ordinary, finished her meal and swapped back with Tracey. The conversation had been subdued and inane, about the weather and the local area. In the back of everyone's mind was concern about where they were headed, or more precisely their lack of options.

Fred had kept to the beer and after the meal was now nodding off. He excused himself and shambled off to the room he would be using for the night. He had set his phone to wake him at 4 am so he could head back home in time to do a normal day's work. Jessica was still suffering a degree of discomfort from her arm. Fred had recommended she start gently exercising it the next day. She was tired and grumpy, especially as she had been denied any of the wine because of her medications.

Tracey had wandered off to get changed and relieve Sara Jane whose lookout shift was coming to an end. That left Ms Bowman and Joe. They sat in silence for a while.

'I am not sure I can deal with all this,' said Joe, realising the wine had allowed his inhibitions to slip and for the first time was discussing his situation rather than planning his next move.

'Yeah, I cannot see you drifting back to your old existence.'

'I don't see how I am even going to get the fucking choice,' stated Joe staring into his glass. The answer wasn't in there either. 'I mean, who are we up against? Where can we run? Is that the only choice we have, to run and hide? How can we turn it around? As far as I can see we are fucked unless we can get on the offensive.'

'Well let's look at this. They know who I am,' said Ms Bowman taking her time. 'The only person who IDed you was the Foreman who is now on the run from the Syndicate. Jessica is not even assigned to me. She was seen in that meeting but probably as a drone, and hopefully no one has bothered to follow up her involvement. Sara Jane is a loose end they need to tie up. I believe she will "die" over in the Himalayas as per her Facebook posts, but they will be frantically searching for her locally. Tracey will be partially on their radar. They know they sent her to the facility and they probably know she is not with the mob they evacuated on that bus.'

Joe ambled over to the whiteboard. It was hinged in the middle so he flipped it over leaving the previous days notes on the back. In black he wrote down the right-hand side their names.

Across the top he listed the threat levels: red, amber, yellow.

Against Ms Bowman he put a cross in red.

Against Jessica, amber

Against Sara Jane and Tracey, between red and amber.

Against himself he placed the cross in the yellow column.

'OK, that would seem to be fairly accurate. Let's leave it to the morning, I'm relieving Tracey about 12.30 am. Then Jessica will have a short stint after me, then you're back out there on lookout duty. Time to hit the pillow.'

Joe agreed. A couple of beers and most of the bottle of red was not a good foundation for decision making.

CHAPTER 28

Joe surfaced reluctantly. He had been shaken awake; it was still dark and maybe he should have left the last two glasses of red in the bottle. Jessica was sitting on the side of the bed shaking his shoulder with her good arm.

'OK, OK what time is it?' Joe struggled up and out of bed before realising he was naked. 'Shit, sorry Jess.' He quickly shuffled into his underwear then jeans. Looking for a clean shirt it occurred to him that a limited wardrobe was another of the hassles of being in hiding.

'You have about an hour and a half of dark before dawn, Joe,' instructed Jessica, pretending not to watch Joe's clumsy gymnastics. She found it a pleasing sight with a nice comic twist. 'It's all been quiet. Not even any wind to rustle the leaves. I can stay with you for a bit. I'm not tired enough to get back to sleep yet, so might as well keep active.'

Joe wasn't about to complain. It did seem a likely time for a raid if someone had found them. He also found himself wanting Jessica's company more than he was prepared to admit. Joe cleaned his teeth and drank a full water bottle, before going to the kitchen for a refill. Jessica had returned outside and was standing on the darkened veranda looking out across the fields to the road. Joe stayed on the veranda for a few minutes to let his eyes adjust. When he could discern the trees from the driveway he ambled out towards the road.

'We need to get those cameras and microphones set up today,' said Joe referring to the DIY home security package Fred had left behind. It contained four wireless cameras with microphones leading back to a base controller linkable to a laptop or a smart TV. Although it was wireless, Joe still suspected it was only good enough to stop honest crooks, not the heavy hitters after them, but it was better than nothing. They didn't have the personnel to keep a constant look out. Joe also felt uncomfortable staying where they were for too long. The exercise last night with Ms Bowman left him feeling vulnerable. He was going to have to devise a way forward, and he would need to ensure there was no link from one hideout to the next. He would have to take the lead on this; he could tell Ms Bowman's training had not prepared her for working without back-up or logistical support. They had booked the current place for a week, today would be the third day, a Tuesday, so they would need something new before the weekend. He also thought they needed a permanent solution, but all that could wait to later. Now he was going to share a sunrise with a beautiful woman. By his reckoning he had about a sixty per cent chance of stuffing this up!

He knew the sun would rise over the Watagan escarpment behind the property, so their sunrise would be delayed. The stars were just starting to fade as the sky moved from night through to twilight.

'So why did you join the RFS?' asked Jessica, eager to break the ice. The last week or so, and the near miss on the motorway, had turned Jessica a little introspective the last few days. She had begun to feel there was something more to life than her career, possible because she had come to suspect her career had just launched itself off a cliff without deciding whether it could fly, or not.

'Well, I had sold up and left Sydney. It was OK for a while finding my way around and starting on the house, but it was, I dunno, a bit empty. I have a couple of brothers, and we keep in touch, but both my parents passed away. They married late, as Dad got caught up in Vietnam. I never missed the hustle and bustle and being "someone". Funny, I could never go back. As soon as I stepped back, I realised that I was just not interested anymore. So I started looking around for something to do up here, and the RFS seemed like a good start. The brigade I am with have a solid commitment to training, so quite soon, after a couple of years, I had made it to the elite level. I also had the advantage of being semi-retired so I could put the extra time in during the week. Then of course along came this fire season, whereupon everything just went nuts.

'That was probably more than you wanted, Jess. So how about you? How did you end up being a cop? And working undercover for Ms Bowman ?'

'It seemed a natural. There was nothing unusual about our upbringing. There is only Sara Jane and myself. Our parents were fairly strict. Well, on me. I always reckon SJ was on a looser leash.'

'Now that I know SJ, I'm guessing, as tight a lease as they dared,' interjected Joe.

Jessica had a brief chuckle at that, 'Yeah as tight as they dared. So, I wanted something where I was outside, helping others and, I'll admit, with a bit of excitement. So after finishing school I took a few casual jobs. My favourite as a sailing instructor at the local sailing club.'

Jessica took a moment to gather her thoughts. 'After a while, when I started to look for something with a bit of a future, and I will admit on a bit of a whim, I joined the cops. Now, about eight years in, and with a degree, I was seconded to what I thought was a Federal Police Task Force but has since gone off the books, and now it appears completely off the rails. As for Ms Bowman, Fred probably knows more – she knows all about him. I don't even know her first name, although I suspect she is still in the armed forces.'

By now the sun was rising above the ridge to the east, turning the haze below the Watagans pink and orange. The twilight was morphing into full daylight, the trees and paddocks changing from grey tones to full colour. They had ambled to the front gate, turned and were making their way down the drive back to the house, into the sunrise. They passed round the house to the left, briefly checked the outbuildings for any sign of trespass and continued towards the back gate. The dew on the grass would have picked up any movement. They wandered to the back gate and then up and down the lane running behind the property. They could see no evidence of anyone entering the property from the rear.

'Fuck it, Joe, I am not normally like this.' Jessica started to sob quietly.

Joe was taken aback. He had not considered the emotional toll of the past few days. Jessica had lost her sister, found her again, then been shot and had her world turned upside down. He was drawn to her but did not want her to think he was taking advantage of her and the situation. He took her in his arms and held her.

Jessica pulled her head back and looked up into his eyes. 'Please, Joe, here and now, just live this moment.'

She locked her mouth onto his. His remaining resistance crashed like a shot duck.

It was as clumsy and exciting as clandestine teenage lovemaking. Joe took off Jessica's coat first, after easing her arm through the sling, then his own, throwing them on the grass behind some trees out of sight from the road. They lay down together. He kissed her deeply, letting his hands slide up under her shirt gently massaging each breast as he pushed her bra higher up her chest. Her hands had reached his belt, but she could only use one arm effectively. He knelt back on his knees and reached for her jeans. Jessica laid back. He undid her belt and fly and pulled her jeans and panties down to her ankles in one movement. She let her knees roll apart He dropped his own jeans and underwear and shuffled up between her knees. He gave her three quick kisses on the lips then they kissed in earnest. He ran his hand down between her legs and gently rubbed her sex. She was wet. Jessica made a mewing sound and thrust her hips up at him. He let himself slide inside her. When they finished, she held him tightly down on top of her with her good arm. They waited for their heart rates to settle down.

The sun was now fully on them. Joe thought to look around and check they could not be seen from the house. It was private for the moment. Neither said anything, neither wanted to ruin the moment. Joe pushed back from between her legs and onto his knees. He carefully pulled her pants back up and did up her belt. He stood and pulled up his own pants. He held out his hand, she passed him her good arm and he helped her up. They hugged, picked up their coats and readjusted Jessica's sling. They then spent a minute adjusting their clothing. He smiled, she smiled. They hugged again.

Joe still had an hour of his lookout duty to perform. Jessica felt ready for bed. She wished Joe was joining her, but knew he had to complete his rounds. They held hands as they walked up to the house.

The sun was now shining on the back of the house leaving the windows opening onto the rear verandah dark and impenetrable. In one of the back rooms an elfin face was peering out from under the sheets. A grin appeared on her face.

Sara Jane nudge Tracey awake.

'Whhat?' yawned Tracey, still feeling mellow from their own lovemaking.

'I reckon those two just did the dirty!' replied Sara Jane pointing across to Joe and Jessica walking across the back paddock. Tracey leaned up on her elbows.

'Reckon your right. What you gunna do about it?'

'Well, it's about fucking time. But I am still going to give him a hard time in training today,' chuckled Sara Jane as she rolled across on top of Tracey, pleased with her pun.

CHAPTER 29

Joe returned to the house once his shift was over. He declined joining the others for breakfast and returned to his room. He needed to catch a bit more sleep. Then he needed to think. He was hoping his subconscious would kick something loose or divine a new tack out of their current situation.

He was just nodding off when Jessica entered. 'You OK?' she asked.

'Yeah, I am good. Maybe it is this pressure-cooker situation, but I do want to be with you. If we ever get through this and return to some semblance of normality, it may not work, but here, now, I think we both need the support. But you will have to guide me in regards to Ms Bowman and your sister.'

'I wouldn't worry about that. SJ saw us walking back towards the house. She took immense pleasure in "congratulating" me this morning in front of Ms Bowman. I do love my sister, but sometimes she is a fucking pain in the arse.'

'Is that a problem with your boss?'

'I don't think so. Ms Bowman seemed very down this morning. She has always been military. That means she believes in the chain-of-command. We had a few words in private; she acknowledges that you are now the one moving things forward. You got us off the radar and into this place. She cannot reach out to anyone; she doesn't know who the traitor is. You are used to working alone and finding creative solutions, then selling those ideas.'

'I'll have a chat with her later,' mused Joe. 'We need a strong leader, and it has been her up to now. It needs to stay that way. I am sure she will rally, but in a situation like this I can see why she should suffer from some self-doubt. But any kind of leadership challenge is just going to leave us floundering. Just now I need a power nap.'

'Wow, one quick roll in the hay and you're fucked?'

'Nah, it's bad pun overload. A few drinks last night and up hours before sparrow fart to see Fred off has left me a flat,' replied Joe. He sat up, pulled Jessica to him and kissed her on the lips. 'I need to rest my mind. Can you suggest we have some sort of brainstorming session this afternoon? We need to find a way out of this mess. We can't keep running.'

'OK, Joe,' Jessica stood and made her way to the door, 'I will come get you in an hour'.

Once again Joe felt his shoulder being shaken. 'It's time to get up,' said Jessica.

Joe realised he crashed out for an hour.

'Coffee. Then bacon and eggs. That's what I need,' Joe mumbled to himself, staggering out of bed and into the ensuite shower.

Showered, fed and moving forward, Joe felt almost human. Breakfast had done the job. Sitting at the dining-room table, Joe was working through the instructions for the DIY security system. It looked straightforward. First job would be to scout the property for good vantage points for the cameras. Attach them with cable ties, string or whatever they could find, turn it on and see if they could get it working.

Sara Jane was working with him. Tracey was on lookout and Jessica and Ms Bowman were in conference, Jessica in the unusual position of attempting to bolster Ms Bowman's self-confidence.

Joe could feel Sara Jane almost bursting at the seams, frustration with Joe for not wanting to talk about Jessica oozing from her pores. He was sitting on the first fork of a gum tree to the left of the driveway, trying to position a camera so it would have a clear view of the stock grid bordering the property from the road. 'Pass me a couple of screws and a screwdriver, this branch is too big for the cable ties to work.'

'Bet that's not what you want to be screwing,' answered Sara Jane, the challenge clear in her voice.

'The Phillips head driver not the slot, please,' Joe deadpanned. He grinned into the tree; he knew taunting Sara Jane was like playing rugby with an unexploded bomb.

'I can shove them both up your arse from here, Mr Fireman. Now, what you gunna do about my sister?'

They had all tried to alter their appearance. Sara Jane's hair had been cut short into a pixie cut. It made her look even more petite and harmless. He knew how deceiving the new look was. They had been training together every day, Joe feeling he needed serious help updating his skill set for this new world he found himself occupying.

They had become friends, a friendship that Joe valued.

'I dunno SJ, treat her with respect? I mean what are the ground rules surrounding relationships forged in desperate circumstances?'

'How the fuck would I know? I'm just glad she's finely getting some. But you hurt her, I hurt you.'

'Got you. Now steady the ladder while I get down from here, and we can see if this is going to work. Leave the ladder here, once we have it working you can direct me from the computer with the handheld radios while I get the aim right.'

Joe returned to the kitchen and began to make himself a cup of instant coffee. He asked around if anybody else would like one, but they all declined. Coffee in hand he made his way to the desktop they had brought from the warehouse.

The cameras contacted their control box through Bluetooth and the control box was linked to the computer by wireless router, so theoretically it was not visible outside the local vicinity and was protected by a password. All four cameras showed up on the screen. Joe took a sheet of paper and noted the adjustments he would need to make to each camera for the best coverage.

With Sara Jane seated at the computer directing him, Joe repositioned the cameras. Once she had signed off on each camera, he returned the ladder and tools to the shed where he found them. He glanced at his Subaru, noting the dust that was gathering on it. They were assuming as only the Foreman knew about Joe, his identity was secure. It meant the Subaru was still usable. It was a risky assumption so the car was kept out of sight unless absolutely necessary. All five team members kept their meagre possessions packed and ready to load into the car. They were going to use the back road and the track over the Watagans as an escape route. Joe was hoping they could find a way to hit back before they had to run.

The five of them gathered around the computer screens. One screen filled with the images from the cameras. Joe turned up the volume from each feed and set up a loop so the speaker repeated each feed on a ten-second cycle. The soundtrack lacked any cohesion, but it gave them another way of listening for drones.

*

Joe stepped away from the computer. Sara Jane took the seat and accessed a web browser.

'Wow, don't do that!' exclaimed Ms Bowman. 'IPs can be traced and used to track us. These a very sophisticated people we are up against.'

'I am using TOR, a web browser with higher levels of security and anonymity, and therefore also the favourite navigation tool for the dark web. It takes longer but keeps our IP address and therefore the location hidden,' replied Sara Jane.

'Does it search content as well as URLs?' asked Joe.

'Yes, but that will make it slower,' replied Sara Jane.

'Try these numbers. They are the public key to a bitcoin account I think was being used to hide the profits from their operations.'

Sara Jane opened a separate tab and typed in the nine digits. She returned to her original page and typed in the address of her news blog. She had a link where her audience could leave private comments. There was a new message there; it looked quite big.

Sara Jane began to download the message. The text showed first, some pictures were still downloading.

'Tomorrow you return what's mine. Otherwise they die. Transfer the bitcoin back and close the auto-move instruction. Reply when it's done. Otherwise they die before they order their fucking coffees. I don't see my money tomorrow, they die anyway.'

That's all it said. The pictures downloaded. They showed Jessica and Sara Jane's parents entering a café. The last picture was of the front door of their house. Subdued, Sara Jane said, 'They go there every afternoon when they are not doing anything. It's their exercise.'

'It has gotta be the Foreman. He is the only one who'd know you were still alive and that we had his money,' said Joe.

'I need to go now. Right fucking now,' Sara Jane replied as she pushed past the others and ran to her room. The others looked at each other. No one had any idea what to do.

Next, they heard the unmissable rattle of a boxer engine. The Subaru shot out of the garage and down the drive. The brake lights flared for a second, the car thumped over the stock grate, turned left and accelerated hard. 'Shit she climbed out the window. She knew we would want to discuss this and try and stop her.'

'It's a fucking ambush,' stated Tracey. For a minute there was silence.

'Joe, Tracey, after her. Take the property ute. I checked it's registered, and the owner won't miss it. Jessica's still injured and I am too well-known. Tracey take your gear,' Ms Bowman broke the silence.

Tracey had shaved her head and Joe had grown a few days' worth of stubble. He grabbed what he thought he would need: his phone, his wallet and a hoodie to hide under. Tracey returned to the main room with an attaché case and her own hoodie. 'You know what to do?' asked Ms Bowman.

'Yes, Major,' replied Tracey formally. Joe again felt out of his depth.

The four of them trooped out to the shed. Joe let Tracey and Ms Bowman take the lead. 'You OK?' he asked Jessica.

'No way. We're fucked aren't we? It's like the walls are closing in on us,' grumbled Jessica. Joe could see she was on the point of crying.

'Get your cop head on. Shift the evidence, examine what we know and what we don't, write down some assumptions based on that,' replied Joe. He knew she needed something to do. Sitting and waiting would be devastating.

But first, 'Where is she going?'

'It's a café down from our parents' place. It's on the beach they moved to when Dad retired.' Joe gave Jessica his phone.

'Type it into the map app. What time would they take their afternoon stroll?'

'Three-ish on an afternoon like this. They would wait for the sea breeze to make it more comfortable.'

Joe continued into the shed. Ms Bowman had found the keys and started the farm ute. It was another Japanese twin cab 4WD. Even in the city these utes were everywhere and unremarkable.

'Joe, give your phone to Tracey and drive. This is Tracey's specialty,' instructed Ms Bowman. 'GO!'

Tracey opened her case and threw Ms Bowman a phone. 'One of a matched pair. Never used and off the books. We can use them to stay in touch. The numbers are preset.'

Joe shoved the ute into first and released the clutch as the vehicle shot forward and took off after the Subaru.

'Fuck, Fuck, FUCK,' screamed Jessica. She knew Joe had given her work to do so she wouldn't fall to pieces. But she wasn't going to just do it as a distraction, she was going to find answers. This needed to be turned around.

'OK, 1039 hours now. That location is about two hours away and your parents visit the café about three. If we have not heard anything we call them at 1430 hours, two-thirty, and warn them. Their lines are probably being monitored so we leave it until the last minute so they can find cover, but without alerting the opposition. There's a strong possibility the Foreman is working alone, but we do not know if the Syndicate is focusing on SJ, you or your parents. The Syndicate don't know your connection and they probably think SJ died in the fire at the facility, there's no record of her leaving.'

'Agreed,' sniffed Jessica, noticing Ms Bowman was back in charge now she had a mission. The hiding and waiting had been bad for everyone.

CHAPTER 30

Tracey studied the target area on the phone. Based on the information provided by Jessica, there was a beach with a kiosk attempting to upmarket itself into a café, a carpark, then a ridge running behind it. The ridge was a national park with walking trails from the lagoon on the north side. Sara Jane's parents walked across the ridge most days, had a coffee and returned home.

'I have a tracker on the Subaru. Go to www.trackmyride.com.au, the username is Subaru14 and the password is Triumph13.'

'Got it,' replied Tracey. 'SJ's about twenty kilometres ahead of us. Looks like she is playing it smart and staying under the speed limit. She will still be at the café at least an hour before her parents.'

'Shit, that's a surprise,' scoffed Joe.

'You know that's one of the things that she says really pisses her off. Everyone underestimates her.'

Joe thought about that for a minute while navigating around a semi pulling a double trailer. 'Seems like a massive advantage in the current circumstances. How is she going to do this, you reckon? Just walk in and take a table? He needs the new private code to the bitcoin account so he has to meet her. He also is going to want to kill her.'

'He can't do that at the café. He will have to lure her into the bush, I would think. He will also need a vantage point. First on site and first to the high ground would be my strategy,' said Tracey.

'Interesting skill set for a soft serve dispenser,' quipped Joe. He was amazed at her calm, analytical approach; after all it was her lover in the crosshairs.

Tracey ignored him. She was examining the map application on the phone. 'OK, he is most likely up on this ridge. There is an access road to this lookout running across the top.' She switched to satellite view and examined the terrain. 'That's where we need to go. You're an Australian bloke taking an Asian visitor on a sightseeing trip, hopefully with benefits. My guess is that along here we will find his vehicle.' She pointed to a spot on the map. Joe understood the general idea but kept his eyes on the road.

'OK, we should be there in another hour. Would that be too early?'

'If I was him, I would already be there. He has no idea how soon SJ will arrive. He has to have his trap set before then. According to the GPS we are about thirty minutes out from the target.'

They drove in silence through the hamlets of the Central Coast. Joe found the laneway atop the ridge and turned towards the lookout while Tracey watched the screen to confirm their position. The lookout was about two kilometres away, and halfway along a motorcycle was parked beside the road. Innocuous enough as the area was riddled with walking tracks.

'That's him, I'll put money on it. Go around the corner, turn around and park on the outbound side closer to the intersection. We can block him if he makes a break for it.'

Leaving the ute as directed, Joe returned to the motorcycle. Kneeling down he removed the spark plug lead from the lead cylinder of the V-Twin. He knew from experience the bike's engine computer would not let the engine start until the cap was refitted to the spark plug. Tracey nodded her approval.

She had her attaché case with her. She raised a finger to her lips in the universal sign for silence and began to creep down the pathway hidden behind the bike. Joe followed. A short distance in, they reached the edge of the ridge, below which a boulder protruded from the face. It offered a panoramic view of the café and the carpark. Exactly as Tracey had guessed.

Lying prone on the rock was a man. He was scanning the carpark with binoculars. Joe realised Sara Jane had held back and not rushed into the trap. She must have been trying to invent a plan. Whatever her reason, it helped them. Joe's blue Subaru entered the carpark. The man below them tensed and focused his binoculars. Sara Jane had parked near the toilet block, the driver's door nearest the entrance to the Ladies. She exited the car and entered the Ladies change rooms. The man below was fully focused, they now had no doubt he was hunting Sara Jane. It was the Foreman.

Tracey lowered the attaché case to the ground. Unlatching it she quickly assembled a deadly-looking rifle with a suppressor attached to the end of the barrel. Casually, still kneeling, she braced her elbow on her knee and brought the butt of the gun up to her shoulder. Before Joe could think she had shot the Foreman in the back of the head. Joe studied the scene; no one appeared to have noticed.

'What the fuck!' Joe exclaimed, his brain trying to comprehend what his eyes had just seen.

'What did you think I was going to do?' said Tracey, surprised at Joe's shock.

'I...I... what the fuck, you just shot him.'

'Yeah, we should have just said "hello" and asked him down for a coffee,' replied Tracey sarcastically.

She dissembled and repacked the gun into its case, making sure to pick up the shell casing. 'Let's get down there and tidy up,' she said, not waiting for Joe, but sliding down the scree to the platform below and the Foreman's corpse.

Joe followed, gingerly. He knew what he was about to see he would never be able to unsee.

Strangely there was little mess. 'Half-powered round,' explained Tracey. 'No through and through. The bullet's still in his head.'

'Isn't that traceable?' asked Joe.

'No, the suppressor would have left the final markings and it is only single use.' Tracey took a look over the edge. 'Roll him over the cliff into the lantana, could be years before anybody looks.'

Joe did as instructed. Tracey picked up the rifle the Foreman had been lying next to. Joe recognised it from the facility. On the inside of the rock platform next to where they had slid down was a guitar case and a backpack. Tracey packed the Foreman's rifle into the backpack. Joe rummaged through the pack finding a wallet, mobile and a motorcycle key. The Foreman had used blue contact lenses to match the licence photo contained in the wallet. With the beard and brown hair, the licence photo looked close enough to pass as an unkempt version of Joe. He assumed it was a clean ID.

He showed Tracey. 'I'm going to take the bike,' he said.

'Wait a moment,' Tracey picked up her phone and called its twin.

'Can you check police database for Matthew Johnson born 12 July 1973? Also, any vehicle registered in that name.'

Tracey waited for a couple of minutes. 'Total cleanskin. And Suzuki DL650 motorcycle,' she repeated for Joe.

'I'll go down and let Sara Jane know. She doesn't have a phone,' Tracey continued. 'Get going the way we came down. Stop every ten kilometres so we can leapfrog each other, hopefully picking up any tails.' She repacked the two guns, placing them and the binoculars on the ute's rear seat. Sliding the driver's seat forward, she started the engine and drove down to surprise Sara Jane. Joe slipped into the Foreman's bike gear and helmet, replaced the spark plug cap, started the bike and followed her down the laneway. At the first intersection he turned away from the beach, twisted the throttle and headed for their temporary base. He couldn't think of it as home.

It was nice to be back on a bike.

'The boy has a new toy!' Sara Jane burst into the room, grinning from ear to ear.

Jessica and Ms Bowman jumped. Ms Bowman snatched at the handgun on the table. They had seen the procession enter the property and were watching the motorcyclist carefully.

'Sorry we didn't contact you,' Tracey interjected, 'we didn't want to use the phone again unless it was an emergency. It's Joe on the bike, so don't shoot him. He does come in handy.' She smirked at Jessica.

Ms Bowman considered shooting someone, anyone, to restore some semblance of discipline, but decided it was hopeless.

Joe was last into the house. He went straight to the kitchen and poured himself a glass of wine. Coffee was not going to hack it. Every day he felt further out of his depth. 'She just shot him.'

'And I fucking love her for it,' exclaimed Sara Jane.

'What other choice was there?' asked Jessica quietly. She understood how lost Joe was. His ordered world view had just been put through the shredder yet again.

Joe sat, sipped his wine and pondered the question. He turned it around, he turned it upside down. He couldn't see a choice. The Foreman and the Syndicate had made this world, they had dictated the rules. The others were all looking at him. He looked inwards; would he lose sleep over the death of the Foreman? He didn't think so. Some wine would help.

'OK, I fucking get it, I can fucking live with it. I just need to get fucking used to it.'

Joe took his glass and the bottle and headed to his room for a hot shower. He was sweaty and dirty from the day. When he stepped out of his steaming ensuite, Jessica was waiting for him. She had brought her own glass. They shared the last of the wine, sitting next to each other on the bed, then he put his arms around her and they kissed.

He felt her hand stroking his inner thigh. He could feel himself becoming aroused. He pulled away. 'You not going to get pregnant, is it safe?'

Jessica appreciated his concern even if it was a bit late. 'No, I am on the pill. Can't have a police officer with a loaded gun having bad PMT, or having bad cramps at a critical moment. It's standard procedure.'

He relaxed and slowly undressed her. This time they took their time. More affection less desperation.

Evening was descending before they re-entered the lounge room. The others were all showered and changed and sitting round the coffee table enjoying drinks of their own.

'Good thinking bringing the bike. Matthew Johnson must have been his back-up identity; I would assume he created it to disappear. I think he was cunning enough to know the operation would be exposed one day, and he would be the scapegoat,' reflected Ms Bowman.

'I doubt, now we have the ID, the name will be associated with the corpse when it is found. We can track it in the police database, but logic tells me he will be identified under his original name, probably from fingerprints and a long criminal record.'

The others accepted her theory. They could follow the news on the computer. Jessica still had her police log-ins, so they could follow the developments from there as well.

Joe went over to the desktop. He opened the TOR window and examined the results from the search he had initiated earlier in the day. He clicked on the first result. He was looking at a fake bedroom. The video paused, a message superimposed itself across the scene, Taming of the Slut deposit to bitcoin wallet to view and then the bitcoin public address for the wallet Joe now controlled scrolled across the screen.

'We're still making money,' he said.

The others gathered round the screen. The video resumed. The Foreman had not had time to complete the set-up. It was loaded but the payment routine had not been completed. It was a freebie.

On the video a door opened and Sara Jane was pushed into the room. Her hair was still down past her shoulders, she was dirty, and she looked scared. It was not a look Joe associated with Sara Jane. He looked up and saw the colour drain from her face, her fists were clenched. Tracey had her arms around her holding her tight. One of the thugs entered the room. His sadistic smile said it all; he was anticipating some serious fun. Moments later he was on the floor and two other thugs were restraining Sara Jane, with murder in their eyes. The Foreman rushed in before Sara Jane was destroyed.

'Holy Fuck,' said Joe. He glimpsed down at Sara Jane's boots. They were the same ones.

'Holy Fuck,' he said again, 'glad I'm on your side.'

'Oh, love you too, Mr Fireman,' gushed Sara Jane, slightly embarrassed by Joe's comments, but pleased he had broken the ice. The video had shocked them all.

Ms Bowman closed the browser and turned to the group. 'We need to debrief. Standard procedure after a mission.'

'Yep, same with us,' replied Joe.

'Tracey and Sara Jane have debriefed us on how the operation evolved. Now let's look at the outcomes. What did we gain, lose or discover?'

'The Foreman is gone. Threat removed,' started Sara Jane.

Joe grabbed his whiteboard and started writing.

'Joe has a clean ID and transport,' added Jessica.

'Income stream is still intact,' added Joe.

Tracey interjected, 'We are undetected at this moment.'

'We still have the Foreman's data,' Joe responded.

'OK, where to from here?' asked Ms Bowman.

'First we must look to our own safety.' Joe started a new column. 'Then, we must climb the ladder. The Foreman was no longer part of the Syndicate. They are still after us. We now need to discover and disable the next level.'

'As Jess said we now own the Foreman's identity,' Joe explained, 'at least until his body is found and identified. We can use it distract them away from us. He must be a bigger worry. While they chase him, we are free to move.'

Ms Bowman considered this for a moment, then added 'Threats: who can the Syndicate identify and who is below the radar. After the other night we can say I am definitely on their radar. Jessica: they know what she looks like but not who she is. Tracey and Sara Jane are still unknowns, still missing, and Joe is our own loose cannon.'

Joe looked up from the whiteboard not sure if he had been insulted. Ms Bowman continued, 'You are completely off their radar, and you are missing presumed dead.'

'I think we make SJ and Tracey dead as well,' piped up Jessica. Looking at the reports, they have found mountains of DNA in the furnace on the facility. 'There must be a way we can slip in a report identifying them, then they are off the radar. I can see the reports against the case, we just need to doctor two of the unknowns, and move them to the knowns. One of the techos is a friend, I think she will do it, she hates crimes against kids with a passion.'

'Do it,' ordered Ms Bowman.

'Hold the fuck up. I'm not that easy to kill off. What about you Trace?' interrupted Sara Jane.

'Well, it's happened before,' replied Tracey sheepishly, 'at least twice.'

'Who are you?' asked Joe.

'Just an orphan who was sucked down into a bad place, then rescued. Now I fight back.'

It was a cryptic answer, but Joe was sure it was the best he would ever hear.

'I have an idea: let's check Sara Jane's Facebook page. Last we saw she was on a hiking holiday in Tibet.' It was Jessica's turn to interrupt.

Jessica navigated her way to Facebook until she was looking at Sara Jane's page. The last entry was, Sara Jane Marlowe, while hiking with her boyfriend, is believed to have been killed in an avalanche on a remote route five hundred kilometres north of the capital Kathmandu. Her friends are linked in prayer as the search continues.

'I always hated fucking mountains,' responded Sara Jane. Joe was chuckling into his wine. 'Nearly as much as I hate smartarse firemen.'

'Well won't it confuse things if we kill her when she is already dead?' asked Joe. He was starting to enjoy this.

'The Syndicate knows she is alive,' answered Ms Bowman. 'Maybe we kill her off, but only release the news to a select few. We know someone at that meeting is either part of the Syndicate or working for them. I'll feed it to them, let them know it is sensitive information and not for general release. Who knows, we may even be able to backtrack it to the leak.

'OK, I will organise those doctored reports. It will confirm the Syndicate's suspicions. Then there will be three of the five of us off the radar,' stated Ms Bowman picking up her beer bottle and stepping away, effectively closing the meeting.

CHAPTER 32

Joe returned to his room after completing his turn as lookout. With the cameras linked to the computer it was easier, but still necessary. Dawn was approaching, and although he had been up for two hours on watch, he didn't think he would be able to sleep again. He had a new problem. After yesterday's unplanned action, they were a day closer to their moving date and as yet had nowhere to stay.

Joe also considered it was time to create a permanent base. He would need to discuss it with Ms Bowman and Jessica; he respected their strategic outlook. So, he now had two tasks for the day.

Find a new temporary base and organise the logistics, and research a permanent solution. First, coffee. The first assignment would be straightforward; find a suitable holiday rental for two weeks and organise the move. The second would require more research. Joe would need to find a way to purchase a property under the radar.

Sara Jane entered the room. She handed Joe a cheap mobile phone. It had been turned off and the battery removed. Joe had found a similar phone in the backpack. He had done the same. 'Looks like he was going to call and demand the private code for the wallet you hacked. Then blow my head off.'

'I would have to agree with you there.'

'A bit fucking depressing, all this shit,' muttered Sara Jane. 'You know, where's the end, how do we get our lives back?'

'Coffee, it's too early for alcohol,' quipped Joe. He did not have a real answer.

In his head Joe outlined a plan, even if it was only for today's problem. He would find them a new temporary location using the same ruse as before and begin the process of acquiring a permanent base using the Matthew Johnson identity. He typed up an outline of his plan to clarify it in his own mind before presenting it to the group.

Ms Bowman entered. She had just completed a walking circuit of the property as part of her watch. 'Doesn't look like we had any visitors during the night,' she reported, 'I'll finish my watch using the cameras.' She sat in front of the computer. 'I take it that you will be working on our next move, Joe?'

'Yep, under way.'

'I don't want to use the ute again. It's not ours and could be embarrassing if someone recognises it. Better hire a van or something locally.'

'I have found a place about ten minutes away. Pretty much the same as this one. I was going to use the same cover as we used to rent this one.'

'Yeah, it's still undetected so let's do it,' agreed Ms Bowman.

'I'm also looking at using the Matthew Johnson ID to purchase something permanent,' added Joe.

'OK, but let's not rush into that. See if any red flags turn up over the next couple of days. Fred should be here later to check on Jessica's shoulder. We can see if he has heard any gossip. Sometimes the unofficial channels are more informative than the official.'

Ms Bowman's last comment reminded Joe he still had access to the Foreman's data. He would do some more digging. First see if there was any documentation supporting the Matthew Johnson identity, and secondly see if he could expose any more useful information.

Within an hour Joe had organised the new location and a small rental truck to facilitate the move. Time to blow off some steam. He went in search of Sara Jane. Together they were working on his self-defence skills. Tracey decided to join them. He could see

Jessica also wanted to play, but she was waiting for Fred to arrive and assess her shoulder. They started with some stretching, then a jog to the front gate and back, then a run to the front gate and back and twenty push-ups, then a sprint to the gate and back and another twenty push-ups. It developed into a race. An hour later they were sweaty, dirty, Joe had a acquired a couple more bruises and the three of them were grinning from ear to ear. The physical release from the stress of the previous day.

'Right, we need to remove any trace of us being here. Moving day is tomorrow, with the same protocol as last time,' Ms Bowman ordered. Joe knew she was right. There was no point being off-grid if you left signposts behind, even if it was a single hair.

Joe was also toying with ways to use the Foreman to ghost the Syndicate. They knew eliminating the ex-employee would be the Syndicate's priority, and as Ms Bowman's team were the only ones who knew he was dead, they had an asset.

Ms Bowman approached Joe, 'Hi, mate, I am thinking of a special dinner tonight for morale.'

'How about a roast lamb? I can nip into town on the bike and grab the bits and pieces,' responded Joe.

'Let's do it. Hello, this must be Fred.' The white Camry was entering the property.

'I hope so,' said Jessica, 'I just want to get out of this fucking sling. I feel so useless being sidelined like this.'

'Joe, you should talk to him. You need to lay some false trails. The whole missing in action cover after the bike "crash" will start wearing a bit thin. In fact, it will start drawing attention to you. So, maybe an overseas business trip for you,' instructed Ms Bowman.

He hadn't thought about it, but it did suddenly seem important. He would ask Fred if there was any interest in his wellbeing or whereabouts back in the real world, as he still thought of it.

Fred parked, and everyone gathered in the main room of the

property. It was comfortable and roomy. Jessica pulled off her shirt and sat in a sports bra. Fred knelt down at her side and examined her injury. It was healing quickly and cleanly. 'Time we started moving this arm again, otherwise the joint will start to lock and you will lose muscle tone,' Fred spoke while finishing his examination. 'Start with gentle stretches, I'll show you a couple of basic ones. Slow down if you feel the stitches tightening up.' They all watched as Fred worked through some stretches with Jessica.

Fred finished with Jessica and looked up at Joe and said, 'People are starting to ask about you.'

'Funny, we were just talking about that. We need to move on from "Missing in Action" after the bike crash to "urgent overseas business trip",' replied Ms Bowman. 'We are still working under the assumption the Foreman was the only one who knew about Joe. I think that assumption is still good. So, moving him completely out of the picture is probably a good thing.'

'No worries. I will let people know I was hospitalised for a day or so "under observation" before leaving the country on business. It fits with my job anyway,' Joe replied.

'OK, that works. Jessica, can you update the police reports into the bike crash to match the scenario? It will close that loose end off as well. The shortfall in the body count was going to start raising flags. It also means Joe can contact his family and friends. I believe they are already raising some questions.'

Ms Bowman was a natural leader with years of experience and training. They all nodded their agreement. Joe was relieved. He had just returned to the living. Now he could attend to such prosaic matters as having his lawn cut and his mail collected.

Joe was hoping Fred could stay the night again, but Ms Bowman insisted Fred leave as soon as he was finished. She saw any contact with the outside world as a security breach, and Joe had to reluctantly agree.

Instead, he would ride into town, go to the supermarket and purchase the makings of an old-fashioned, home-cooked roast. A couple of bottles of red would also find their way into the V-Strom's panniers.

The day lapsed into routine. Joe returned from his shopping expedition, his preparations for dinner would soon start, and devoted the rest of the afternoon to immersing himself in the life of Matthew Johnson. The Foreman had been meticulous in building and maintaining the identity. Joe was happy to inherit the fruits of his labour. Matthew Johnson was his ticket to freedom.

Mid-afternoon came and went. Joe put the joint in the oven and soon the house was filled with the aroma of the baked dinner. The others gathered round the kitchen bench drawn by the bouquet. 'Grab a glass of what pleases you and let's sit on the balcony. I have cheese and dips and crackers for starters,' Joe suggested.

They trooped outside and found seats on the verandah in the shade. They were going to sip their drinks, nibble on the snacks and pretend they were just a bunch of friends enjoying an evening in the countryside.

CHAPTER 33

They moved only ten minutes down the road. The move had gone smoothly. Joe and Jessica were scouting the property installing the surveillance cameras. Tracey and Sara Jane were seated at the computer providing feedback.

'Holy shit, they're raiding the warehouse at Morisset,' blasted out of the radio. Joe nearly fell out of the tree where he was installing the last camera, but he climbed down and with Jessica jogged back up to the house. The computer was placed in an alcove of the living room. Sara Jane, Tracey and Ms Bowman were gathered around it.

The industrial park in which the warehouse was situated looked deserted. It was Sunday afternoon. However, as the film crew closed in it captured a knot of activity around their old base. A tilt-tray tow truck was in the process of dragging the damaged LandCruiser back out into the daylight. The camera focused on the damaged rear of the vehicle.

'A police operation is taking place in Morisset Industrial Park,' the announcer intoned. 'They are acting on a tip-off a major drug ring was operating out of the premises. However, the warehouse was empty except for this abandoned vehicle.'

'How close are they behind us?' asked Tracey.

'It's a dead end. The warehouse was organised through the department. Since then, Joe has been organising our accommodation off the books. There is no link, I am confident of that. But what it does prove is that the department has been infiltrated or the committee we report to has been compromised. My thinking is that it's the committee,' explained Ms Bowman. 'If it had been from within the department it would have happened sooner. I have been delaying reports to extend the timeline. The committee would only have just received the information regarding the warehouse; the department has known all along.'

'Who or what makes up the committee?' asked Joe.

'Basically, a joint operation between ASIO, the Armed Forces and Federal Police. The committee runs the Task Force. The focus is globalised organised crime. The Task Force reports to the committee chaired by the Federal Attorney-General. The full committee attended the briefing the other day. That's two strikes. I don't need a third. Someone associated with that committee is the leak.'

Joe's next question was obvious, 'So at least one of the people on the committee has been turned? Who are they?'

'Federal Attorney-General, head of ASIO, head of the Armed Forces, head of the Federal Police, some adjuncts and secretaries, and a Queen's Council to provide legal advice.'

'Anyway we could get a list of names?' Joe asked. 'Maybe the leaker was reporting to the Foreman? Or possibly the Foreman was reporting to him?'

'Or possibly they both report to a third person, like the head of country or something?' added Jessica.

'Therefore, they most likely know Jessica's identity?' added Joe.

'Not necessarily, I had Jess's details changed when she came on board. So, they are looking at another New South Wales state police officer who died a couple of years ago. Quite frankly, my money is on the committee leaking, not my department,' explained Ms Bowman. 'We were being white-anted the whole time. In the end, Jessica and I were the only field operatives left; one disappeared and the rest were disbanded. The Attorney-General and the QC, Brightly, were very eager to shut us down. I'll type you out a list, Joe. What are you going to do with it?'

'Crossmatch it to the stuff I uploaded and the phones we have confiscated. With a bit of luck, we might join some dots.'

'We still have the camera set up outside their Alexandria place,' added Sara Jane. 'It saves a week to the cloud. It's another avenue, maybe some more dots.'

The group's confidence started to scrape itself off the floor. What had seemed another blow was starting to look like an act of desperation by the Syndicate, possible providing the link taking them to the next level.

A mobile phone started ringing. They all looked at each other. Once a normal part of life, mobile phones were now shunned by the group. To hear one ringing could indicate a serious security breach.

Ms Bowman answered the phone. It was a prepaid sitting on the kitchen benchtop. She put it on speaker.

'Sorry wrong number,' squawked the phone. Ms Bowman hung up, switched off the phone and removed its battery and SIM card.

'Sergeant Shan will be sending an email shortly. We agreed on a Gmail account. It is attached to this phone. Joe, take this about twenty kilometres away on the bike, reassemble it and download the email. While you are out, can you purchase another laptop and download Fred's message to the laptop. Then disassemble the phone and dispose of the pieces. That sounds convoluted but our survival depends on us being anal about our security.' Ms Bowman noted the glum expression on Jessica's face. 'For God's sake dig up some extra gear and take Jess.'

Within minutes Jessica had found an old helmet in the back of the garage. They would be able to purchase her some decent bike gear and the laptop in town.

It felt almost normal. Riding through the countryside, wineries spread across the rolling hills on both sides of the road. A beautiful woman on the back of the bike, the ever-reliable Suzuki V-Strom purring away underneath them. He would make it a bit of an outing.

The bike shop offered free coffee on Sunday afternoons to tempt the weekend warriors. Joe knew how it worked. Last time he had been there was a few years ago. He had entered planning on sipping a free coffee, and before he had finished had traded his existing ride for the nearly new Triumph Explorer parked next to the coffee machine. He just hoped the same salesman wasn't on duty.

Jessica felt light-headed. They were behaving like normal people. It was so unexpected, she squeezed Joe gently, relaxing and enjoying the ride. Fifteen minutes later they were seated at the bike shop, mugs of coffee in their hands. Joe had steered them into the riding gear section to avoid running into the salesman who had sold him his last bike. Jessica was going to take her time and enjoy doing a bit of shopping.

Completing the rest of Ms Bowman's instructions didn't take long. Returning to their current home, Joe, took a detour, and stopped outside one of the large supermarkets on the edge of town. He quickly purchased some steak and vegetables for the evening meal. Some bottles of wine also found their way into the V-Strom's panniers, again. They took the long way home.

Once back at the current safe house, Joe opened the new laptop and clicked on the file Fred had sent them. It consisted of an audio file and some pictures.

Fred's voice could be heard coming through the speakers, 'These two clowns came a-knocking this morning. They claimed to be cops and flashed some badges, but they smelt like pure thug to me. They were asking about the Major and the General. Apparently, they were linking me, through my military service, to the Major. I don't think it had anything to do with my current activities. I didn't know the General was mixed up in this. I was going to tell them to be scared if they were in the General's sights but thought, fuck it, let them find out for themselves. I have attached some photos of them from our home security system and their vehicle from the driveway camera. I have also sent through a copy of a police business card with a mobile number.'

'Hey who is the General?' Joe asked the room.

'My husband,' replied Ms Bowman.

'Well, it appears the bad guys are interested him. We better warn him to be careful.'

'Better warn the bad guys to leave the country. He can look after himself.'

Sara Jane was looking at the picture of the two thugs and the car Joe had left on his screen. 'Look at this.' She unplugged the laptop and took it over to the alcove where the PC and its two screens were sitting. 'This is the feed from the camera across the road from the Alexandria warehouse. Here are those goons leaving this morning. You can see them walking over to the black van through the open warehouse door. Money on, these are the bastards that grabbed us,' she said looking at Tracey.

'Any ideas how we can use this? I mean, if we just pass the information on nothing's going to happen. They are obviously protected by someone who was in that meeting,' Tracey replied.

Joe thought for a few minutes, blocking out the discussion going around the room. It was a trick he had learnt in corporate boardrooms. 'Let's have the Foreman set a trap. Good chance they are still in the car on their way back to Sydney.'

'Or,' interrupted Ms Bowman, 'we test our leak theory. I will send a message to the heads of the committee exposing these two bozos as being turned. I'll say we pulled them into custody, and they have talked under some quality narcotics I just happened to have in my possession. Then after we had milked them dry, we let them go. It will be interesting to see what happens.'

'I say go for it. Better than my idea,' said Joe.

'I agree,' added Jessica.

'Same for us,' added Tracey looking at Sara Jane.

Ms Bowman opened a program on the desktop computer. It would allow her to send a text message through different servers randomly selected from around the globe, making tracing the source, and therefore their location, impossible.

She hit send. 'OK, only the heads and the Legal have received the text.'

'Well, that was a good day's work. I have some steaks for dinner.' Joe wandered into the kitchen and began assembling the makings of dinner. 'First, marinate the chef.' He opened a bottle of red, set it on the benchtop, found some glasses. 'Who wants some?'

'Rough red. I'll have some,' replied Sara Jane from the computer.

Summer twilight was falling. They had eaten and enjoyed two glasses of wine each. Ms Bowman insisted they stop there. She did not want anyone falling asleep on watch-duty. It was Sara Jane's watch. She had walked the grounds looking for any signs of trespassers in the last of the light. She was now seated in front of the computer; one screen showed their surveillance cameras, the other the feed from the hidden camera outside the Alexandria warehouse.

As she watched the warehouse's roller door began to rise. Even on a Sunday evening light escaped from under the door. Sara Jane idly wondered how much the staff in the front of the building knew. Were they an unknowing part of the ruse or part of the Syndicate, providing back-up and cover? As the door wound up, a large American pick-up truck, its front pointing towards the street, was exposed. It appeared to be empty. The black van could be seen driving towards the door from the right side of the picture. They must have made some other calls on their return from Fred's place as the trip had taken a couple of hours longer than it should have.

The black van entered the warehouse. The driver parked it in the centre of the empty space, front in, leaving space for the pick-up truck to leave without being impeded. Sara Jane could not hear what was being said, but she could see the two men who exited the vehicle were in no hurry. She felt her chest tighten. 'Fuckwits. Hope you get what's owed to you,' she mumbled. There was no doubt in her mind they were the thugs who had abducted her.

There were two bright bursts of light from the load bed of the American pick-up truck. The two men were on the floor, and even from across the road it was obvious they would never be getting up again.

'Fuck, fuck, the fuckwits are dead,' exclaimed a shocked Sara Jane.

A man could be seen stepping down from the pick-up truck's load bed and climbing in the driver's door. The headlights flared and the truck left the bay. The door rolled closed.

CHAPTER 34

Joe switched the TV channel to a late-night news program. It was about 10 pm.

'Two men were shot dead in Alexandria this afternoon. Police believe it was the latest in a series of shootings relating to the gang wars in Sydney's western suburbs.'

'That settles that. No one gives a fuck about drug dealers shooting each other,' commented Sara Jane. 'Easy peasy; conveniently pigeon holed; problem solved.'

'So, what does that mean?' asked Joe.

'My guess is they were foot soldiers for the Syndicate. The message we sent was leaked, it exposed them, and they were neutralised.'

'Yeah, but, Ms Bowman, it was a bit extreme.' Joe still felt out of his depth.

'Two reasons: first the Syndicate did not trust them anymore, and secondly, to send a message to the rest of the troops. "Any lapse of loyalty will be punished". A more important question as far as I am concerned is: who was the executioner? A contractor or the next rung up the ladder in the Syndicate's hierarchy?'

Joe stood, went to the kitchen and opened the laptop on the bench. While out sending the phone message he had downloaded the Foreman's files to the laptop. He was now able to view the files while maintaining their digital blackout.

'In the Foreman's files there is a man he calls the Boss. He was gathering information on this Boss as part of his insurance policy. In the files, there was a vid, which believe me you do not want to see, where the guy was wearing a balaclava, and some gossip column stories he had downloaded. It looks like he was comparing the two sources to expose the Boss's identity.' Joe opened the files and browsed through them a number of times. 'He seemed to be zeroing in on this bloke, Quentin Brightly.'

'QC assisting the Attorney-General regarding oversight of our Task Force,' stated Ms Bowman.

'Now there's a fucking coincidence,' snarled Sara Jane. Pushing Joe away from the laptop she opened the video the Foremen had made in the Alexandria facility. The colour drained from her face. She spoke quietly, 'We need to destroy this fucking monster.'

'We need to determine his position in the Syndicate first. Then we need a plan to take him out, causing the maximum damage to their operation,' cautioned Ms Bowman. 'We need to focus on the big picture, destroying the Syndicate's operations in Australia. If we become obsessed with this monster, we may destroy him and lose our pathway to the next tier.'

Jessica was still watching the late news broadcast on the TV; she turned up the volume. 'The Australian Embassy reports that no sign or communication has been received from Sara Jane Marlowe since she lost contact trekking with her partner in the Himalayas ten days ago. Rescue services have declared large areas no-go areas since heavy rainfall made many passes and valleys subject to avalanches and flash floods. Local authorities hold little hope of finding the pair alive.'

'Bizarre, officially killed off in the Himalayas to cover up being unofficially killed on a chicken farm just out of Wyong. Well, I suppose it's good in a way. I'm off their books. Makes Tracey, me and the fireman all dead!' You two are the only ones still in the land of the living.' Sara Jane pointed at Ms Bowman and Jessica. 'It's time we started haunting these pricks.'

'I'm going to recover,' interjected Joe.

'Mum and Dad must be beside themselves. We need to contact them,' said Jessica.

Ms Bowman spent a few moments thinking how best to respond, 'It would be best coming from you, Jessica. They would believe the message. Anyone else and they might start asking questions which wouldn't be safe for them or us. Joe, take Jessica and SJ out in the Subaru, twenty kilometres in a different direction from this afternoon. Jess, call your parents on the prepaid phone. We are going to have to assume their phone is tapped. SJ, you can't be heard on the phone in case the bad guys recognise your voice. They have probably listened to your blog multiple times. Try to use some code they will understand.'

Joe was glad he had sipped only a couple of glasses of wine with dinner. The three of them walked over to the car. Climbing in, Joe was wondering how he would explain driving a dead man's car should he be pulled over by the police. Luckily the car had not been reported stolen or missing so the chance of being stopped by the police was low.

Jessica was wondering how to convey Sara Jane's survival to her parents without tipping off any listeners. 'Is Mum's cat, Twinkles, still alive?' she turned and asked Sara Jane in the back seat.

'Last I knew it was still alive,' replied Sara Jane. 'What's your plan?'

'Along the lines of SJ is now gone and with Twinkles? I better speak with Mum. Dad will be inconsolable and probably won't understand the message.'

'OK,' said Joe, 'here should do. Actually, I will keep the car moving in this direction, hopefully the call will move between a couple of towers, and as soon as we are finished, I'll turn around and reverse direction.'

Jessica fitted the battery to the phone and hit the on button. She dialled her mother's number from memory. Her mother answered.

'Hi, Mum,' Jessica sniffed, 'I just heard the news. SJ's gone to join Twinkles in heaven. Our sweet little angel is gone.'

The threesome in the car held their breath. Her mother sounded like she was sobbing. 'She was such a sweet, sweet child, never in any trouble like you were,' her mother spoke while sobbing and sniffing. 'At least she has her beloved Twinkles with her in heaven to keep her company.' Jessica broke the connection. She could hear Sara Jane snorting from the back seat attempting to hold back laughter.

'Fuck she's smart. Got it in one. At least I can now paraphrase Mark Twain *Reports of my death are greatly exaggerated ,*' Sara Jane gasped, attempting to hold back laughter. 'We all know how fucking much that cat and I hate each other. At least the "sweet child" and "you being a trouble-maker" bits were true.'

'My fucking arse,' countered Jessica. Joe agreed. Even though he had only known the sisters a short time he could not imagine Sara Jane being described as a sweet, sweet child, no matter how blinded a mother was by maternal love.

'Turn off the phone and pull out the battery so I can turn around and head back to the house,' Joe instructed Jessica. Ms Bowman's digital tracking paranoia was contagious.

The twenty-minute return journey was a happy one. The conversation with their mother had brightened the sisters' moods. Joe, however, was left wondering how he was going to re-enter the land of the living.

Joe let the sisters out of the car by the front door and drove the Subaru into the shed. By the time he entered the lounge room, Sara Jane was surfing the internet using TOR. 'Fuck me, they are not wasting any time. Now I'm dead the bastards are trying to destroy my credibility.'

'What's that?' asked Joe. He hadn't been paying attention as he was contemplating going to bed. Joe turned around and joined the others gathered around the computer desk.

'Sara Jane Marlowe, self-proclaimed investigative journalist or narcissistic fraud? it says here. Sara Jane Marlowe, unable to hold a steady job with a mainstream publication, created her own blog to expose alleged organised crime. However, most of her articles have been disproven with a senior police spokesman quoted as saying "these sort of unsubstantiated allegations, published by pseudo-journalists do not help us combat crime. Valuable resources have to be deployed to verify these claims, and when, as usual, they turn out to be smoke and mirrors, real leads to real crimes have gone cold. Friends who wish to remain anonymous have told of a party girl whose increasingly erratic behaviour was possibly due to an undisclosed drug problem. Her need for self-aggrandisation triggered increasingly unsubstantiated, sensational stories designed to draw in sponsorship funds.'"

Everyone was silent. They were waiting for the explosion. Sara Jane started to chuckle, 'They've vindicated me. This is such a heavy-handed attempt to discredit me, it's just going to fall flat on its face. When this is finished, I'm going to fucking frame it so every morning when I wake up the second thing I see will be this.' The way Sara Jane looked at Tracey, they all knew what the first thing would be.

Joe checked the accounts. The drain on the Syndicate's bitcoin account he had redirected from the Foreman was working. They could afford a permanent base.

To remain anonymous, he would need to create an Australian shelf company. A subsidiary of a foreign-registered company to ensure his name did not appear on any searches. For now, he would keep his plan to himself. He was not sure exactly for whom he was working. Ms Bowman was leading them, but was he an employee, a conscript or a consultant? Indeed, who was he, his new alias, Matthew Johnson? His gut instinct told him to keep his real identity as far away from this mess as he possible. Once he had finished his look-out duty for the morning he would start.

The run of sunny days had ended. A monsoonal low had been pushed down from Australia's tropical north, drenching the Hunter Valley as the cold air from the south forced the clouds to drop their moisture. Joe decided he would walk the perimeter at the beginning of his shift. The time alone would help him contemplate his requirements. He also had to decide when to brief Jessica. He wanted to bring her in at the planning stage, but he was sure any plans he made needed to be removed from official channels. They knew the committee to which Ms Bowman reported was compromised by the lawyer assisting, but was that the only leak? How far had the Syndicate penetrated the Australian Government and institutions? To survive and have a future, Joe had to stay invisible.

He contemplated the rain. They had only one old umbrella between them. No one had had time to pack clothes and personal items, so they were having to purchase clothes as they needed them. As it was the first rainy day they had encountered since being on the run, they found themselves woefully unprepared. *Maybe the property's shed was unlocked and he could find something in there*, Joe thought, looking across the driveway. Leaving the umbrella behind as it was more of a hinderance than a help, Joe sprinted across the driveway and twisted the handle of the shed's side door. It opened. Joe entered the dark building, found a light switch and turned on the power. It was a normal farm shed slightly larger than a double garage and stacked full of tools and supplies warehoused against a rainy day.

It didn't take long for Joe to find what he needed. A Driza-Bone raincoat, a hat and a pair of gumboots. Joe changed his shoes, donned the raincoat and hat, and let himself back out the side door. This property was on a corner block, a typical hobby farm with room for a few horses and, as it was the Hunter Valley, a field of grapevines. There were two exits: the main driveway and a second gate onto the second street. Even an accountant like Joe could see it would be easy to trap the team as both exits were visible from the junction of the two roads. Their safety depended on their vigilance and, he hated to admit it, a fair bit of luck. Joe decided to walk the perimeter of the property on the roads forming the corner of the block. He was looking for any disturbance indicating they were under observation. After twenty minutes he had found nothing. He felt a little happier, but he was still wary. Their survival depended on taking the initiative and would not happen while they were running and hiding.

In his mind he began listing the attributes of the property he believed would make a secure base. He would like a degree of isolation, but in proximity to a major town for supplies and quick access to major transport routes. He realised his thinking was mirroring the Syndicate's. The facility they had closed down filled most of the criteria. Joe decided he would begin his search in the same general area.

Joe considered his options. A trip into town and the local library would do the trick. The library would have public access to computers. This would add another layer of anonymity. Even if the transactions were traced to a particular computer, the search for the user of the computer would stop at the library. Most members of the team needed a trip into town to update their wardrobes for wet weather. The problem with being in hiding: it was the basic things, usually taken for granted, that tripped you up.

As far as he could tell, there had been no intrusion into the property. He would return to the house and spend the rest of his two-hour shift watching the computer screens. Then, as Tracey had the next shift, he would have a chat to Jessica. He would plan the trip into town for tomorrow.

At the end of his shift he showed Tracey the gear he had borrowed from the shed. Tracey climbed into the wet weather gear. One look and it was obvious neither Tracey nor Sara Jane would be able to wear the wet weather gear he had found. It was just too big. Joe was happy about this; he now had a reason to go to town.

Although he trusted Ms Bowman, he had decided he would keep this part of the operation from her. It was well through the grey zone and close to black, completely outside the law, and he was not sure where she drew the line. He knew her first loyalty was to her country and therefore its institutions. He also acknowledged that it was a contradiction, trusting Jessica with the information, but he knew in his heart for their relationship to have a chance, he was going to have to trust her.

'Hey, guys, I was planning a trip into town tomorrow. This weather might hang about for a few days, so I was hoping to find some wet weather gear.'

'Who are you calling a fucking guy?' responded Sara Jane.

Oh ho, thought Joe. He tried again, 'Hey, people, I was planning a trip into town tomorrow. This weather might hang about for a few days, so I was hoping to find some wet weather gear, and we are woefully unprepared,' he quickly amended.

'Who are you calling a fucking people?' responded Sara Jane laughing.

Joe realised she was toying with him. Bandying words with Sara Jane was always a losing proposition. She was just too damn smart, bloody minded and bored of being a captive of their circumstances.

'Everyone, stop yelling,' yelled Ms Bowman. Joe kept his mouth shut; not everyone appreciated irony.

'Seems like a good idea, Joe. Before you go, let's check the police internal broadcasts for any mention of any of you or the car,' Ms Bowman continued.

Sara Jane opened up TOR. Jessica navigated to the NSW Police internal website and searched for any alerts or notifications on any of them. 'We appear clear,' she said.

'OK, I will stay here. After the attack on the freeway, I think I need to keep a low profile,' stated Ms Bowman.

'Done, we'll leave about 9.30 am. The town of Cessnock is only twenty minutes down the road,' added Joe. 'I might grab a nap. I never got back to sleep properly after my shift last night.'

Joe wandered off to the room he was using. He had his notebook and a pen on the bedside table. Lying on the bed he started to develop a wishlist for their new hideout. He did not want to search online as he did not want to leave a trail. The precautions they were taking could be excessive, but he was not about to underestimate the opposition. *"It's not paranoia when someone's trying to kill you" must be their new mantra*, thought Joe.

Jessica wandered into the room. 'There's nothing more on the shooting in Alexandria,' she said. 'I searched the case files and the shooter appears to be a ghost. The official story is still the gang feud. Though they have linked the guys who tried to push you off the cliff to the same narrative.'

'Whose side do you reckon the shooter's on? Is he after the Syndicate on some kind of vigilante mission or is he part of the Syndicate closing down loose ends?'

'Oh, he is Syndicate for sure. If he was a vigilante, they would have him pinned down by now. Someone with some heavy-duty juice is mis-directing the investigation. What I don't know, and don't like, is this: why is the investigation being linked to the guys in the ute? It is not a big jump from there to dragging you into the frame, Joe, as their intended target. I can't see how the Syndicate could know about you, but it's a strange coincidence. The only link I can see would be the payment the Foreman made through his bitcoin account. Or maybe it is just a redirection? But it's a coincidence none the less and therefore a threat.'

'Can they track you through the cop intranet?' asked Joe.

'They would know I logged in, but I just read the alerts. As I am supposed to do every day. I didn't conduct any searches or dig down at all,' answered Jessica. 'Do you think they may be on to me? Using me as some sort of Judas goat to expose our little gang?'

'Don't know. But they must know you are tied to Ms Bowman, and there's your blood all over the seat of the LandCruiser. I have no idea how they would use the information. Have the police arrest you, or pass it on to the Syndicate? For myself, I am thinking it's time I became Matthew Johnson.'

'Well, I'm getting used to the beard.'

'Glad you are. Fucking thing irritates the shit out of me!'

'So, what next?' asked Jessica.

'I was thinking about that this morning. One of the reasons I want to go into town tomorrow is to find us a permanent base. I can use the computers at the library to search for likely places. The daily drain I installed on the Foreman's bitcoin account has proven very profitable. Now I am going to build some corporate veils to hide behind. I can then use them to purchase a place. Something like this but closer to the motorway and Wyong. Keep this between you and me. I trust Ms Bowman, but the bad guys are onto her. I don't want her to become a pointer, indicating our plans.'

The rest of the day passed slowly. They each took their turn as lookout. Mostly scanning the property through the cameras. Joe's turn came around again in the early evening. He donned the raincoat, hat and boots; he was the only one they really fitted. Being the only male in an all-female household, he did occasionally feel the need for a bit of solitude. He again walked the perimeter, digesting the information Jessica had given him. He trusted the cameras, but they were static and there would be blind spots. He spent the first hour of his watch on foot, and when satisfied there had been no intrusions he returned to the house. He would use the cameras to complete his shift. He could see the computer screens from the kitchen as he prepared dinner.

Once his shift was completed, he opened a bottle of wine and felt his beard. The song *Cheap Wine And A Three-Day Growth* came to mind. He smiled to himself and grabbed the remote for the TV. Using the Apple TV he navigated to YouTube and searched for an Australian rock channel. Red wine, a spag bol on the hob and classic rock. He felt nearly normal. Suddenly he felt lonely. He knew what was missing. He missed his dog.

CHAPTER 36

It was still drizzling the next morning when Joe had completed his shift. Once again he had donned the raingear and walked the boundary. Still no intrusions or suspicious activity as far as his untrained eye could detect. By the time he returned everyone was up and about, even though they had all lost two hours of sleep during the night on lookout duty. He could actually feel the excitement in the air. Jessica winked at him. They had started out in the same bed the night before, until Jessica's shift, then separated so as not disturb each other changing shifts.

He looked them over. They had all subtly changed their appearance, and with the rain, Joe was confident they would go undetected. 'Right, let's load up. Tracey, grab the shopping list. We will buy some groceries while we are out.'

'OK, children, behave and have fun,' said Ms Bowman, surprising Joe with a joke. He kept forgetting under the impeccable middle-class, middle-aged matron, there was a lifetime Army officer covering the human underneath. Joe laughed; the mood was infectious.

Luckily the garage was attached to the house. Being a country estate, the garage was big enough for four vehicles. The Subaru and the V-Strom were parked up one end; the balance of the space contained the gym.

Joe was glad they would be giving that a miss this morning. While he felt fitter than he had in a long time, training with Sara Jane was definitely a contact sport. Training with Jessica was not much better, except for sharing a shower afterward. Jessica worked on fitness more than fighting. Training with Tracey was just scary. She never seemed to try very hard or raise a sweat, but no one could keep up with her. 'I love a lover with stamina,' Sara Jane would gush. Tracey would then blush in embarrassment and throw Joe onto the floor, as a distraction, no matter how prepared he was.

They piled into the Subaru, zapped open the garage door with the remote and headed out into the rain.

'Are we there yet, Dad?' yelled Sara Jane from the back seat before they had reached the end of the driveway.

Joe turned to Jessica, 'I can see why she has been killed off twice already.'

The rain had kept most sensible people at home. Finding a park in the centre of town was no problem. 'Meet at the pub for lunch about twelve-thirty?' suggested Joe.

'Sounds like a plan,' replied Tracey.

Sara Jane and Tracey quickly blended in with the crowd. Joe took Jessica's hand, 'Let's find a coffee shop first. I could do with a brew.'

'Do you know where the library is?'

'Yeah, it's on the edge of the shopping centre, over there,' pointed Joe. 'My plan is to spend as little time as possible shopping and then hit the library's computers. I plan to have a shortlist by eleven, we can go over it together.'

A quick run through the local discount department store and Joe had supplemented his wardrobe to his satisfaction. He left Jessica to complete her shopping and to grab the groceries. Once seated in the library he had no problem getting online. Searching the various real estate sites Joe quickly found several properties he thought matched his requirements. He saved them so he could show Jessica for a second opinion.

One property stood head and shoulders above the others. It was on a decent acreage, had two road frontages on two through-roads, a modern seven-bedroom house and some large sheds. Better still it was operating as an Airbnb, and was being sold as a walk-in, walk-out corporate retreat or convention business. It was only ten minutes from the centre of Wyong and equally close to Morisset.

While he was convinced it was the one, he wanted Jessica to come to the same conclusion independently. He saved a list of seven properties for her to look at. His favourite in the middle.

Jessica wandered into the library, pulled up a chair and sat next to Joe. 'Here's my shortlist. What do you think? I'm going to wander over to the shopping centre and use the loo. You chose which one you think is best.'

Joe was back after a lazy ten minutes. Once he was seated, Jessica pointed to the property Joe had selected. 'This one,' she said, 'it's perfect for us.'

'Agreed,' said Joe. 'I'll call the agent. We better do this outside.'

Joe used the prepaid phone to make the call. 'Wyong Valley Real Estate, Bob speaking.'

'Hi Bob, my name is Matthew Johnson, I represent the Elite Corporate Retreat Group and we are interested in moving into the Australian market. I am looking at your property in Dickson Road, Darrun Darrun.'

'Yes, I know that one well, we have had a lot of interest,' replied Bob.

'We'll take it at the listed price. We will also take all the outstanding Airbnb bookings until we can settle, paying the current owner at the going rate.' There was silence from Bob the real estate guy.

'Arggh err don't you want to view it?' asked Bob.

'I'll also need a local solicitor to organise our side of the purchase. Is there someone you recommend?'

'Yes, there's a local firm we recommend.'

'Good. Text the details to this number; also your bank details. I'll organise a ten per cent deposit today.'

'I'll need to check with the owners, but that should all be doable.'

'OK I'll be round to sign the contract about two this afternoon.' Joe hung up.

'Poor Bob, you ruined all his fun, he was about to hit you with the big sales spiel. I could hear him deflating from here,' Jessica laughed.

'Let's head to the pub for lunch. We should be just in time to meet the others.'

For an hour they forgot about everything except enjoying a meal. The three women enjoyed sharing a local chardonnay, while Joe limited himself to one small glass. He still had a bit of driving to do.

He figured it was about an hour to Wyong, so had them up and moving at ten minutes to one. They had yet to tell the girls, as he thought of Tracey and Sara Jane, about their plans.

Joe explained in the car.

'So, you're using their money to pay for it?' asked Sara Jane.

'Yes, lock, stock and barrel. Hopefully we will be able to move from our present digs straight to the new place,' answered Joe.

'Won't we be more vulnerable,' asked Tracey.

'Yes and no,' replied Jessica. 'We will be in one place. But we won't be making as many transactions. We will also be able to plan and implement better electronic security to fortify the place.'

'Well I'm for it on two counts. First I'm sick of running. We dig in we can fight back, and second I love using their fucking money against the pricks!' Sara Jane exclaimed.

'Have we an unused prepaid phone in the car?' asked Joe.

'Yes, I have this one. It has never been used,' replied Tracey.

'OK, I will use it for the transactions, then we'll destroy it. I want to keep as anonymous as possible.'

'Whose name will you use?'

'I'll use "Elite Corporate Retreat", Matthew Johnson as the representative. I'll need a driver's licence as ID for the contract exchange. We can't use one of ours. Jessica, can you set up a Gmail account for Matthew? Make it a bit obscure. We'll use it to communicate with the agent and the solicitor.'

Ten minutes later Jessica replied 'Done'.

'Great stuff, here we go,' said Joe as he reversed into a parking spot, careful to leave the car positioned for a quick exit.

'You three, go grab a coffee in that small shopping complex across the road, use this phone to contact me in an emergency, otherwise I'll come find you. Shouldn't take too long.'

Joe was right. Bob the agent, hadn't been sure if it was a hoax or not, but could not risk losing the deal. When Joe walked in, he had the contract ready to go and a local solicitor on hand to act for Joe. In under an hour he had arranged the exchange of contracts and a shortened settlement period. Luckily the owner of the property had cancelled all Airbnb bookings so Joe was also able to rent it until full settlement could be made.

Bob looked on as Joe made the deposit into the agency trust account using the prepaid phone as a modem for his laptop. On completion he purged the IP address from the laptop's system. The next time he connected with a different phone it would generate a different IP address. Once again the digital trail would be dead ended. They had a new place to stay, and the luxury of a week to do some preparatory work on their security and defence systems before they needed to leave their existing base.

He left the estate agent's office after much hand-shaking and congratulations and found the three women enjoying a coffee. 'Come on, let's get out of here. I don't want the agent or solicitor seeing the car.'

CHAPTER 37

The drive back was uneventful. Joe had told them he would explain everything once they had returned to their current accommodation. Ten minutes into the trip he peered in the rear-view mirror. A couple of drinks, and weeks of disturbed sleep, had taken their toll; Sara Jane and Tracey were asleep. He looked over at Jessica, 'Hey, stay awake. You can keep me awake.'

Sara Jane began to snore.

'Not many people can sleep through that,' giggled Jessica. Joe couldn't help but laugh out loud.

The rain had settled in, no longer a downpour, just a steady drizzle. Jessica and Joe spent the drive talking about their childhoods, just getting to know one another better.

Proceeding down the driveway, Joe was surprised to see the rental Camry parked in front of the house. Parking the Subaru in the garage and waking his passengers, Joe wondered again about Fred and his connection to Ms Bowman. He opened the hatch and started unloading the groceries and clothing purchased in town.

Entering the kitchen, he spied Fred lying on the floor in front of one of the floor-to-ceiling windows in the open-plan lounge room. He had a pair of binoculars glued to his face. Fred was chuckling to himself. Ms Bowman was in the kitchen, an inscrutable expression on her face. Two strangers walked into the room, they looked like they had just finished showering. One male, one female, both in their early twenties. The young man was dark haired and brown eyed, a stubbly beard and a ponytail; the young woman looked like an elite soldier, blond hair, blue eyes and an upright posture.

Jessica, Sara Jane and Tracey stopped with Joe and looked around at the newcomers and Ms Bowman. 'Meet the twins,' she said, 'my kids. Their father decided to bring them up for a visit.'

'OK,' said Joe, not sure where to go from there.

Fred rolled over onto his back. 'Reckon we can call the General in yet? He must be pretty damp by now.' He was obviously enjoying himself.

'What's going on?' asked Jessica.

'I noticed you were under surveillance. So I borrowed the bike and rounded up the off-duty crew,' said Fred gesturing towards the twins who seemed to be studying the kitchen benchtop.

'I had them drive in the back entrance and park behind the house. The General doesn't know they are here.'

Fred dug out his phone. He sounded the message out as he typed. 'Time to come in out of the rain, old man, there's a neat scotch sitting on the counter with your name on it.' Fred gestured out the window. The others gathered round.

A mound of vegetation in the middle of the field across from the house stood tall and started to walk towards them. 'Better find some scotch,' he said to the twins. 'I'm thinking he will need two glasses before he sees the funny side of this.'

Luckily Ms Bowman had some scotch; it was not something Joe had thought about. The mound of vegetation jumped the fence and made its way towards the garage doors. Joe looked at Ms Bowman, 'It's OK, you can open the door,' she said to Joe. He hit the remote and the garage door opened. The twins walked into the garage to assist the new arrival.

A middle-aged man entered. His grey hair buzz-cut, military style, his piecing grey eyes seeing everything at once, his military bearing making him seem taller than his average height. Joe didn't know him, and wasn't in the military, but felt he needed to salute the newcomer.

'Sergeant, I should have fucking known,' he grunted, a smile creasing his face as he strode across the room and hugged Fred. 'Sharpest eyes and mind I ever met. How did you pick us?'

'Wrong colour grass, your ghillie suit's too green. The drought has only just broken. Plus, I spiralled in and saw the camper a couple of properties over. Watched you doing a shift change. Then, when you marched back over the hill, I drove down and said "G'day" to the twins and brought them back here.'

'You bastard, how long did you leave me on the damn hill in the rain?'

'Only about three hours,' snickered Fred.

The General sauntered over and hugged Ms Bowman. 'Good to see you, Fi.'

'How did you find us?' she asked.

'Well, I heard about that meeting; the Army chief reports to me. Then, we heard about the shooting on the expressway and decided we were needed in the field. We picked you up at the warehouse you were using in Morisset and have been watching for the last three weeks.'

The General saw Joe's embarrassment. 'Don't worry about it, son. We are the best team there is.'

'Except for Uncle Fred,' added the male twin.

'Yes, and it's damn hard to beat the best.'

'Was a while since I was playing soldiers, General. I reckon you've just gone soft on the younger generation,' teased Fred.

'Kids, I think Fred would like to have a chat with you outside,' replied the General.

The twins moved towards Fred who returned the banter. 'Sorry, have to say "No" this time, can't damage my doctor's hands on your chins.' The twins moved menacing towards Fred and put their arms around him. 'You were the only one who could put shit on the old man,' said the girl laughing.

'Well, I did get a leg of lamb while we were at the shops. Heaps of veges too. I reckon I can make it stretch for all of us,' said Joe. He really hoped they would all stay for dinner. The company would do them all good.

'You're on,' replied the General. 'Fi, why don't you give me a full debrief in private?' Ms Bowman's eyes lit up as a smile spread across her face. 'Thought you would never ask. This way, soldier.'

She led him away towards her room.

'Hope it's going to be a stealth mission,' snickered Sara Jane.

'Reckon she's got him standing at attention yet?' replied Tracey.

It took Joe a minute to understand. He looked towards the twins; they were both blushing.

'Ahh, parents bonking, how embarrassing.' Joe looked at the twins. 'So, what do we call you? Did they give you names?'

Fred stepped in, 'This is Jodie and Keith Anderson. Fi is Fiona Anderson but works under her maiden name, Ms Bowman or Major Bowman, depending on the assignment. I think the General had to give her a first name when they married.'

Joe stepped into the kitchen. The lounge and kitchen area of the house was open-plan, so they were all able to join in the conversation as Joe and Jessica began to prepare the dinner.

'I've just started with an advertising agency in town,' explained Keith. 'I did a stretch in the Army after school and they put me through a media communications course. I did my time but the lure of the outside world became too strong. It's taken some adjusting but I'm getting there.'

Fred found some white wine and some cold beers. Once everyone had a drink Jodie spoke, 'I stayed in the army, Fred was my inspiration. I have nearly completed my medical degree with a specialisation in trauma medicine.'

'Dad called us together the weekend before last. He explained Mum's predicament and his conclusion that the committee was compromised. We decided to all take leave and become her unofficial back-up. We had seen Fred visit a couple of times at the last place. But we thought no one would detect us. Next thing you know Fred's knocking on the door of the camper and offering us a hot shower. Leaving Dad out in the rain was his idea.'

Once the meat and vegetables were in the oven, they all returned to the lounge room. Tracey took up station at the computer, watching the video feed from the cameras while sipping her wine. By mutual agreement the conversation stayed light, no one wanted to break the mood and speak about their current strife.

Joe decided he needed to bring Ms Bowman up to date. He had learnt from experience when to trust people and when to keep his own council. If they were going to work as a team, they all needed to be included.

Ms Bowman and the General returned to the lounged room, showered and relaxed. 'We have our next base,' said Joe. 'This one's a keeper.' Joe had taken some glossy flyers from the real estate agent's office. He did not want to view the property online.

'Is it traceable to you or us?' asked Ms Bowman.

'It's as safe as I could make it,' replied Joe. Ms Bowman nodded. They both knew there was no cast-iron guarantee. Nothing could make them one hundred per cent safe while the Syndicate existed.

CHAPTER 38

It was great to have company. It was not only a great dinner party, but the first uninterrupted night's sleep in what seemed eons, the General and the twins taking over the night-watch duties. Refreshed, Joe wandered into the kitchen as the sun crested the mountains to the east. The General was examining Joe's musings on the whiteboard.

'How deep do you reckon these guys are embedded into Australia?' the General asked.

'Not sure. We have only identified the parts we have butted heads with. If the facility we closed down was the only one, they still would need logistical support, and they would have needed people in authority to keep them covered. We now suspect the QC assisting the Attorney-General and we know about the bloke who took out the help at the Alexandria warehouse. But who else?'

'Do you have a plan?'

'Well, I thought I would backtrack from the facilities we know they operate. The "Chicken Farm" and the charity base. The investigative work I will leave to the others. I think finding the "Fixer" needs to be their priority because we have probably become his priority,' said Joe.

'I would have to agree with that assessment. Basically, a two-pronged attack. By the way, when I'm off-duty please call me John. I have to play by the rules when I'm the General. I think the only way we are going to draw out the Fixer, as you call him, is to expose someone as bait. And to do that we need to let them know we are a threat. But we need all the intel we can get our hands on first.'

'I'll get on it as soon as my brain's kick-started,' responded Joe. He poured coffee for Jessica and himself and returned to the room they were sharing.

An hour later, another coffee in his hand, freshly showered and having enjoyed a cooked breakfast, Joe was again pondering the whiteboard. An idea struck him. 'Hey, Jess, can you use your police log-in to do a title search? Let's see if they own any other properties.'

'Yeah, we can access that information through the Land Titles Office. Usually I just ring them, provide my badge number and they're happy to do a search. We can do it as members of the public as well. Just go to their website and enter the street address. It will give you the title deed details, then you can do a title search.'

'Great, so we can do it without exposing you?' Joe asked.

'Yes. We will need to provide an email address. But we can use a Gmail or Yahoo one, so we can stay invisible. Then we can delete the account when we finish.'

'I think we can risk using the internet for this. I'll use the wi-fi on this prepaid phone as the internet connection, and we will run through the TOR browser. Our time here runs out in two days, but I don't want the ruse I used to rent this place to be exposed. It leads to my client. So, we still need to be careful.'

It took Joe about ten minutes. 'Well, would you look at this! They own another property in the same area. Let's see if we can find it on Google Maps.' A few clicks later Joe was staring at the screen. 'Fuck me, the second place is on the other side of the spur we used to attack the first place, and looking at this, it is also a chicken farm.

'I bet it's a legitimate chicken farm! It would provide cover for the facility. It would be the legitimate business, sharing its sales and costs across both properties, so the facility would appear genuine. Being so close I bet the plan was to evacuate one to the other in case of a search, but the Foreman bailing out stopped that from happening.

'Well, let's see if we can expand the net. Any connections we make to the second property could have a link to the facility. Hah, look at this, they even have a webpage with contact details and everything.'

Joe picked up one of the prepaid phones and rang the number. The call was answered on the fourth ring, 'Hi there, it's Bob Vincent here, from Hunter Water, it appears your November water rates instalment is thirty days plus overdue.'

'You'll need to talk to our bookkeeper, the useless bastard probably forgot again. Here's his phone number.' Joe wrote down the phone number as it was recited.

'Does he have a name?'

'Brian Johnson, Brian Johnson Accounting and Bookkeeping.'

'Thanks for your help.' Joe ended the call.

'I think a personal visit may be the best bet,' said Jessica.

'OK, I agree,' added Ms Bowman. 'Jessica, take Joe and Tracey. Tracey does a very believable bad cop to your good cop Jessica. Joe can feed you the questions.'

Joe remembered Tracey dealing with the Foreman, *still waters run deep and dangerous*, he thought.

'The rest of us, let's see what we can find. We need to expand our picture. John, can you and the kids look after the security? I'll work with Sara Jane to see what else we can dig up. Well done, Joe and Jessica, every piece of the puzzle leads to the next one.'

'Brian Johnson lives and works from his house down on the Central Coast. We can be there in less than an hour,' Joe said to Jess and Tracey.

It was a beautiful day for a drive. The air had been purified by the rain and was so clear a traveller could count the trees on the nearby mountain range. Ten minutes short of their destination, Joe pulled into a roadside café-cum-service station. 'Coffee stop,' he announced. His real reason for stopping was to plan their interrogation of the Bookkeeper. Joe had no idea how this worked, but he did have some thoughts about the questions he would like answered.

Once they were seated, he asked, 'What do we want to find out?'

'Anything we can,' said Jessica. 'We start by asking general questions so we can see how much of the big picture he knows. Then we start to drill down to the details. It's also good practice to jump around. Keeping him off balance increases the chances of him making a slip. I will sit in front of him asking questions in a gentle manner. Tracey will stand and lean in with menace if she feels he is stalling. You keep track of the questions and feed us new ones when a particular line of information opens. So, what general questions do we ask?'

'I suggest we start with the chicken farms. See how much he knows and see if we can guide him into talking about the Syndicate. We go from there. He might know about the whole Australian operation or he might think he is working for a legitimate chicken farming operation. One thing points to him knowing more. The Foreman had copies of the details of those bitcoin accounts. The only source of that information, I can see, is this bloke. Where else could he have got it? If my guess is right, then the Bookkeeper is seriously involved with the Syndicate.'

Returning to the car they made their way into the village. Finding the address was not a problem. There was a plaque by the front gate identifying the business. Joe parked the car down the street. They would walk up to the house. There was a risk he would be out visiting clients or having lunch, but they were prepared to wait if necessary. A surprise visit would be more productive.

'Put these on,' ordered Tracey, producing a box of disposable nitrate gloves. 'We don't want to leave any trace of evidence.'

As they reached the front door, they noticed it was ajar. The house was eerily quiet. Tracey went first, she had drawn her pistol. He looked over at Jessica, she had also drawn her firearm. From where Joe did not know; he hadn't realised either of them was carrying a gun. He felt a bit sheepish being the only one unarmed. He saw an old cricket bat on the verandah. *Better than nothing*, he thought.

While Joe was grabbing the cricket bat the two women entered quietly through the front door. 'Hold it right there,' commanded a voice. 'Hands in the air and drop the weapons.'

There were two thumps as Jessica and Tracey dropped their guns on the floor. Joe wasn't sure whether he had been seen or not. Ducking down to pick up the cricket bat could have kept him out of sight.

'OK, both of you through that door into the office. I need a hand,' continued the voice.

Joe peered cautiously round the door frame of the front door. A man, his back to Joe, was leading the two women through a doorway on the right, a metre or two down the passage. Joe stepped through the doorway lifted the bat over his head and smashed it onto the man's head. The old bat snapped, the stranger's gun went off as it bounced off the floor, blasting a hole in the wall. Tracey swung round, pulled two plastic cable ties from her pocket and tied the gunman's arms and legs together. Joe knelt down and scooped up the two guns, passing them to Tracey and Jessica. He bent down again and picked up the intruder's gun.

Together they proceeded into the room, cautiously checking the corners in case the intruder had a partner. A man was sitting in a chair in the centre of the room. He had been beaten. There was a noose around his neck. Not knowing if the gunshot had attracted any attention, they removed the noose, 'Brian Johnson, I presume?' asked Jessica, showing him her police badge. The man nodded. 'We need to leave now.'

Joe saw a laptop on the desk. He unplugged it and stuffed it under his arm. He quickly scanned the office for any flash drives or similar, saw two in a desk tidy and dropped them in his pocket.

Tracey skipped to the front door over the prone gunman. 'Clear,' she said back into the room. With Tracey leading, her gun hidden behind her back, Jessica and Joe led Johnson to the car. Tracey shoved their prisoner into the rear passenger seat. Jessica blocked the door as Tracey ran around the car and jumped in behind the driver. Jessica took the shotgun seat, Joe scrambled round to the driver's door, handed Jessica the laptop, climbed in and started the engine. He looked around. He did not want to drive straight into an ambush. No one seemed to be paying them any attention.

He was about to drive off, when the intruder burst out of Johnson's house. He had managed to free his feet but his arms were still bound by the cable ties. 'Not hitting hard enough. Amateur mistake,' said Jessica. Joe drove off in the opposite direction and down the first side street. He took the first left and left again, regaining the main road on the opposite side of the Bookkeeper's house. He was about to turn right and head back out of town when a blue F100 American pick-up truck screeched onto the main street several blocks down and headed their way.

'Floor it,' yelled Jessica. Joe complied, ignoring the screeching brakes of a car approaching from their right.

'Same truck as Alexandria?' yelled Joe. 'How come?'

'We are the only ones who know about it,' Jessica replied, 'Remember we have been fucking incognito.'

'Shit,' said Joe. He assessed the situation. Bigger engine, two-wheel drive, has to weigh nearly three tonnes pursuing smaller engine, four-wheel drive and better handling. Four passengers added a bit of weight. Single carriageway B-road twists and bends would be helpful. 'I'm going over the top of the Watagans. We have four-wheel drive; he has two, lots of trails for us to disappear down.'

'He was going to hang me in the back yard,' squealed Johnson. 'He made me write a suicide note and leave it on the table.'

'So, you know about the Syndicate?' asked Jessica, as though it was a normal conversation despite the car bouncing and jigging all over the road.

'Yes, the fucking Foreman hacked my computer, stole the bitcoin details, so they think I am working with him to steal all their money. Problem is if they don't kill me, he will.'

'No need to worry about him no more. I blew his head off,' Tracey casually interrupted.

The Bookkeeper, startled by her casual turn of speech, turned to her and gulped. He looked at Tracey, he looked again, 'Shit, you were one of the stock.'

'And I remember you, I might have been drugged so I couldn't fight back, but I remember EVERY FUCKING DETAIL. You fucking raped me.' Tracey glared into his face.

The F100 was gaining, Joe hoped the dirt road to the Watagans was close. The Subaru seemed to have a slightly higher top speed than the low-geared truck, but the F100 could accelerate quicker out of each corner. It was going to be close.

'Hang on,' he shouted, mashing the brake pedal and turning the wheel to the left, then slamming the accelerator all the way to the floor, reversing the lock as he swerved down the dirt road. The Subaru's 4WD and stability systems fought for control as the car flew down the neatly graded dirt road.

The F100 didn't make the turn. As soon as the front wheels hit the dirt, halfway through the corner, it understeered off the road, both front wheels buckling under the chassis as it bounced over the road verge and into a brace of saplings. Joe put another two corners behind them, narrowly missing an oncoming vehicle before slowing down and looking in the mirror.

The Bookkeeper's head had dropped to his shoulder. Tracey was poking him with a pen.

'I think the fucking dickhead just died of a fucking heart attack.

I was looking forward to killing him slowly. Dump his body off a cliff. He is no fucking use to us and he shat himself.'

CHAPTER 39

They had thrown Johnson's body off a cliff beside an isolated dirt road while driving through the Watagans. There was only one thing Joe was certain about; he was not suited to this "James Bond" lifestyle. Tracey and Jessica were also quiet. The adrenaline hangover was affecting all of them.

Returning to their rented hobby farm, Joe zapped the garage door open and parked the Subaru. He was wondering what he should do with it. He suspected it was now tainted. There had been gunfire, a car chase and now a man was missing. Even disregarding the Syndicate's "Fixer" as Joe thought of him, residents of the Bookkeeper's village, and the other vehicles they had narrowly missed during their escape, would surely have reported their exploits to the authorities. He also suspected the Syndicate may have infiltrated the system to such an extent they would be able to control the story, painting Joe and the team as the bad guys.

Joe entered the house and powered up the kettle. Coffee was needed. 'Well, as disasters go, this morning was up there with the best of them,' Joe stated. 'Total clusterfuck.'

Ms Bowman, the General, the twins and Sara Jane were sitting in the adjoining lounge room. Fred must have returned to his practice after they had left. 'What happened?' asked Ms Bowman.

Joe tried to think of the best way to explain what happened. 'We walked into a situation. The Fixer was already there and we surprised him as he was setting the Bookkeeper up for a suicide. We extracted him and were making our escape when the Fixer broke free and came after us. We were able to get away on the dirt roads.

It was too much for the Bookkeeper, he had a heart attack after recognising Tracey from the facility. He had raped her while she was drugged. I have his laptop, not sure if there is anything on it that will help.'

'Have a look at it anyway,' instructed Ms Bowman.

'I think we may have been exposed in a number of ways,' continued Joe. 'The Fixer saw Jessica and Tracey and the Subaru. Also, there was gunfire and the car chase, so the police were probably called. I am thinking we may have to ditch the Subaru. If anyone reported the registration number, it will lead to me.'

'Jessica can check the police net for any reports. Until we know better, we will need to assume the car is tainted and Jessica and Tracey are known to the Syndicate.' Ms Bowman's instructions made sense, they needed good information to make good decisions.

Joe looked around the room. Tracey was cuddled up to Sara Jane, silent tears leaking from her eyes, Jessica was paler than he had ever seen her. He needed two hands to hold his coffee steady. Fred had lectured him about this while fighting the fires. Post traumatic stress disorder, PTSD, Joe could see it creeping into the room. They would all have to face their demons, but for now they needed to move forward.

'We need to start planning the move. As the next place is permanent, security will need to be paramount,' Joe stated, attempting to refocus their minds. If they let the doom and gloom prevail, they were lost.

The room was silent. Joe looked around the room. Enthusiasm and motivation had definitely fled the scene. The General marched up to the whiteboard, picked up the eraser and cleared Joe's previous musings.

'Run and hide: they will hunt you down and put you down. Return to your normal lives: they will hunt you down and put you down. Change your identity, move overseas: they will find you and kill you.

No, we cannot beat them globally, but we must teach the Syndicate that Australia is just too damn expensive. We need to hurt them and hurt them bad.' The General now had their attention.

'All of us in this room are committed whether we like it or not. They wrote the rule book, not us. The Syndicate is responsible for the misery it causes, not us. They are the bad guys; they taint everything and everyone they touch. They are the cancer; we are the scalpel.'

This was leadership. Joe could feel the room revitalise. They were going to have to deal with their demons eventually but not now. Normal people faced with abnormal situations had to step forward, but there was always a cost. The General was going to force them forward.

The General continued, 'What's our overall objective?'

'Defeat the Syndicate, throw them out of the country,' piped up Jessica.

'Kill the pricks,' added Sara Jane.

'Get our lives back,' was Joe's contribution.

'All good.' The General wrote on the whiteboard: DEFEAT ENEMY, RETURN NORMALITY

'So how do we achieve any goal?'

'Little steps,' answered Tracey.

'And the first ones are?' asked the General.

'Secure our base,' said Joe.

'Gather information,' added Ms Bowman.

'OK, two assignments for tomorrow. Joe, take the twins to the new base, start mapping out the move and security. Before the ponytail, Keith was one of the best electronics guys we had. Jody can reverse engineer an attack strategy better than anyone, she'll advise on defences. Take the camper.'

'Second: Jessica, Sara Jane and Tracey, list what we know in summary on the back of this board. I see someone has started on the other side. If possible, plan a visit to the twin facility, the chicken farm, I assume its purpose was to provide a cover for the actual facility, providing a legitimate business with deliveries and shipments, sales and expenses. Then follow the money and corporate trails to see where they lead.'

'Who cooks here?' The change of direction surprised everyone.

'I do usually,' answered Joe.

'Plan a comfort meal for this evening. Single "rum" ration tonight. It's too easy to hide in the bottle, and too damaging to our operational efficiency,' ordered the General.

'I could try a lasagne; I have the ingredients here already.'

'Do it,' finished the General.

Joe sat in the rear of the campervan. Keith and Jody occupied the two front seats. It was another glorious summer's day. Joe was beginning to wonder if the bushfire danger would start to rise again. There was another cold change forecast for the end of the week; by then the bush would have just about dried out from the last soaking. It could go either way: if there was rain and little lightning the fire danger would stay low, if there was little rain and lots of lightning strikes, well, best not to think about it. Joe snapped back to the present. He wouldn't be fighting any fires with his mates for a while, not until this mess was wiped clean.

Joe had organised with the solicitors to handle the settlement of the new property. They were able to take possession by paying the previous owner a rental for the short period until settlement. The Matthew Johnson identity was fronting for an offshore corporation. Joe hoped there were enough degrees of separation between stealing the funds from the Syndicate and using them to purchase the property to keep them safe.

'Hey, where's your ponytail?' asked Joe looking at Keith's short back and sides.

'Couldn't stand being a cliché anymore. Last night I decided it just wasn't my thing. Mum was an expert at buzz cuts when we were kids, so when I found a set of dog clippers in the shed, I asked for a tidy-up, and five minutes later it was all done. Guess I'm not cut out for civvy street.'

'You reckon the army's going to take you back?' asked Jodie with a snigger.

'Why not, they haven't thrown you out yet!' retorted Keith.

Joe was reminded of the times he spent with his own brothers.

They arrived at the property. Jodie asked Joe to drive. 'Take us around the area, on the roads closest to each side. I understand there is a road at the rear?'

'Here we go.' Keith showed Jodie a map of the property on his mobile phone.

'Can you switch that to satellite?' asked Jodie. Keith complied. 'OK, now terrain.' Keith complied again. 'If I was to attack or mount surveillance on this place, the way the property slopes down this northward-facing slope front to back, I would base myself on that hill on the far side of the road across the back or north boundary in those woods. The road across the front is on top of the ridge line, it is too obvious and open for surveillance, but you would be out of sight on the far side if you wanted to mount an ambush. The two sides are rugged bush and gullies.'

Keith took his sister's tactical appraisal and using a pad he had brought with them began to sketch out a surveillance system. He then wrote out a list of materials. 'We can purchase all this stuff from the local agricultural supplies shop and electronics place. But let's not do it locally. The nearest city is Newcastle, about an hour up the motorway. We should source our requirements up there from multiple sources.'

'Let's go. By the time we collect everything on this list, it will be time to head back and report to the General. By the way, what do you call him, the General or Dad?'

'Depends whether we are operational or on a family picnic,' replied Jodie, deadpan. Her humour was dryer than the Simpson Desert.

By late in the afternoon the campervan was full of boxes, from battery-powered cameras with their own solar panels, hundreds of metres of electric fence, again with its own power source, to a device that transmitted their phone and internet communications offsite to a remote transmitter. For anyone attempting to track them they would be using a cell tower remote from their actual location.

Joe had them pick up some steaks, some vegetables, wine and a premixed salad. Tonight, he was going to light up the barbeque. Stuff what the General thought, they had earned a night of relaxation.

Joe was hoping a permanent base would lift the team. Having the General and the twins join them also boosted his morale. Having a permanent base may not be the soundest tactical decision, but psychologically it was a turning point. They were no longer running.

It was late in the afternoon by the time they returned to base.

Jessica, Sara Jane and Tracey were waiting in the lounge room with the General and Ms Bowman. The General insisted on a debrief as the first order of business for the evening. Jessica started:

'We were tasked with investigating the twin facility. First, we checked all the police databases and the Roads and Traffic databases: the Subaru is clean. There is a report regarding the incident yesterday and a missing persons alert has been issued for the Bookkeeper, however as far as I can see it all revolves around the F100 that was chasing us. There is no report of a second car or of us.

'So we consulted with the General and Ms Bowman and decide to use the computers at the Cessnock Library for our search, just in case we raised any flags. The facility seems legitimate, and we found an employment ad for casual farm hands. I called and arranged an interview today. The farm manager showed me around. He seemed to have no idea they were providing cover for the shadow operation over the hill. In fact, he seemed perplexed about how high his expenses were and how low his sales. They did not align with the product leaving the farm and the feed and supplies he ordered. He had questioned the Bookkeeper about it and been told it was above his pay grade. He was definitely suspicious of the corporate owners. I then told him I was a journalist not really looking for work on a chicken farm but investigating the corporation. He confirmed they usually had little contact from the owners. But the day before yesterday a man had arrived unannounced declaring himself a representative of the corporate owners, wishing to inspect the operation.

'The farm manager was clearly scared of this man. He would not tell me why,' said Jessica. 'He realised he had told me too much. He clammed up tight and was suddenly very nervous. I advised him to take a holiday, take his family and disappear for a while.

'I think I may have fucked up. I feel I have dropped him in the shit big time.'

'Let's think about this,' declared Ms Bowman. 'I think in reality you may have saved his life. They were already looking at him. He is an outsider in the midst of their operation, supposedly legitimising the twin facility and its human trafficking operation. The Bookkeeper must have reported his suspicions and the Fixer was sent round to scare him. Knowing they are under scrutiny, there is a good chance they will attempt to silence anyone who knows their operation. Hopefully he takes your advice and runs.'

'It's a move forward. We now know how they covered the operation of the facility. Joe, what are you doing?' asked the General.

'It's the Bookkeeper's laptop. I already have all the information on it.'

'How?' asked Ms Bowman.

'I've been running an anti-virus program on his laptop. I have it on this USB stick. Jessica updated the virus definitions while she was at the library today. According to the report, this laptop has been cloned, and I recognise the cloud account it was cloned to. It's the Foreman's. This is how he knew the bitcoin private and public keys; he stole them from the Bookkeeper.'

Ms Bowman decided to summarise and close the discussion. 'The dots are joining. Soon we will have a better picture of the enemy. Great work everyone. Tomorrow's a rest day. The day after, we move.

General, can you organise watch-duty between yourself, the twins and myself tonight. The civilians look like they need a night off.'

'Beer and wine in the fridge, I'll clean the barbie, someone make some salads,' piped up Joe.

CHAPTER 41

The rest and recreation the night before had worked wonders. Joe had had his best night's sleep in a while. Jessica was still asleep beside him when he woke. He climbed out of bed as quietly as he could. He didn't make it. Jessica dragged him back into the bed. Twenty minutes later Joe again climbed out of the bed; Jessica was indulging in a lie-in, enjoying the sunlight streaming through the window onto the bed. Joe returned fifteen minutes later showered and with two cups of coffee.

'Ms Bowman wants everyone in the main room for a briefing in twenty minutes.'

'Jeez for a minute there, Joe, I felt like a normal human being.'

'Yeah, Jess, for a few minutes.'

'Any idea what's next?'

'None, I'm not even going to speculate. Just gunna try and steal a few more moments of peace and quiet.'

'Well, I better grab a shower, are the others all up yet?'

'I only saw the General in the kitchen. He passed on the message.'

With a sigh Jessica climbed out of bed, stretched and preened, enjoying Joe's eyes on her naked body. She sashayed into the ensuite bathroom attached to their room.

Ten minutes later everyone gathered in the main room. Ms Bowman walked into the kitchen and stood behind the island bench facing the rest of the team. 'I have been trying to determine a way forward. Everything we have done so far has hurt the Syndicate, but we still need to find a way to regain our freedom. While we are running and hiding we are just gifting the Syndicate more time to regroup. Once they regroup, our chances of defeating them in Australia will be limited.'

'What about globally?' asked Sara Jane.

'If we can push them out of Australia that will be a start, then we can consolidate and communicate with other countries for a global push. But let's not be naïve, these guys corrupt governments and in some countries are the government. If we can make Australia unprofitable for them, maybe we can make them abandon Australia.'

Ms Bowman turned to Joe, 'Joe you have been researching the "corporate structure" of the Syndicate in Australia, what have you found?'

'Well, tracking the bitcoin transactions through the account, or wallet as Bitcoin calls accounts, linked to the video, we were able to trace where the bitcoins were exchanged for cash by Bitcoin exchanges based in Australia, then, through not quite legal means, we were able to follow this money as it made its way through the Syndicate's normal business accounts, paying for goods and services. We were then able to create a rough sketch of their organisation in this country. There is a lot of supposition here, we have based our study on tracing the transactions from the bitcoin wallets we discovered at the facility. There is a possibility there are other branches which were kept quarantined from the organisation we found. Personally, I do not think so, based on cost and given we have tracked the organisation to the QC assisting the Attorney-General as the head of the Australian branch. I doubt there would be two people of that stature to head two quarantined branches without some overlap.'

'Joe, please outline how you tracked this information?' asked the General.

'Well most of the work was handled by Keith. Keith has a background in electronics and cyber warfare. Keith was able to backtrack the bitcoin transactions, through the exchanges where they are changed to real money, and through to the IP addresses of the computers used to manage the transactions. Some we were not able to track further, as they were probably using TOR, so were able to hide their real IP addresses. But we discovered enough to be able to basically "follow the money" as they say.'

'Joe, can we scroll back a bit. Please clarify for an old bloke. IP address? TOR?' interjected the General. 'Is it something to do with that super hush hush software Keith had me borrow from the FBI?'

'Keith may be the best person to explain this,' replied Joe, beckoning Keith to stand and answer the General's questions.

Keith stood. 'An IP address is the individual internet identification given to a connected device. It is the equivalent of a phone having an individual number. This allows a hacker or investigator to follow the connections. TOR basically bounces a connection from one computer to another making it impossible to find the original computer's IP address, and therefore difficult to track that particular computer. However, Dad, sorry, the General, was able to procure us a piece of software the FBI has developed. This software attaches itself to the bitcoin transactional commands issued by a particular wallet, or account in analogue terms. In other words, a very specialised virus. The virus then backtracked and planted itself on the originating computer. As with many government-developed viruses, it is ignored by antivirus software. So, when the target computer or device connects to the internet using a normal browser such as Explorer or Chrome, the virus sends us not only the IP address of the device but also a backdoor into that device.'

'Holy shit, Big Brother is on the case,' added Sara Jane.

'He's not a big brother just an annoying twin,' responded Jodie.

There was silence in the room. Keith had already explained all this to Joe, allowing Joe the luxury of watching everyone else digest the information.

'So, in a classic case of following the money, we painted a picture of the Syndicate's corporate structure in Australia,' Joe continued. 'However, there are gaps. There must be someone else involved with enough juice to pull strings. Our assumption is Quentin Brightly has control over others, probably through blackmail as we cannot find evidence of any financial transactions. However, just because we have not found something does not mean it does not exist.'

'If we attack Quentin Brightly will we destroy the Syndicate in Australia?' asked Ms Bowman.

'Depending on two things: one, Quentin Brightly's operation is the only operation in Australia, and two, we convince the Syndicate it is too expensive to operate in this country.'

'What operations have we found so far?' asked Jessica.

'In Australia, all we have found is related to the human trafficking, organ harvesting and the pornos. No sign of drug trafficking or arms dealing, or anything else. We know from looking at their global operations they operate in those markets. We just can't find any evidence they are doing it in Australia,' Joe explained. 'The operation appears to be continuing according to the movements of bitcoin, but we have yet to discover how. We think the actual facility is offshore, but we cannot pin it down at the moment.'

'What about the guy who came after us?' asked Tracey.

'Again, looking at the movements of bitcoin, he is not being paid through Brightly's wallet. My current thinking is he has been brought in by "Head Office" as a fixer, basically cleaning up after Brightly,' answered Joe.

'Maybe he will take Brightly out for us.'

'Not sure, but I do have an idea how we can turn the Syndicate against Brightly. I still have the codes for the bitcoin accounts, and I haven't touched the main account, the one we believe belongs to the Syndicate itself. I would like to drain it through Brightly's account. If Brightly were to rip the Syndicate off, their reaction may well tell us his position in the Syndicate. My guess is they will kill him.' Joe drew a breath.

'Before I go ahead, I would like you all to agree. If this backfires, if any of my assumptions are incorrect, or if we have underestimated Brightly's authority, we will be hunted down and killed. I think we need to vote on this. Let's have a cuppa and call a vote once we have all had a moment to consider where we stand.'

'Before we do, I have another proposal to add,' Ms Bowman addressed the room. 'To flush out any other Syndicate operations and to increase the pressure on Brightly, I plan to meet in private with the Attorney-General and persuade him to squeeze Brightly from the other side. Hopefully, we can pressure him into a mistake.'

Joe filled the electric jug and made tea and coffee for the group as they digested the information they had just received. A few minutes later they broke up into two groups: Sara Jane, Tracey, Jessica and Joe, and the Bowman family as Joe thought of them.

Jessica spoke first, 'You know this is a dangerous strategy?'

'I can't think of anything else?' answered Joe.

'I for one want my life back. If we don't go on the offensive these fuckwits will win,' Sara Jane answered. 'We can chip away at the edges, but it will only end badly for us. The more time we give the dickheads, the more time they will have to hunt us down and destroy us. We need to stand and fight or we might as well blow our own brains out now and be fucking be done with it. What do you think, Trace?'

'I agree. We have been lucky so far. I don't see it lasting.'

'What about the doctor? They must have had some sort of medico helping them? I thought you mentioned one visited the facility?' asked Jessica.

'We could search for him. But I think we would just find another corrupt minion,' replied Tracey. 'The Foreman and the trustees held him in contempt, not awe or fear, so I think all we would find would be some pathetic, disbarred doctor they were blackmailing or paying under the table. Later today, if we can move off site, I can call my people, see if they can add to the picture.'

'Who exactly are your people?' asked Joe.

'They are a bit like us. Theoretically we are part of the United Nations. Started out official but driven underground by corruption. There are about a dozen of us left and we are spread across the Asia-Pacific region. They can be trusted, but, because the Syndicate has corrupted so many officials across so many nations, we have limited ourselves to information gathering. We are trying to assemble enough verifiable data to be able to dump it in the public domain and force the powers that be to take action.'

'Once we have decided our course of action, we should draft a list of questions for you to ask them,' suggested Jessica.

'Good call, let's go see how our Army buddies went,' Joe added, finishing his cup of coffee.

They all gathered back in the main room.

'Before we commit to this, do we all agree to the two courses of action discussed this morning?' asked Joe.

Joe surveyed the room. Everyone returned his gaze.

'I don't see how we have any fucking choice,' Sara Jane responded.

The group was silent for a minute or two. Ms Bowman stepped forward. 'OK, so listen up, we are going to beef up our operational security. Once we have put these two attacks into motion, we are going to have to go mobile. We will need to leave here, but we will be unable to take up residence at the new place until we are sure we have not been compromised during the operation. There is a risk in each attack. Firstly we are assuming we are the only ones with access to sophisticated tracing software and viruses. Secondly, we are assuming the Attorney-General is clean. That's two assumptions. The collateral we are staking is our lives, so we cannot assume anything. Joe, once you have actioned the bitcoin transfers take Jessica, Sara Jane and Tracey and drive, stay off the grid. The General, Jodie, Keith and myself will take the camper and do the same. Keith, you work with Joe on some communications protocols. But first we must sanitise this place. Aim for a departure time of 1300 hours.'

'You had better rent a small truck for the excess equipment, clothes and so forth. We will need to travel light, but minimise our shopping expeditions. Also, we can't leave anything here for them to trace. The truck can stay in a storage yard until we retrieve it. Make sure you pack the security cameras and computer into the bike and Subaru. It will be your first priority when you arrive at the new base. Joe, you organise that so we can put tracks down to Goulburn,' ordered the General.

It took fifteen minutes. If their assumptions were correct, the Syndicate would believe Quentin Brightly had just stolen from them nearly a billion US dollars' worth of crypto currency. The daily transfer protocols Joe had put in place still existed. The funds would end up draining through the money-laundering system Joe had implemented. He thought he had better dismantle his system the next day. Making it inactive would add another layer of security.

Ms Bowman had organised a clandestine meeting with the Australian Attorney-General for the next day at midday, meeting at a motel on the highway outside Goulburn, a town halfway between Sydney and the national capital, Canberra. The group discussed which questions she should ask and information she should share with him. Keith went to his room and returned with a small black canvas bag. Opening the bag, he produced a small brooch shaped like a lizard with two small sapphires as eyes. 'Wear this, Mum. The body is a small transmitter and the pin is the aerial. It is good for about two hundred metres. We will be around the corner listening.'

Keith then produced two cheap mobile phones. 'These are prepaid, registered to the army. Once the meeting is finished, we will call you and arrange the next step. As things are fluid at the moment, we will not make any further plans until we know the lie of the land. I have paired them by saving the number of the corresponding phone in the contacts. We will call about 1400 hours tomorrow.'

'OK, let's sanitise this place and disappear,' ordered the General, signifying the end of the meeting.

'For civilians they're not too bad,' commented the General. They had just left the hobby farm for the last time. The four of them were in the campervan heading for Goulburn.

'Keith, how secure is this van? Can it be traced?' asked Ms Bowman.

Keith was sitting in the front passenger seat, Jodie was driving. He turned around to his parents in the back seat which, being a campervan, folded down into the double bed. 'Well, it should be OK. But, for the purposes of operational security we will need to stay off the toll roads. The electronic toll collectors will track our progress, and although the account is in a bogus company name, we should still take the back roads.'

'You can take over the driving when we hit the suburbs then,' said Jodie, 'I don't feel like driving a manual stick shift through the hundred and fifty traffic lights we will traverse between this side of Sydney and the other.'

'Calm down, there is no rush. We will arrive in Goulburn around 1800 hours. Looking at Google Maps we have found a motel across the road from the meeting place. It has parking round the rear so we will be able to stay out of sight. Fi, did you have any trouble convincing the Attorney-General to meet with you?'

'No General, the mention of the attack on the motorway where Jessica was injured, and the link to our previous meeting was enough to convince him that our Task Force is compromised,' replied Ms Bowman. 'In fact, he agreed a bit too easy.'

'OK go in assuming it is a trap. If he is clean, he will never know we are across the road. If he is dirty, we will be twenty seconds away. Kids, you both carrying?' asked the General.

'Two silenced Saturday night specials in the galley cupboard. They are good for a single use. There are also four combat knives in the cutlery drawer,' replied Keith. 'What about you, Dad?'

'I have a service pistol on me, but no silencer. We need to avoid gun play. The last thing we want is local cops becoming involved. What about if he has a security detail?'

'My guess, if he has a security detail, he is clean. If he has left them in Canberra, we can assume he is dirty,' added Jodie.

'OK, so looking at pictures of the motel room I'll be using, it looks fairly standard. Door to the left, window to the right. I will leave the door unlocked, and if I think the meeting is compromised, I will hug the left wall while you lot charge in and take down any black hats.'

'Well that's probably the best we can do. Just to add another layer, say "It sure is smoky outside," if you do not like what you see when you walk into the room,' added Keith.

Once they had navigated their way through Sydney, the run down the dual-carriage Hume Highway to Goulburn was like a family holiday. 'Wow, this is the first time we have been away as a family in years,' commented Ms Bowman. 'Maybe we could try it more often.'

'Yeah, the family that hunts together stays together?' added Jodie.

'About another twenty minutes,' said the General.

'Until what?' asked Jodie.

'Until you kids start squabbling,' Ms Bowman chuckled.

'Keith always starts it.'

'Bullshit,' said Keith, now driving.

The four of them shared a laugh.

'We can watch the sunset from the Hilltop War Memorial. With all the smoke from the bushfires it should be quite spectacular from up there.'

'And we can have a family dinner,' added Ms Bowman.

The further south they travelled the smokier the atmosphere became. The fires that had plague the state since August were still burning down in the Alps and far south coast. The countryside was still barren from the drought. Patches of dried reddish-brown soil broke through clumps of wispy straw-like grass. The farms they passed were all handfeeding their remaining stock. The small amount of rain that had fallen had been drawn into the parched soil, disappearing without a trace.

The more the farms suffered, the more the regional towns suffered. Being just off the motorway and located just far enough out of Sydney made Goulburn a popular stop for lunch or even overnight. This transient income stream helped the town's economy, but not enough to mask the run-on effects of the most severe drought the east coast of Australia had ever endured. Several stores in town had closed while the pubs appeared to be nearly full of men and women nursing drinks while they waited for better times.

Keith parked the campervan around the rear of the motel where they had chosen to base themselves. It was directly across the road from the motel where the meeting was scheduled for the next day and their rooms stared straight across the highway at their target. After being in the van all afternoon the four of them decide to walk into town and have some dinner. With daylight savings they still had a least two hours to sunset. The café they chose was spacious in the way only a café in a country town can be. The décor was nineteen-fifties, as was the menu.

'Real hamburgers and real chips,' exclaimed Keith.

'Look at the milkshakes,' added Jodie.

'God, it is so hard to find places like this these days. They all think fucking McDonald's is the preferred business model.'

'Keith, watch your language.'

'Sorry Mum.'

'OK, just don't say the M-word and food together in the same sentence again.'

They ordered, they talked and they ate. 'It was so good to sit back and enjoy a meal together. It seems years since we all sat down like this,' sighed Ms Bowman.

'Look at you, Mum, coming over all sentimental,' responded Jodie.

'Well it is true; your mother and I have been so busy with our careers, we never really spent enough time together as a family. It's only now, with hindsight, we realise how much we missed.'

'We understand, Dad, but what you guys do is different, it has meaning. It's like Joe the fireman; he quit his big corporate job, now he protects his community for free. Jodie and myself admire you two so much we joined up ourselves. Now look at us all four working together to take down the bad guys.'

'Your support means a lot to your father and me. Let's change the subject before we get all gushy and gooey. We should grab the van and have a recce from the lookout. We need to know all the exits from town. Not just the obvious ones, but the back lanes.'

With still an hour's daylight left, they had time to retrieve the van and drive up Rocky Hill. From there Goulburn was laid out before them.

'OK, north we have the highway to Sydney, south to Canberra, east down to the coast and west inland. So far all our interactions with the Syndicate have been north of Sydney. So, if tomorrow's operation goes to shit, they are going to expect us to run north up the highway. I say we head west, then swing north and return to our base from the northwest. In fact, I think we should go west regardless. It is the road over there; it intersects with the main road through town three blocks south of the motel.'

'Sounds good, Dad, we should also stock up on food, water and a serious first aid kit,' added Jodie. 'We may need to disappear if this goes pear-shaped.'

'OK, let's hit the supermarket, and there should be a large pharmacy in town,' the General concluded, leading the family back to the campervan. The sky above them turned orange and red as the setting sun shone through the smoke and ash in the sky. 'Hope that's not a bad omen.'

Ninety minutes later they gathered in one of the two motel rooms they had booked. 'Early night. I want to maintain surveillance on the meeting room from 4 am. There has been no light on in there yet, but, if they are going lay a trap it will be in the morning before they expect us to show. Fi, does he know your background?'

'I don't think so. These guys are usually lazy, so I doubt he's dug deep. No one appears to have requested my record, probably because they assume I am part of the police or Justice Department. It's one of the reasons I don't use my rank.'

'What weaponry do you intend to carry into the meeting?'

'I can't decide. I was going to wait and see if our reconnaissance discovered anything.'

'OK, we will decide our final tactics based on how the situation develops tomorrow. Kids take the other room; your mother and I will share this one. Surveillance starts at 4 am. Keith, you and I will take first shift.'

By 4 am they were all awake. Their training meant they had all fallen asleep immediately their heads hit their pillows. Rested, it was time for action.

'No lights,' whispered the General, staring out the window at the motel across the road. 'A car has just pulled up with no lights on. Would have been less obvious to drive in with them on.'

'OK, looks and walks like a male, just over average height, looks fit. No excess weight, he's heading to the room, looks like he has the code to the keypad on the door. Hang on, sloppy, he didn't cover the keypad. I have the room code, 6087. He is letting himself in, no lights. Definitely not the Attorney-General, any guesses?'

'None good,' replied Keith. 'Private security the AG hired or if the AG is in the Syndicate's pocket, maybe the Fixer.'

'We have to assume your mother is entering hostile territory. First, we need to survey the surrounds, looking for any indications he has back-up. The Fixer works alone, so far?'

'Yes, we have seen no back-up. But, Dad, I agree we need to find a way to patrol the area without giving ourselves away.'

'OK at dawn, go for a jog. Note any cars with occupants or running engines. Any vans or trucks with a sight line to the motel. Any rooms like this one as well. Hopefully we are the only ones with eyes on the target. An hour later have your sister reverse your tracks, brief her on anything you see so she can provide an update. It's not perfect but it's about the best we can do. After your sister returns, we'll go through our options.'

Keith returned to his room. Jodie sat down next to her father and continued watching the room across the road. Nothing was happening. Was the mystery man catching up on some sleep, waiting for his support team to appear or watching them watching him?

It may have been a year or so since Keith had joined the private sector, but he had maintained his operational fitness. He was able to jog at a respectable pace and survey his surroundings. His training in reconnaissance kicking in automatically, he was able to survey, analyse and memorise the details of any threats as he ran.

Twenty minutes and he was back in the motel room. 'A few parked trucks, all have cold engines and no direct sight lines to the target. I didn't see any one at all. Of course, there is still the chance there are black hats with eyes on us who were too dug in for me to see,' he reported.

'OK, show your route to Jodie. Highlight any parked vehicles, she can do a reverse loop in forty-seven minutes. I'll go on a walk say eighty-three minutes after her, keeping it random. We don't want them setting their watches by our passing!' instructed the General.

'Fi, this bloke over the road is odds-on a bad guy. I don't think you should go in. I think we should wait for the AG then grab him and take him elsewhere.'

'I disagree, the AG is a pawn, the bloke in the room is probably the Fixer. I think he is the bigger prize. He is part of the Syndicate, not just a paid-off hack. Although I'll wait until the AG has entered the room. The Fixer being here instead of the AG's security does indicate the AG is bent. Get both of them in one swoop,' answered Ms Bowman. 'As long as we have the perimeter secure, I'm going in.'

Jodie completed her circuit. 'I didn't see anything obvious,' she reported back. They continued to watch the room across the road. The General completed his own circuit. 'I can't see any support,' he stated when he returned. 'Lucky the doors to our rooms face the rear. He can't see us coming and going.'

'Jodie, watch the cleaner over there. Maybe you can use her trolley as a disguise. You could be in closer when the meeting occurs. Keith, have the van started and ready behind the south corner of the building. We may want to leave in a hurry. We filled up last night, so what sort of range will we have before we need to refuel?'

'It's good for about six hundred kilometres. The water tanks are full, and we stocked up on supplies. We should be able to go off-grid for a couple of weeks if need be.'

'OK, everyone have a shower, it may be the last chance we have for a while. Then we will sanitise these rooms. Regardless of what happens we will leave immediately after the meeting by the road to the west.'

The morning ticked by slowly. The dry heat was still with them, the smoky air trapped by an inversion layer. 'There's a southerly change forecast for later in the day,' noted Keith. 'Possibly a thunderstorm, but mostly wind until rain comes around midnight.'

'Fi, do you have your questions ready?'

'Yes, General, though I doubt I will be needing them if the Fixer is in there.'

'What about your comms? Have you run a test with Keith?'

'Yes, we tested it with me inside this room and Keith out the back, twice the distance from the corner of the building you will hiding behind and the target room.'

'I still don't like this. Deliberately walking into an ambush.'

'OK, General, I cannot see any other way. If we go in hard, we will blow our cover. We know it's an ambush, they don't know we know it's an ambush. Remember, they think I am an ambitious civil servant, and will act accordingly.'

'1000 hours, three hours to the meeting. Two on watch, two resting. We will eat at about 1100 hours; we want to be at our peak performance at 1300 hours for the meeting and bear in mind we may not be able to stop once we leave until well after dark.'

The hours crept by, nothing moved across the road. Keith prepared some sandwiches, half they ate at eleven am, the rest he packed into the van. Jodie had noticed the cleaner had left the motel opposite. Her trolley was parked in a utility room at the end of the complex, luckily on the far side from the office. She would go over around half-past twelve as the "afternoon shift". At one pm she planned to be hovering around the car belonging to the occupant of the target room. If she could, she would use her knife on the tyres, disabling the vehicle and therefore hampering any pursuit.

At noon the General ran them through another test of their earbud radios. The four of them then searched and sanitised the two rooms they had occupied. 'There's a car turning in to the motel opposite,' Jodie called from the window. 'Whoever it is, is stopping in front of the target room. It's the AG; he just left his car and entered the room. I'll be about ten minutes. I'll head over now, loop around, and approach from the north.'

'OK, Fi, go with Jodie. You will be able to blind-side them. You should be about ten minutes early. Don't knock unless the door's locked; hopefully you can walk straight in catching them off-guard. Fi, wear your sunglasses, the room will be dark, no lights on and curtains closed, take them off as you enter the gloom and hopefully you will have some sight before your eyes adjust to the low light.'

'Keith, get the van ready. Everybody out, I'll leave the room keys in this room. Just pass me the cleaner so I can wipe them down. The rooms are booked for another night, so no one will look until tomorrow.'

'Unless it goes to hell across the road,' added Keith.

They separated at the rear of the motel. Jodie and Ms Bowman headed north up the rear lane crossing over the main road a hundred metres up. They were able to walk down the footpath on the target side, blocked from view from the motel room where their quarry waited.

Keith started the van and moved it to the rear south corner of the motel they had been using. He waited in the driver's seat, the side door open and the engine running. The General crept forward until he could see around the corner of the building across the road. It was a dry 35 degrees Celsius, and smoky. Sensible people were indoors with their air-conditioners on max.

The utility room was unlocked. Jodie was able to remove the cleaning cart and make her way down the front of the motel building. There were only two cars parked out front of the motel. The one that had crawled in about 4 am with its lights doused. Up close it looked like a rental Camry. The second had just arrived and parked in front of the target room. The Attorney-General's car, the one parked in front of the room, inadvertently gave Jodie extra cover as she slashed the two tyres on the right-hand side of the Camry.

Ms Bowman walked past Jodie hugging the front of the building, out of sight of anyone watching out of the window. The TV in the target room came on, the sound blaring. She was ten minutes early. She held her breath, turned the handle on the door and pushed. It opened, the Attorney-General had not thought to lock it, she barged into the room.

The lights were out and the curtains closed, she was able to swipe off her sunglasses as she entered the room. She was not totally blind. The Attorney-General was sitting on the bed , facing away from her, the second man was standing in front of him.

'Afternoon, Mr Attorney-General, smoky outside.' She stepped into the room and pressed herself against the wall. The man standing pulled his trigger, the Attorney-General's body jerked and collapsed onto the bed.

Jodie crashed the cleaning cart into the room. She had her pistol sitting on the top tray under a towel. Her hand was on the grip. She raised the gun, slipped her finger onto the trigger and squeezed. The shot went wide as she hadn't aimed, but it sent the gunman diving for cover. He fired from the floor around the corner of the bed as he landed. Jody let the cart's momentum take it further into the room blocking the gunman's view of her and her mother. She dived across the bed, reached over and pulled the trigger twice. She saw the gunman's extended arm droop to the floor and the pistol fall from his hand.

The General crashed through the door and took in the scene, then quickstepped past the bed and kicked the gun across the floor away from the gunman. He then turned to his wife.

Ms Bowman was sliding down the wall. A trail of blood streaked the wall behind her. A crater could be seen where the bullet had passed through her and into the wall. The General snatched two towels from the cleaner's cart and pressed one to the front and one to the back of his wife's body.

'Keith, bring the van across,' he screamed into his throat mike. Jodie checked the other two. The Attorney-General groaned. The gunman was dead, her second shot removing the top of his head.

Jodie went through his pockets shoving everything into her own pocket. She went across to the Attorney-General. Ms Bowman barging through the door had saved his life, the distraction caused the shooter's aim to drift, hitting him in the arm.

'Throw him in the van,' yelled the General. 'Grab anything you can in one sweep and jump in the front with Keith, I'll carry Fi.'

Within seconds. They were in the van. No one had paid any attention. The General turned the TV volume down to a reasonable level. He placed the "do not disturb" card on the door handle. Hopefully it would buy them some time and distance.

'Go, Keith, but keep it legal until we are out of town. We don't want to draw any attention to ourselves. Change of plan. We are going to go east, take the Braidwood Road. About twenty kilometres past the racecourse take a right following the signs to Queanbeyan. About thirty kilometres later there will be driveway with an old red milk urn out the front. Turn down it. It's a Special Services medical facility.'

'How's Mum,' asked Jodie.

'I need to keep pressure on the wound. She's lost a heap of blood and is in shock. I'd take her to a local hospital, but I don't think they would keep her safe.'

The Attorney-General groaned. The General threw him a towel. 'Push that on your arm.'

Keith had driven out of Goulburn. He pushed the van as fast as he could along the secondary road. The Wakefield raceway flashed past within ten minutes, the turn-off would be another ten down the road. The camper was not built for this speed.

Jodie climbed out of the passenger seat and squeezed into the rear of the camper. The General had Ms Bowman wedged along the rear seat. The Attorney-General was sliding around the floor on his and Ms Bowman's blood. 'Tell us everything you know about the Syndicate. You set my mother up.'

Jodie reached up into the galley of the camper and pulled a combat knife out of the cutlery drawer. She pulled out her phone and pressed the recording app. The Attorney-General remained silent. She jabbed the knife into his calf muscle.

'Fuck, you crazy bitch, don't you know who I am?' he screamed.

'I'm a soldier and you sold out my country. And you nearly got my mother fucking killed.' She jabbed him again.

'OK, OK, they traced me through some porn I was watching. They said if I didn't do as they instructed, they would expose me,' he whimpered.

'Looks to me they decided you were a liability. The Fixer was sent to silence you permanently,' Keith shouted across from the driver's seat. 'We saved your miserable cock-sucking life.'

'We know about your mate, Quentin Brightly,' added Jodie.

'Hold on, here's the intersection.' Keith down-shifted three gears as he slowed to make the turn across the traffic. The General held Ms Bowman steady but Jodie and the Attorney-General slid across the van on the blood. The Attorney-General's eyes flickered towards the knife Jodie was holding.

'Come on fucking try something, dickhead. Give me a fucking excuse to jam this into your heart.' Jodie spoke quietly. The Attorney-General's face went white.

'Fifteen minutes to go,' shouted Keith, slamming the gear stick into top gear, calling the distance to go from the GPS on the dash.

'You won't get anything useful out of him.' the General spoke quietly, 'He's as weak as piss, they would have sucked him dry, but not told him a thing.'

'He's fainted anyway. Or faking it,' said Jodie. She knelt on the floor and shuffled over to help her father. 'Hang in there, Mum. We'll be there in a minute,' she whispered gently. She looked at her father. She could see the tears streaming down his face.

The van was bouncing around the B-road. Keith was keeping it on the road by sheer willpower and the advanced driving courses the Army had insisted he take. He heeled and toed through a down shift then another, 'Turn coming up,' he yelled.

Two more down shifts and he hauled the wheel over. He had

judged it just right; the van made the corner and he was accelerating back up the gears. He slowed down again to take a cattle grid.

'Stop,' yelled the General. 'There should be a bloke working on an old tractor to your right. He's the guard. Hit the horn. I can't see from back here.'

The van stopped. A man appeared at the window, looked inside. 'General,' he saluted.

'Sergeant, tell them we are coming in hot. The Major's been hit.'

'What about him,' asked the guard.

'You can put him through the shredder and use him for fertiliser as far as I'm fucking concerned. He's a fucking traitor. Have them hold him until you hear from me.'

'Go, Keith, up to the main building. The Sergeant will radio ahead.'

The van pulled up in front of the building, a medical team were rushing out with a pair of stretchers. 'The Major is the priority,' the General shouted as he flung open the side sliding door of the van.

Ms Bowman and the Attorney-General were rushed inside. The General and twins stood dejected outside the van. An officer approached the General.

He saluted 'General.'

'Colonel,' replied the General, 'we need to keep travelling, can you make our visit off the books? The Major's life depends on it.'

'You know that is our specialty.'

'We also need a vehicle.' The General pointed at the camper, the rear floor was covered in blood and steam was floating out from the engine compartment.

'No problem, take one of our vans. They are unmarked and look like any other white delivery van. They have been decked out as stealth personnel carriers.'

Fifteen minutes later they were leaving the facility.

'What is that place?' asked Jodie.

'The best non-existent hospital in the land. It's for Special Forces and the like, injured in operations we want to keep off the books.'

'Will Mum be all right?'

'This Syndicate better hope so. If anything happens to her we won't be just putting them out of business, we will be fucking exterminating them.'

CHAPTER 44

'Those movie doctors work miracles every day. People are shot, see the doc and are back shooting bad guys before the sun goes down,' commented Fred. 'Unfortunately I was never good looking enough to make it into the movies. So you are stuck with real world doctoring.'

'Do your kids think you are funny?' asked Jessica, attempting a push-up.

'They do groan a lot. But only rarely throw food.'

'So, you were really lucky as the bullet had spent most of its energy by the time it hit you. It only damaged some soft tissue, and no tendons, arteries, nerve bundles or bones were damaged. It just lodged in the fleshy bit at the back of your arm. But the fleshy bit is muscle. So now we must re-engage and strengthen the damaged muscle. Other muscles are compensating for it as much as they can, but this will cause an imbalance. I bet you are feeling muscle aches in your neck and mid-back.'

'Yes, I am.'

'What's needed is an exercise and stretching regime to overcome the damage. I fear it will always feel a bit tight and you will feel the occasional twinge. The scarring on the surface and underneath will be there permanently. I have downloaded a set of exercises and stretches recommended by the Physiotherapy Association. I would start gently with those and gradually increase the load.'

Fred handed over a sheaf of papers. Jessica and Joe had a look through them. 'They look fairly straightforward,' Jessica commented. 'Thanks for all you have done.'

'No problem, my dear, in future just don't get shot. A couple of inches over and you would have probably lost your arm.'

'OK. Note to self: medical professionals advise being shot is bad for your health,' replied Jessica.

'Sorry to change the subject, any news on those two thugs from the other day?' asked Fred.

'They are dead. We were looking for a leak in the Task Force Jessica works for, and we hinted that those two may have been turned and were providing Ms Bowman with information. They were shot dead by a third man. We are calling him the Fixer. He appears to be working independently of the existing operation. We suspect he has been sent here from overseas to close off any loose ends incriminating the Syndicate,' explained Joe.

'Do you have a suspect on the Task Force?' asked Fred.

'The Task Force reports to a committee. The committee is assisted by a Queen's Council called Quentin Brightly. We believe he is the link. We believe the Attorney-General is also compromised. Ms Bowman and family are having a private chat with him today. Our thinking is Quentin Brightly is the head of the Australian operation and the AG is his puppet.'

Fred contemplated this information. A minute later he spoke. 'Corruption is a cancer. Like with cancer you have to damage a lot of healthy tissue to remove all the corruption. Hopefully it has not spread too far, because like a cancer it can consume and destroy the whole system.'

It was a sobering analogy.

Fred had met them in a lake-side park. Even with his beard and sunglasses, Joe was still not comfortable entering Morisset. Too many people knew him, and being a regional town everyone wanted to stop and chat. Not a good way to stay off the radar.

'Look, I need to get back to work. Stay healthy.'

'Thanks, Fred, I was going to say "love to the cheese and kisses and tin lids", but it will have to wait until this is over,' said Joe.

'Cheese and kisses? Tin lids?' asked Jessica.

'Wife and kids,' answered Fred and Joe together.

Fred had driven his own car to the meeting. Joe and Jessica announced themselves only when they were sure Fred was not under surveillance. Fred's car was an early 1970s Australian muscle car. It had been updated to make it a comfortable daily drive. It was bright purple.

'I suppose its reverse psychology. Nobody would suspect he was up to anything nefarious driving a purple Falcon GTHO.'

'Fred's pride and joy. We need to join the others,' answered Joe.

Jessica and Joe walked back to the park bench. They began donning their motorcycle gear. Once they had their helmets on, Joe reconnected the intercom.

'All set?' he asked Jessica.

'Ready to roll,' she replied.

Joe piloted the bike along the blacktop and then down the access road to the Watagan Mountains National Park. Just over the west side of the ridge line there was a secluded campsite on an intersection of two fire trails. On leaving the last Airbnb they had driven into town and purchased camping gear, food and water enabling them to stay off the grid until they heard from the General and Ms Bowman.

They found Sara Jane and Tracey sitting at park bench preparing a cold lunch.

'Shame we can't light a fire,' sighed Tracey.

'One whiff of smoke on a day like this and you'll have twenty fire trucks, six national park rangers and ten cop cars here in under twenty minutes. We are still in a period of maximum fire danger.'

'Bloody goody two shoes, Mr Fireman, no wonder you and Jessica are together,' responded Sara Jane poking out her tongue.

It was pushing one o'clock in the afternoon. 'We should hear from Ms Bowman soon. If everything has gone to plan, we can head down to the new place,' said Jessica emphatically ignoring her sister.

Once they had eaten, they turned on the prepaid phone Keith had provided them.

They waited; an hour passed. The phone rang. Jessica answered.

It was Jodie, 'Mum's been shot by the Fixer. So has the AG. The Fixer is dead. We have dropped Mum and the AG off at a secure facility run by Dad's people. We are heading to base via the long way. Will see you there. Please confirm and deploy.'

'Confirmed,' Jessica stated. The line went dead. Jessica removed the back of the phone, extracted the battery and SIM card. She smashed the SIM card with a rock, then battered the phone. 'We can't leave the pieces here in case it was traced. We will need to dispose of them on the way. Let's pack up and get out of here!'

The tent and sleeping gear were quickly packed into the Subaru. Together they walked through their campsite from the previous night attempting to remove any trace of their presence.

'I'll take the bike; I can cut across the trails along the ridge line and drop down behind the new base. Why don't the three of you head back down to Cessnock and grab some supplies. You can also pick up the rental truck from the storage yard. I'll call you on the phone Jessica has if there is an issue. Neither of these have been used before,' suggested Joe.

'This shitfight sure chews through the phones,' answered Sara Jane. 'What price privacy?'

'You mean what price living!' stated Tracey. 'Come on let's get out of here, this place gives me the creeps. I can't wait for a hot shower.'

Joe jumped on the bike, started the engine. He turned to the Subaru. Jessica had beaten Sara Jane to the driver's seat. After staring down her sister, she started the engine. At the first fork in the track, Joe turned to the south, behind him the Subaru turned to the west.

Joe followed the fire trails running across the ridge line in a southerly direction. The map in his head guided him through the national park and state forests. Within half an hour he was parked in a clearing gazing down at the corporation's new property. His corporation, well his corporation when he was Matthew Johnson. He would talk to Keith about hanging a security camera up at this lookout. It gave an eagle's eye view of the property sitting on its north-facing slope five kilometres to the south and one kilometre below the level of the lookout.

The real estate agent should have left a side door key in a key safe attached to the door of the shed. The rest of the keys for the house and outbuildings should be on the kitchen bench. He took out his phone and snapped some photos. He hoped they would help Keith set up the security. This was a permanent base so Joe wanted a full suite of security measures in place, plus serious defensive capability established across the grounds. No more running.

A permanent base could easily become a trap. They would need not only to monitor the countryside surrounding the property but also the internet for any digital searches. There was no doubt in Joe's mind, the Syndicate was coming after them. You don't steal a billion dollars from a global criminal organisation without retribution.

How soon the Syndicate connected the missing funds to the closing of the Australian facilities was the question. As far as Joe was concerned, the team had to assume it would happen sooner rather than later, and now, with the Fixer dead, identifying the source of the next threat to Joe and the team would be problematic.

Joe did a slow scan of the countryside around the property. Next he examined the photos he had just taken. He expanded them until just before they pixelated. He was looking for any randomly parked vehicles. He couldn't see any. Nonetheless he would circle into the property. He picked out his route from the lookout. By utilising a couple of fire trails, he could cover all four sides. He started the V-Strom, left the lookout and descended out of the mountains. He felt it was the start of a new chapter.

It took forty-five minutes to ride the outside boundary of the property. His observations from the lookout were confirmed. Nobody appeared to be taking any interest in the property or the area. He opened the front gate, passed through and headed for the shed. He left the gate open. Jessica and the girls would not be far behind him and they were expecting the General and the twins later in the evening.

Keith had drilled him on anti-surveillance techniques. Joe had cleared the area for any physical spies, but now he needed to track any digital ones. From the right pannier of the bike Joe removed a handheld device. According to Keith it would pick up any transmissions from hidden cameras, bugs or movement detectors hidden around the property.

Keith had instructed Joe to close in on the buildings in a spiral pattern, starting well clear of the house and outbuildings, slowly closing in while walking around them. Joe followed the instructions. He could find no evidence of radio signals leaving the property. Opening the flyscreen, he unlocked the deadlock then the door handle. He entered the kitchen. Slowly swivelling through three hundred and sixty degrees he again scanned for transmissions. None.

He walked through the house scanning every room. Nothing. He put the scanner down on the kitchen bench. He looked across the open-plan living areas through the floor-to-ceiling windows and across the paddock to the Watagans. The estate agent had provided an inventory, but Joe knew he wasn't going to have time to check if everything was there. He did a second walk-through checking off the major items against the duplicate copy he found on the bench under the keys. They would be renters for the next few weeks until he settled on the property. It would be totally automatic; he had already deposited the funds in the solicitor's trust account and all the documents were signed. The solicitor would register them and finalise the sale.

He hoped the Subaru and the truck were only half an hour away, but could not be certain. There was nothing to eat or drink until they arrived. Joe would use the time familiarising himself with the property and would start in the shed.

He was pleasantly surprised to find the shed contained a fully equipped workshop, a ride-on mower and a quad bike and trailer, hopefully saving him a trip to the hardware store. Across the gravel quadrant at the rear of the house was a large barn. Joe opened the oversize roller door and found it to be empty. There was room for multiple vehicles. He returned to the V-Strom and rode it into the barn. The Subaru and the rental truck would also fit in with room for at least one more. He opened the panniers and laid out the security cameras they had been using on the concrete floor. They would have to do until they installed a permanent system.

By the time Jessica, Tracey and Sara Jane arrived he had installed four cameras in close to the house, covering the four sides. The next ring would be further out focusing on the four sides of the fence line. The four of them unloaded the car. Then Joe concentrated on reconnecting and booting up the computer. Within ten minutes he had the images from the four cameras on one of the screens.

Time for a coffee. The food supplies had been left on the island bench separating the living area from the kitchen. Joe was happy to pack them away himself. As the designated cook he had a proprietary interest in the kitchen. He left the coffee, sugar and milk out on the counter and fired up the jug. 'Coffee in five minutes!' he yelled.

'Yes please.'

'OK'

'Make mine a tea.'

They had been living out of each other's pockets for long enough; Joe knew how each member liked their brew. Five minutes later they were lounging comfortably around an oversized coffee table.

'Nice place, but I'm a city girl, sick of all this fucking green,' Sara Jane opened the conversation.

'Argh, the smell of crumbling concrete and old asphalt,' sighed Tracey. 'Take me to paradise, lover.' She put her arm around Sara Jane.

'I'll finish my coffee and mount the rest of the cameras. We should still have few hours of daylight left.' Joe said. 'Then I'll do some vegies, rice and mince for dinner. I can spice it up a bit and it's an easy meal to reheat for the others when they arrive.'

'Any update?' asked Jessica.

'Not yet, I would not expect it either,' answered Tracey.

'If we have the full team back tonight, we can pick up the rest of the gear tomorrow. It's still sitting in the truck we rented. We didn't have time to collect it. We also need to resume the watch system between us. The General and twins will most likely be too knocked about to help tonight,' added Jessica.

Joe finished his coffee and headed out to the shed. 'Wait for me,' called Jessica, jogging to catch up to him. Together they loaded the trailer attached to the quad bike with a ladder, strapping, some brackets, screws and a screwdriver. 'Makes it easy with everything left here!'

'Yes, one of the reasons this place grabbed my attention. It was set up as an Airbnb slash corporate retreat, and was for sale on a walk-out walk-in basis. Saves us a whole mountain of pain shopping for furniture and everything else,' replied Joe.

'Personally, I don't mind a bit of shopping, setting up a house can be fun,' countered Jessica.

'Yeah, I agree, but not when you are trying to keep a profile lower than a bluetongue lizard's belly,' replied Joe.

'Talking of lizards, do you reckon there is much wildlife round here?' asked Jessica.

'Do you mean as in nightclubs or flora and fauna?' teased Joe.

'Ha-ha, funny man.'

The day was still humid, however the sea breeze was reaching them and taking the heat out of the air, and for the first time since the last rain, clearing the air of smoke. 'I heard on the car radio that the smoke from these fires is now completely circling the southern hemisphere and is so bad in New Zealand they are warning people with respiratory problems to stay inside,' commented Jessica.

'Yeah, five hundred kilometres south of here on the New South Wales – Victorian border there are still major fires burning out of control. The worst in living memory.'

'Can't they stop them?' asked Jessica.

'The only thing that stops fires like these is the weather or the ocean.'

They finished loading the trailer. Joe turned to the quad bike, looked it over, and he found the starter. 'Hey, this thing's electric,' he exclaimed. 'Didn't even know they made them.'

'It was in the blurb.'

'What blurb?'

'The one about this property. The one you should have read before you purchased this place.'

'Hah, yes that one!' replied Joe.

He unplugged the power lead and walked round the vehicle. The controls looked straightforward. Front and rear brakes were managed by levers on the handlebars, a normal twist throttle and a lever next to the cowling for low, high, neutral and reverse.

He turned the key to light up the dash. A glance told him it was in neutral and fully charged. There was a slight hum emanating from the bowels of the vehicle. 'Come on, jump on!'

'I'll open the roller door first. Luckily it's facing the door.'

Jessica opened the door and Joe slowly turned the throttle. There was still no discernible engine noise. The quad started to move forward, creeping out into the daylight. Jessica jumped on the back of the bike. Joe left the gear selector in low and inched forward. He slowly opened up the throttle. The hum and speed increased; the response was virtually instantaneous. Joe turned down the hill away from the house and accelerated down the track leading to the bottom gate.

The fence line ran along the secondary road near the bottom of the gully. Across from the road was a creek. Joe could hear it running despite the drought. He noticed a pipe submerged in the creek running through a culvert under the road, through a pump house and continuing up the hill to the top of the property where two large water tanks stood. 'Permanent water. Apparently, there is a third tank for rainwater captured off the barn, shed and house.'

'And,' added Jessica, 'full solar power backed up by batteries. The place is not connected to the grid. There is also supposed to be a diesel generator and a diesel fire pump.'

'More study needed, my girl!'

'So, one camera in the north-east corner looking west across this lower frontage. The tree just over the fence line should do as a mounting point.' Joe rode over, placed the ladder against the tree and climbed. In minutes he attached the camera. 'We'll place the left side one in this tree as well. I'll angle it so it shows the back of the house.' The second camera soon joined the first. Nestled in two forks of the tree they were invisible from the ground.

Joe decided to try high range on the ride to the top of the property. Without the noise of an internal combustion engine it was an eerie experience. The torque of the electric motor was unlike any other vehicle he had ever piloted.

From the top of the property, running alongside a more substantial road, there was a view back down the slope encompassing the whole property. Joe placed one camera in a tree in the south-west corner facing east back down the road, and the second one in a different tree on the south-east corner facing north-west across the property.

Joe pulled the radio out of his pocket and called the house. 'Can you see all four on the computer?'

'Yep, looks good, nearly no blind spots. Best you are going to get with four cameras,' crackled the UHF radio in reply.

'OK coming back to the house. See you in ten minutes, once we have put everything away.'

I t was approaching midnight when the cameras relayed the glow of headlights approaching the property from the east. No one had gone to bed. They were all waiting for the General and the twins to arrive and report. There would be no sleep until they knew all the grisly details.

As the vehicle's lights passed the camera its right indicator began to flash. The large white van reduced speed, turned right and stopped at the locked gate. Joe jumped up and ran to the quad bike parked just outside the kitchen door. Invisible in the night, Joe followed the boundary until he was adjacent to the left-hand flank of the van. He dismounted from the bike, climbed over the fence and knocked on the left-hand sliding door of the idling vehicle stepping towards the rear as he did so.

The sliding door flew open, no one was in sight. 'Hey, General, Keith, Jodie, it's me,' yelled Joe before silently sliding round the rear of the vehicle.

'Stand down, son.' Joe recognised the General's voice. He returned to the left of the vehicle as the General and twins were dismounting.

'Good to see you, General, Jodie, Keith. Bad day at the office, I take it?'

'Had better. Open the gate so we can move out of sight.'

Joe opened the gate while the General and twins re-entered the van. 'The barn is open, drive straight inside. I'll meet you there.' The van went through and Joe relocked the gate before following on the quad bike into the barn on the far side of the house. Once inside, Joe closed the roller door and looked at the Bowman family.

They looked hollowed out, the day had taken its toll. 'Grab your stuff and follow me into the house. Hot showers and strong drinks and comfort food await.' Joe was desperate, as were the others, to know what had happened, but one look told Joe the new arrivals needed reviving first, and once they were comfortable, a debrief could be held.

Soon the team were all seated in the comfortable main room. The General described their day.

'So is Ms Bowman going to be OK?' asked Jessica.

'Most likely, but it will take a few months. She came out of surgery about five hours ago. The doc seemed quietly confident, but it's too early to tell. The AG lost his arm. We are the only ones who know his whereabouts. We will need to appraise the situation in the morning and consider how best to use his capture to our advantage. But first we need sleep.'

Joe spoke for the group, 'No worries, General, we'll take the watches tonight, you and twins catch some sleep. I take it you found the rooms OK?'

'Yep, all good. Days like this remind me I'm no longer as young as I used to be,' replied the General, before leading the twins away to their rooms.

Joe turned to Sara Jane and Tracey, 'Two hours on watch, two hours off, split by couples? Jessica and I will do the first shift if you like.'

Sara Jane and Tracey looked at each other before nodding their heads in agreement. 'Night, see you in a couple of hours.' Sara Jane led Tracey down the corridor to their room.

Joe led Jessica back to the lounge area. They had arranged the sofas so the computer screen showing the security cameras was visible. 'I'm tired but wound up tight. Won't be able to sleep until I can relax,' commented Jessica. She lay back against Joe on the sofa.

'I can relate to that, too much happening too quickly. My brain feels like it is trying to catch up, while the rest of me just wants to hide under the sheets for a couple of days,' he replied.

Slowly their hands started to wander over each other's bodies. 'How about a back massage? Lie on the sofa and take off your top,' Joe suggested. It seemed like a good idea to Jessica. They had two hours to fill.

Slowly, gently then urgently and demanding. They took each other away from the stress and demands of the world they now inhibited. For an hour or so there was only each other. Relaxed, breathing accelerated, a sheen of sweat covering their bodies, they rested.

'We better get our clothes back on before our shift ends,' suggested Jessica. Joe glanced at the clock hanging on the kitchen wall. There was less than twenty minutes left of their shift. She gathered her discarded clothes and quickly dressed. Joe did the same.

'What will happen to us when this is all over?' asked Jessica.

'This feels special, between us. It feels like it will last forever.'

'But, Joe, how do we know if what we have is just a reaction to the stress of our situation, or something that will survive in the normal world?'

'Well, Jess, I am so far out of my depth in this situation, I just don't know. But we need to stay positive and part of that is accepting what we have is real.'

'I guess you are right. It is easy to be overwhelmed by all this. In my mind I see us together in the future doing normal things, like walking the dog and going out to dinner. It's what's keeping me going.'

'Same here, same here.'

Holding each other they tried to imagine their future.

Jessica was first to return to the present, 'We better do a double check over the security footage. We were a bit distracted there for a while.'

They both returned to the computer. Jessica watched the live feed on one screen, while Joe scrolled back over the last hour and ran it through quickly.

Jessica nudged Joe's arm 'Look at this, what are those shadows? They don't move like people.'

Joe moved over to Jessica's screen. A mob of grey kangaroos was crossing the property, leaping the top and bottom boundary fences. 'They must be on their way to the creek,' Joe commented.

'Wow, that's not something you see in Sydney.'

'The drought probably means they have to travel considerable distance for water.'

A door slammed; exaggerated footsteps could be heard slapping down the hallway.

'Shift change, make sure I don't see anything I won't be able to unsee.' Sara Jane entered the room followed by Tracey.

'What's that?'

'Skippy and his mates going for a drink,' answered Joe.

'Who the fuck's Skippy?' asked Tracey yawning.

'You know *Skippy the Bush Kangaroo*, the old TV show from the 1960s.'

'Wow, the bastards can move. Look at that bloke standing watch. He has to be topping six feet, nearly two metres tall.' Sara Jane was watching the live feed.

'Time for us to hit the sack.' Joe stood and assisted Jessica up from the couch. 'I'll see you two at 4 am.'

The day started late. Joe had relieved Sara Jane and Tracey at 4 am. He stood the 4 am to 6 am watch himself, letting Jessica sleep. He had then snatched another two hours' sleep. After showering he staggered into the kitchen about half-past eight. The others were all gathered round the picture windows looking north towards the bottom of the property, across the back road to the stream. The mob of kangaroos had stayed. The water pumped from the stream up to the tanks on the south side; uphill from the house fed a drip irrigation system keeping the paddocks green even during the drought.

'The kangaroos will probably head into the bush once it heats up, but they are loving the green grass,' Jodie said.

'We should encourage them; they will act as a natural intruder alarm,' Keith added. 'We could also add some bird hutches in the trees and some natural bird food. Attracting a bunch of screaming galahs would be a bonus.'

Joe spoke up, 'Yeah, speaking of which, I installed some basic security yesterday, but I would like to work with you today on improvements, and ways and means of securing our communications.'

'Let's work on some comms first. We need information. It's the only way forward, but now we are static we can't afford to leave digital footprints everywhere, and that includes the library. We need to be totally off the fucking radar.' Keith wandered over to the whiteboard. 'I was thinking of using a laser transmitter to move our signal away from the property, then use a 5G modem to connect to a cell tower. Better still, use two or three far enough apart they use different towers. Joe, would you be able to set up dummy accounts to pay the Telcos?'

'Yeah, I'll have the bank in the Cayman Islands open us some Visa or Mastercard debit card accounts. As long as there is cash in the account, they should be fine. I'll use different names unrelated to this place.'

'OK, boys, you get the hardware mounted. Jessica, Sara Jane and Tracey, you're investigators, go into town and access some free wi-fi and start our research. We need to find them before they find us. We have the Foreman , Quentin Brightly and the Attorney-General as starting points. See if we can confirm Brightly as the head of the Syndicate here in Australia. While you are out, I'll nip down the road in the van so I can receive an update on Fi. Jodie can stand watch here, and I'll relieve her when I return.'

'Sounds like a plan, General,' agreed Jessica.

The General took a quick glance around the room, his eyes settling on Sara Jane. She was glaring at him intently. He had dealt with unexploded bombs before. 'It's a suggestion not an order. I know you are not military.' He added hastily, 'Even I'm not military as far as this goes.'

Sara Jane relaxed. 'Sounds like a good proposal to me. Keith, would it be digitally secure?'

'As long as you do not log on to any of your own internet sites. They could have tracers on them. If anyone was watching they would know you are alive. Though, at some stage that could be to our advantage.'

Joe looked around, 'Has everybody eaten? I'll just have a quick breakfast and be right with you, Keith. Jess, can you give Keith and me a lift into town so we can pick up the rental truck? We can source any additional equipment Keith needs once we are in the truck.'

'Yeah no worries,' replied Jessica.

After breakfast, Joe and Keith made their way to the barn. Keith led Joe to the white van, 'With a bit of luck there will be some sort of disguise in the van,' he said.

They opened up the van and began searching the various compartments built into the rear. Joe found magnetic signs that could be attached and removed and matching hi-vis vests carrying the logo of a major telecommunications company.

'OK, stage one, now let's go back inside. I will draw up a plan and then we can purchase the equipment. It should be fairly easy. I will use off-the-shelf stuff so we don't draw attention to ourselves. Joe, have you a clean way of purchasing the equipment?'

'Yeah, no problem, I'll use the Matthew Johnson identity, but let's make the purchases in Newcastle. It's a major city so we will be more anonymous.'

'Good call.'

It was a bit of a squeeze, but they all five of them managed to squeeze into the Subaru for the trip into Cessnock. They dropped Joe and Keith off first at the storage yard where the rental truck was parked. Jessica, Sara Jane and Tracey prepared to continue into town. 'Let's aim to have everyone back by four pm so we can share everything we have found,' Jessica suggested through the driver's window of the Subaru as she drove away.

'No room for discussion there, you two already married? I can see the white picket fence going up as we speak,' asked Keith innocently.

'At the moment a quiet suburban life is very fucking appealing,' chuckled Joe. 'OK, what do we need and where do we get it?'

'Electronics store, I dunno, try a supercentre. We can park once and shop around.'

'Gateshead, on the opposite side of the lake?'

'Yep, that should do it.'

Joe and Keith set off. Driving to the other side of Lake Macquarie would add an hour or two to their mission. But Joe could see the sense. The further they kept away from the property, the less chance of anyone finding them. The rental truck was air-conditioned and had automatic transmission. He could pretend he was a normal Joe doing a normal day's work for the next few hours. It would be like having a holiday!

*

'So, what's it like playing with the fireman's pole?' They hadn't even driven as far as the end of the street. She could still see the storage yard in her rear-view mirror. Jessica could understand why Sara Jane had been killed off twice so far.

She thought about Joe. What they had felt real, but was it real or a reaction to their circumstances? She was unsure. Jessica had had a few boyfriends, but nothing serious. Between school, sport then university and work, they had always been a side dish not the main course. She could feel her aspirations and ambitions changing. When she thought of her future, Joe was in it. The whole thing was very unsettling.

'When's the wedding? When are you going to make me an aunty? Every family needs an embarrassing aunty. I wouldn't even have to try hard,' taunted Sara Jane.

Jessica felt herself blushing. Sara Jane had hit home. It must be the insecurity of their predicament. 'Wow, you're actually blushing, Jess. What, this one more than a pleasant distraction? Tracey, I think big sis is serious about this bloke. Wow again, wait till I tell Mum and Dad. Dad will start knitting baby socks and Mum will be looking for her fucking shotgun.'

'Huh?' the last comment sparked Tracey's interest.

'Modern parents. Mum wants her daughters to have careers and conquer the world. Dad wants to play with the grandkids,' explained Sara Jane.

'Well Joe could be a house-husband and Jess could still work. "Ms

Jessica Marlowe NSW Police Commissioner." "Mr Joe, homemaker." Sounds pretty cool. She could give you all the scoops. Joe could stay at home and look after the kids. And I think after the last couple of weeks I might join him. I could be your nanny.'

'Then I would have to come and live up here as well. Someone's gotta keep the nanny out of trouble. You know, with a bit of this and a bit of this.' Sara Jane started tickling Tracey. Jessica could see where this was heading. She realised she should have made one of them sit in the front when Joe and Keith had exited.

'Thank God, here's the library carpark.' Jessica slotted the car into the first vacant spot she found. 'Come on, everybody out. Meet back at the car about three pm so we have plenty of time to get home.'

'Home now, is it? Not the base or property, but "home". Sister, you're gone hook, line and fucking sinker.' Jessica knew Sara Jane would have the last word. She didn't care, it was as though the teasing had forced her feelings for Joe out of her subconscious into the open. As she walked away, she was smiling to herself, no longer blushing.

Jessica would use one of the library's computers, Tracey and Sara Jane would use the one Joe had purchased in a café with wi-fi. First, Jessica logged onto the police intranet. With Ms Bowman out of the picture, she was wondering if she would be reassigned. She didn't know how much her commander knew of her work on the Task Force because it had been so secret.

Scanning her messages, she sighed. There was nothing significant there. She felt like a drowning person coming to the surface of the ocean and seeing the rest of the world continue on as though nothing had happened. On reflection, she realised she shouldn't be surprised. Her colleagues knew she was undercover on a special Task Force. They knew to stay clear. Next, she scanned the bulletins for the last few days. Again nothing, nothing about the Foreman's body, nothing more about the disappearance of the Bookkeeper, nothing about the closing down of the facility and nothing about the shootout in Goulburn. The whole lot of nothing was suspicious in itself. Someone was keeping the lid tightly clamped. She hoped it was someone from their side.

OK, thought Jessica, *let's have a look at the Attorney-General.* Jessica checked all the news sites she could access first, then the social media sites. There was not a lot. Apparently, he had suddenly retired due to ill health. He had then disappeared. She tried a Google search next, hoping to discover any rumours, conspiracy theories or innuendo floating around the web. Not much, just speculation; one source hinting he may have had a sudden cancer diagnosis costing him his arm. Neatly done, she guessed the General was responsible for that piece of gossip. She returned to the search engine.

Quentin Brightly, she typed. The man in the video had been wearing a mask, but his hands were clearly visible. She would start there. Quentin, it seemed, liked having his photo taken. She expanded a few images of his hands holding champagne glasses at various functions and events. She was looking for a crescent-shaped scar on the back of his left hand between the thumb and forefinger. And there it was. Not conclusive, but definitely enough to encourage further digging.

He was a darling of the Sydney glitterati. 'There for the opening of a dunny door if there is a camera present,' she whispered remembering the old slang cliché. 'Let's see what we can discover about his professional life.'

Jessica trolled through several sites. He sat on a few committees and semi-political investigations. He didn't appear to be doing much court work. In fact, as far as she could see he had only one case coming up for mediation. It actually seemed beneath him. Then she read some of the commentary. Then she read between the lines.

A pair of young men were suing the Rural Fire Service for damage to their vehicle. Some of the communities worst hit by the fires in the Central Coast hinterland were watching the case closely.

From what she could tell, the two young men were responsible for the Rural Fire Service being unable to back-burn and contain the Gospers mega-fire. For this reason, they had retained a Queen's Counsel. Quentin Brightly's job was damage control. 'Well I'll be fucked.' The Rural Fire Service had called Joe and Fred as witnesses. She read some more; it had happened at the café Joe liked to visit on his motorbike.

Joe and Fred were going to come face to face with Quentin Brightly.

CHAPTER 48

Jessica was hungry. Time to grab a bite to eat. It was hot and sunny outside. She decided to eat in one of the air-conditioned cafés in the mall across the carpark. Sara Jane and Tracey were somewhere in there, but she determined to stay away from them. Every little misdirection helped.

She decided on a sandwich and coffee. She was looking forward to Joe's cooking. She had no idea what he was going to prepare for dinner, and she didn't think he did either. She had a suspicion a bottle of red wine would be involved. Joe seemed to like a bit of marination, of the chef. She grinned at the thought.

The afternoon's research would start with one Joseph Burnett. Jessica finished her lunch and returned to the library. She searched for Joe Burnett; there wasn't much, and he had already told her all of it and more. She had been in the library long enough. She had no idea if anyone could backtrack her searches, but she had no intention of finding out the hard way. Now they had a semi-permanent base she could purchase some clothes. Living out of a suitcase had its limitations.

A pleasant hour later she wandered out of the shopping mall. She found a seat in the shade at the bus stop where she could see the car and prepared to wait for Sara Jane and Tracey. They were only five minutes behind her. She followed them to the car.

Standing instructions were to circle into the base, including one run along the road at the bottom of the hill. They couldn't risk being followed. 'Talk about the long way home,' grumbled Sara Jane.

'Operational security,' answered Tracey.

The rental truck was in the barn parked next to the General's van. The motorbike was gone. Inside the house Keith was in front of the computer screens. On one screen there was a panoramic view of the property, on the other an error message: No Internet connection.

Keith was speaking on a handheld radio. 'OK, the top button turns the laser red, press it.' Keith turned and yelled out the window. 'Jodie, ask Dad if he can see the red light. We need it to hit the receiver plate.'

Jodie could be heard passing the message on to her father.

'Joe's on the cliff, aiming the laser wi-fi at a receiver we have attached to the TV aerial. It will look like part of the aerial, and there is an uninterruptable line of sight to the transmitter. However, the plate is a few centimetres wide and Joe is about five kilometres away, so aiming the transmitter is really fiddly,' Keith explained to the newcomers.

'Wait, the software is starting to respond. We must be getting close.'

A muffled yell could be heard from outside. 'Dad can see the red dot on the receiver,' Jodie conveyed.

'The software is responding too.' Keith grabbed the radio. 'Joe, we need fine adjustment, use the Allen key on the vertical and horizontal grub screws. You need to move the focus up and to the left.

'Vertical first. Nearly there. Whoa, stop there. Now the horizontal. You're fifty per cent there. Twenty. Stop now!' Keith released the talk button on the radio. 'Jodie, ask Dad if the red dots are on the centre cross hairs of the plate.'

'He heard you, it's spot on, a bullseye.'

'That's it Joe, just turn off the red light, it was only for aiming. See you back here.' Keith switched the radio off. 'Jodie, tell Dad we are finished.'

Jessica walked into the kitchen; 'Hey everyone, let's have a debrief ten minutes after Joe returns. That'll give us time to have everything packed away.'

'You make the coffees; I bought a cake while we were in town,' piped up Sara Jane.

'Once we debrief. Then we can all have a rest and wash up before dinner,' finished Jessica.

'And a little private debrief,' added Sara Jane quietly to her sister.

Before Jessica could respond, Keith looked up from the computer screens, 'Joe's on the last lap, here in five minutes. Jodie, can you watch the screen. I'll go help Joe pack up.'

The shadows were beginning to lengthen, the seabreeze was beginning to trickle through and the edge came off the heat.

Jessica was in the kitchen facing the others in the open-plan lounge room. She waited for everyone to settle with coffee and cake. The whiteboard was equipped with a printer in its base. Joe saved and printed both sides in case his previous musings were pertinent. He wiped it clean.

'So, do we all agree? Is Quentin Brightly our number one candidate for the Australian boss of the Syndicate? What evidence do we have?' asked the General.

'He is on the Task Force's Guidance committee, which we know is compromised,' started Jessica.

'The Foreman also fingered him. And he had met The Boss in person, but with a mask. He has a significant amount of evidence on his computer. He was about to send Brightly a copy of that video with the kid,' added Joe.

'Didn't he send it?' asked Jessica.

'No, it was still in the unsent file.'

'I looked at as many photos as I could find. And the man in the video raping that child has the same scar on his hand as Brightly,' added Jessica.

'Well, do we all agree the next step is to push Brightly and see if he reacts?' asked the General.

'We examined his Facebook and other social and professional media accounts,' added Sara Jane, 'and the fireman is going to spend some quality time with him very soon.'

'Yes, I was about to bring that up,' Joe responded.

'While we were out and about today, I contacted Fred. The two of us are to appear at a mediation session to settle a claim by a couple of dickheads against the Rural Fire Service for damaging their car and causing personal stress and suffering. The media is frothing at the mouth, because these are the two wankers who stopped the back-burning the RFS was about to light to stop the Gospers mega-fire. The media wants someone to blame for the fire impacting the Central Coast and they are hoping to use this case as a bridge to blame the wankers or the RFS. So, these guys, realising they have dug themselves into a hole have engaged Quentin Brightly to represent them at the mediation hearing. Normally it would be way below his stature but the potential lawsuits and media coverage have upped the stakes considerably.'

'According to Fred, the RFS did not initially take this very seriously as it was only about a car window, so they decided to let Fred and I represent ourselves. I have told Fred to let everyone know I will be "returning to the country" in time for the hearing. With the Foreman gone, I can return from the dead, as he was the only bad guy who knew my identity. Fred has also contacted Tommy, the proprietor of the café where this happened and Tommy has sent Fred some CCTV clearly showing the wankers doing the pushing and shoving. We have not let them know we have the footage in case they drop the case. We could pay for the car window but I thought we could use this as an opportunity to spend some quality time with Mr Brightly. The mediation session is next Tuesday, five days from now,' concluded Joe.

'Brightly has had no previous contact with you or Fred?' asked the General.

'None, we don't move in the same circles,' answered Joe.

'So, we can keep things moving, hands up all those think this is a good idea,' asked Jessica.

There were no dissenters.

Joe wrote on the board, Joe and Fred to mediation.

Sara Jane stood and started speaking, 'Tracey and myself concentrated on his social calendar, which is quite busy. We found an event, the opening of an exhibition at an art gallery he will be attending as a sponsor. It is scheduled for a week on Saturday. We would like to buy some tickets.'

'Another chance to get in his face,' added the General.

Joe wrote on the whiteboard, Art Gallery function.

'I think we should resurrect the Foreman,' said Jessica.

Joe added Resurrect the Foreman to the whiteboard.

The General stood, 'I've called a meeting of the Task Force's Oversight committee, I have appointed myself Fi's stand-in, Jessica should come with me.'

Joe added Task Force committee to the list.

He then rubbed out the art gallery function and moved it to the bottom of the list. 'You know I think it's time we all indulged in a bit of culture. He would have seen us all individually and then to see us all together should give him a good old-fashioned kick up the arse.'

Joe drew a line under the task list he had just written.

'What else do we have?' he asked.

'I'll go first,' said the General.

'I spoke to the people looking after Fi and the Attorney-General. They are pleased with Fi's progress and believe she will make a full recovery in time. She will be recuperating there for a while yet. I was able to speak to her, and she is in good spirits and apparently working on the Attorney-General, well the ex-Attorney-General, since his shock resignation. She has convinced him she is his only hope of survival. He is singing like a bird, but it appears he was nothing but a tool, used by the Big Boss to assist in covering up the Syndicate's operations. He has admitted his instructions came through Brightly. So, you may want to add that to your list of evidence on the board.'

'Done,' replied Joe writing in another line at the top of the board.

'My people also were able to take control of the Fixer's body. Some of our friends in the intelligence services of our allies were able to provide an identification. He was a known KGB agent who was only starting his career when the Berlin Wall came down and the KGB was officially disbanded. What is not known is if he went private or became part of the one of the organisations the KGB morphed into, some of which are still not known. Speculation is rife within western intelligence services, many believing the Syndicate is controlled by forces within the current Russian hierarchy. A bit like a self-funding infiltration,' finished the General.

'I have one more suggestion,' added Jodie. 'Why don't Keith and myself start tailing Brightly. We can make it obvious. Just a bit more pressure.'

'Sounds like a good idea. I can't see us being able to take him down using the police and the courts. His overt and subverted influence would make it nearly impossible, so we have to force him into mistakes so his minions abandon him; then he will be exposed and we can present the evidence against him to the authorities. Come on let's all grab a rest and a shower. Tonight's for R and R, tomorrow we will start to put our plans into motion,' ordered the General.

The group broke up. Joe and Jessica made their way down the hallway to their room. 'I think I will have a swim. I've been sitting all day and need to stretch my muscles,' Jessica mused.

Joe agreed. 'I'll be in that. There's plenty of time. I'll throw together a BBQ for dinner tonight. It will set the right atmosphere, laid back and relaxed.'

'Why do I think it will involve red wine?' asked Jessica.

'I am assuming that's a rhetorical question, so I won't bother answering!'

Minutes later they were swimming lazy laps in the sparkling pool. Joe was wondering how he was going to keep it that way. What about the lawns? Could he get people in and maintain operational security?

He decided those were problems for another day.

'Incommminng.' Sara Jane landed with a bomb a couple of metres in front of him, followed by Tracey seconds later. 'Jess said you're going to be my brother-in-law,' she announced when she surfaced. 'I always wanted a brother to kick around.'

CHAPTER 49

The room faced east. The sun broke over the nearby hills and through the window just after five-thirty in the morning. Joe laid back in bed oddly content. Neither Jessica nor Joe had taken Sara Jane seriously; they knew not to raise to the bait. But Joe reflected that his life had changed. Was Jessica a permanent part of that now? He didn't know the answer. He was adrift in unchartered waters. Only time would tell.

But, looking out the window, it was clearly time to do some yard work. Lawns to mow, edges to trim, pool to clean and probably a hundred other jobs he would discover as he went along. He was actually looking forward to it; a bit of honest toil instead of all the planning and scheming. But first, coffee and some breakfast.

He quietly climbed out of bed, threw on some clothes, and headed to the kitchen. Jodie was just finishing up her watch, Keith was preparing to take the next two-hour shift. 'I'll have a coffee then do a run around the fence line, check for any signs of visitors,' Joe offered.

Keith looked up, 'Good idea, I'll watch from here, see if we have any blind spots in the CCTV coverage.'

Joe finished his coffee. He decided to take the electric quad bike. He would keep the speed down and not worry about the helmet and other protective clothing. Joe wandered over to the shed opposite the barn where the quad was stored next to its charger. It had charged up over the last few days, the charger was connected to the solar panels and battery pack so this would be a free ride. He rode over to the back door: 'Keith, I'll start from the fence adjacent to the north-west corner of the house and track down the hill to the north.'

'Gotcha,' replied Keith.

Joe also used the time to survey the property, not in terms of security but in terms of maintenance. It was something he had failed to consider when he purchased the place. He would need to consult the inventory, see what equipment had been included in the sale. Any extra trips into town were off the agenda. Joe was becoming bored of the 'Operational Security' mantra, but knew the moment they were blasé about it would be day the bad guys appeared on their doorstep.

A full circuit at a fast crawl took a bit over an hour. Joe had also stopped to take some photos of some maintenance issues. The mob of kangaroos watched him warily. The soundless quad and Joe following the fence lines put them at ease and they returned to munching the well-irrigated lawn. A pair of dirt bikes roared across the top road on the southern border of the property. The kangaroos scattered, jumping the fence and disappearing into the eucalyptus forest on the east and west boundaries. Joe stopped and listened; the dirt bikes could be heard disappearing into the distance. They had not hesitated as they passed the property. He relaxed; it was not unexpected. There would a steady stream of bikes heading into the forests around the area for a bit of fun.

The day had begun to warm up by the time he returned to the house. He went over to where Keith was sitting in front of the computer screen. Keith had drawn a rectangle on a piece of paper and sketched a rough representation of the property. By following Joe on the screen, he had been able to discover the blind spots in the CCTV coverage. He showed Joe. 'Here's one job for today. We need to position cameras to cover these blind spots.'

'Great, did you track the two dirt bikes that passed by on the top road?' asked Joe.

'Yes, worked fine tracking them coming and going, and was able to follow them for quite a while using the high-definition camera you placed on the cliff with the router unit.'

'So, we have internet as well?'

'Yes, through the 4G slash 5G network. We are using a focused beam to one tower so it cannot be triangulated but will only give its location as a straight line, and a long line at that, as we are not using the nearest tower. Though as an added precaution I would keep using TOR,' explained Keith.

Some of the team were still drowsy as they made their way into the kitchen. The night watches led to disturbed sleep. Joe looked around. 'Maintenance day, boys and girls. I'm going to do some gardening today. You are welcome to join me or have a rest day.'

'What about prepping for next week?' asked Sara Jane.

'Well, I'm up first with the mediation on Tuesday. Tomorrow I'll go into town and buy a suit. We need to take the truck back as well. Fred thinks we should turn up looking like executives. He's hoping the opposition will assume we are a pair of yahoos from the bush, so he wants to surprise them. His theory being, as we are representing ourselves, they will assume we are out of our depth and will be easy pickings. We don't plan to tell them about the footage from Tommy's, hopefully wrongfooting them again. Also, I was hoping to set up a burner with a message from the Foreman for Brightly, which I will send in the middle of the proceedings while we are watching Brightly's face.'

'There was an Oversight committee meeting for next Thursday, I'll confirm today,' added the General.

'The art exhibition will be the Saturday evening,' confirmed Tracey.

'How about we start surveillance from about halfway through the week prior to the exhibition?' asked Jodie.

'OK, that's our timeline in place. Let's start the day properly with eggs and bacon,' concluded Joe. Joe could see the General was tempted to lecture the team again about operational security, but looking at the group, hesitated, probably realising nagging would not help.

The two dirt bikes were parked on a fire trail five kilometres west of the property. They were looking at the playback from a Go-Pro video camera. It had been mounted on the helmet of the second rider. They had twisted it round so it no longer pointed forwards, but ninety degrees to the right.

'Reckon it was the same guy on the quad?' The second rider lifted his phone. 'The tracker from the truck shows it parked behind the house, probably in the barn.'

'Well according to this the job is still open. We on?'

'Maybe we should do a reccy first? We don't really know who he is. Just the job on that black site. How many you think are in the house? And did you see the cameras as we rode past?'

'For fuck's sake. We both agreed on this when we saw him yesterday at Gateshead. There was him and the other bloke. The target looks like a bloody accountant, though the other bloke looked pretty handy. Two of us, take them one at a time, should be cool.'

The first biker was looking at his phone. 'There's a fire trail down this side, just in from the fence in the forest. We could follow it down and attack from there.'

'Yep sounds like a plan.'

Keith was showing Joe the blind spots in their CCTV footage when a dozen or so kangaroos jumped the western fence and hopped across the property before disappearing into the forest on the eastern side. 'Something's spooked them,' muttered Keith.

Keith switched one of the screens to the feed from the cliff face looking down on the property. He zoomed in on the area to the right of the screen corresponding to the west side of the property.

Joe looked over Keith's shoulder, the two bikers could be seen dismounting from their bikes. 'I didn't hear a thing! We should have heard their bikes.'

'How the fuck did they get onto us?' asked Sara Jane to no one in particular.

'Dunno, the more urgent question is what are we going to do about it?' responded the General. 'They are obviously interested in us. But that's not a capital crime. We can't just kill them outright. We'll have to capture them, then decide. I think we need a bit of authority. Jodie, Keith, let's grab our uniforms make this look official. Someone make sure the two tasers are fully charged.'

Joe kept an eye on the screen. The two interlopers were making their way cautiously through the forest. They would be entering the property behind the barn.

Jessica scampered through the connecting door into the garage, returning with two tasers. She handed the second one to Tracey. 'You know how to use one of these?'

'Yes, we were trained on them.'

'Great, because I don't think anyone else here has any idea.'

Joe was watching the two men creep through the forest. 'As far as I can see they are unarmed.'

'OK, before they get any further let's go down behind the barn,' ordered Jessica, looking over Joe's shoulder. 'Sara Jane, take a radio, stay in touch with Joe.'

The three women left quietly. Joe scrolled back and used the mouse to reposition the video feed. He split the screen so he could bring a second camera online, looking down the fence from the house. Between the two views he could see the four sides of the barn.

'They are coming out of the woods and are approaching the fence. Still no sign of weapons. One of them is caught on the barbed wire strand across the top of the fence. The second one climbed across OK,' Joe reported. He watched Jessica and Sara Jane come around the barn from one side while Tracey stayed around the corner of the third.

The radio came alive. Sara Jane must have hit transmit. 'Hello, boys,' she crooned, 'what can we do for you this lovely day? Barbed wire's a bitch, isn't it guys?'

The two bikers stopped and starred at Jessica and Sara Jane who were smiling at them. Tracey snuck out from behind the barn, stepped lightly up behind the intruder who had crossed the fence, held the taser to the back of his neck and pulled the trigger. He fell to the ground shuddering. His mate was shocked into action and tore himself free of the fence stumbling to the ground beside his shuddering partner. Jessica pulled her taser out from behind her back and fired.

Both women withdrew the prongs back into their tasers. Tracey then produced a pistol she had tucked into the waist of her jeans. 'Get up and walk towards the house.'

Joe watched the procession approaching the house on the screen. He heard a sound behind him, turned and saw the General return to the room in full uniform followed quickly by the twins.

The General took a seat at the head of the dining-room table flanked by his offspring. The screen door opened, the two bikers wobbled into the room, followed by the three women.

'Take a seat,' ordered the General gesturing to the foot of the table. 'Who do you work for, the Russians or the Chinese?'

'No one,' stammered the man on the left.

'Bullshit, this is a top-secret military facility,' the General replied sternly.

'We planted a tracker on the rental truck when we saw that bloke in Gateshead yesterday.'

'Why?'

'Because there was a reward offered for him on the site.'

'What site?'

'It's a black internet site where you can pick up standover jobs and the like.'

'That job was cancelled,' added Joe.

'What do mean?' asked the second intruder.

'The guy who placed the ad got cancelled. Hollow point to the back of the head. I guess he wasn't able to delete the ad after I deleted his fucking brain,' sneered Tracey.

'Take their phones. Pull out the batteries and the SIM cards. Throw the phones in a bucket of water and destroy the SIM cards. Grab the keys for their bikes, we can hide them in the shed or the barn. We will need to call HQ; these guys will have to disappear for a while,' added Jodie.

'You're not burying them on my place,' chirped in Joe.

'At ease team. I'll just make a call,' said the General.

He left the room, returning ten minutes later.

'Get him to write down the name of that site. We need to take that ad down,' Jessica said.

'Give it to her,' demanded Sara Jane, jabbing the reloaded taser in the leader's face.

Jessica passed him a piece of paper and a pen. 'Write. Plus, the log on instructions. Joe, you still have the Foreman's login somewhere. If we log on as him, we should be able to take the ad down. Otherwise every idiot under the sun is going to try for a piece of you.'

Joe took the piece of paper over to the computer. He opened TOR on one screen and the Foreman's files on the other. Using the Foreman's details, he erased the ad. It made him feel like a free man!

The General returned. 'I have arranged for a vehicle to meet us around 1400 hours this afternoon; they will take these two bozos into custody. There was some duct tape and cable ties in the shed we can use to secure them. We will have to leave around noon to make the rendezvous.'

'What about a lawyer?' stammered one of the prisoners. His accomplice was starting to cry.

'This is a black national security operation. We don't deal with lawyers. You ceased to exist when you crossed that fence. Have a nice day,' concluded the General.

'How did our bounty hunters fair?' asked Joe.

'They're spending some quality time with the ex-Attorney-General,' replied the General. 'What time are you leaving in the morning?'

'About 6 am. I'll pick up Fred and we'll travel down together. Jessica and Keith have checked and the Subaru is still clean.'

'Well, take an early look-out shift tonight. You'll need a good night's sleep.'

'Did you load the emails from the Foreman?' asked Jessica. 'Don't use that phone for anything else except the Foreman and make sure it is turned off, the battery and SIM card removed.'

'Got it.'

Joe watched the security screens from 8 pm to 10 pm, before Jessica and he turned in for an early night. He had set his alarm for 5 am.

Tuesday morning. Joe woke with the dawn. He switched his alarm off before it rang. Jessica stirred and rolled over; Joe kissed her before heading to the bathroom. Within twenty minutes he was climbing into the new suit they had purchased on Saturday. Dark charcoal, with a faint blue pin stripe, white shirt with a conservative tie and a pair of shiny black shoes. 'Wow, I look like an accountant. Funny I never dressed like this when I was an accountant.'

'What did you wear back in your wheeler-dealer days?' asked Jessica.

'Jeans and a shirt. I was strictly backroom. As all the deals were done internationally, it was all by phone. Plus, I was in the internet, media tech business. No one who wanted to be taken seriously ever wore a suit.'

'Well, good luck, and give my love to Fred. I'm going to catch an extra hour of sleep if I can. Sara Jane and Tracey want to do some training today. It's bound to be painful.'

Joe kept the speed down as he headed to Fred's house. He was a little early so he cruised past his house on the lake. The house was looking neat and tidy. He hoped he would be able to move back in soon, but at least the maintenance company he had hired was looking after the place.

'Morning, sunshine,' beamed Fred as he jumped into the car. 'Ready for our big day?'

'Wouldn't have bothered except to get close to Brightly. With the media coverage they've received so far, I reckon they are going to want to shut the whole thing down as quickly and quietly as possible.'

'Yeah, idiots, the Rural Fire Service and the Government are looking to point the finger. The media needs someone to blame, and these turkeys dream up this stupid claim. So now the focus is on them, talk about digging yourself a hole. I suppose that's typical of their arrogance. So used to Daddy and Mummy's money shielding them, they are surprised when reality bites them on the arse. Pushing this so far for some sort of petty intimidation has backfired spectacularly.'

'I'm guessing they will try and settle in about five minutes. They'll drop the claim as long as we agree to silence,' mused Joe.

'Mate, I had my mechanic quote me to replace the window. The window's about five hundred bucks, but it costs a grand to have a Porsche dealer fit it. So, I have fifteen hundred in cash in my pocket. I'm happy to pay up and then talk to the press.'

'With you on that, Fred. But I'll cover the cost of the window. I broke it. It was worth every cent.'

'Here's the entrance to the expressway. Sydney here we come.'

As friends do, they chatted and joked their way through the two-hour drive. 'That's the building.'

Fred pointed to a newish office block in central Sydney. 'There's a parking station across the way, we can leave the car there, and since we are early, we can grab a coffee and a pastry.'

'Sounds like a plan!'

They parked the car, wandered over to the café, ordered coffee and pastries and watched the crowd shuffling into the surrounding office buildings.

'Do you ever miss it?' asked Fred.

'At the time it was exciting,' answered Joe. 'Afterwards, I really enjoyed the quiet time living by the lake. But it all feels a lifetime ago, hardly real compared to the present dramas.'

'Anything for the quiet life,' agreed Fred ruefully.

'Yeah, boredom never sounded so good.' They both grinned.

Joe looked at his watch. 'Time to go up'.

As they had prepaid, they stood, left a tip, crossed the road and walked into the marble foyer of the building opposite. 'It's at the solicitors office on the sixth floor,' Joe said as he pushed the lift button.

The solicitors leased the whole floor so the reception desk was immediately in front of them as they exited the lift. 'Fred Shan and Joe Burnett here for a mediation session,' announced Fred.

'Please follow me,' replied the receptionist. 'Your session will be held in meeting room two.'

They entered a generic meeting room. 'Looks like we don't even rate a fancy boardroom,' commented Fred after the receptionist had shut them in the room.

'Grab the seats in the middle of the table in front of the window. They are going to keep us waiting as a bit of a power trip. The expectation is we will stand around waiting for them to enter and let them give us permission to sit. But we can turn it against them,

I'll open the blinds so the natural light is behind us. We'll be seated with our folders open and won't stand when they enter. We'll make them feel as though they have been sent to the headmaster's office. Leave your jacket on as well.'

Fred grinned. 'The Joe Burnett in its natural habitat,' he quipped in a really bad David Attenborough accent.

Joe grinned back.

A solicitor entered the room and sat at the head of the table. 'Bob Simmons, I'll be your mediator today, I'll be chairing this meeting and minuting any decisions made.'

'No worries,' responded Joe and Fred together.

Ten minutes later, Joe noticed the mediator looking at his watch and scowling. Joe could see he didn't appreciate being kept waiting. There was a knock on the door and the receptionist poked her head in. 'Here are the rest of the attendees Mr Simmons,' she said speaking to the head of the table.

'Send them in,' he ordered.

Quentin Brightly and the two young men entered the room. No one stood. They milled around for a few seconds until Brightly guided them to seats opposite Fred and Joe. Brightly was dressed in a dark power suit; the two young men in designer jeans and shirts.

'Let's get started,' Simmons broke the silence.

'Because of the trivial nature of this matter, normal practice is to attempt mediation and avoid wasting the court's time. I take it Mr Shan and Mr Burnett will be representing themselves and Mr Brightly QC will be representing Mr Spencer and Mr Jamieson.'

'Can all parties please state their names, ages and occupations for the record.'

'John Spencer, twenty-three, marketing exec.'

'Robert Jamieson, twenty-three, social media consultant.'

'Fred Shan, fifty-eight, GP.'

'Joe Burnett, thirty-two, accountant.'

'Thank you, gentlemen. Brightly would you please begin the proceedings.'

'Thank you, Mr Simmons. First of all I would like to request that the outcome of this session be kept confidential.'

'No,' said Joe.

'No,' said Fred.

'Gentleman, all comments to be addressed through the Chair. Mr Shan or Mr Burnett can you state your reasons for not agreeing to confidentiality.'

'We won't be part of a cover-up. This matter is already part of the public record,' said Joe. Fred nodded in assent.

'Mr Brightly, please continue.'

'Mr Spencer and Mr Jamieson claim they were assaulted and abused by Mr Shan and Mr Burnett while trying to purchase coffee. They claim compensation for a broken window on Mr Spencer's car plus damages for assault and damages to their reputations, due to unfounded rumours spread by Mr Shan and Mr Burnett.'

'Mr Shan or Mr Burnett, do you have a response?'

'Yes, Mr Chairman, we have the CCTV footage from Tommy's café where the alleged events occurred. Can Fred connect his phone to your AV system?'

'I'll have our IT guy hook it up, if you don't mind,' replied the chairman. He reached behind and pressed a key on the phone behind him, 'Can you send Angus in, we need the AV set up.'

'Objection, we were not advised about this video footage.'

'This isn't a court of law, Brightly, we are here to determine the facts not who has the most expensive lawyer.'

A young man entered the room, Fred handed over his phone. 'No problems, this is simple.' He turned the system on, pressed a few buttons on Fred's phone. 'Done, what you see on your phone's screen will be duplicated on that screen on that wall.' He pointed to a screen behind the chairman.

'Thanks, Angus. Let's have a look, shall we.'

Fred ran the footage on his phone. With Tommy's café being remote, it had a high-end CCTV system so the images were clear and high definition. There was no sound.

It started with Tommy pointing and gesturing at two men standing beside a Porsche SUV. It was obvious he was asking them to go, and they were refusing. Two trail bikes were seen entering from the right side of the screen, the riders wore yellow, with the initials RFS in large black print on their chests.

They parked their bikes and walked up beside Tommy. There was some talk and gesturing. One of the two protagonists was seen to push one of the RFS riders. He was seen falling beside the far side of the SUV with his arms windmilling. The other rider pointed to the torch on his helmet, the two men looked round jumped in the SUV and sped off the screen to the left.

'Well, that was pretty conclusive,' said the chairman.

Joe hit send on the phone in his pocket. Quentin Brightly's phone pinged, he looked down towards the top of his thigh.

He had been keeping it on his thigh so he could surreptitiously follow his messages. He jerked upright, his face went white and he pushed back from the desk. His phone fell on the floor.

'Looks like you just heard from a ghost, mate!' grinned Joe.

Brightly bent down, snatched up his phone, stood and went to leave the room. 'I have to deal with this,' he said over his shoulder as slammed the door behind him.

There was silence in the room.

'Let's continue,' said the chairman.

'The vid's a fake. They pushed us around and deliberately smashed the window,' shouted Jamieson.

'Why?' said Joe.

'Through the Chair please, gentleman,' interjected Simmons, 'answer the question'.

'They are trying to blame us for their incompetence, saying we stopped the back-burning, that was supposed to stop the fire.'

'Can one of you please explain?'

'Yes,' said Joe. 'There was a weather window the RFS could use to burn off the fuel in front of the Gospers mega-fire. Defying restrictions these two snuck into the area for some "selfies" for their social media profiles. One of the reconnoitre teams found their vehicle. For their safety the back-burn was stopped until we could find and evacuate them. They were not located until the next day. The weather window had closed as the westerly airstream and high temperatures had returned and the back-burn could no longer go ahead. It took another two weeks to control the fire, in that time it burnt huge areas of the Central Coast hinterland. Causing millions in extra damage and incalculable suffering to those impacted.'

'Would the back-burn have worked?'

'The incident control team estimated a seventy-five to eighty per cent chance of success,' responded Fred.

'Bullshit. And who cares about some bogans living in the back of nowhere,' commented Spencer.

The room went silent. The two young men looked around like rabbits in the headlights. Joe hoped they wouldn't be smart enough to shut up.

'It was a pratfall. You damaged my Porsche. Nobodies like you know you will never have one, so attack your betters whenever you can. What do you drive, eh what do you drive?'

'Subaru,' said Joe.

'Falcon, bought it when I was twenty, it was fifteen years old then.'

'Shitbox,' sneered Jamieson.

'Hold on,' said Simmons. 'That would make it about a 1970 model?'

'Yes, it was the spare automatic GT that didn't race at Bathurst in 1969,' said Fred.

'Don't start him on his car. We will be here all day,' said Joe laughing.

'I was going to buy the wife a Porsche Mecan,' Fred continued, 'but she said "No", she thought it would be bad for business.'

'You're a GP?' asked Simmons

'Yes, but the wife and kids run the four medical centres we own. She thought being seen by the patients in such a car would be bad for business.'

'OK, well I can't see car envy as a viable excuse. And I do see an assault against Mr Burnett. Do we need to continue?'

'No, we're cool. We will not be taking the matter any further,' said Joe, Fred nodded in agreement.

Mr Simmons turned to face the two young men. 'I would advise you two to keep your mouths shut.'

He looked at Spencer and Jamieson for a minute. They couldn't meet his eyes. 'Matter closed then.' Spencer and Jamieson stood and left the room without a word.

Fred's phone was still connected to the AV equipment. Angus entered the room preparing to disconnect it.

'Any photos of the car on there?' asked Simmons pointing at the phone.

Fred flicked through some photos of the car and his family.

'Wow, she's something special,' sighed Angus.

Joe wasn't sure if he meant the car or Fred's daughter.

CHAPTER 52

'Anything else you want to do while we are in town?' asked Fred.

'Nothing comes to mind,' replied Joe. 'Let's reclaim the car and hit the road. We can stop at Tommy's on the way through and grab some lunch. I'm sure he would like to know how it went.'

'Won't the others want to know about Brightly's reaction?'

'I was filming him with my own phone.' Joe pointed to his top shirt pocket; his phone could be seen protruding out of the breast pocket. 'I forwarded it to a secure email account Keith opened for us while you rev heads were drooling over your car.'

'Wow, that was some reaction. What did the message say?'

'Thanks for the redundancy package, having a great time splashing your bitcoins around. The Foreman. Would have shaken him on a number of levels. Firstly, he thought he had hidden his identity from the Foreman, then he's contacted on his personal mobile number, and now he knows the Foreman has accessed his bitcoin account. I'm guessing he had the Bookkeeper manage that for him. Now the Bookkeeper has disappeared as well. As far as the Syndicate is concerned, Brightly is the one who has stolen their funds. Including a screen shot from the video of him raping that child would've been the clincher.'

'So, what happens next?'

'We'll have to wait until we get home. You haven't seen the new place, have you, Fred? We'll stop off on the way to your place and have a bit of a debrief.'

They escaped the city before the lunchtime crowds swarmed onto the pavement. A quick lunch at Tommy's and Joe and Fred returned to the base just after two in the afternoon. 'I'm sure we were going around in circles for the last ten minutes,' claimed Fred.

'That's because we were. I was checking for tails and so was whoever has look-out duty at the moment,' explained Joe.

'Makes sense.'

Joe nosed the car through the top gate, rumbled down the hill and parked in the barn. 'Impressive, nice spread,' commented Fred. 'Though never imagined you as a country squire.'

The team were gathered in the main room. Although they had all seen the video, they wanted to hear the live report. Joe filled in the details while Fred mingled with the crew.

'So, what next?' asked Jessica.

'We need to reconvene the Oversight committee. Now we have a new Attorney-General, there should be no more stonewalling and misdirection. As Fi's replacement, I have made an appointment with him on Thursday morning. He will be flying up to Sydney. I have requested the committee be there. It will be interesting to see who shows up. Jessica, you will be coming with me.'

'But, General, were you ever made Ms Bowman's official replacement on the Task Force?'

'It's not a problem, Tracey. There is no one in a position to refute my claim. It is, as you know, an undercover operation, so the people who know about it are limited. I'll use the secrecy to drop myself in the role. I'll just announce that as Fi's commanding officer it is my responsibility.'

'I didn't know you were Ms Bowman's commanding officer?' queried Jessica.

'I'm everyone's commanding officer,' responded the General. 'But I wasn't going to explain specifics with them.'

'Do we know much about the new Attorney-General?' asked Joe.

'I have had Intelligence have a dig around. They haven't found anything, but as you can appreciate it had to be done on the quiet. Not knowing who has been compromised by the Syndicate and Brightly does handicap us to a certain extent. Thursday's meeting should hopefully stir things up a bit. Then on Saturday evening, we all have tickets to the art gallery event, possibly a good time for Sara Jane to introduce herself. Afterwards we will keep him under surveillance.'

Later Joe was dropping Fred home. 'Come in, Chitra would love to see you. No idea if the kids are in or not.'

Joe agreed. 'Yeah, I need to make sure you are not spoiling my dog.'

'Hi, Joe, lovely to see you,' Chitra, Fred's wife, greeted him as he was taking his shoes off in the entrance way. Joe hadn't seen her for a while. She was petite with greying hair, deep, brown, wise eyes and a love of bright clothes. Before he could answer an energised bundle of fur skidded around the corner on the tiled floor and crashed into Joe's legs. 'Hey, old mate, how are you going?' Joe knelt down and hugged his dog.

'Can you stay for dinner?' asked Chitra, 'We haven't seen you in ages and you look like you've lost a few kilos. We can't have that. Fred tells me you have been hanging around with the Commander with no name? His twins were about the same age as our two and seemed to spend most of their time at our place while their parents were out saving the world.'

'He's a General now,' added Fred. 'Still doesn't have a name, and Keith and Jodie have turned out to be chips off the old block. Army to the core. Old mate you want a beer?'

'Yeah why not?'

'In fact, stay the night, just tell them you will see them in the morning. Doctor's orders!'

'Robert and Amy are still at work. Both now working in the business. I can put my legs up and let them get on with it these days,' said Chitra, 'Robert completed his Master of Business Administration and Amy is just completing her internship as a general practitioner. They should be home any minute.'

'No worries, I'll just let the General know.' Joe ducked out and called the base, happy they now had secure communications.

'Can I have a shower? These days I've been keeping a change of clothes in the Subaru,' asked Joe.

'Yeah, use the guest room down the back. It's got an ensuite,' answered Fred.

While Joe was changing, he heard a car pull up, doors opening and closing, and people entering the house. 'Hey Mum, hey Dad, we're home,' he heard a young man yell, 'Hey isn't that Joe's car parked out front?'

Shit, thought Joe, *half the peninsula knows the car.* He dressed quickly and walked back into the kitchen. 'Can I slip the Subaru round the back; I'd like to keep a low profile.'

'Good thinking,' replied Fred. 'I should have thought about that when we arrived.'

While Joe was moving the car Chitra turned to Fred, 'Things still a bit iffy? I know you were trained to handle this shit, but how is Joe handling it?'

'You could say he is out of his comfort zone, but he is turning out to be a bit of a natural. I think he has found love as well.'

'Speaking of which, Amy would love to hear how Keith is doing.'

'What?'

'You stupid man, Amy has Keith pegged as the world's most eligible bachelor. They have been together for a couple of years now,' chuckled Chitra.

'But, but, how and when did that happen?' stuttered Fred.

'She has had a crush on him since way back when they were kids. They caught up while she was away at uni, and Amy decided he was hers.'

Fred grinned, 'So *Amy decided*, poor Keith, bugger didn't stand a chance.'

Joe re-entered the kitchen through the back door.

There was another knock on the door. 'Wait here until I check out who it is,' said Fred, opening up the security feed on a screen mounted on the wall. 'Speak of the devil, it's the man himself, Keith.'

Light feet were heard running down the stairs and Amy rushed past, opening the front door wide and throwing herself into Keith's arms. 'I was so glad to discover you were in the area,' she gushed.

'Come in, Mum and Dad will be pleased to see you, and Dad's mate from the RFS is staying for dinner as well.'

'Hi, Keith, is it? Joe Burnett,' Joe stood and extended his hand. 'You remind me of a bloke I had breakfast with. I'm amazed the General let you out.'

'Dad's a pushover; Mum's the tough one,' replied Keith with a smile.

'So, everyone knows everyone?' asked Robert entering the room, 'And let me guess, if you tell us how, you will have to kill us?'

Joe glanced round. You could see Amy and Robert were Fred and Chitra's children. They were a bit taller than their parents, and had beautiful toffee-coloured skin and black hair: Amy's straight and long, Robert's short and complimented by a short beard. Soulful brown eyes, with dark lashes. Amy was a touch shorter than her brother: her body was curved, his was harder. When she smiled at Keith, Joe could see he did not have a chance.

'Pizzas!' said Fred. 'And more beer.' He turned to his children, 'So how was your day?'

'Not too bad,' replied Amy, 'There were a couple of patients who asked for me specifically today, which made me feel I'm being accepted.'

'And I did some more work on the Allied Health proposal,' answered Robert.

'Why don't you give us a brief presentation?' suggested Fred, 'I would be interested in hearing Joe's views.'

'Actually, I would like that, maybe he has a suggestion. It would be good to move this forward,' replied Robert.

'Let's all grab some fresh drinks and sit down.' While the others sat in the open-plan lounge room, Robert took a position leaning against the kitchen's island counter.

Smart, thought Joe, *he has taken command of the room, standing and, as the centre of attention, he now controls the discussion.*

Robert started. 'The building next to our Morisset Medical Centre has come up for sale. It used to be a bank with offices upstairs. My proposal is we buy it and convert it into an Allied Medical Centre. Then our doctors could send referrals to our physios, our psychologists, our dieticians and so forth. In other words, vertical integration. At the moment we refer them to other practitioners.'

'The problem is, Dad does not believe we should be referring to ourselves. He feels it is a conflict of interest and could lead to over-servicing.'

Fred interrupted, 'I would also like to use the space to employ more doctors. Our wait times are blowing out and our existing practitioners are struggling. I'm seeing a couple of them are starting to become quite stressed.'

Amy responded to her father, 'But Dad, the issue is not space, it's finding the doctors. There are three vacant rooms on my floor and four on the floor above. And, it's not just us, in fact we are one of the best staffed practices in the region. Some are really struggling.'

'Your father has always treated his staff like family,' added Chitra. 'It pays dividends, we are now a favourite employer. But our patients need to come first, so your Dad has also demanded high service standards.'

Robert continued, 'Which all adds up to decreased margins, which is why I am suggesting the additional revenue streams.'

'Maybe use a different approach,' suggested Joe. 'Purchase and renovate the building, but become the landlord, rent the rooms to allied health practitioners, provide the services such as booking, billing and reception, and leave the practitioners to run their own businesses. You could have shared facilities such as a gym and possibly a hydrotherapy pool the practitioners could book as required.'

'A managed suite type of model?' asked Robert.

'Yeah, something like that,' said Joe.

'What about quality of service?' asked Amy

'Well allied health practitioners wouldn't be part of the same company, so the only reason you would be referring patients to a particular practitioner would be quality of service,' mused Robert. 'We could also write service quality expectations into the service agreement. I like it. It would reduce our administration burden as well. Thanks, Joe.'

'Maybe we should think of asking Joe on board as a consultant?' suggested Fred, secretly pleased. His children had identified the problem, sought advice, accepted the advice and formulated a solution to the problem all without any assistance from him. Now he just needed to organise for them a guiding hand they respected and would listen to, and his retirement was a step closer.

'I need to free up some time first,' Joe replied.

'I'm for it,' added Chitra.

'Me too,' responded Amy.

'I'm in,' was Robert's reply. 'But, the first step is negotiating the purchase of the building.'

'Let me know how it goes. The pizza should be here soon. More beer anyone?'

Chitra looked at Fred, 'Nearly time to buy those golf clubs'.

CHAPTER 53

It was the next morning. Joe was having breakfast at Fred's house. He had let Keith return to the base ahead of himself. Keith had spent the night with Amy, obviously with Fred and Chitra's blessing. Joe realised Keith and Amy's relationship must be serious and long term. 'What are you going to do with property out in the sticks?' asked Fred. 'I can't see you living out there.'

'I dunno, it was a corporate convention centre and I purchased it as an ongoing concern. So once we have this mess sorted, I think I will move home, find some managers and see if I can ramp up the business side of it.'

'Keith has suggested it might be a nice place for Amy's and his wedding,' ventured Fred.

'Well, I can't see it being a big jump from corporate retreat to wedding venue. The big issue is sorting this mess out, so we can return to our normal lives. Though unknowing and unseeing some of the things I've seen and now know after the last few weeks is going to be difficult,' mused Joe.

'Changed your world view?'

'Yes, I knew in abstract that shit like this must go down, but not in Australia and not under my fucking nose.'

'Yes, Joe, I wish I could say otherwise. Unlike in the movies or TV, going back to your normal life after a clusterfuck like this is not going to happen. We will need to spend some time together. Post traumatic stress disorder is a real possibility.'

'What about the others?'

'They will as well. Everyone involved is going to be affected by this. It is worse for you "civilians". The professionals should have the training these days to know they will need counselling. You civilians will be the ones trying to tough it out,' replied Fred.

'Thanks, doc, I better be on my way. Thanks for last night.'

Joe returned to the property via the usual circular route. He was sure he did not have a tail, but they could not take any risks. He knew a member of the team would be monitoring his progress to ensure he was not being followed. A small box was sitting in the centre console and was monitoring the car electronically, searching for any signals or unexpected transmissions in case a bad guy had placed a tracking device on the Subaru.

Joe was looking forward to reuniting with Jessica. He hadn't meant to be away for the whole night, but it was hard to say 'No' to Fred and Chitra, especially after Fred's help the previous day. He found Jessica in the makeshift gym they had assembled in the garage, training with her sister and Tracey. 'Want to join us?' Jessica asked.

'Maybe later, first I need a shower and a coffee,' answered Joe.

'Well now you're back the General will probably want to detail tomorrow's escapade.'

'No worries, I'll be in the main room in ten minutes.'

Joe was back in seven minutes, showered and changed. He thought his beard could do with a trim; he would prefer to shave it off completely, but he just needed that extra bit of anonymity at the moment.

The team had gathered in what Joe called their briefing formation. The speaker in the kitchen on the far side of the island bench, the rest of the team in the lounge room seated on the sofas and the dining-room chairs.

The General was to conduct this briefing. He had taken his position behind the island bench. The rest of the team made themselves comfortable.

'Good morning all,' started the General. 'Let's get started.'

'As some of you will know, Jess and myself had a planning session last night to decide how we should let tomorrow play out. So tomorrow, Jess and myself will travel to Sydney and hold a meeting with the new Attorney-General and the committee's Queen's Council Quentin Brightly. We have two agendas: the first is to reopen the investigation into the Syndicate's operations in Australia and bring the new Attorney-General up to speed. The second agenda is to increase the pressure on Brightly. The first is the cover and overt reason for the meeting, the second is the primary but covert reason for the meeting. Does that make sense?'

The audience nodded in agreement so the General continued. 'The meeting will also provide Jess with an opportunity to let Brightly know how much of his organisation we now control. My suggested strategy is to inform him we have the Foreman, the Bookkeeper and the Attorney-General. I will also detail who the Fixer was, his history and that we have beaten him twice, the second time killing him. We will not be accusing Brightly outright, the evidence we have is circumstantial and a lot of it would be inadmissible in a court case as we gathered it illegally. Our intention is to spook Brightly into making a mistake.'

'He's a QC, which I suppose is about as senior as you can be as a lawyer. Aren't you worried he will see you coming and set an ambush?' asked Joe.

'The General and I believe he has run out of resources and doesn't have the skill set or the stomach to take us on directly,' replied Jessica, walking round to stand beside the General. 'In fact, our research shows a man who has never had to deal with real pressure his whole life. His wealth and position in society have always cleared the path for him. A situation he has always exploited. We are hoping by keeping up the pressure we can force him to run, force him to run to the Syndicate's offshore facility.'

'Do we know it actually exists?' asked Jodie.

'All the evidence points to it being a container ship sailing a route round the western Pacific. We strongly suspect, and conversations with the detainees we rescued from the facility confirm our suspicions, that a number of other detainees were transferred out of the facility in a pair of modified forty-foot shipping containers. They were transported by road to Newcastle harbour where they were loaded onto a small freighter. The freighter was away from harbour for about ten days, returning empty. Harbour records show this freighter regularly follows the same routine. However, inquires of all ports it could possibly reach come up negative. It does not seem to unload anywhere. Hence we suspect it is the Syndicate's supply ship.'

Jessica let the information sink in for a minute or two. 'However, it is a landing barge style of vessel, so it could beach on a supposedly uninhabited island or coastline, or in some natural harbour, and off-load the container using its own cranes, but the harbour records show voyages of varying length, whereas if they were frequenting the same harbour, we would see some consistency.

'We also looked at the problem from the angle of the most efficient way to run their operation, and a small container ship again appears the most logical. A land-based operation would also be subject to the legal system of the host nation, which would need to be managed through bribery, fear and corruption.'

'Maybe he will just leave the country,' suggested Sara Jane.

'That is a possibility, and we have an alert out to all airports and ports. He is to be stopped from leaving the country. On Saturday evening after the art exhibition he will receive a call from one of his minions in Philippines' Customs letting him know his passport has been flagged by Interpol. We will also be keeping him under observation. If he looks like using some other route out of the country, we will pick him up and let the General's people have a chat with him.'

'So, Jess, how will he run?' asked Jodie.

'He has purchased a sailing vessel, a forty-one-foot German production boat called a Hanse. Seaworthy and easy to sail single-handedly. He has used a company to purchase it, but it was one we had already identified,' continued Jessica.

'So how do we track him? I don't know much about boats,' asked Joe.

'While Dad and Jessica are in their meeting, I will go down to the marina and make sure the AIS is permanently on,' replied Keith. 'We can use it to track the boat, without planting any device. All commercial ships must have their AIS activated at all times. We will be able to track it from below the horizon and we should see the rendezvous on AIS,' explained Keith.

'For us landlubbers, what's AIS and how will follow him?'

'AIS stands for Automatic Identification Systems. Each vessel over a certain tonnage has a transponder that is linked into the system. Anyone can view it online. In fact, if we could discover the AIS signature of the offshore processor we could follow them and even backtrack their path. But there are hundreds of ships in that region of the ocean. The only reason a cargo vessel can turn off its AIS is if the security of the ship is threatened by pirates, possible up around the Philippines, but not likely between Australia and New Zealand. In fact, turning off the AIS would actually bring the ship to the attention of the authorities. The exception is vessels under three hundred gross tonnes, which is why we couldn't track the trading vessel. They weren't required to have an AIS transponder as they were under the minimum tonnage limit.'

Continued the General, 'I have persuaded the Navy to lend us some of their new toys. They are currently moored at HMAS Waterhen, Sydney Harbour ; we are booked for training on Friday. Nothing an old soldier loves better than a new toy,' concluded the General, smiling,

'So, Thursday, Friday, Saturday in Sydney? We might as well book a hotel or something. Would be nice to see some concrete after all this green,' suggested Sara Jane.

'I'll make us a corporate booking. We can train it down and use hire cars while we are there. Should provide us with a degree of anonymity,' suggested Joe.

'I think that's probably a good idea,' agreed the General.

'Does Brightly have any muscle?' asked Tracey.

'We think a rent-a-thug. But we can't be sure. His minder could be from the Syndicate,' replied Jodie.

'So, what about your presentation to Brightly and the Attorney-General?' was Sara Jane's next question.

'We are going to script it this morning and role-play it this afternoon. We want everybody involved so we can fine-tune the script for maximum impact. I still haven't decided whether or not we should show the video of him raping the kid or keep it for the art exhibition,' explained Jessica.

'I want to show the fuckwit the video, right after I introduce myself!' interjected Sara Jane.

'I agree, it's high impact and hopefully will be the final straw,' added Jessica.

'Any questions, doubts, or problems you can see, please let us know now. Otherwise, we will get started on the script. As Jess said, we will role-play the meeting this afternoon, at the end of which we will decide to green light the mission or look for a Plan B,' the General concluded.

'I'll take lookout until lunch,' offered Joe. 'While I'm at it I'll book us some accommodation and, I think, three rental cars.'

'Yeah, and remember you owe us an extra shift tonight after disappearing all of last night,' added Sara Jane.

'No worries,' smiled Joe in return. He would be taking Jessica's shift anyway as she would be on stage for the next act.

But, back to the here and now, to this morning, and Joe decided it was time he inspected the boundary. He assumed no one had breached their perimeter, but complacency was probably more dangerous than Brightly at present. The episode with the trail bike riders was a stark reminder of their vulnerability. That made him think it was probably a good idea to initiate some searches of the dark web to ensure no other contracts had been issued for the death or capture of other members of the team

CHAPTER 54

Joe finished the cup of coffee he had been nursing during the discussion. He had confidence in the electronic security Keith had installed, but still liked to run the fence line on the quad bike each day. The General concurred and between them they completed a sweep of the grounds each morning and afternoon. For Joe it was his quiet time, a chance to reflect and fortify his mind and soul.

'You need to pace yourself. Constant stress without breaks leads to mistakes. Think of your mind as another muscle; if you constantly overexert it will fatigue and fail you when you need it most,' as the General explained.

The day was warming up, it would be another fine day. The fires were still raging in the south of the state, and smoky haze still dominated the upper atmosphere. The paddocks surrounding the base were lush and green due to the drip-feed irrigation supplied from the creek. They now had a regular mob of kangaroos keeping the grass mown. They had become accustomed to the silent electric quad bike patrolling the property, but they were still wild animals and would shy away from any intrusion. It was another level of security.

Joe took his time. This morning he would work through the logistics for their next push against the Syndicate. He wondered if it would ever end. The only realistic goal was to make Australia financially unviable for the Syndicate's operations. Joe wasn't confident his life could return to normal when this was achieved. He wasn't confident the Syndicate would just pack its bags and abandon Australia without at least some retribution. Globally, he didn't think they could be defeated. There would always be some corrupt regime happy to give them a home.

Joe stopped the bike. Enough of this gloom and doom bullshit. He needed to concentrate on the here and now. He'd steal just a few more minutes in the sun, watching the roos sunbaking on the lawns.

Returning to his station in front of the security screen, Joe used the desktop computer's second screen to book a mid-range, inner-city hotel for the group. They would be travelling down to Sydney by train in the morning with the rest of the commuters. He then booked three rental cars under a different corporation. They would secrete these in three separate parking garages close to the hotel. Every degree of separation would help them stay alive if their plans disintegrated and they needed to leave town quickly.

Lunch was a subdued affair. The General had planned a practice session for the afternoon. The goal was to increase the pressure on Brightly by revealing information he would know exposed him, but in a subtle way so only a guilty person would feel threatened.

Afterwards Joe and Jessica strolled the lawns of the property. 'Confident?' asked Joe.

'I don't think you can be confident in a situation like this. Too many variables, too many unknowns and too many theories based on suppositions.'

'Any other way to move things forward?'

'No Joe, we need to flush him out and if he has support, we need to flush them out as well.'

'Looks to me as though our plans are based on Brightly being the last man standing. I suppose we need to assume, for own defence, that the Syndicate has a team in place.'

'Most definitely,' agreed Jessica as they re-entered the house. 'Think of it like sport. In most games a good defence is better than a good attack, and our best defence is stealth, staying off the radar.'

'No alcohol this evening or at dinner tonight. First thing tomorrow morning we are going to be fully operational. Please try and have a good night's sleep,' ordered the General.

Joe was not sure how that would be possible. Everyone would need to relax first.

'Do you have a plan for our commute tomorrow?' asked Tracey.

'Yes. You, Keith and Jodie take the van, you will be our surveillance team. Once Brightly leaves the meeting, we want him under surveillance. If he doesn't do anything interesting straight away, start making the surveillance a little more overt.'

'Overt?' asked Sara Jane.

'Yes, as in obvious. It's a tactic designed to increase the pressure on the target. We want him to do something to incriminate himself, or if has back-up, to draw them out into the open,' explained Jessica.

'Sara Jane, Jessica, Joe and myself will take the Subaru to Morisset Station and catch the train to Sydney. I will change into uniform at Central Station. Jessica will be dressed down, as an undercover operative; unremarkable will be more believable. Joe and Sara Jane, please head to the hotel and stay out of sight, you will be fresh ammunition for Saturday evening at the art exhibition.'

The van left the next morning as Joe was rising. He had taken extra shifts as lookout so the main players could have an uninterrupted night. He looked around; the place had yet to feel like home. He hoped one day he would be able to stay in one place long enough to feel like a resident, not a guest. *Funny*, he thought, *nearly all his visions on the future included Jessica. Both of them leading a sedate, boring middle-class life*. A man could dream.

The General, Jessica, Sara Jane and Joe travelled to Sydney with the rest of the Thursday morning commuters, each in a separate carriage. Joe hoped they would all manage to reunite at the hotel at the end of the day.

Once she had arrived at Sydney Central Station, Jessica waited at the same table, nursing a coffee, as she had while waiting for Ms Bowman before the last meeting. She hoped Ms Bowman was recuperating and would soon be able to rejoin them. She looked up from her musings as the General strode to the table in full dress uniform, complete with a full chest of medals.

'Wow, you look like you have been in the wars with all that bling,' exclaimed Jessica.

'Yes, some earned, some awarded for campaigns that will never be disclosed and some I bought on eBay. I have always found most civilians are impressed by the full fruit salad,' he explained while gesturing to his medals. 'Most military would take one look and write me off as a wanker and a fake, which can come in handy at times as well.'

'Today's meeting is in the same conference room in the same shared office space as the last one. Are you sure I should go like this?' Jessica was dressed down. Unlike the last meeting where she was dressed as an office drone, this time she sported plain jeans, a pink pastel blouse, little make-up and generic sand shoes.

'Yes, today we want you to look like nobody. We want Brightly to be unsure if he has ever seen you before, so your name will be Miss Shaw. We should enter fashionably late.'

'That name's a Fred-level pun,' groaned Jessica. 'Last time we were here they put trackers on us.'

'Yes, it will be interesting to see what happens this time. It'll indicate how isolated Brightly is. If we pick up any hitchhikers, electronic or human, we will know he has some back-up.'

They located the building, took the elevator to the correct floor and were shown to the conference room by a receptionist. She knocked, opened the door and left them to introduce themselves.

'Good morning Mr Attorney-General, your Honour, good to see you. This is Miss Shaw, who has been working undercover on this case.' The General spoke as entering the room, his hand extended to the Attorney-General, who was standing to shake his and Jessica's hands. Brightly remained seated.

The General and Jessica took seats on the opposite side of the conference room. 'I assume you have read the minutes of the committee's last couple of meetings; I will let Miss Shaw continue the story.'

'There is no story,' interjected Brightly, 'The operation was closed down, this nonsense about an overreaching super crime organisation is pure fantasy.'

'Fantasy or not we have an obligation to hear her story. I am well aware my predecessor attempted to close this matter down, and had his arm shot off and his reputation destroyed. Now his freedom is in jeopardy for his troubles. Please proceed, Miss Shaw.'

Jessica outlined the events triggered by the last meeting. 'We now have in our control the Foreman, the Bookkeeper, and the last Attorney-General. They all believe that we are their only chance of staying alive. The Fixer is dead. The two operatives working out of the Alexandria charity are dead. We believe we have dismantled nearly all their operations in Australia. All that remains is to destroy the head.'

'Bullshit, as discussed last time, the Foreman was the head, there is no international conspiracy,' interjected Brightly.

The General was watching him closely. He could see a sheen of sweat on Brightly's forehead. Brightly was clenching his hands tightly on the desk in front of him. A white crescent-shaped scar showed clearly on one hand.

'Please continue, Miss Shaw,' responded the Attorney-General. Brightly did not object again, he did not want to draw too much attention onto himself.

'Thank you, your Honour. The Foreman directed us to a video on the dark web of a man raping a young child. A child he claimed was a captive of the Syndicate. A child, incidentally, we picked up when we raided their facility north of Sydney. The Foreman claimed this man was the Boss, as he called him. He had videoed the rape at their Alexandria centre, and while the rapist is wearing a mask, we have examined the footage frame by frame and identified some distinguishing marks on the man's hands. We also have been able to determine his height and weight.'

The General watched as Brightly slowly removed his hands from the table. He turned away before Brightly realised his actions had been seen.

Jessica continued, 'The video and other information the Foreman has provided us with has allowed us to build a profile of the Boss. We are in the process of using the profile and associated information to narrow our search and identify this perpetrator.'

The General continued, 'The Syndicate we are chasing is international. It is unlike other crime gangs in that it's operated purely as a business, with no emotional input. With help from the UN, Interpol and the security services of other nations we starting to appreciate its scope. In some cases, it controls governments through blackmail and corruption, and in other cases the government is actually part of the Syndicate, controlling certain nation-states. We can only hope to make Australia too expensive for its operations to be worthwhile. Once we have done that, we will be assisting other foreign agencies to do the same.'

The Attorney-General turned to Brightly, 'Mr Brightly, do you have anything to add?'

'Only that the General and his cohorts appear to be holding people illegally. Denying them their rights under Australian law.'

'Not so, Mr Brightly, we are holding them for their own protection, at their request,' answered the General.

The Attorney-General looked at his watch, sighed, and rose from his seat, 'I must leave for my next appointment, thank you for your time. Please keep me informed of your progress.' The General and

Jessica stood, walked round the desk and shook hands with him before he exited the room. Brightly then rose and left without a word.

The General looked at Jessica and put a finger to his lips in the universal sign for silence. He feared Brightly may have bugged the office and Jessica may say something to tip their hand. He signalled her to leave the room with him.

They travelled down on the elevator and walked out onto the street. The quickly checked their pockets and clothing for any trackers or bugs. They began walking, doubling back and using shop windows as mirrors. They appeared to be alone.

'It would seem he has no support, but we are trying to prove a negative. They may just be keeping a low profile,' mused the General. 'What do you think, Jess?'

'He's shitting himself. He is still arrogant enough to believe we don't know who he is, but we have definitely shaken his cage. Saturday night's party should be fun. I know Sara Jane's looking forward to it.'

'And the Emmy Award for best performance in a secret briefing goes to Jessica Marlowe,' announced the General as they returned to the hotel. Joe, Keith, Jodie, Tracey and Sara Jane stood and clapped their appreciation. Jessica took a bow. The reunion took place in Joe and Jessica's room at the hotel.

'How's the surveillance going?' asked Joe.

'I followed Brightly from the office building where you met with him to his own office. He walked straight there. Initially it didn't occur to him that he may be under surveillance, but I rushed a couple of pedestrian crossings and even earned a honk from an impatient driver. By the time we arrived at his office he was turning and glaring at me every hundred metres or so. Jodie and Keith are going to resume the surveillance outside his house this evening. The van is already there, we found a spot for it across the road from his house. They have dressed like a pair of TV detectives in cheap suites. They plan to be moving around with their Bluetooth earphones, talking into their lapels.'

'Thanks, Tracey,' replied the General. 'We don't need to watch him round the clock. Keith has alarmed the yacht and we have the AIS to track it, so if he runs early, we will still have him.'

'Let's grab some lunch. Then this afternoon we'll visit Waterhen Base. The Navy insist on an orientation before they'll hand over the keys to their new toys.'

'Don't let Jess steer, I remember sailing with her as a kid. She made Captain Bligh look like a pussy.'

'Sure thing, SJ. I seem to remember mutiny was your default setting,' responded Jessica.

'There's a café down the street where we can get something light for lunch,' added Joe. 'The meals here look a bit big, especially if we are planning on being on the water this afternoon. We can catch the train across the Harbour Bridge and walk from the nearest station. I take it you would like to keep our trip to Waterhen undercover?'

'Yes, thanks, Joe, good idea. We don't want him knowing we have the capability to follow him on the water. We must assume he has a team watching us, even if it seems unlikely.'

The team found a table at the café. Being out in the open, they maintained a conversation about the weather and the fires. There was a low forming to the south of the Australian continent. It was hoped this would move across the south-east corner and douse the remaining fires. It looked promising. Melbourne, to the south, was already reporting a drop in temperature and rain developing. A few days of rain was needed to extinguish the last of the blazes.

They took their time over lunch, so it was early afternoon before they made their way to the train station singly and in pairs. Fifteen minutes later, they were walking down towards HMAS Waterhen, a small naval base on the north side of Sydney Harbour. The General was in civvies, so the guards on the gate asked the team to wait while their credentials could be verified. Before long a middle-aged man approached from the building across from the parking lot.

'Captain King at your service, General. I have been instructed to demonstrate the *Gazelle* to you.'

'I thought it was a boat?' asked Joe.

CHAPTER 56

'It's a code name, if we named it after a fish or something technical it would be obvious it was a boat. It's just a basic redirection,' replied King.

He led them through the door into a large warehouse opening to the harbour on its water side. A large boat ramp and a pair of wharves ran out into the bay. They followed King to a corner of the warehouse where a matt black craft was sitting on a launching platform. It was only seven metres long, built on a two-hulled catamaran platform with a closed-in, binnacle-style cockpit towards the bows.

'The engines are in the hulls. It can take a maximum of eight crew, or for longer voyages two and enough supplies to keep them alive for a month.'

'What about fuel? Surely it can't hold enough fuel for a month,' asked Jessica.

'The engines are top secret. They are electric, using jets. Now seawater has a negative charge, so the boffins have devised a way to use the exhausted seawater from the jets to generate electricity, which in turn charges the batteries,' explained King.

'But you would lose some energy through heat and resistance, which I think would mean you would always be running at an energy deficit?' asked Keith, fascinated by the technology.

'Yes, and we have the most advanced solar panels in the world on the roof creating enough charge over a twenty four-hour period to manage that deficit. Well, that is the theory. Our best run has been to Brisbane and back: six days and sixteen hundred kilometres.

Gazelle returned with a ninety per cent charge. But that was after dark, about two in the morning. We believe if it had returned in the evening as the sun was setting, it would have had a full charge. We only let it in the harbour after dark, when it is virtually invisible.'

'How easy is it to drive, sail?' asked Joe.

'It's about the same as an automatic car. The only difference is the navigation. We have built a simulator. It's in the smaller shed over there. I suggest you spend some time in there this afternoon. How many of your team do we need to train, General?'

'All of them would be best. It gives us extra flexibility to be able to switch the crew in and out. Especially since some of them have a habit of getting shot.'

King was not sure if the General was serious or not. 'OK, um, yes, please follow me.'

'So how do we address you?' asked Joe.

'Sir, or Mr King will do fine,' answered King.

Joe realised King wasn't his name and no other information would be forthcoming. He was expecting a lecture on national security any second. He wasn't disappointed.

'You all are in here under the General's security clearance, which is the highest there is. Needless to say, but I will say it anyway, this project doesn't exist. You talk about this to anyone and really bad shit will come down on your head,' Mr King explained.

'What sort of bad shit?' asked Sara Jane.

'Even that's classified,' answered King with a grin.

'Well, since I'm officially dead twice, I'm not too worried. Just wait a sec while I take a selfie for my Facebook page.' Sara Jane pulled a phone from her pocket.

'I can understand why people keep making you dead,' chuckled King. 'I know about the avalanche but not the other one.'

'You know who I am?' asked Sara Jane, amazed.

'It's my job,' answered King.

Sara Jane poked her tongue out at him and pocketed her phone.

King kept his silence for a minute or two, a slight smile growing on his lips as he watched Sara Jane wrestle with his last statement. 'Actually, I'm a fan, a subscriber. A lot of people thought that avalanche story was bullshit. You should see the comments on your Facebook page.'

Sara Jane gave King a brief hug, a large grin creasing her own face. 'You had me going there for a minute, mate.'

By this time they had reached the building housing the simulator. King unlocked the door and entered, switching on the overhead lights. In front of them was the cockpit of the *Gazelle*, a pair of large screens mounted in front of it.

King walked over to the simulator. 'OK, first a quick induction. This simulator is laid out the same as the *Gazelle* cockpit. There is room for a pilot and a co-pilot. Or skipper and first mate.

'The cockpit cover hinges down from the left side, latching down by the skipper's shoulder on the right coaming. There is a rear hatch for passengers to board or for stores to be loaded. It is operated from within the cockpit, like the remote hatchback release on a car, or from a handle recessed into the hatch. It can be locked from inside the cockpit should hostiles board the vessel.

'The rest is as straightforward. The skipper has steering, trim tabs and the throttle. The first mate has the navigation and ballast tanks. Both are managed by the touch screen in front of him.'

'Ballast tanks?' asked Joe, 'Is it a submarine?'

'No, but the ballast tanks help with the trim and also the stability when the sea is rough. The hull is designed as a wave piercer, so it can slice through the seas instead of bouncing across the top of the swell or chop,' answered King.

'Also, being electric, as long as the batteries are charged it is ready to go. Just turn it on here, by flipping this switch. To launch, just roll it down the ramp, it will float off the cradle once it hits the water.

Just remember to jump in or tie a rope to it. It's a bit embarrassing watching a top-secret toy float out into the harbour unattended. And now, for the important stuff, tea and coffee is over there, and the loos are through that door. Please don't wander around the base; stay in this building. Practise on the simulator. Who's first?'

Sara Jane and Tracey were first to try the *Gazelle*. The screens in front of the simulator played video from out in the harbour, hydraulic rams moved the cockpit about as though it was the chop on the screen.

'OK, Gilligan, little buddy, where are we?' asked Sara Jane hamming it up for the audience.

Joe sensed it was going to be a long afternoon. There was a lounge setting over by the tea and coffee. He wandered over and made himself a cup of coffee. Jessica wandered over to join him.

'We should be able to follow a yacht, with that, basically undetected especially at night,' commented Joe.

'With AIS activated we will be able to follow him from over the horizon. Hopefully he will lead us straight to their offshore facility. We should find out, if we can, what stores have been loaded onto the yacht. That will give us some indication of the distance he expects to travel.'

'How far could it be? What's the range of the yacht?' asked Joe.

'The yacht's is theoretically infinite, it's water and food for the crew that's the issue. The downside is its speed is limited, an average of six knots or twelve kilometres an hour would be tops.'

'Looks like our turn, Jess, let's not channel *Gilligan's Island*.'

'Sorry, mate, you're the Mary Anne to my Professor,' grinned Jessica.

'Couldn't we be, say, Captain Cook and Joseph Banks?'

'You know, Sir Joe was a real goer, first bloke to fuck his way round the world?' replied Jessica.

'Yeah, but not on a *Gazelle*!'

'I dunno, plenty of room in the back. Like an aquatic shagging wagon.'

'Shagging wagon?' asked Joe.

'Yeah, those old panel vans from the 1970s. Dad just spent a fortune buying a restored one so Mum and he can relive their youth.'

Joe had no answer to that, and really didn't want to think about it too much. They walked over to the *Gazelle* together.

'I'll drive,' Jessica said to King as they approached.

'Where are the sick bags?' asked Joe.

'It's easier if the navigator jumps in first. Up the front and over the console between the two seats. There are a couple of steps built into the rear of the console to access the companionway behind the seats. The waterproof hatch at the end opens into the rear area. Once the navigator is in his seat the pilot can climb into the driver's seat.'

King spent ten minutes taking Jessica and Joe through the various controls. 'Good luck,' he said closing the hatch.

The screens in front of the simulator showed the scene from the end of the boat ramp. There was a gentle rocking as the hydraulic rams imitated the movement of water in the bay. Jessica carefully eased the throttle forward and the video screens reacted. After about twenty minutes, Jessica returned to the virtual boat ramp. 'Swap, now you try.'

Joe didn't have much experience with boats. He was a touch tentative at first and the virtual vessel began to drift with the wind. He tried to correct with steering and throttle as though he was driving a car. He clipped a patrol boat moored to the wharf. 'OK, remember the rudder is at the stern, the opposite of a car, so it's like steering a car backwards. The rear of the boat takes a wider line than the front.'

It wasn't hard. Jessica soon had Joe performing virtual figure-eights around a pair of buoys sitting in the virtual bay. 'Now I get it,' exclaimed Joe. He pushed the throttle all the way forward to its stops and flew round the bay. He didn't allow for the vessel's sideslip at full speed, skimming across the top of the water sideways, before slamming into a breakwater.

'That's about ten million dollars' worth of carbon fibre littering the shoreline. I expect you'll be receiving a hefty fine from the Environmental Protection Agency,' commented King.

'No worries, King, in the virtual world I can just reverse out of here, not even a scratch.'

'I'm going to insert the offshore scenario. Jess, experiment with the ballast tanks to see if you can flatten the ride out,' instructed King. 'They will start empty.'

Before them the ocean tossed and turned. Underneath them the hydraulics operated in tandem. It felt real. Joe eased the throttle forward and the simulator jumped from virtual wave to virtual wave. 'Hang on, I'll fill the tanks. There are four. I'll fill them evenly, see if it works.'

The ride became smoother but then as Joe increased speed, the front was ploughing into the seas and they were stalling in a bow-down position, the drives shooting water into the air. Jessica reduced the volume of water in the front ballast tank of each hull. The simulator began to run smoother, Joe increased speed again. The screens in front of them showed the top of the waves passing over the top of the craft. The wave-piercing hull-shape was working. Suddenly they nosedived, Joe pulled back on the throttle and bobbed backwards into a trough. 'You need to steer and throttle for each wave. Jess has the trim about right, and you can't change it fast enough for each wave. It's all about throttle control and steering.' King's voice came through the speakers, 'Try again'.

Like the bike, thought Joe, *it's all about anticipation*. Slowly he moved into a rhythm, then increased speed.

'You've got it, well done. Now, can we have the next two contestants onto the stage please!'

Joe shut down the simulator and once it had stopped moving around on the rams assisted Jessica from the cockpit.

Jodie and Keith were awaiting their turn. Keith was nearly jumping out of his skin with anticipation.

'Wow, and I still have my lunch. Good luck, guys,' commented Joe.

CHAPTER 57

Friday dawned hot and muggy, the sky crisscrossed with wisps of high-altitude cloud. The smog and smoke from the bushfires were trapped by the inversion layer sitting over the Sydney basin. Today the weather would change. A Sydney southerly buster would be storming through some time in the afternoon; lower temperatures, rain and wind were forecast for the weekend and into the following week.

Joe thought of the bushfires raging to the south of them. The next few hours would be critical. The change would initially fan the fires in new and unpredictable directions, lightning strikes could start new outbreaks before the lower temperatures and hopefully some rain, and, then, some more rain would eventually begin to quell the flames.

He stretched in bed. Jessica was still asleep. They had no reason to rush today. The opening of the art exhibition was tomorrow, Saturday. Keith, Jodie and Tracey would be letting Brightly see them every so often; the van was still parked over the road from his house. If he was the Syndicate's lead in Australia, hopefully he would be starting to feel the pressure. So far, his actions and reactions were confirming their suspicions.

Jessica stirred and began to awaken. Still half-asleep she reached for Joe. It was another twenty minutes before they were ready to climb out of the bed. They shared a shower, dressed and made their way to the dining room. Breakfast was still being served. The General greeted them as they entered. 'My room 10 am for a SITREP.'

'Good morning to you too,' mumbled Joe.

'Even the General is starting to feel the pressure,' observed Jessica quietly as they joined Sara Jane and Tracey at a table for four. Jessica had opted for fruit and muesli from the self-serve bistro. Joe had gone for the bacon and eggs.

'Top of the morning to you!' announced Tracey in a really bad Irish accent.

'And to you,' answered Jessica, not bothering to mimic the accent.

'Anything interesting planned for today?' asked Joe innocently.

'Well, bit hot and muggy for outside stuff today, might have a look see round some of the museums and galleries. There's a heap of brochures sitting in a rack at reception,' replied Sara Jane, maintaining their cover as tourists.

'Mind if we join you?' asked Jessica.

'Not in the least,' answered Tracey, before Sara Jane could interject.

The rest of the meal was spent in companionable silence and the occasional smattering of small talk before both couples returned to their rooms until the they were due to meet for the General's Situation Report.

They knew better than to be late. 'Thanks for coming, everyone,' the General started.

'Smart man,' thought Jessica. 'He's savvy enough to realise Joe and SJ will push back if he starts talking to them like soldiers.'

'Tomorrow's the big day. It's the day we let Brightly see us all together. We are hoping he will run and lead us to their offshore facility.'

'What if he doesn't?' asked Sara Jane.

'Well, first we will have to re-evaluate our evidence, make sure we have the right man, and if still think we do, we will need to re-evaluate him. If he doesn't react and we still think he is the Australian head of the Syndicate, we will have to be very careful. He would be showing a lot more backbone than we give him credit for, or he could have back-up that we are unaware of. Both scenarios increase our risk.'

'Also, we are assuming he is going to escape in the yacht. Personally, I am not sold on that idea. It's just too slow,' observed Joe.

'We are assuming it is a stealthy retreat. If Keith had not altered the AIS so it was on permanently, he could disappear over the horizon and, as long as he kept out of the shipping lanes, could stay out of sight indefinitely. However, I see your point. I think, as a precaution, we will start twenty-four-hour surveillance on him. We will make it discreet instead of overt, and we will start it from the time he leaves the art exhibition. Good point, Joe.'

'That's all good for tomorrow, any plans for today, General?'

'Well, Keith, Jodie, Tracey and the van will still be in his face today. This evening, I think we will pull the van out and Keith and Jodie can keep an eye on his place electronically.'

'Why don't we resurrect SJ?' asked Jessica.

'How?' asked the General.

'How about a text requesting an interview?' suggested Sara Jane. 'Good morning, Mr Brightly, my name is Sara Jane Marlowe and I'm not dead. I know my readers would love to hear your views on people smuggling, organ harvesting and child pornography. Can I make a time to see you on Monday morning?'

'Let's wait until Jodie or Keith have him in sight, with a bit of luck he might read it straight away and they will see his reaction,' added Joe.

'Good thinking.' The General picked up his phone. 'Hi Jodie, do you have Brightly in sight?' He listened to the reply, 'You do, he is sitting in a café having a coffee. Great. Hold the line we are going to send him a text'.

The General handed Sara Jane an unused phone. 'Here open that up and fire off the text. Here is the number.' He handed her a business card.

Sara Jane quickly assembled the phone. Typed out the message and pressed send.

'Done.'

A minute passed. Then they could hear Jodie's raised voice on the phone. The General switched the phone to speaker, so they could all hear. 'Holy shit, I don't know what you did, but you definitely gave him a jolt. He is leaving the café, hasn't finished his coffee and pastry. It's like he saw a ghost.'

'Not seen, heard a ghost. Well just another gentle little prod. Thanks, Jodie, keep an eye on him.'

'No worries. See you later.' She broke the connection.

The General concluded the session, 'Well, I think our work is done for today. Down time today. My gut tells me it will be game on from tomorrow evening, so rest now while you can.'

'What about prepping the *Gazelle?*' asked Jessica.

'Being done as we speak. It's being fully prepared with enough equipment and supplies for a crew of seven. They will have it in the water, moored in one of their pens,' replied the General.

CHAPTER 58

'What am I going to wear?'

'What for Jess?' asked Joe

'Tomorrow night of course.'

'Well, let's see if we can find something while we are out today.'

'What are you going to wear, Joe?'

'Dunno, shorts, flipflops and a singlet,' answered Joe. 'I could make a statement regarding the democratisation of modern art.'

'You wouldn't get in the door. Looking at the ticket, it looks damn formal. What does "Black Tie" mean precisely?' asked Sara Jane.

'It means we are all going shopping,' Jess replied.

'We'll need to have a change of clothes stashed nearby. If he runs straight away, we could be caught out,' added Joe.

The General walked into the room. 'Good point. Let's all have a change of clothes in the vehicles. There are three rentals, right Joe, all parked nearby?'

'Correct, General.'

'OK, Jessica and you in one, Tracey and Sarah Jane in the second, and Jodie, Keith and myself will take the third. We will drive them to the exhibition, so we have the option of separating should we need to cover multiple bases.'

'Here are the keys and parking chits for each vehicle. They are all white Camrys. The number plates are on the key tags, and I have written the parking station and parking bay on the chits. They are all within a kilometre of here. The exhibition is being held over in Donnington House, across the Harbour Bridge, in Mosman. Allow about half an hour travel time; it's about the slowest road in Sydney.

They have parking on site. We should also all know the route to Waterhen, in case we need to go straight to the *Gazelle*.'

'Good work, Joe. Anything else we can put in place now? What time should we leave here?'

'About three, General. The exhibition opens around four pm. I was thinking we would enter in twos and threes, then slowly surround Brightly and begin to introduce ourselves. Any ideas regarding what order?'

'Tracey and I last, as we are dead,' jumped in Sara Jane. 'Maybe start with the General and Jessica, then Jodie and Keith. Joe can just hang around and look menacing.'

'I'm going to shave off this beard. Not sure if he will be able to place me after the mediation the other day.'

'Keith, Jodie and myself will wear our dress uniforms. I'm guessing, in his eyes, that will formalise the pressure. Show Brightly we are officially sanctioned.'

'Well, let's go shopping. Still time to be finished by lunch, and we can enjoy the afternoon.'

'Joe, this will take most of the day. Shopping has to be done properly. Maybe us three girls will go it alone. We will meet you back here later this afternoon. Can we trust you to organise your own outfit?'

'I have been dressing myself for a number of years, you know.'

'From what I have seen, I wouldn't be bragging about that,' jibed Sara Jane.

Joe considered defending his style but thought better of it. If he wasn't careful the women would insist on doing his shopping with him. He was planning on completing the mission within thirty minutes, something that could only be achieved if he was allowed to shop unsupervised. It had been a while since he had been in central Sydney, and he felt like having a look around before the weather changed.

It was a short walk from the hotel to the Pitt Street Mall. The pedestrian shopping area contained all the big brands and some so exclusive no one had ever heard of them. Joe quickly found himself a black tux, a white dress shirt and a black bow tie. He finished the ensemble with a pair of black shoes and a black belt. He toyed with the idea of buying some fire engine-red socks to liven things up a bit, but knew he just wasn't brave enough to try.

All done and he had beaten the lunch crowd. Joe, wandered back to the hotel, stored his purchases in his room and ordered a room service lunch. He took his time over lunch before strolling through the Royal Botanic Gardens along the harbourfront, wandering from Bennelong Point where the Opera House stood, along the foreshore boardwalk to the next point along, Lady Macquarie's Chair. It felt good to do something normal for a change.

It was nearly 3 pm before he re-entered the hotel. Jessica, Sara Jane and Tracey had still not returned, so he ordered a coffee and the daily newspapers to read on his balcony. He was still amazed, with all the events and dramas they had fought their way through, there still appeared to be no trace in the press. He could not make up his mind whether this was good or bad.

Joe heard voices. Looking over he saw the General and the twins relaxing on the General's balcony. They were seated around a small table with a phone lying on it. The phone was set to speaker. Joe recognised the voice; it was Ms Bowman. He decided he did not want to accidently eavesdrop on the family's conversation, and took his coffee and papers inside. He continued to scan the papers but was soon bored. Time to turn on the television and do some channel surfing.

Joe dozed. The door was flung open and Jessica, Sara Jane and Tracey walked into the room, loaded down with shopping bags. 'Wait until you see these,' proclaimed Jessica, her eyes smiling.

'No worries, why don't you change in SJ and Tracey's room? Then you can do the full runway exposé.'

Jessica was the first to return, entering the room as though she was strutting down a high society catwalk. The red gown she was wearing cascaded to the floor. Red high heels were just visible under the fluttering hem. Sara Jane was next, strutting down the imaginary aisle in the same dress, just a size or two smaller. Tracey followed, same dress, same shoes. The effect was simply stunning, and the statement was bolder than the red of the three ball gowns. They were together, they were a team and they were dangerous.

Joe gaped. All three were slim; Jessica was slightly taller, Sara Jane and Tracey were the same height. Jessica still wore her hair long, Sara Jane's was still in a bob, both had sun-streaked brown hair. Tracey's shaven head was shining in the light from the window. When they stood together every eye in the room would be drawn to them, and if they were circling Brightly every eye in the room would be on him.

'Wow, I nearly feel sorry for the guy.'

'Don't you go fucking soft on us, mate!' responded Sara Jane.

'Don't worry, SJ, he won't be receiving any sympathy from me. Anyway, with the General and twins in uniform, you three in matching outfits, I reckon I'll just fade into the background. Why don't you lot change into something more comfortable, seems to me that a quiet drink before dinner is in order.'

Sara Jane and Tracey left the room, Jessica followed behind but quickly returned carrying her jeans and T-shirt. 'Of course, we also bought the make-up and accessories to bling the rigs up to their full potential. I forgot how much fun a shopping expedition is with your girlfriends, even if one of them is SJ.'

'Did she behave herself?'

'Tracey's made her really happy. Mind you I think she is also in love with the danger. Or addicted to adrenaline. One or the other. Hopefully, she will settle down once this is over.'

'Jess, don't know if that will be possible. Tracey will still be employed by whoever she is employed by, and while we may have put a dent in the Syndicate's Australian operations, in the Asia-Pacific, according to Tracey, they are huge. Australia was only ever a sideshow. If we can achieve some level of victory against them in the next few days it will be great. Hopefully the General and the new Attorney-General will broadcast a strong enough message, "Australia is too expensive to do business". It still leaves the other nations of the Asia-Pacific region. How many of them have the strength to push back against such an organisation? And the stronger the Syndicate becomes in the region the more vulnerable Australia will be. And we still are only speculating about the existence of the offshore facility.'

'Come on, where's my glass-half-full fireman. I can see your point, but I don't see we have a choice. We need to follow this through, if we take the pressure off, Brightly will disappear and a new Boss will be inserted, one we don't know, one we will have to find all over again.'

'Yes, I agree. Jess. Probably just last-minute jitters before an operation.'

'Actually, I know exactly what you mean. I think we all have them. Let's go downstairs and have that drink. Joe, what's that noise?'

'It's the southerly buster. It must have just hit. You'd feel the temperature drop soon if you were outside. I better close the balcony door before it smashes itself to pieces. The wind is slamming it against the door frame.'

Joe was just finishing his first beer; Jessica was nursing a chardonnay. The General entered and joined them, ordering a beer for himself. 'Single ration each this evening. We are going to need to be at our best tomorrow, and we must also be prepared to take off at a moment's notice. He may bolt sooner than we are expecting.'

Sara Jane and Tracey entered the room and joined them. 'Where are Jodie and Keith?'

'Still on surveillance. Some of the team from the hospital where we left Ms Bowman will relieve them at 8 pm. They will also pick up the van and take it back down the Southern Highlands.'

'What about our tracking equipment?' asked Tracey.

'All downloaded onto two laptops. One will be the primary, the second will be a back-up in case we lose the primary. They will be in separate cars, one with Keith and one with Joe.'

'Toys for the boys?' retorted Sara Jane.

'No, just the two people who have taken the trouble to understand the software. If we have problems, we may not be able to call on anyone else for support. Also, Keith and Joe are not on Brightly's radar to the extent you three girls and myself are. Therefore, they will have greater freedom of movement,' replied the General.

'But Keith and myself are still going to the exhibition tomorrow night?' queried Joe.

'Oh, yes, definitely. You will be our eyes and ears. Your number one priority will be to ensure we have an exit route at all times. If Brightly surprises us with security or some kind of goon squad you need to let us know and be ready to call a retreat. We can't have any shoot-outs in the middle of a public gathering. The Syndicate will have no such qualms.'

'So, we are still gambling on Brightly being isolated?'

'Yes, Joe, it's our underlying assumption. And, if it is wrong, we will need to retreat, not to save our own skins, but to ensure there are no innocent victims. I cannot emphasis that enough. So, I will repeat, if at any time we sense Brightly has reinforcements or support, we retreat. We do not attempt to fight it out in a room full of civilians. Can you please all acknowledge?'

'Copy, we retreat before engaging,' replied Joe.

'Understood,' Jessica added.

'Roger,' from Tracey.

'SJ?'

'If you insist, but I want that prick so fucking badly I can taste it.'

'So do we all,' continued the General, 'but we can't risk making the situation worse. We fall back and we observe. I repeat. No action to be undertaken in public.'

'Change of subject, how is Ms Bowman? I thought I heard her voice this afternoon?'

'Pissed off, Joe. She is not happy being benched. However, she is getting stronger and her injuries are healing. She is assisting the ex-Attorney-General and some other players with their memories. Unfortunately, none of them know anything about the offshore facility. But, on a positive note, they all are designating Brightly as their only point of contact.'

CHAPTER 59

Saturday dawned grey and stormy. One of Sydney's famous summer storms had arrived early the night before. Joe watched as the wind drove sheets of rain past their hotel window. No breakfast on the balcony this morning, he mused.

The phone rang in the room. Joe answered.

'Meet in the dining room in about twenty minutes,' said the General. Joe was not sure whether it was an order or a request.

'No worries, we will be there,' Joe hung up the phone. 'Jess, time to get your arse into gear.'

'What now?'

'Our presence has been requested in the dining room for breakfast in twenty minutes. Sorry make that eighteen minutes.'

'Really? What time is it? Too much excitement, I had all sorts of trouble sleeping last night. Tell them thirty minutes.'

'Down to seventeen.'

'For fuck's sake.' Jessica stomped across to the bathroom.

The room had a small kitchenette with coffee-making facilities. Joe turned on the kettle as it would be easier if they had a cuppa before going down to breakfast.

Jessica reappeared trailing steam from the bathroom. 'I'll have a proper shower later this afternoon, before the main act.'

'Likewise,' Joe replied shucking off the hotel dressing gown he was wearing and heading for the shower.

They entered the hotel's dining room with a minute or two up their sleeves. The General, Keith and Jodie were seated at their usual table. The makings of breakfast in front of them. Sara Jane and Tracey had yet to appear. Joe and Jessica walked up to the servery. They both opted for bacon and eggs on toast. A substantial breakfast seemed like a good investment.

'It's Saturday and it's not even seven o'clock in the morning,' a voice commented from behind them.

'Morning, SJ. Morning, Tracey.' Joe spoke without turning from the servery.

Once they were all seated and had started their breakfasts, the General addressed the table. 'My room 07:45. We will be going out, wear casual gear.' They nodded in agreement. The conversation returned to small talk, mainly about the change in the weather.

The team drifted into the General's room. Keith was checking the room with a handheld electronic device. 'All clear.'

'What's all clear?' asked Sara Jane.

'No bugs,' answered Keith. 'This gizmo picks up any electronic devices.'

'I have arranged for us to do some weapons training this morning. We have a discrete surveillance on Brightly. They'll let us know if he leaves his house. There will be a van picking us up out the front in ten minutes. It won't be much as we need to be back here for a late lunch, then prepare for this afternoon.'

There wasn't any time for discussion. The team trooped out of the General's room and headed down to the foyer. Joe was impressed. Everyone held their tongue. There was no discussion of the day's planned activities in public spaces. Though he did note, by looking closely, you could see a quiet determination on their faces which was out of place on a bunch of tourists. As they exited the hotel a plain white van stopped in the pick-up zone. The door slid open and they entered. The door slid closed and the van re-entered the traffic stream.

The General commenced his briefing. 'We are being driven to a secure facility where we will have a cram session on some stealth weapons. The same weapons are waiting for us on the *Gazelle*. We are assuming the offshore facility is a ship and have prepared accordingly. The same principles should apply if the Syndicate are using a deserted island or remote harbour.

'Tracey, Keith has organised a drone for you. A sniper's rifle is not practical in the seaway. It will have three tranquiliser darts, so your job will be to neutralise any lookouts, or gunmen, using the ship's super structure or cranes, or any other high ground. Keith, Jodie and myself will have assault rifles. These will be the weapon of last resort. Our success and safety are dependent on stealth. If we need to shock and awe then start looking for a means of retreat.

'All of us will carry stun sticks and tasers. Logic tells us the target will not be expecting an attack. So, stealth will be the key.'

'How will we board?' asked Joe, imagining a rusty, red, steel wall towering above them ploughing through a tossing ocean.

'Probable the hard way. Once we have reconnoitred the target with the drone, Jodie will use a grappling hook to board. Once she has secured the rope, we will use a winch and pulley to hoist everyone on board. We may get lucky, as they will need to stop and lower a gangplank of some sort for Brightly to board.'

'Why not attack them using Special Forces?' asked Sara Jane.

'Deniability. The Government cannot be seen to participate in an act of piracy. The more research we do the more it appears the Syndicate controls or is controlled by some nation-states. Our private force is off the books. Also, remember these people have corrupted multiple organs of the Australian Government. We still do not know who else is on their payroll. No one knows why I am requisitioning the *Gazelle* and the equipment loaded into it. They also know well enough not to ask.'

'Bullshit, you're doing this off your own bat, calling in favours, using your position to purloin equipment. No one knows what you are up to. This isn't sanctioned by the government. This is you acting alone,' responded Sara Jane. 'And I agree, it's the only way we can fucking stop these arseholes.'

'SJ, I think the General was saying the same thing. It's us and no one else,' summarised Joe.

The van was proceeding down a street in an industrial park. Joe guessed they were somewhere south-west of the city. The driver indicated and turned through a gate into a fenced compound. The person guarding the gate looked like a rent-a-cop, until you were close. The man's face was chiselled, his stare hard and penetrating. The uniform was deliberately padded and wrinkled. The General showed the guard his ID. Joe grinned, he had seen the guards right arm twitch, about to perform a parade ground salute, willpower holding habit in check. They drove into a warehouse where some trestle tables were set up in the middle of the floor. Further down you could see a gun range with targets on a pulley system.

A man stood behind the table. 'There are two types of weapons on this table,' he began without a greeting. 'A stun gun, or prod, and a taser.' He pointed to the second table. 'Here we have a drone, three automatic weapons and two handguns. I believe three of you are trained on the automatic weapons and two on the handguns, from police service? All these weapons are sanitised. The drone has been tested to ten kilometres, though accuracy will suffer due to the signal delay. The closer the better.'

'Correct. Him, her and myself,' the General gestured towards Keith and Jodie, not using any names, 'are military trained, those two are police trained,' indicating Tracey and Jessica. 'The last two, him and her,' pointing towards Sara Jane and Joe, 'should just have the tasers and stun guns. Our training time is severely limited.'

Jessica picked up a handgun. 'I haven't held a gun since I was shot. I would like to try a shot or two. My right arm is still a bit twitchy. I wasn't much of a shot before, probably more danger to our side than the opposition now.'

'Take it over to the range and have a go,' suggested the General.

Jessica picked up the handgun and a box of ammunition. She checked the gun was unloaded before heading over to the range. She loaded the gun, donned eye and ear protection, took up a double-handed stance and pulled the trigger until the gun was empty.

As the echoes died down, she returned to the table. 'Yep, the barn doors are safe from me. I'll just take the prod and the taser.'

The instructor continued. 'The prod or stun gun works by pushing it against your target and pulling the trigger. The taser can shoot to about ten metres, and there are three charges in each load. Additional cartridges can be loaded like this.' He quickly demonstrated how to drop out a used cartridge and insert a new one. 'Remember though, if you want to re-shock the existing target and the barbs are still attached to him, press the button on the side, here, and if you really don't like him hold it down. The charge will travel down the wires already attached to your target.

'Wait here, I'll grab a couple of dummies and you can try them out.' The instructor walked over to the wall and dragged a pair of manikins over to the group. 'Have a go.'

Sara Jane immediately picked up a taser and took a shot. Nothing happened. 'And remember the safety,' added the instructor.

They each tried the stun gun and the tasers. 'Easy enough,' said Joe. 'Not sure if I could shoot a real person with one.'

Sara Jane looked at him. 'I can guarantee I won't have that fucking problem.'

Joe decided not to say anything. At least until Sara Jane had returned the taser to the table.

'You and you, have a look at the drone,' the General instructed Keith and Tracey.

Tracey would be the principal handler, Keith her back-up. Tracey hefted the controls, toggled the switches and turned on the power. The drone lifted off the table with a slight whirling, quieter than any she had flown before. 'I really need to try it outside, in the weather.'

'Good point, there's a space out the side door. It's like a courtyard so it's blind from the road.' The instructor led the way, Tracey flying the drone behind his back as she walked. The rest of the team following in her wake. The wind was still blowing, swirling around the enclosed courtyard. Tracey quickly had the drone under control, holding it steady and practising aiming the darts. She landed the drone at her feet and handed the controls to Keith. He soon proved proficient with the device.

A solid steel gate slid across opening the far side of the courtyard. A garbage truck drove in heading for the large bin in the corner. Two men jumped out of the cab and started to wrestle the steel bin away from the wall so the driver could scoop it up and empty it. One of them looked over towards Tracey, 'Hey you want to come play with my toggle stick?'

A sudden seizure shook the man and he collapsed to the ground, not breaking his fall, his head banging off the ground. Sara Jane stood holding the taser, two thin wires stretching to the twitching victim's chest. 'Yep, good to about ten metres,' she commented, ejecting the spent cartridge, leaving the barbs in the prone man.

'You in charge?' the General turned on the driver. 'Your men harass one of my staff again I'll have all three of you sacked.'

'Got it, mate. He's a dickhead anyway. About time someone zapped him,' the driver answered. 'Just hope he didn't crap himself. He mentions this to anyone we'll see to it he gets the boot.'

The instructor walked over and pulled the taser barbs out of the prone man's overalls and led them back inside without a word. They left the driver and his offsider to assist their still-drooling co-worker back into the cab of the garbage truck.

The team's van was waiting for them.

'Good hunting, sir,' the instructor saluted as the van drove back out through the roller door.

Once more they were gathered in the hotel's dining room enjoying a light lunch. The General had deliberately steered the conversation away from the afternoon's activities. An hour or two of relaxation was more advantageous than repeating the same briefing over and over again.

'So, if you didn't become a cop, you would have been a professional sailor? Like in the Navy or on cruise liners or something?'

'No, Joe, as in the sport of sailing.'

'I didn't know there was such a thing.'

'Not so big in Australia, but it's huge in Europe. And Australians are very much in demand.'

'I didn't know it was such a big sport in Australia. Never mind the rest of the world.'

'Well, in terms of participants, sailing is Australia's most successful Olympic sport.'

The General stood, 'OK, gang, we leave at two. It's twelve-thirty now, so an hour and a half to make yourselves beautiful. I suggest we move all our luggage to the cars, beforehand. We still have these rooms for another night, but if events move quickly we may not have time to return. Make sure you have a change of operational clothes ready to change into once we leave the exhibition. Remember to stagger our departure from here and our arrival at the exhibition.'

Once Joe was showered and shaved, Jessica claimed ownership of the bathroom. She was going for the full glam look. Not only for the mission, but also to upstage Sara Jane.

'I wish I had time to for a proper session at the hairdressers,' lamented Jessica. 'I managed some time yesterday, but so did SJ.'

'I wouldn't worry, Jess. Trace will upstage both of you.'

'Fuck off. Only SJ counts.'

Joe decided to concentrate on tying his bow tie. He knew when to retreat. He thought he had done a workman like job on the tie, so started to pack their bags. Firstly he organised a backpack containing cargo pants, a long-sleeved T-shirt and a hiking jacket of many pockets, plus, lightweight boots with non-slip soles. All in black and all created out of some lightweight miracle fibre. They were courtesy of the General.

They decided to leave a little early. They both knew Saturday afternoon traffic in Sydney could be a nightmare. Between the kids' sports ending, the DIYers scouting materials, and the Saturday afternoon barbequers, everyone was going somewhere without the discipline of a work-day peak hour. He left Jessica in a café around the corner from the hotel with their bags while he retrieved the car. In a matter of minutes, they were loaded and on their way.

Crossing the Harbour Bridge, Joe decided to take a scenic route to their destination. He was still not convinced Brightly would escape by yacht. And, even if it was his plan, would he move the boat closer than its current berth on the western side of the Harbour Bridge? Joe hoped Keith was keeping an eye on its position using the AIS he had hacked.

'We have some time. Let's just scout out the marinas on this side of the harbour. There appear to be at least two within five minutes of the exhibition. The AIS will tell us where the yacht is. We will just need to know the quickest way to each marina so he doesn't give us the slip.'

'I'll record the routes on my phone. Let's do a quick recce to check access; some of these gin palaces are worth a fortune so there will be security gates and alarms to bypass. Joe, why don't you call Keith, see if the yacht is moving?'

Joe opened his phone, used speed dial, spoke for a few minutes and terminated the call. 'Still parked. How long do reckon it would take to move it from where it is to here?'

'Ten minutes. Five if he met it out in the harbour.'

'Well, it's five to three, let's head up to the exhibition. Jess, do we know Brightly's connection to this show?'

'The gossip magazines weren't clear, but art is a popular way of laundering money, especially if, like Brightly, you have the inside running. A bit like insider trading on the stock market. I believe it's a political fundraiser as well,' explained Jessica.

'Here's the parking lot, take that spot over there and park rear-in to the curb, so we have a clear shot at the exit of the carpark. I saw the General parked out on the street just back from an intersection so he cannot be parked in. No sign of Tracey and SJ yet, though they could be around the corner.'

As they were walking to the entrance of the grand old hall the exhibition was being held in, Joe opened the e-tickets on his phone. The security scanned the bar codes and unclipped the red rope from across the entrance way, letting them pass. Donnington House was, for Sydney, an old building, having been built in the 1850s. It was originally a private hospital, then was converted to flats, and finally was restored as an exhibition and reception centre. The hardwood floors were recently stained, the walls recently painted a flat off-white, the lighting was all modern LEDs, focused and discreet, highlighting the paintings on the wall. They were all emerging artists, so the pricing was erratic as far as Joe could see.

They spotted Brightly. He appeared to be holding court in the main hall. While Joe was watching, the General, Keith and Jodie strolled up to Brightly. The General appeared to be greeting Brightly as though he was an old compatriot, then, while still gripping Brightly's hand in his own vise-like grip, he was introducing

Keith and Jodie. It was clear Brightly recognised them but could not place them.

'And action,' mumbled Joe as he took Jessica's hand and entered the room.

The General indicated Jessica as they wandered into Brightly's circle, 'Ha, Brightly, you remember Jessica? She's on the Task Force with me. Jess, you remember the Honourable Quentin Brightly QC from our meeting the other day?'

'Yes, Mr Brightly, how are you? Let me introduce my companion. This is Joseph Burnett. I met him while we were rescuing those poor kids from that facility up north. He's also an accountant and knows his way around crypto currencies.'

'Mr Brightly, my pleasure, we actually met a few days ago. What a coincidence! I was one of the fireys at a mediation the other day. You were representing those two yahoos claiming we assaulted their Porsche. You left in a hurry after receiving a text, I recall?'

'Ah, over here,' waved Jessica. Sara Jane and Tracey walked up. Brightly was now surrounded by three military personal in uniform and three women in identical, bright red ball gowns. 'Mr Brightly QC this is my sister Sara Jane Marlowe and her companion Tracey, although you may remember her as Lui Chin. She was working undercover for a UN anti-people-smuggling operation when a pair of goons kidnapped her.'

'I heard you two were dead,' stammered Brightly.

'Actually, I'm the only one who is officially dead, twice actually,' hissed Sara Jane. 'No one knows what happened to Tracey except those involved. But, not to worry old buddy, we got better. I am looking forward to our interview. There a few pertinent matters I would like to discuss.'

'That's a nasty scar you have on your hand, there, being crescent shaped makes it quite distinct,' interjected the General. 'By the way, did you know Ms Bowman is my wife? Yes, she is still alive and doing well. Jodie, here, killed the Fixer. We have the facility Foreman, the Bookkeeper and the recently retired Attorney-General. They are all singing like canaries, hoping we can save their miserable lives from the Syndicate.'

Jessica stepped forward, 'We are closing in on the Australian head honcho, just don't yet have enough hard evidence to take him in. Or, as Joe here raided the Syndicate's bitcoin accounts, syphoning their funds through the Australian boss's account, we may just leave him out for the Syndicate to deal with. Once they find the embezzlement I am sure he is going to die eventually, but not before they attempt to recover the money with, shall we say, maximum pressure and pain. I hear they are pretty good these days, can keep a client alive for days. Until the pain collapses his mind.'

'You people are insane. You know shit and you can prove less. Now fuck off!' he quietly jeered. He turned and yelled. 'Security, remove these people. These uniforms are fake, they are not real Army, and they are with these others. Toss them out, now.'

Brightly slipped out from the centre of the group as a posse of security guards surrounded them. He made his way quickly to the exit. Jessica slipped through the closing gauntlet of black-suited muscle and swiftly followed.

The General spoke clearly 'OK, OK, we will leave quietly. I suggest you get out of the way.' The security team paused, unsure what to do next. This was supposed to be a quiet, upmarket event. They weren't expecting a downmarket brawl.

Unseen, the guard nearest Sara Jane decided to shove her towards the exit, assuming she was a soft target. His sudden collapse stunned everyone. Joe noted Sara Jane was wearing her favourite boots under her ball gown. She was shaking her wrist, stretching out the strain from the impact her fist had made with his nose. Knee and nose both busted was Joe's guess.

'Once again for the dummies. We are leaving, move out of the way.

If you want someone to complain to, ring this bloke.' The General shoved a business card into the nearest guard's hand.

The group walked purposely towards the exit. The guards stood aside. Once outside, the General instructed, 'Find Jess. See if she has a lead on Brightly. Keith, has that boat moved?'

'Yes, Dad, sorry General, it just crossed under the Harbour Bridge. Should be just off here in about five minutes.'

The General looked around; Joe was running for the car. 'Joe, wait, where are you going?'

'There's a marina five minutes away. I'm guessing he is headed there. I'll go check it out. You grab the *Gazelle*.'

'That works. We will try and pick you and Jess up on the way. We have five times his speed so shouldn't be a problem. Let's go,' ordered the General.

'Just hope he's using the fucking yacht. Where the fuck's Jess?' Joe mumbled to himself as he started the car.

He speared out of the carpark swerving around a couple of cars standing on their brakes to avoid him and headed down the side road to the marina. He kept his speed down, only slightly above the speed limit, too much traffic and he didn't want to alert Brightly to his pursuit.

The bus went through every half hour. The roads had been designed for horses and carts. Not forty-foot behemoths. It threaded its way through the gaps in the oncoming traffic. Each car it encountered had to pull off the road to let it through. Joe looked for a way past. Someone had parked across the next bus stop; the bus was forced to stop in the middle of the road to allow a group of teenagers to board. Joe looked across the footpath. There was a drop-off then the marina parking lot. A large black car had just arrived and was parked near the gate blocking access to the wharf. The driver jumped out, ran around and opened a back door. A second man appeared dragging a woman in a red gown; somehow they had snatched Jessica. Joe watched as the second man, who he recognised as Brightly, plunged a hypodermic into Jessica's thigh and squeezed the contents of the syringe into her body. She was still struggling, but the more she struggled the quicker the drug circulated. The second man used a swipe card to open the gate.

Joe snatched his backpack from the back seat, checked he still had his phone, and leaped out of the car. He heard the cars behind him honking as he leaped the fence, dropping four metres to the grassy bank then rolling down to the carpark. He dragged himself to his feet and sprinted for the gate. Brightly and Jessica were through the gate, the second man pushed through and slammed it in Joe's face. He heard the lock engage. He threw himself at the gate, bouncing back onto the pavement, tripping over his backpack and falling to the ground. The bullet skimmed over his head as he was falling and struck the car behind him. He rolled sideways and around the back of the car as two more bullets followed.

He heard footsteps echoing down the planks of the wharf, then there was silence. He risked a peep around the corner of the car's rear bumper. A powerful outboard started, clunked into gear and disappeared into the late afternoon.

Jessica was gone.

CHAPTER 61

Frantically Joe turned around. A stranger was pulling up in his rental car. Joe ran to the car as the driver was about to park it. 'Get out of my car,' he screamed.

'Hey, mate, someone dumped it in the middle of the road, I was just clearing it out of the way,' the man replied.

'Thanks,' Joe grabbed a handful of the man's shirt and pulled him out of the car, jumped in the driver's seat and slammed the gear lever in reverse. Screeching backwards, he spun the wheel and jammed on the brakes. The car spun round, its front now pointing towards the exit of the carpark. Joe slammed the transmission into drive and accelerated out. He was desperately searching for a vantage point. Driving one handed he hit the General's speed dial on his phone.

'They left the marina in a power boat. I'm trying to find a vantage point so I can see where they are going. I saw Brightly drug Jess and drag her through the marina gate. I didn't see the boat.'

The car mounted the footpath and hit a sandstone garden wall. 'Fuck,' Joe again slammed the car in reverse.

'What was that?' asked the General.

'I just fucked the car.'

'Can you get to a wharf? We just crossed under the Harbour Bridge.'

'Yeah, there's a public wharf at the end of the street. Sign says Mosman Public Wharf.'

'Get down there.'

Joe snatched the bags out of the boot of the mortally wounded

Camry and jogged down the pedestrian pathway to the ferry wharf. Sirens could be heard converging on the area.

As he stepped onto the wharf the *Gazelle* slid silently up to the dock. The rear hatch popped open as Joe jumped onto the roof of the craft. With a whoosh of water jetting from its rear the craft turned within its length and sped from the bay out into the harbour.

The harbour was starting to clear. A light sou'easter was all that was left of the previous day's storm. Most of the pleasure craft had returned to their moorings; their crews heading for the yacht club bar for a cleansing ale.

'That's it,' yelled Keith from the co-pilot's seat. 'It's Brightly's yacht.' He pointed at his screen at a yacht heading down the harbour under full sail.

Jodie opened up the throttle, the *Gazelle* jumped forward, it's wave-piercing hulls slicing through the chop of the harbour.

The General opened the rear hatch, he prepared to climb out, Joe and Sara Jane right behind him.

'Sailing vessel on our port bow. Heave to. This is Australian Border Patrol. Prepare to be boarded.' Keith's voice burst from the loudspeaker.

'Repeat, heave to immediately.'

The yacht continued on its way.

'They are not going to stop,' he yelled back into the cabin. 'Jodie, come along side to leeward and nudge their bow into the wind. General, strap a line around their stanchions up near the bow. I'll be able to hold their bow into the wind with our engine while you board her.'

Jodie performed the manoeuvre as ordered. The crew of the yacht tried to tack away, but the General had fastened a line from the front of the *Gazelle*'s hull to the bow fitting of the yacht as she came head to wind, Jodie used the *Gazelle*'s engines to hold her there, sails flapping. The General, Joe and Sara Jane leaped aboard; the General in full dress uniform, Joe in his tuxedo and Sara Jane in her red ball gown made their way to the cockpit of the yacht.

'Who the fuck are you? You can't do this,' demanded the skipper.

'We can and we just did. Joe, SJ search below,' replied the General in a quiet voice.

It only took a minute. 'She's not here. Neither are Brightly or the thug,' yelled Joe.

There were two young men and two young women on the yacht. 'Hey aren't you the arseholes from the mediation the other day? Brightly represented you.'

It took a while but one of the young men recognised Joe without his beard. All the fight went out of him.

'Yeah, Brightly asked us to move his boat to Pittwater an hour up the coast. He said we had to leave at three-thirty so we would arrive at the right time,' replied the skipper meekly. 'He said it would be good for us to get away for a week or so after the hearing, you know, until the publicity died down,' he explained meekly.

'It's a fucking decoy.'

Sara Jane was desperately scanning the harbour. From behind one of the islands scattered throughout the harbour a seaplane began its take-off. 'There, taking off into Rose Bay, from behind Shark Island. I swear I saw a flash of red while they were boarding.'

'Keith, track that plane. Everyone, back into the *Gazelle*.'

Sara Jane's gown snagged on a cleat. 'Fuck it,' she cursed, unzipping and ripping clear, she dashed ahead in her panties and boots. Joe and the General clambered after her, the General freeing the line from the yacht's bow as he dived onto the back of the *Gazelle*.

Jodie slammed the throttle forward as the three boarders crashed to the floor in the rear of the craft.

'He's flying low, below the height of the cliffs. He'll stay under the radar. If we go offshore, our over- the-horizon radar should track him. We can silhouette him against the coast. It'll take us about ten minutes to be in position,' Keith yelled over his shoulder.

Tracey clambered to the front of the crew area, sticking her head between Jodie and Keith in the pilot seats, 'I activated the Track my Phone app on all our phones. I just got it working for Jess's,' she handed Keith her phone. 'There she is. She must have turned her phone on. I couldn't see her before.' It showed a dot moving up the coast.

'There's just been an all-points broadcast, Coastal Seaplane has just reported one of their planes stolen. The transducer has been turned off, and it's reported flying under the radar. They estimate it has around two hundred kilometres of fuel left.'

The General considered the information, 'Thanks Keith, they can't land a plane like that on open water. They have to be heading for a lake or harbour.'

'Well the sou'easter's behind him, there's a number of options with that range. We're leaving the shelter of the harbour now; we can do twenty-five knots, about fifty kilometres an hour. But it will be rough.'

'What's his speed? About five times ours?' asked Joe.

'Roughing out the possibilities, if he goes for maximum range, they will be about five hours ahead of us when they land.'

Joe continued, 'Any ideas on their final destination? Do we still think he will run to the offshore facility?'

'What choices has he got?' asked Tracey.

'Fuck it, I think I know where they are going!'

The General turned to Joe. 'Where Joe?'

'The supply ship. You know the containers they trucked out of the chicken farm. They went to Newcastle. They were shipped out on a small coastal trader, like an oversized landing craft.'

'Bit risky, needs your logic to hold. Can we get some land support up there?'

'Sorry, Tracey, it would take forever to organise as we are off the books. There is no back-up. This Task Force doesn't actually exist. It was closed down by the old AG and Brightly, remember, and never officially restarted,' explained the General.

'OK, we are tracking them, let's just go with it for the moment. Should anything change disproving the assumptions we are employing, we will need to change our plans. Now try and get some rest. Joe and Sara Jane, you can relieve Jodie and Keith in two hours,' instructed the General.

The swell was still out of the south, though decreasing now a day had passed since the southerly had blown through. The *Gazelle* was overtaking the waves as it headed north. Its motion, thanks to the wave-piercing hulls was reasonably smooth for a small craft on the ocean. It would accelerate down the face of each wave before slowing down as it climbed the rear of the wave ahead, before repeating the process over and over again. The overcast day and the claustrophobic nature of the *Gazelle* were the perfect recipe for motion sickness.

The General issued instructions, 'Lie down on the benches along the inside of the hull and keep sick bags handy. If you can, use the head or the port in the rear of the cabin. It's going to be a rough ride. Sip from your water bottles. I suggest no one eats until your bodies become used to the motion. Sleep if you can, conserve your energy. We will swap pilots every two hours. When we have an objective, we will consider our options, no point wasting energy on speculation.'

There was no argument.

Night was creeping in, the grey light of the overcast day fading to black. Joe was in the driver's seat, Sara Jane in the co-pilot's, tracking the plane. They had taken their shifts early as both could feel the onset of motion sickness.

'The plane's disappearing, it's blinking in and out of the radar screen,' Sara Jane commented.

She looked at Tracey's mobile phone, now mounted on the console, it showed the red tracking dot turning across Newcastle

Harbour. 'They appear to tracking along the Hunter River. Your guess is looking good.'

'We're still three hours behind. But, if they use the supply ship, they will need to exit the Newcastle Harbour, and it will be slower than us. We should be able to intercept them. Though we will need the General and the twins to guide us, a bit out of my area of expertise. This not knowing is the worst part, for all we know they could have thrown her out of the plane as soon as they were clear of The Heads.'

'Doubt it, Joe. Brightly needs her, he needs her to prove he didn't take the Syndicate's money. Without her he's fucking dead meat. I reckon the muscle is there mainly to ensure Brightly makes it to the offshore facility. That little hack of yours is probably the only thing keeping Jess a-fucking-live.'

'Hope you are right, SJ. I know we keep talking it through, and it all makes sense, but I still can't help breaking out in a cold sweat, trying to justify the risk.'

Sara Jane scanned her displays, 'Nothing on radar, but the mobile is tracking again. It's heading back down the river, but only at about five kilometres an hour. Hopefully we can be in position to pick it up on radar when it leaves the harbour and before she is out of mobile range. There appear to be several parked ships off the coast of Newcastle.'

'Yeah, waiting for the coal loader. The supply vessel should be smaller, but we won't see it until it is clear of the harbour.'

The General's voice stunned them, speaking from between the seats just behind their heads. 'Joe, take the speed up, every time you near the crest of a wave throttle down, then as you start to climb the wave in front, throttle up. It's going to be rougher, but as long as we don't porpoise out of the water over the top of a crest or nosedive into the wave ahead we should be able to make better time. SJ try and assist with the trim tabs, I'll watch the radar and the phone tracking from here.' He slid between the seats, sitting with his arms gripping the arm rests.

Joe steered with both hands. Using the foot throttle he powered up the rear of the wave in front, lifting off a second too late. The *Gazelle* leaped over the crest then fell into the trough, Sara Jane just managing to flick the bows up before they ploughed into the wave ahead.

'OK, I'm going to cross diagonally across the face like a surfer,' Joe twisted the wheel slightly as the bow crested the next wave. Surfing diagonally across the face, he gained an extra five kilometres an hour.

'That actually works. Well done, son. And better yet your course is now closer to the mouth of Newcastle Harbour. We keep this up we should see them as they exit,' exclaimed the General.

'Cowa-fuckin-bunga,' chanted Sara Jane as they slid down the next face.

CHAPTER 62

'The flashing light, it's Nobbys Head lighthouse. The harbour entrance is behind it, facing north. Hard to see because of the city lights, but if we hang out here, we should be able to see their masthead lights as the pass the sand spit.'

Joe eased back on the throttle, the *Gazelle* was drifting on the dying swells just north of the city of Newcastle and south of Nobbys Head. They were separated from the north-facing harbour mouth by the sand spit joining Nobbys to the city. A pair of lights stacked vertically could be seen gliding northwards on the other side of the spit. The General hoisted himself up from his position wedged between the pilot and co-pilot seats. 'The signal is definitely coming from the vessel under those lights. Hang here, we will confirm as they head out to sea and have them on radar before Jess is out of mobile range.'

Joe squirmed around in his seat, 'Let's just board them and rescue Jess'.

'She'd never fucking forgive you, mate. We take the scumbags now we'll never find their floating base,' Sara Jane responded.

'I agree, that's the prize,' added Tracey. 'No way Jess would let this go. General, Jodie, Keith?'

'Follow them,' from Keith.

'Find the base, kill the disease, not treat the symptoms,' from Jodie.

'OK, sorry Joe. We go after their base,' ordered the General.

'Fuck it,' mumbled Joe. He eased the throttle forward and aimed to seaward off Nobbys Head. He was planning to use Stockton Beach, thirty miles of pristine sand dunes glowing ghostlike in the faint moonlight, to backlight their target as it slipped between the breakwaters guarding Newcastle Harbour. 'And there she is, looks like she's heading east-nor'-east,' he noted, 'Looks like she's quartering the waves like we were.'

'Yep, have them on radar, the following sea has added a knot or so to their speed,' added Sara Jane. 'About two kilometres an hour, for the landlubbers,' she added in response to Joe's questioning look. 'Takes her up to about ten to eleven kilometres an hour or six knots. If the seas flatten out maybe they will push a bit harder. Closest point to international waters would be two hundred nautical miles east. About a day's travel time.

'I'm guessing we are looking for a disguised container ship or similar. It can probably be inside the economic exclusion zone. They would have some kind of manifest, dropping the odd container here and there. I think this supply ship is only for sensitive cargoes and passengers they want to transfer off the books.'

'The only way to find out is to follow them. The seas are settling so let's see if we can keep some food down, the rations on board are designed for energy and to be easy on the stomach. Keep hydrated. We have a water tank and water-making facilities on board. We will start a watch system. Those off watch try to sleep. It could be four hours, twenty-four or forty-eight hours before we have a target. We will be no good to anyone if we arrive exhausted,' instructed the General.

CHAPTER 63

Jessica was locked in a small cabin on the supply ship. Once she was sure she was alone she opened her eyes. She pulled her phone out from inside her panties. It had not been comfortable, but her options had been limited. She risked a text. You following?

Yes was the reply. She switched the phone off. They would be out of mobile range very soon, she would conserve its battery, she would be able to use the camera to document evidence. She knew she was taking a risk, but letting herself be taken was a free ticket to the centre of the Syndicate's operations.

Initially she had resisted, but, as Brightly's driver grabbed her from behind and forced her into the car, she chose spontaneously to go with them. With Joe chasing them, Brightly and his thug had been too distracted to drug her thoroughly. She had seen the syringe coming and jerked her leg away at the last second. The contents had squirted onto the skin of her thigh not into it. When she pretended to swoon, they had seen what they had expected to see.

Once through the gate, while Brightly held Jessica, his man found a twenty-five-foot runabout in one of the marina's berths. He was about to strip the wires from the simple ignition switch when he felt a small box taped to the underside of the dash. It contained the spare key.

They were gone within a minute. Jessica was thrown about in the rear of the runabout as the driver blasted out of the marina, through the bay and out into the harbour. Jessica realised very quickly he had no idea how to drive a boat. Brightly quickly came to the same conclusion. 'Give me the helm, idiot,' he bellowed over the motor, as the boat landed awkwardly after smashing through a ferry's wake. The boat slowed and the men swapped positions.

They had not bothered to tie Jessica's arms, so she was able to steady herself. She knew Keith had the yacht tracked through its hacked AIS, she was waiting to see how they would handle the transfer. The runabout crossed the harbour and continued up Rose Bay, on the south-east corner of the harbour. Brightly was following a taxiing seaplane.

He approached the seaplane from the rear, coming up alongside its left-hand float under the high wing as the plane slowed. 'Wrap the bow line around the float support,' he yelled at his minion.

The plane slowed further. They were barely moving through the water. Brightly jumped onto the aeroplane's float from the runabout, reaching up he reefed open the door. The pilot was alone in the plane. Holding the door with his left hand, Brightly reached into his jacket pocket and produced a small handgun. He pointed this at the pilot. 'Leave the engine running and jump out the other door,' he yelled waving the gun to reinforce his instructions. The pilot took one look at the gun and did as he was told. As soon as he heard the splash Brightly turned to his henchman, 'Get her up here, the drug won't knock her out entirely, just make it impossible for her to make a decision.'

With Brightly dragging from inside and the henchman pushing, they bundled Jessica into the rear of the plane. 'Untie the boat and get in for fuck's sake.'

Brightly buckled himself into the pilot's seat, 'Leave her on the floor in the back, jump in the co-pilot's seat. Let's see if those flying lessons were worth it. Can you fly a plane?'

'Basics only, boss.'

'Then just watch the instruments. If you see anything that looks wrong let me know.'

'Now, I'll push the throttle back a bit and the use the rudder to turn into the wind. Seems to be working!'

Jessica realised Brightly was going to attempt to fly the plane. She had no idea whether he could or not, but it meant the yacht had been a decoy, Brightly had had another plan for his escape, or was maybe so arrogant didn't think he needed one, and was improvising. Regardless, Joe and company would be following a red herring while she was disappearing over the horizon.

The plane began to accelerate. Jessica was wedged between the pilots' seats and the second row. She was bouncing on the floor and against the seat mounts. It was painful. She used the movement to retrieve her phone. All she needed to do was turn it on and mute the sound. It only took a second and she slipped the device back inside her panties. Tracey had briefed her on the Find My Phone app and how they could use it to track one another. She just hoped it worked.

'Bet those chumps on the yacht are going to get a surprise. Arseholes thought I was too stupid not to notice the AIS had been reset. I was going to drive but this came along and is even better.'

'If you say so, boss,' the offsider didn't sound so sure.

'Check the bitch, make sure she is out of it.'

'Why don't we just ditch the slut?'

'Because she knows where the money is. I know your instructions are to get me to the *Shenandoah* with or without my cooperation. This bitch and her mates framed me, and they stole the Syndicate's money. I need her alive so we can get the money back. Without her I'm as good as dead.'

The co-pilot didn't bother replying. *You useless prick. Once we have the money back you're fucking dead anyway, and I'm going to enjoy making it happen,* he thought to himself. A small grin creased his lips.

'We'll keep low and just offshore. We'll be at the supply ship in under an hour. We'll just have enough fuel,' continued Brightly.

They flew on in silence. Jessica agreed with the co-pilot, it was as though she was reading his thoughts. One way or another Brightly was dead, only his arrogance and stupidity were blinding him to his fate.

It was growing dark outside the plane. Jessica remained prone on the floor. She would have bruises for her trouble. Suddenly, lights were reflecting off the ceiling, the plane banked and turned to the left, headed inland. *Maybe Newcastle Harbour*, thought Jessica.

'Do know how to land this fucking thing?' asked the co-pilot.

'Just do as I say. I'll bring her in long and slow as soon as we cross the Sandgate Bridge.'

The bridge stretched across the Hunter River behind the port of Newcastle, where the biggest coal loader in the southern hemisphere occupied the southern shore. At this time on a Saturday night it was still working, but with the noise and floodlights the seaplane crossed over without being noticed.

'Now I'll ease her down. There's the supply ship up ahead. Nice and slow, throttle back, flaps, and here we go.'

Brightly completely misjudged the distance the plane needed to land, once it was skimming across the water, he realised he would hit the mangroves before he could stop. There are no brakes on a seaplane, just the friction of the water draining off its speed.

The mangroves were only just starting to reclaim the bank of the river. They were young and flexible. The plane smashed through them before hitting the ancient seawall. It pitched up on its nose, the propeller disintegrating before the plane collapsed back on its tattered floats where it settled slowly in the mud with a list to port.

Jessica had braced as best she could. As soon as the plane stopped moving, she resumed her posture on the floor, groaning quietly.

'Get the tender over here now,' screamed Brightly into his phone, while unbuckling. 'Grab the bitch. Let's get on the boat and out of here.'

Between them they manhandled Jessica out of the plane. A

dinghy and outboard were following the trail they had cut through the mangroves. The dinghy pulled alongside the right-hand float. Two additional sets of hands pushed and shoved Jessica onto the floor of the dinghy between the seats.

'We need to set sail before they find the plane. We probably have until morning.'

'On it, boss. We have a secure cabin ready for her. No one following you?'

'Nah we're all clear, the fuckwits are chasing a sailing yacht heading towards Pittwater.'

CHAPTER 64

There was a small porthole above the bed. Jessica climbed up and looked out over the rear of the small supply ship. Newcastle Harbour was fading into the darkness behind her; Nobbys lighthouse periodically flashing. As far as she could tell they were on a course just north of east. The southerly swell was pushing them from the rear right-hand corner of the ship, making it corkscrew briefly with each wave.

She hoped to catch a glimpse of the *Gazelle*. Logically she hoped they would stay out of sight, but emotionally it was nice knowing she was not alone. Her best strategy was to conserve her energy. She had no idea whether her captives would feed her or not, or how long she would have to wait until they made contact with the mothership, as she now thought of it. Lying down and resting was her only viable course of action.

Up on the supply ship's bridge , the Captain was not happy. 'Kidnapping, you fuckwit, now we are a party to a kidnapping,' he bawled at Brightly.

Brightly smirked, 'I wouldn't worry about it. What do think was in those containers you shipped out last month? About twenty-five people. You're not a kidnapper, you are a full-on people smuggler. One more won't make the slightest difference. Your only chance is to work with me. I'm the only one who can keep you out of jail. Anything happens to me the authorities will have you on toast. The records are all there waiting for the cops to raid my house.'

The Captain's face went ashen under his tan. Not knowing had always been his defence; now he realised his greed had been his undoing. Worse still, the busted-up seaplane sitting on his doorstep, and him slipping out of the harbour in the dark, were just too much of a coincidence to be ignored. He was going to have to do some serious thinking.

'Who is she?'

'Just some cop who's been closing in on our operation.'

'This just keeps getting better and fucking better. You kidnapped a cop? Fuck you're a fucking moron, mate.'

Brightly was enjoying the Captain's consternation. Being able to bully the man returned some normality to his life. 'There's only you and your mate onboard?'

'Yeah. We left so quick we didn't have time to pick up the other two who usually sail with us,' replied the captain, defeated. 'We'll have to split the watches, Bob, with your friend there.' He pointed to thug currently lounging against the back wall of the bridge, 'And, me and you, four hours on four hours off during the day, two hours on two hours off during the night.' We should pick up the *Shenandoah* tomorrow evening. She's up north of Lord Howe Island, hiding behind a couple of reefs up that way, outside the shipping lanes. Once we are clear of Newcastle Harbour's radar, I will turn off the AIS. If I turn it off while they can see us on radar we might as well post a neon sign on the roof saying "Look at me, Look at me".'

Brightly walked out to the side of the bridge. He opened the door and stepped outside onto a small platform that allowed the Captain of the vessel an unobstructed view across the bow of the vessel and out to the rear. In front was inky blackness; behind the lights of Newcastle were slipping below the horizon. 'What about pursuit? Anything following us? How good is your radar?'

The Captain went to the radar screen, it was integrated with the navigation system and showed the coast sinking towards its bottom end. 'These reflections have not moved,' he said pointing to two blips to the south of them. They are cargo ships waiting to enter the port in the morning. You can see the AIS signature of each one when you press this button. Nothing else is moving. There were a couple of blips earlier on, probably a fisho just off Nobbys trying his luck. But whatever it was they have faded below the horizon now, so can't be following us.'

Brightly studied the screen for a minute or two. He turned to his thug. 'Come here. I don't trust these arseholes. When you are on watch keep a close eye on this screen. I want to know straight away if anything pops up,' he ordered.

'Yes Boss,' answered the thug before returning to his corner. He had no intention of sleeping until they were back on board the *Shenandoah*. He didn't trust a soul on this glorified landing barge.

CHAPTER 65

'Watch change. Jodie and Keith, can you take the next two hours? We are going to want to drop back a bit as we clear the shore. How far can we track him on our radar?'

'General, we can see him from about fifty kilometres. He can probably only see us from about five, unless he has something special,' explained Keith.

'Then let's drop back about twenty klicks behind him,' replied the General. 'If we see him approaching another vessel or heading for shore, we'll close the gap. This thing is supposed to be stealthy, but let's not take any unnecessary risks.'

Joe was still uncomfortable leaving Jessica alone on the supply ship. However, he could not think of any arguments powerful enough to change the minds of his teammates. He was empathetic enough to appreciate his motivation was slightly different from his compatriots. He had been thrust along by events and was doing whatever was necessary to return to his normal life, while for the others, the destruction of the Syndicate was their motivation. The slightly divergent goals only became an issue in situations like their current one. Where his primary goal was the safe return of Jessica, they saw it as an opportunity to hurt the Syndicate. He could understand, but it didn't make him happy.

Leaving the driver's seat, he used the head to relieve himself then lay down on one of the benches lining the side of the crew area. He was head to toe with Tracey.

'So, who do you work for, Trace?'

'Well, we are a semi-autonomous division of the United Nations, originally tasked with combating human trafficking. But the more we learnt the more we came to realise that the main players were a new style of international gang. Like many corporations they had embraced globalisation and have slowly been swallowing the smaller, ethnic-based criminal organisations like the Mafia, Triads and the Yakuza. Unfortunately for us, to be effective we have to be off the books, so most of what we do is merely intelligence gathering. Then if we can make a case, we try to pass it on to a local national police force. It doesn't always work, as very often the Syndicate has corrupted the government or the police forces we hand our findings over to, basically achieving nothing but tipping our hand. Then, lately, our budgets are being cut, as those under the influence of the Syndicate attempt to take us out of the game.

'Our current chief is running more and more of our operations off the books. Recently our enemies have started to openly attack him. Forcing him into hiding. But not only are they trying to destroy him physically, they are trying to destroy his reputation and the integrity of our unit. We are now virtually an underground organisation. Quite frankly, we probably have about three months before they close us down completely. Every success we have is actually another nail in our coffin. The corruption is just too rampant.'

Joe thought about this for a minute, 'Well Trace, your mob should become private.'

'There's a whole smorgasbord of issues going private. From funding to governance. I mean who would stop us going off the rails? The sums of money are huge, and then there are the risks of kidnapping and extortion. You know that can bend even the most honest of people.'

'I still control the Syndicate's bitcoin account. I could hand the keys to your lot.'

'Why would you do that, Joe?'

'Because Trace, the Syndicate is always going to be searching for the group or individuals who stole its funds. And I want to return to a normal existence. I'm not a soldier or saint. But for your team, it would allow you to operate against the Syndicate using their own money, and it will help you identify them as they come after you and their money. Hopefully, I will then be out of the equation and will have returned to boring lakeside life.'

'I thought the trail you laid was untraceable?'

'Only to a certain extent. Untraceable by anyone restrained by rules and regulations, codes of practice and the rule of law, but privacy regulations and corporate reputations are nothing when some arsehole is holding your daughter hostage sending her home one small piece at a time. So, the anonymity I currently have cannot last forever, but for your team I see it as a bonus.'

It was Tracey's turned to sink into contemplation for a few minutes. 'I can see how that could work. Apart from the money, the General, Ms Bowman, Keith and Jodie will be joining us. He has gone out on a limb, operating without any authority or oversight. This operation will destroy all their careers.

'This will also be my last field operation. Not only is my cover blown by those movies they uploaded, for the first time in my life I have someone else to care about and someone who cares about me. I plan to join SJ as a researcher on her blog. If nothing else it will provide some cover. I think most of the research I will be doing will be for my old boss anyway. I don't think I will ever be out entirely. The debt I owe is unrepayable.'

'Aren't you worried that she may be a target as well?' asked Joe.

'Yes, we are brainstorming different approaches. SJ realises now that she is going to have to hide behind some kind of veil of secrecy to keep us safe. We don't have the answer yet. Hopefully it is something you can help with. You seem pretty good at working behind the scene. So what are your plans, Joe?'

'I'm just hoping Jess and I can make a go of it in the normal world. You know, where the biggest drama you face is having your car door dinged at the local supermarket.'

'After this I don't think any of us will return to normal lives. Well, those of us who had normal lives to begin with Joe. SJ and I feel the same. It will be a new normal. Can we make it work? I don't know. None of us do. All we can do is try and make it work.'

Joe thought for a moment or two, then he picked up on one of Tracey's earlier points. 'I think you have alluded to this debt before. Why do you owe your boss such a debt? In the last month or so you have nearly died for him multiple times.'

'Yeah, and now I am bouncing round in a floating coffin trying to distract myself with this conversation so I don't perform a technicolour yawn over the stern. Twenty odd years ago I fled Vietnam with my family on a broken-down old fishing boat. It was a set-up from the start. As soon as they had our money, they owned us. I was dragged off the boat and shunted round from one evil owner to another until I was rescued by the group I now work for. My mind has blanked most of my early life, and drugs they fed me to keep me compliant have blanked out the rest. I have never seen anyone from that boat or my village again. I owe my boss my very existence.'

'Sometimes it's easy to forget how easy some of us have it. You have given me a better understanding of what drives people like Jess and you. It is something I will need to understand if we are to have a life together.'

'Yeah, Joe and most importantly it's taken our minds off our heaving stomachs.'

'Yeah, that too. By the way does SJ always snore like that?'

'Yep, never a quiet moment with her, even when she's unconscious. I find it a comfort.'

CHAPTER 66

'Fuck, this is boring.'

'SJ, most soldiering is,' replied Jodie. 'Hours of boredom punctuated by minutes of intense fear.'

The *Gazelle* had been trailing the supply ship through the night and halfway through the next day. They were working the boat in shifts: two hours on and four hours off. The supply ship had been travelling in an east-nor'-east direction, diagonally away from the Australian coast for twenty hours, sitting steadily on ten knots, about twenty kilometres an hour.

'Where are we?' Sara Jane asked, poking her head into the cockpit.

Joe pointed to the map on the co-pilot's console, 'About a hundred kilometres straight east of Port Macquarie.'

'Isn't Port Macquarie the city everyone retires to? Average age is about ninety in the shade?'

'Yeah, about two hours drive north of Newcastle, three-and-a-bit from Sydney, reputed to have the best climate in Australia.'

'Still not doing it for me, Joe.'

'Yeah well, it's a twenty-hour swim dead west of us, SJ. So, don't think we will be visiting today.'

Sara Jane was still looking over Joe's shoulder. 'Hey, what's that?' A faint echo was showing at the extreme edge of the radar screen. The supply ship appeared to be heading directly toward it.

Keith peered across from the pilot's seat, 'Another ten minutes and we should pick up its transponder. We can then back track it through the AIS system.'

'What's the AIS again?' asked Tracey from the rear of the *Gazelle*.

'Automatic Identification System, it's a marine anti-collision system. Basically, each ship transmits a signal so other vessels know where it is.'

'Reckon it's their "offshore facility"?'

'Could be, but it's fairly busy out here so could be anyone. Don't get your hopes up, Joe.' Keith continued watching the radar for a few more minutes. 'It's stationary. Which definitely is not normal.'

'*Shenandoah*, registered in Panama, owned by Shenandoah Shipping, a Cayman Islands registered company.' Keith read off the screen. He continued searching, 'Doesn't appear to go anywhere quickly, basically floats around between Sydney, Auckland and various ports in the Philippines. The supply ship will be alongside it in an hour. About three hours before sunset.'

The General contemplated this information, 'Well, let's close up to about ten kilometres, keep up-sun of the supply ship. With the sun setting behind us we will be nearly impossible to see. What's the range of the drone? We want to be eyes on as soon as they raft up, my guess is Brightly and Jess will cross to the *Shenandoah* as soon as they have tied up.'

'I'll go ready the drone. SJ can you take the helm?'

Keith clambered out of the pilot's seat. Sara Jane climbed in and took control.

'Increase speed and come around to the north a bit, so we can curve in from up-sun. In another hour it will be fairly low to the horizon,' ordered the General.

Keith read the drone's specifications from the rear of the Gazelle. 'Radio range twelve kilometres, speed just over sixty kilometres per hour and battery life sixty minutes. At ten k's out, best case is ten minutes there and ten minutes back, leave ten in reserve so we have a dwell time of thirty minutes. There are two spare batteries, but we will lose twenty minutes at least doing the changeover. Once it's dark we can move in close, the infra-red camera will allow us to identify lookouts.'

'OK, that works. Keith, once we are close you will need to stay with the *Gazelle*, the rest of us will board. You are not only our best driver but also the only one who can operate half these systems. You will orchestrate our movements as much as you can using the drone.

'Tracey and Jodie follow me. We will check and prepare our gear. Then I want you two to swap with SJ and Joe. Jodie, Tracey and myself will lead the attack. We will leapfrog each other so two are always covering the third. SJ and Joe follow behind and keep your heads down. We will take out the combatants. You two will need to find Jess and bring her back to the *Gazelle*. Now, if we are right about this ship, there are going to be several non-combatants and possible trustees as per the chicken farm. Keith, is there any way you can find a schematic of the ship? Even if it's generic, it's better than nothing.'

'I thought Tracey was to fly the drone?' asked Sara Jane.

'We need her on the assault team as we don't have Jess with us,' the General explained. 'Though she can work with Keith until we are ready to board.'

Keith searched the internet using the satellite phone as a modem. 'Here's the basic information. She can carry three hundred and fifty TEU, her bottom is about seven metres under the water, about one hundred metres long and just under twenty metres wide. TEU stands for Twenty-foot Equivalent Units. She was last sold roughly two years ago to her current owners. She has the capacity to self-load and unload with her own cranes. Looking at the photos, her bridge tops the stern castle at the rear of the ship with, it looks like, four levels of accommodation below it. This all sits above the engine room.

'Given we suspect the *Shenandoah* to be carrying people, I am not sure how they have configured the container load. We will have to use the drone for a closer look,' Keith concluded.

'Hey, guys, the supply ship is closing in on the *Shenandoah*,' Joe yelled from the cockpit. 'They are coming up behind it and are aiming to raft up on the left-hand side. Looking at the radar image her bow is pointed roughly north-west, keeping the wind and sea behind her.'

'Conserving fuel, letting the wind and seas blow her along just enough to maintain steerage-way,' explained Keith. 'We should be in drone range in ten minutes, which will be about the time they raft up together.

'It's coming up to 7 pm, so the sun should be behind us now. How far out are we?' asked Keith, snapping the battery unit into the drone, turning it on and checking the charge level. 'Fully charged,' he mumbled to himself.

'So, SJ, turn downwind and sea. Try and match the speed of the *Shenandoah*, I'll need to go topside and I don't want to be washed overboard by a freak wave.' Keith made his way to the hatch and started undoing the clips. He pulled the ladder down and prepared to climb onto the roof of the *Gazelle*. 'Jodie, this will need two of us. One to launch the drone, the other to hold the controls. Joe, I am turning on the camera and cloning the feed to the screen on the bulkhead. Once we're over the target probably best to set the boat on autopilot and make your way back here, so we can all see the target.'

Keith handed the drone and controller to Jodie before climbing out the hatch until he was bracing his buttocks against the rear lip. 'OK, pass up the drone.'

Jodie passed the drone to Keith. He straightened up until was holding it above the roof of the *Gazelle*, 'Turn on the control,' he instructed. 'You should see a green light and a video feed looking over the bow.'

'Got it,' replied Jodie.

'Start the motors.'

'Started,' confirmed Jodie.

Keith was now holding the drone down, 'And releasing.'

'I have control, gaining altitude.'

'OK, Jodie, I'll observe on the screen. I'll also record. Can you pilot the drone?'

'Roger that, ascending to one hundred feet. Proceeding in direction of target.'

'I have you on the screen, tightening up camera focus. It appears the supply ship has just thrown a couple of lines to the *Shenandoah*. Deck hands have caught them and made them fast. A gangway is being lowered. They have swung it out enough so it's sitting on the deck of the supply ship.

'Here's Brightly, he has just pulled Jess out of the superstructure and is now pushing her to the gangway. Jess is climbing the gangway. It looks like her hands are tied, otherwise she looks OK and is moving well. They are being followed by Brightly's thug, the guy who was driving the car.'

Joe stared at the screen hoping for a closer view. As he watched, the drone rose and Keith adjusted the focus to provide a wider view. He flew the drone over the container ship. 'I'm about fifty metres up and slightly up-sun, no chance they would be able to see me.'

As he flew over the top of the outermost row of containers, he saw the innermost rows were lower, forming a walled-in courtyard running most of the length of the deck. People could be seen moving around the makeshift platform. Mostly women and children wearing rags, as far as the *Gazelle*'s crew could determine.

Jessica, Brightly, Brightly's minion and a couple of men wearing orange overalls entered the *Shenandoah* through a small tunnel between the containers. As they approached, one of the men in orange unlocked a door in the superstructure towering above the rear deck and pushed Jess through. The rest of the group followed and the door slammed shut.

'I don't think we will be able to follow the same route,' commented the General, 'Let's have a look at the supply ship and the outside of the target. This set-up appears to be more about keeping people in, not keeping them out, our best route maybe across the supply ship, up the gangway then around the outside of the containers to the fantail, behind the superstructure. Keith, can you fly that route? Everyone, watch closely. We need to spot any lookouts and CCTV.'

Keith flew the drone back to the supply ship, 'One person keeping watch on the bridge. It looks like the other one is preparing to follow Jess and Brightly onto the *Shenandoah*.'

The General continued, 'I'll board first and take him out. Then we will regroup on the deck of the supply ship under the wheelhouse. We should be out of sight from the bridge of the bigger ship.'

Keith let the crew man climb the gangplank and disappear through a gap between the containers at deck level. He flew alongside the container ship. The General continued his commentary, 'There's a walkway along the top of the gunwale, on top of the box section. It runs the length of the ship, round the outside edge of the deck.' Keith pulled back and up, 'There do not appear to be any cameras or lookouts watching it. The way they have set up the courtyard in front of the superstructure, they can keep an eye on their prisoners from the bridge. We should be able to access the fantail no problems and regroup there.'

'How many bad guys?' asked Joe.

'Impossible to tell. If they remain true to form, it will be a small number of crew in charge of trustees. Why pay for crew when you have a ship full of slaves? A minimum of a captain and a couple of officers to drive the ship across three watches, plus an engineer, is my guess. Plus, two crew men on the supply ship, plus Brightly and his thug.'

'Mind you, that's pure conjecture' added the General, 'so our attack will need to be based purely on stealth and surprise.'

'Keith, bring the drone back. We will want it fully charged for the attack. You will be our eyes and ears and drive the *Gazelle* when we board.'

'SJ, once Keith has retrieved the drone, take us a little further out. No point ruining the surprise party due to some random sighting. It will be fully dark in another hour. We will make our move then.'

'Wait,' ordered Keith, 'The guys in orange are leading a bunch of kids onto the supply ship. They just locked them into one of the containers on the supply ship's deck.'

'Good catch, they must be shipping them somewhere. Unfortunately, we need to concentrate on our main objective,' replied the General.

CHAPTER 67

Sara Jane let the *Gazelle* drift behind the *Shenandoah*. The windage of the four-storey aft castle under the bridge acted like a sail, pushing the container ship ahead of the *Gazelle*. The General looked over his team. Mentally he divided them into experienced combatants and non-combatants. He began his final briefing.

'Keith, sorry mate, I know you would prefer to be in the action, but you're our best tech guy. You'll also be responsible for defending the *Gazelle*. If things go wrong, we will need it for our retreat. You will also be our drone pilot and comms guy. And the only one here with half a chance of doing all three jobs at the same time. We will leave you a taser, a stun gun and a handgun.

'Jodie, Tracey and myself will make up the attack team. All three of us have combat experience. Our job will be to find and neutralise the bad guys. We will have stun guns and tasers. Jodie and Tracey can have handguns. Make sure you have extra cartridges for your tasers. Each cartridge has three shots. Also carry a spare battery. The handguns are last resort, use them only if we are retreating. We need to avoid the noise and ricochets.

'Joe and Sara Jane, contain the bad guys once we neutralise them and find Jessica. My guess is she is in a lockable cabin. The only problem, given the nature of this beast, is there could be multiple lockable cabins.

'Radios: each one has an earpiece and a microphone you clip to your collar. The ship is made of steel so they will probably be useless once we are inside. The two teams are not, repeat not, to split up. I know we can cover twice the ground individually, but you are more likely to be taken out by the opposition with no one watching your back. We also have no idea what armament they have on board. Again, we assume the worst. If we run up against automatic weapons, we will have no choice but to bail out if we survive. Stealth, stealth, stealth, people.

'So, let's get dressed people. Please sip an energy drink and go to the loo before we kick off. There won't be time for a piss once we board. I'll lead in, I'm hoping we will find a schematic of the ship inside the rear door. It should be there to document the evacuation procedure, in case of a sinking or fire. If we do, we'll plan our assault from there.

'We can assume, from the top: bridge, chart room, radio room and a conference or meeting room on the top level, then, second level down, Captain's, Chief Engineer's and First and Second mates' cabins, as they would all need access to the bridge. On the third level down, or the first level up, some crew cabins. I believe this is most likely where we will find Jess, and on the main deck level where we enter, the common areas such as the galley and rec rooms. But given the nature of their activities some of the space may have been bastardised for their purposes.'

'What should we do with any captives?' asked Joe.

'Operatives we will need to lock in a cabin, if they are trustees they can go in the general population, in the courtyard. Take some flexicuffs. They are only temporary but they are all we have.'

'Everyone OK so far?' The General looked around, everyone met his eyes and nodded their heads in agreement. 'No point over-planning as we don't have enough intel. We are just going to manage events as they unfold, but most importantly watch each other's backs.

'Keith, it's nearly totally dark now. Take another run with the drone please. Let's see if you can see in any of the windows, particularly on the top level.'

Joe swapped with Keith. Keith re-entered the main cabin and checked the drone. 'It's fitted with night vision and obstacle avoidance radar, but I will still need to be careful,' he commented as he worked. 'OK, Joe, hold her steady as I prepare to launch. I'll try and do it single-handed this time in case I need to retrieve and relaunch it while you're onboard the ship.'

Keith opened the hatch and placed the drone on the deck inside the cabin. Taking the control, he launched it carefully up until it slipped out the hatch into the night. 'Should have thought of that earlier! The obstacle avoidance radar keeps it from hitting the ladder or the hatch, I can launch and retrieve from inside!'

Keith flew the drone towards the *Shenandoah*. The screen showed a shadowy green light as the low-light vision automatically engaged. Keith again flew the route of their attack. A close inspection of the supply ship showed an empty bridge. 'Hopefully, they have joined the others on the *Shenandoah*,' mumbled Joe.

Keith began a commentary, 'They don't seem to have any guards or lookouts. No one is going to escape, there's nowhere to run. But it follows from what we have seen so far. They are arrogant and at this level complacent, assuming their cargo is not going to cause them any problems. I bet they drug the water. It seems to be their standard operating procedure.' The *Gazelle*'s crew watched the screen on the bulkhead in silence.

The drone flew across the roof of the bridge. No one was lying there with a gun looking down. Keith flew the length of the right, or starboard, side of the ship, the side opposite the supply ship. No one was visible. Across the bow and back down the port side, again not a soul stirred.

'See if you can see in the windows behind the bridge. I would assume they are having a meeting somewhere, having just arrived,' suggested the General. Keith flew the drone around the rear of the stern castle. There was a row of windows, smaller than those on a house but larger than the portholes on the levels below. Light flooded out, and the curtains were open. Keith manoeuvred the drone closer to one of the windows until he was looking inside.

'Looks like a conference room.' He turned the drone diagonally across the front of the window and let it hover. 'They all appear to settling in around a large conference table. Four guys in orange jumpsuits, three in blue slacks and shirts, plus Brightly, his thug and the crew of the supply ship.'

'Check the bridge,' instructed the General. Keith flew the drone to the front of the stern castle. The bridge was fully lit with fluorescent lights, and empty. 'Even if there was anyone there, their night vision would be shot,' observed the General.

'Try the windows on the next levels, maybe we can see Jess,' suggest Joe.

Keith looped the drone round the third level, all portholes dark and covered. 'No luck there.'

He repeated the exercise on the next level down. One window showed a light. He flew closer, a face could be seen looking out into the night. It was Jessica. Joe was elated, he had been sick with worry ever since watching her being bundled into the car outside the exhibition.

Keith flashed the mini spotlight in the front of the drone. Jessica jumped back in shock. She reapproached the window and gazed out as Keith gave a second flash, she waved back. She held up her hands all fingers extended, then closed them and showed one finger.

'Eleven, just as we thought,' commented the General. 'We need to move now! Before their meeting breaks up.'

Keith again replaced Joe at the helm. The remainder of the crew dragged on their clothes. 'Buddy up, I want everyone checking everyone's gear,' yelled the General.

There was a bump. Keith was holding the *Gazelle* against the hull of the Supply ship. 'Jodie, you first. Clear the supply ship, make sure there isn't anyone on watch. Keith, keep the drone on automatic hover above her. Once you have cleared it, wave and we will join you.'

The *Gazelle* drifted away from the supply ship as Keith hovered the drone in position. He returned his attention to the controls of the *Gazelle* and brought it back alongside. Jodie sprung up the ladder, through the hatch, then they heard her running across the carbon-fibre roof. Their eyes were riveted to the screen. They saw her slip over the lifelines and onto the deck of the supply ship. She disappeared into the cabin, returning two minutes later. She signalled the all-clear. 'Gather on the far side of the supply ship. Don't board the *Shenandoah* until we are ready. Follow me.' The General disappeared through the hatch as the words left his mouth, followed by Tracey, Sara Jane and Joe bringing up the rear. 'See you on the flip side,' he yelled at Keith as he mounted the ladder.

'What the fuck does that mean?' mumbled Keith to himself.

They crouched on the starboard gunwale, waiting and listening. There didn't appear to be any reaction to their intrusion. The General was first up the gangway. 'Stay put until you hear my signal.'

He took up position on the walkway bordering the *Shenandoah*'s right side, his back pressed up against the side of the outermost container, invisible from the bridge. He pulled up his microphone and whispered into it, 'Up now, all clear.'

Silently the team crept up onto the deck and found themselves positions against the container. 'OK, now I'll move up to the rear corner of the stern castle. We will regroup there before checking the fantail. One at a time. If there's any trouble, slip into the gap between this container and the one in front, where the passageway to the courtyard is.'

The General moved silently up to the next staging position. He tapped twice on his microphone with his finger, not wanting to risk speaking. Again, one by one, the group moved towards the rear of the vessel. Meanwhile, the General was peering around the corner, his taser in his hands and held upright in front of him. It was deserted; their luck was holding.

'The meeting's breaking up. Brightly and his thug are leaving; the rest look like they are planning a bit of a party. They have opened a cabinet and are hitting the drinks fridge.' Keith's voice came over the intercom.

A couple of minutes passed, and Brightly returned without his minder. Keith continued, 'Brightly's returned, but no thug. Brightly's pouring himself a glass of brandy by the look of it and taking a seat. The thug is still missing.

'Hang on they have just pulled a panel back, looks like a large screen TV. There's a picture coming up, a bit hard to tell, looks like the room they made the movie of SJ in. Hang on, I'll move to the next window, I'll be straight across from the TV then and should be able to bring it into better focus.'

He was silent for half a minute.

'I can see better now. It looks like Jess. It must be the cabin they are holding her in. She's still in her red dress.'

Joe nudged the General, 'We need to get up there now. Brightly's thug's going to come through the door any second. We need to stop him before he gets there or we will all be on candid camera.'

'Let's go,' replied the General leading the way.

'The door is opening; the thug is walking into the room. Hang on, I have an idea.'

'Everyone holds at the doorway, we enter the room, they will see us on the TV.' The General entered the stern castle and found the stairs, he mounted them quickly and silently. Jessica's cabin was one level up, and hopefully just above their present position.

Keith watched as Jessica backed up against the wall adjacent to the porthole. He scrolled through the menu on the drone's controller until he saw the option he wanted. He pressed enter. An impossibly thin red light leaped from the front of the drone. Keith manoeuvred it until it hit the advancing thug directly in the right eye. He lifted his hand to block the light but was temporarily blinded. Jessica didn't need a written invitation; she was on him in seconds. She had seen the laser light hit his right eye and she immediately scratched at his left. His hands came up to protect his face from an attack he could no longer see. Jessica lifted the hem of her skirt and ripped off one of stilettoes. She removed the rubber plug from the end of the heel. A metal spike was revealed, she swung at him from the side aiming for his ear canal. The spike went in, he screamed and reefed his head in the opposite direction popping the spike out. Jessica swung again jamming the spike into his eye as his head reached the end of its arc. He fell to the floor convulsed, then lay still.

Jessica looked up to see the General framed in the doorway, signalling with his hand for her to follow him. Turning her head, she saw the camera, a red light showing. It was still recording. She lifted her hand in a fist her middle finger extended, walked over to the camera and smashed it with her shoe. No one on the top deck saw her walk out of the cabin.

CHAPTER 68

Quentin Brightly's confidence started to return. With his minder gone maybe now there was a way out of this mess. Boris, as his minder called himself, had turned up on his doorstep at the beginning of the week. Brightly had initially assumed Boris was there to protect him. He knew he was being watched. A man and a woman kept reappearing outside his home. A white van had remained parked across the road for most of the week. Then there was the Asian girl he was sure had followed him around town after the mediation and the Task Force meeting.

But it soon became obvious, Boris was only keeping Brightly alive until he returned the Syndicate's money. They held him responsible for the funds the Foreman and the Bookkeeper had stolen. What was worse, the damn General from the Task Force had them.

Brightly had convinced Boris the girl was the key, and while the Task Force played their games at the exhibition, he knew he had pulled a master stroke by taking the lady cop. She had been there at the beginning and she was the reporter's sister. She would know where the money went and how to retrieve it. He knew they had escaped cleanly. No one could have followed them. He also knew he could not go back to Australia. He would need to stay off the grid. Luckily, he still had some funds secreted away in accounts in banks in countries that believed in privacy.

He had been impressed with their 'offshore facility' as they called it. The Captain had taken them all into the conference room behind the bridge when they had arrived. Brightly was happy to be off the noisy, slow, old supply ship and on something more substantial. A couple of stiff drinks and a hot meal would be appreciated. Later he could adjourn to the "recreation rooms" as the Captain called them with a "toy" of his choosing.

Of course, Boris had to ruin it. Now they were on the *Shenandoah*, he made it clear, Brightly was as much his prisoner as the woman. Then the Captain began to brag about their operations and how they had an almost limitless supply of risk-free stock. They contracted the people smugglers to deliver their consignments straight to the *Shenandoah*. As long as they intercepted the boats far enough out in international waters, no one missed them. Some countries, especially those with stakes in the Syndicate, were happy to deliver unwanted citizens directly to the *Shenandoah*, the elite of those countries happy to have a steady supply of replacement organs on tap. No questions asked.

Space had been made for film production and a makeshift operating theatre had been built. With access to so much fresh stock, they were able to pick and choose. Unwanted stock was turned into food for the remainder or thrown over the stern rail along with the remains of those whose organs had been harvested.

The Captain saw Brightly's face turn pale. 'Don't worry, old son. We eat proper food.' He gestured towards the crew of the supply ship, 'These guys and their mates in some other countries keep us supplied. Only the stock eats the stock.'

Brightly hesitated, 'Sure, no worries. Though I might leave it for a bit, the old stomach's still settling into life on the waves.'

'Anyway, where are my manners,' added the Captain, 'let's have a drink. Luka, open the cabinet and offer our guests a drink. I'll have a rum and coke'. One of the men in orange stood and walked over to a cabinet by the wall. The top lifted and the front dropped down to expose a liquor cabinet.

'But who's driving the boat?' asked Boris.

'Mate,' responded the Captain, 'first off, it's a ship not a boat.

Boat's what wankers like Brightly over there play about on over the weekend. Second, we are only drifting around, if anything comes within fifty miles of us, we'll pick it up on radar, and an alarm will sound. After we purchased her, we had the radar upgraded.'

Boris reddened. 'Make mine a vodka. Straight. And where are you holding the girl? I need to discuss the missing cash with her.'

'We have her in one of the movie rooms. Two levels down, while you're up Luka, turn on the screen for Studio Two. Unfortunately there's only one camera so far, but its high def and can pan and zoom in. I can control it from this remote.'

Boris grabbed the bottle of vodka off Luka. He lifted the bottle and drank deep of its contents. He thanked Luka in a language Brightly assumed was Russian. 'Now I'll show you fuckwits how a real man deals with a bitch.' He wiped his mouth with his sleeve, stood, finished the bottle, and made his way towards the door.

'Make sure we test the information before you kill her!' yelled Brightly.

'Fuck you. I'll decide what to do with you when I return,' yelled Boris over his shoulder.

Boris had made Brightly's position clear. The Captain gave him an appraising stare, the rest avoided his gaze. The expression "deadman walking" came to mind. 'Have you a brandy?'

The camera showed Jessica staring out of the window. 'I bet she's trying to see Australia! Stupid slut. Nice of her to dress up for us, though, bitch.'

The camera showed Jessica turning around, the door must have opened off camera and Boris was now in the room. They didn't need sound to recognise the fear on her face. 'Remind me we need sound in the studios. The punters like to hear as well as see.'

'Come on, Boris, you stupid, scabby prick, you're blocking the camera. We can't see.' The Engineer spoke, his Scottish accent thickened by lust and whisky.

It was over in seconds. Boris was on the floor convulsing and Jessica was giving them the finger before breaking the camera.

'Fuck, fuck, fuck,' the Captain hesitated. 'You four break into groups of two and find her. You two get back to your ship, it's the obvious means of escape. There's nowhere for the bitch to run. When you find her bring her to me.'

The Captain, First Mate, the Chief Engineer and Brightly remained at the table. 'What you fucking grinning at shithead? Oh, I get it, reckon you're off the hook now old mate Boris is gone.' The Captain looked at his Engineer and First Mate. 'Well think again, we'll make the bitch talk and when she does and tells us where the money is, I doubt your arse will be worth more than a fifty-dollar bill.'

'Even if she does give you the bitcoin accounts, I'm still the only person who can access them.'

'I don't see that as a fucking problem, mate. I bet the bitch proves tougher than you,' growled the Engineer.

Ten minutes passed in silence. Brightly picked up the brandy bottle and refilled his glass. The three-man ship's executive sat listening to the radios.

CHAPTER 69

'Get the drone back up to the conference room. Let's see how they react!' ordered the General.

Keith had the drone back in position in seconds. 'The Captain's pointing to the four guys in orange, now he's instructing the crew of the supply ship. He's walking to a cabinet and handing out radios. Brightly has a smirk on his face.'

'Back down to the fantail, everyone,' instructed the General, 'quietly.'

Jessica took the time to remove the heels from her shoes; a small spring-loaded button allowed her to slip them away from the soles. She now had a pair of flat shoes and two metal spikes with flat handles on their ends. One was smeared with blood.

Once they were all gathered on the fantail behind the stern castle the General began talking quietly into his radio. 'I am going to have to make some assumptions. They could be wrong. If they are, we will need to wing it.

'Based on Keith's surveillance the crew, who we'll call the orange guys, will start searching for Jess, split into two teams of two. They will probably pick up small arms, at least one handgun per team. If it was me, I would send the crew of the supply ship back to their boat. It's the most obvious way off this ship.

'Joe and Tracey, get forward of the supply boat and once the crew board slip the lines. With everyone occupied searching for Jess, there will be no one to help them re-attach. The two of them will be out of the game.'

Joe replied, 'There's an orange lifeboat on a cradle. If we launch it, they'll think Jess has escaped in it. They'll have to send the supply ship after it. The *Shenandoah* isn't manoeuvrable enough and they can't have Jess rescued by the authorities.'

'Good thinking, Joe. Change of plan, let's launch the lifeboat and hopefully the supply ship will chase it. Anyone have any idea how one of these works?'

'General, it'll have instructions on a placard,' suggested Joe.

'OK, Joe and Tracey, forget about the supply ship, let's launch the lifeboat. The rest of us will keep watch. Keith, let us know if anyone approaches from the sides of the ship. Jodie and Jess be ready to take down anyone who comes out the rear door we just used. Sara Jane, watch down the left side of the stern castle. I'll take the right.'

Joe and Tracey slipped over to the lifeboat. It was about six metres long, faded orange and totally enclosed. There was a hatch in the top rear accessible by a ladder. At the foot of the ladder was a placard with instructions detailing the launching procedure.

Joe started climbing the ladder. 'I'll see if I can start the motor. Then it will hopefully move away from the ship, but we must be ready to drop it straight away as they will probably hear the motor and come running.'

Tracey read through the launching procedure. There were numerous steps she needed to take before launching.

First step: *Release the toggle pin.* Most likely a fastening pin so the lifeboat did not sway about on its cradle. Following the arrow, she found a pin holding the cradle to the frame supporting the lifeboat. She pulled it out; the lifeboat swung free of its cradle, suspended in the gantry by lines attached to the bow and the stern. The stern gantry had steps built into it, she hoped Joe would be able to swing across and use them to descend to the deck.

Joe had climbed the gantry and entered the cabin of the lifeboat while Tracey was studying the launch procedure. He was looking at the engine controls. Luckily the instructions were printed in large letters on the centre of the console.

First: Turn on the ignition. Joe turned a key in the centre of the dash to the on position; a red light appeared.

Second: Wait till red LED turns to green, then turn key one more notch to engage starter. Hold until engine starts. A red light appeared above the ignition switch. He watched it turn green. He turned the ignition to the start position and held it against the return spring. The engine started and settled into a rough diesel idle.

The throttle lever was mounted on the right side of the dash. It was marked Forward, Neutral and Reverse from the top down. He moved it all the way forward. The engine noise increased but only marginally. *It must be governed*, thought Joe.

He scampered back through the cabin, through the rear hatch, and grabbed the handholds on the rear gantry. He swung his legs across and shimmied around the gantry until he was on the shipboard side, away from the swinging lifeboat. He slid down to land next to Tracey.

Tracey had been busy while Joe had scrambled inside the lifeboat.

Instruction number two in the launching procedure was Secure the Painter. This was to make sure the lifeboat didn't drift off without its passengers. They wanted the opposite. Using a utility knife attached to her belt, Tracey had cut the line, close to the bow of the lifeboat.

Release cradle clamp. She pulled a pin with a stylised padlock painted on it. The lifeboat swung away from the deck over the ocean. Joe joined her, 'One more step. Pull this.' She handed him a line running from the top of the rear gantry above the lifeboat's hatch to the foot of the gantry. It could be launched from the boat or the ship's deck.

Joe pulled the line. The lifeboat dropped free. It splashed down slightly bow first, before righting itself and motoring away into the night at an oblique angle to the course of the *Shenandoah*. Footsteps could be heard running up to the lifeboat station. Two men appeared down the gangway from the bow.

'She's escaped in the starboard lifeboat,' the first man yelled into his radio. His partner climbed onto the lifeboat deck and swung his torch into the night, trying to find a trace of the fleeing boat. The first man joined him, pulling a handgun out of his pocket. The torch light found the lifeboat; the gunman opened fire. The noise allowed Tracey to step up behind them and shoot both in the back with her taser. Hanging over the gap in the rails left by the departed lifeboat, neither stood a chance, both losing their grip and falling over the side of the ship. The taser darts pulled free as they fell. Tracey unclipped the cartridge and kicked it over the side of the boat.

Joe saw the handgun sitting on the deck next to the gantry and went to retrieve it. 'No. Leave it. Their mates will be here in a second. They'll see it and think the first two fell overboard.'

'Good thinking.' Together he and Tracey slipped behind a large structure bolted to the deck. *A paint or rope locker*, thought Joe. They didn't have to wait long. The second pair of orange jumpsuit-wearing crew ran up, looked at the empty lifeboat station and saw the gun lying on the deck.

*

In the conference room, suddenly a chime could be heard. 'Lifeboats, someone is fucking with one of the lifeboats,' the Captain picked up his radio. 'Check the lifeboats,' he yelled into it.

'We have port side.'

'We'll check starboard, we're up the bow now making our way back.'

Again, there was silence.

'SITREP, what the fuck's happening?' yelled the Captain into his radio.

'Port side's OK, going to assist starboard side.'

Another moment's silence. 'Starboard's gone. Dimitri's gun's on the deck. Can't see them.'

'Supply ship, get out there and find them. Bitch has escaped in a life raft. Find that lifeboat. If she turns on the EPIRB, the last thing we want is the authorities all over us.'

'What about Dimitri and Luka,' squawked his radio.

'Fuck them, they're shark food by now.'

The radio went quiet. The two men could be heard shouting at each other in their own language. Shortly after, they wandered round the rear of the stern castle and entered the door from the fantail the team had used earlier. Tracey and Joe could hear them muttering as they mounted the stairs back to the bridge.

A rumbling noise started off the port side. A spotlight pierced the darkness, highlighting the bollards to which the supply ship's lines were tied. 'Clear the lines. Lead them back to us, get on board and heave them in.' The supply ship's skipper could be heard over its deck speaker. The crewman could be seen highlighted in the spotlight clearing the lines and doubling them back to the ship. He jumped back on board. 'Release the bow line.' The crew member on the bow of the supply ship let go his line. It unwound from the *Shenandoah*'s midship bollard and spiralled back on to the deck of the supply ship. The faster drift of the *Shenandoah* opened a gap between the two ships.

'Release the stern line.' The crew member now stationed at the stern of the supply ship pulled his line free and secured it on the deck of the supply ship. The skipper, from his helming position, turned his spotlight onto the ocean behind the *Shenandoah*. He followed the light with a slow turn to the left away from the *Shenandoah* until he was steaming in the reverse direction of the *Shenandoah*'s drift. The searchlight could be seen probing the darkness.

Joe looked around and motioned to Tracey, 'Let's join the others.' He tapped his microphone, 'Hey, General, we're coming back to you. Clear.'

'Yeah, Roger that. Regroup on the fantail,' came the General's reply. 'Stay in the shadow of the stern castle. Last thing we want is to be silhouetted by the spotlight of the supply ship.'

Once they had regrouped, Tracey gave a brief after action report. 'So which direction did the lifeboat go?' asked the General.

'Off to the side, straight out. You'd think they could find it on radar,' commented Jessica.

'Maybe they have crap radar. And it was the other side of the ship. It should keep them occupied for a little while anyway. Keith, can you see the supply ship and lifeboat on your radar?'

'Affirmative, General, the lifeboat is heading in a north-east direction, about ninety degrees from our course. It is holding a fairly straight course at about six knots, twelve kilometres an hour, and about one kilometre from your position, but nearly two kilometres from the supply ship. They should see it soon as they are clear of the radar shadow of the *Shenandoah*.'

'Thanks, Keith. I think they just received a radar hit. The supply ship has changed direction towards the east and they are searching with their spotlight in the correct direction. If it holds straight, it will take them a couple of hours to catch it and radio back. Can you follow on radar and let us know when they get close? I'm guessing the bad guys are regrouped in the conference room until they hear from the supply ship? Can you have a look see with the drone? Thanks, Keith.'

They waited silently. A minute passed and Keith came back online. 'Yes, can confirm all known bad guys are in the conference room. Will need to bring the drone in for a battery change, so you will be unsighted for the next five minutes.'

'Guys, we have a chance to catch our breath. We can't storm the conference room, and I'm guessing they will stay there until they hear from the supply ship. Once they know Jess is not on the lifeboat they will begin searching again. We need some ideas. They still believe they are only searching for Jess, but they are going to be doubly alert now they have lost three men.'

'And thanks, everyone, for coming to my rescue. I knew I could count on you guys,' added Jess.

'And Jess, nice shoes, bet you didn't buy them at David Jones.'

'Hah no, Joe, but a girl has to have her secrets.'

'Looks like the Captain's laying down the law,' commented Keith. 'The two crew in orange jumpsuits have just left the conference room.'

Keith had changed the battery on the drone and was back in position. The General and his team were gathered on the fantail leaning against the rear of the stern castle. 'Watch the windows, we will see the lights come on if they go to their cabins.'

'Roger, General.'

Tracey was nearest the door. 'I think they are just above us. They must be going to dispose of the body Jess left in the cabin they were holding her in.'

The General considered this for a moment, 'The door to that cabin locks from the outside. Tracey, SJ, run up and lock them in.'

Tracey and Sara Jane scampered up the stairs and rounded the corner and slammed the door. It was secured by a deadlock on the outside of the door, designed to keep people prisoner, not for the occupant's privacy. Tracey turned the key, while Sara Jane pressed her weight against the door handle in case one of the crew attempted to reef the door open before it could be locked.

'Done,' gasped Tracey. She withdrew the key and pocketed it. They could hear the two men faintly through the steel door, wrenching the locked handle and yelling in frustration. The two women slid down the gangway and re-joined the others.

'Done. I have the key,' said Tracey.

'Well done, two more down. There may be a spare key so let's be aware those two may come back into play,' cautioned the General.

'Four left. Keith, can you track them?'

'General, they appear to be splitting up. I'll circle round to the bridge. I would guess at least one of the officers will take up a watch. Brightly is still sitting at the conference table, a bottle of brandy in front of him, though, I have a feeling he is only pretending to drink it so the crew disregard him.'

'A light has just come on, below the conference room, you can probably see the glow if you look up, three levels above you. I'll hover the drone down for a look.'

They waited silently as Keith repositioned the drone. 'It's the First Mate or the Engineer. Looks like he is taking some downtime, probably has the next watch.'

'Two hours maybe before he is missed. Based on two-hour watches. Keith, can you give us a layout of the room?'

'Yes, General, it's like a motel room, just a bit smaller. The bed is below the window, there is a desk and chair on one side and a cupboard on the other. There is a small ensuite up by the door on the right as you enter. Hang on, he looks as though he is about to have a shower. Yeah, he is undressing and heading towards the ensuite.'

'Thanks, Keith. Jodie and Tracey come with me, the rest of you stay here. Let's go get him.' The General led the way into the stern castle. 'It should be the level above the room Jess was in and below the conference room. Looking at the windows it should be the door on the right as we face the rear of the ship. Hopefully the door isn't locked.'

The General, Jodie and Tracey quickly mounted the stairs. They were steel stairs with railings, and as space on the ship was at a premium, so steep they were almost like ladders. Joe could hear them ascending from the doorway even with their rubber-soled boots. He hoped the noise would be swallowed up by the background noises echoing around the ship. Joe, Jessica and Sara Jane could follow the raid via their radios.

'OK, we are outside the door. Keith can you confirm he is still in the bathroom?'

'Roger, General, still in the bathroom.'

'I'm going to try the door handle. It's not locked.'

'Jodie and Tracey stand just inside the cabin door. I'll stand further inside and distract him. As soon as you can zap him with the stun guns.'

The trio crept into the cabin. The General stood in the centre of the room, Jodie and Tracey pressed themselves into the wall between the ensuite's door and the cabin door. With the ensuite being so small the door opened into the cabin, hiding Jodie and Tracey.

'G'day, mate, how you going?' the General exclaimed as the man stepped out of the ensuite. Tracey kicked the door closed, while Jodie plunged her stun gun into the roll of flab round the man's naked waist. Tracey stepped forward a moment later and plunged her stun gun into his neck. The man collapsed. He lay on the floor convulsing. The General snatched a small roll of duct tape from a thigh pocket in his cargo pants. He quickly wrapped it round the man's head and across his mouth. He flipped him face down and taped his hands and wrists together. He left his legs free.

'Now listen and listen well. We are going for a little walk, down two levels. You try anything these two will happily zap you again. Then we will push you down the stairs. Nod your head if you understand.'

The prisoner nodded his head.

'Let's go,' ordered the General, grabbing the prisoner by the elbow and hoisting him to his feet. 'Tracey, take a peek. The head of the stairs is just outside the door. We should be able to hustle down quickly enough. Joe, Jess, SJ, meet us at the door to Jess's cabin. We have another prisoner.'

Tracey led the way down the steep stairs, the General followed the prisoner, one hand holding the man's upper arm, the other the rail. They regrouped on the gangway beside the head of the stairs. 'Only one flight. Keith, bring the drone down a level, let me know if the captives look like crowding the door.'

'Got you, General. In position,' replied Keith. 'They are currently sitting on the bed.'

Joe, Jess and Sara Jane had ascended one flight while the General, Tracey and Jodie forced the prisoner down the steep stairs.

'General, the prisoners are looking towards the door. They must have heard you. Looks like they are making their way towards the door,' Keith reported.

'Jess, and Joe, have your stun guns ready. If you see the bastards prod them. Tracey and Jodie, you push this arsehole into the room as I open the door and push it inwards. SJ, you unlock the door and relock it as I slam it shut.'

'The prisoners are just inside the door, one on the open side, one on the hinge side,' warned Keith.

'On three,'

'One, two, three,'

Sara Jane had the door unlocked as the General uttered 'two'. On 'three' he swung the handle and booted the door inwards. The door slammed into one of the prisoners waiting behind it, hitting him square in the face. His hands went to his shattered nose as he bounced backwards. The impact stopped the door's momentum but left enough room for Jodie and Tracey to shove the new prisoner through the gap, colliding with the crew man waiting in ambush on the open side of the door. The General, his hands still on the door handle, slammed it shut. Sara Jane relocked it as he held it in closed.

'OK, back to his cabin. We should be able to hide in there with some privacy for an hour at least, until they call a watch change. Keith, time to change the drone's battery again. Once we are in the cabin, we'll do a SITREP.'

Keith had the drone fly back to the *Gazelle* waiting just off port side of the *Shenandoah* and used its collision avoidance radar to land it at his feet. He had one battery left fully charged. The last one he had changed out was nearly half recharged. So as long as he could keep cycling the batteries, he was confident he could keep the drone flying for the duration.

The rest of the team quickly made their way up a level and into the now vacant cabin. Jessica, Joe and Jodie squeezed onto the bed, Tracey sat in the office chair by the desk, Sara Jane lowering herself onto Tracey's lap. The General remained standing.

'How's everything on your end, Keith?'

'Good, General. The drone is back and the new battery fitted. The first battery will be fully recharged in another thirty minutes. I'll put the next one on charge then. I'm using one battery every thirty minutes, but taking an hour to recharge. With three batteries we should be able to keep the rotation happening indefinitely.

'I can see the liferaft on the radar. It's holding its course well. The supply ship has closed the gap between them by about a quarter, but I doubt they'll risk boarding until daylight, a good six hours from now.'

'OK, good work, rest the drone until we are ready to move again.' The General looked at the rest of his team. 'Three left, but we will lose the element of surprise soon. We've been lucky so far. While we still hold the element of surprise, I think we win. By my reckoning we have about ninety minutes until the Captain calls a watch change and will come looking for one of the guys we've locked up below.'

'Before we make our next move, let's search this cabin. See if we can pick up any information. First, who was this bozo? Have a look through his desk, you two. See what you can find.'

Sara Jane and Tracey untangled themselves from each other and, standing, pushed the chair away from the desk. Sliding out the top drawer they dumped the contents onto the desktop. Sara Jane provided a commentary as Tracey shuffled the debris. 'Looks like he's a ship's officer, not the engineer. Has an Australian passport, no personal correspondence in this drawer. Next drawer down, a bottle of rum, and not much else, bottom drawer some ships' and equipment manuals, and underneath … Oh fuck. Polaroids of children, not good. If I'd seen these early, I'd have killed the fuckwit.' Sara Jane threw the manuals back into the drawer covering the evidence.

'He'll get his. We'll hand this lot over to the authorities once we have control of the ship.'

'Not good enough, General. Push the fuckwit over the side and sail away,' replied Tracey.

Joe piped up, 'Let's not place the cart ahead of the horse, guys. We have to have control of the ship before we call the authorities. Otherwise, all the poor souls in front of us will be going over the side with chains round their necks before the cavalry appears over the hill.'

'Cavalry? Joe, John Wayne taught his horse to swim?' asked Jessica.

Joe adjusted his metaphor. 'Fucking Navy then, steaming over the horizon.'

'Yes, totally, we need to safeguard the captives, and to do that we must control the ship, neutralise the crew and Brightly,' confirmed the General.

'We'll take the bridge next. Keith, launch the drone, we need to know the location of the last three bad guys. The rest of you study this evacuation plan. It gives a good schematic of the ship,' said the General, tapping the notice stuck to the wall beside his shoulder.

'Drone's in the air, tracking towards the conference room,' confirmed Keith.

'Situation's changed. Brightly's on the move. He is no longer in the conference room. There's a cabinet open at the rear of the room, looks like it's the armoury. Better consider him armed. Right, I'll fly round to the bridge now to see if I can locate the Captain and Engineer.

'Right, in position. The Captain and Engineer are both still on the bridge. Looks like the Captain has a call on the satellite phone.

'Hang on, the rear door is opening, must be Brightly, not sure what he's planning?'

From the deck below and rear of the stern castle gunshots rang out clearly.

'Brightly's opened fire on the Captain and the Engineer. Looks like the Captain's down and the Engineer has ducked behind his console. Brightly's shooting wild, he's all over the place.' Joe was amazed at how calm Keith's voice was over the radio. His own adrenaline was pumping from the shock of the gunfire.

'Assuming the same type of gun we recovered from the deck earlier it's a Glock. Safety is built into the trigger and holds seventeen rounds. Keith, can you tell if there is any return fire? Hopefully the Captain and Engineer didn't see any reason to be armed.'

'No, General, no return fire at present, repeat no return fire.'

The General considered the situation for a minute. 'Jodie, come with me. Jess and Tracey follow us to the top of the stairs. Joe and SJ stay here until we give the all-clear. And, SJ, before you can argue, it's because Joe and you have no firearms or combat training.'

Joe could see the explanation had not appeased Sara Jane. She looked like she was about to explode. 'Roger that, General, we'll stay here until called. SJ, he can't have us up there, we would be a liability.'

'Fucking bullshit,' replied Sara Jane climbing onto the bed and leaning against the bulkhead. Joe was about to laugh as she reminded him of a teenager having a sulk.

'I'll keep watch out the door in case there are any surprises from below decks,' he added. 'I know we haven't seen anyone, but that doesn't realistically prove they are not there.'

The General walked to the door of the cabin, 'Keith, SITREP.'

'Brightly's standing just inside the door. It's open on the right-hand rear of the bridge. The Captain was in the centre front of the bridge when he went down, the Engineer is towards the rear left of the bridge behind what I assume is his console. I counted twelve shots, which would leave five if the gun is standard and fully loaded.'

The General led the way cautiously up the ladder to the next level. The top level contained the bridge at the front, radio and navigation rooms behind, a passage way from side to side, with the conference room to the rear.

Not wanting to make a sound, the General pointed to Jessica and Tracey and to the starboard side where the bridge door was still closed. They nodded. They would surprise the Engineer from behind as soon as Brightly was contained. The General and Jodie shimmied along the wall; the General holding his handgun two-handed and in front of his face, Jodie drawing her taser. He then signalled to the deck beside the door, Jodie lay down on her stomach facing forward but still behind the bulkhead. The General removed his left hand from the pistol, he closed his fist and then extended three fingers. Jodie nodded confirming she understood his signal.

He dropped one finger, paused; dropped another, paused; and dropped his last extended finger.

'Drop the fucking gun and hands up, scumbag,' he yelled from behind the bulkhead. Jodie barrel-rolled until she was peeking round the door frame at deck level, her taser extended in front of her. She pressed the trigger. The prongs penetrated Brightly's dress shirt and completed the circuit. The General's yell had caused him to half-turn so his gun was no longer covering the Engineer, one shot firing into the steel ceiling before ricocheting into the port side bridge window, spidering the glass.

Brightly was down on his face, the gun just out of reach of his right hand. The General leaped over Jodie and kicked the gun out of his reach. 'Hands behind your back, don't move or I'll blow your head off.'

Brightly had yet to recover from the taser attack and couldn't move his arms behind his back. The General grabbed Brightly's right arm and dragged it across his back to his left. The General shoved his handgun into his belt at his hip as he reached into the thigh pocket of his combat pants for his roll of duct tape.

'Strap the fuckwit's arms up nice and tight,' came a voice. The General looked up to see the Captain had snatched up the gun he had kicked out of Brightly's reach. The black hole at the end of the barrel was now wavering at him from ten feet away in the Captain's left hand. The Captain's right arm hung limp and bloody at his side.

The port side bridge door was rattling. Jessica and Tracey were on the wrong side of a locked door. The Chief Engineer rose from behind his console and came forward, the Captain handed him Brightly's gun.

'I don't know who the fuck you are, mate,' he snarled at the General, 'and I don't fucking care, finish taping Brightly's arms, grab your friend on the floor there and come on in.'

As Jodie lifted herself from the floor, the Captain continued, 'Throw your weapons down, girly. Chief, keep them covered.' The Captain staggered to his feet. He was losing blood through the bullet wound to his upper arm.

He pressed a button on the console next to a microphone. 'One, get your arse up to the bridge now.'

He released the button and turned back to the General, he walked over and kicked Brightly in the side. 'Stand him up, tape her left elbow to his right elbow.'

The Captain swayed gently with the movement of the ship as the General taped Jodie's elbow to Brightly's. The Captain pointed his gun at the General.

'Now, Chief, tape this wannabe hero's right elbow to Brightly's. For now, we'll lock them up downstairs. You can all share a room with Brightly's mate, I'm sure he won't be any trouble. Between the three of you, you have two good arms so you can get down the ladders. Try anything and she dies first.'

'Chief, you take his gun, I'll keep Brightly's. Where the fuck is One? Be careful. We don't know who else is on board. We need this lot secured first then we can work out what the fuck is going on round here,' the Captain continued.

Keith turned off the General's and Jodie's radio channels, he didn't want the Captain or Engineer hearing him talk to the rest of the team. The team had all heard the Captain's instructions through the General's and Jodie's voice-activated microphones. Tracey and Jessica looked around quickly, the locked door had stopped them and they had not been able to cover the Captain and the Engineer. Now they were exposed in the companion way once the Captain had pushed his captives out of the bridge through the starboard door.

'Into the conference room,' whispered Jessica. She pushed the conference room door open, and Tracey followed her in, silently closing the door behind her.

'We need to stop them before they reach the lower level. They'll release the prisoners and then we will be fucked,' whispered Jessica.

'I still have the key to the door,' responded Tracey, 'and it's a solid steel door. Even if they have a spare key, one of them will have to retrieve it while the other guards the General and Jodie.'

Using his headset, Joe broke into the conversation, 'Or they could throw them in another room. Looking at the evacuation chart there are four rooms on the lower level. SJ and I will head down now and see if we can slow them down.'

'Good thinking, Joe. I have the drone outside the bridge window and they are about to force Jodie, the General and Brightly through the door. Jess and Tracey, you cleared the passageway?'

'Yeah, we're in the conference room,' confirmed Jess.

The Engineer backed through the door and dragged the prisoners out with him, careful to use them as a human shield should anyone be waiting of them. The Captain followed, leaning against the bulkhead as he did, blood loss and the movement of the ship making it hard for him to keep his balance.

'OK, Chief, you first, clear the passageway below and shoot anyone who appears.'

'Captain, what about One or the rest of the crew?'

'Fuck him, they must have already neutralised him,' answered the Captain. 'There's probably more of them, but we need these ones locked up first. So, shoot anything that moves.'

'Captain, too risky, we only need Brightly alive. Shoot these two in the head and throw them off the bridge wings. We'll be sitting ducks if we try and get down to the studio rooms.'

The Captain thought about the Engineer's suggestion. 'You're right, dead fuckwits don't cause problems.' He looked closely at the General, 'You look like you've been round the block a few times, mate. Shame your young friend ain't gunna have the same luck. If we had more time, we could have some fun with her, but the Chief is right, best option a quick bullet each and over the side. Then we need to find the rest of the crew and deal with your mates.'

Keith's voice came through their earpieces, 'Hang on, guys, looks like they are having a discussion out in the corridor. The Captain's bleeding all over the wall and can hardly stand. Joe and SJ, are you down the lower level yet?'

'Yep, just locked the rooms and threw the keys over the side.'

'Joe, they're heading back into the bridge. There is no way the Captain would make it down the ladders. There are ladders from the deck running up the outside of the stern castle to the bridge wings. Use them, access the bridge wing doors and ambush them.'

'Roger, take left SJ. I'll take right.'

'Jess and Tracey, as soon as they try to re-enter the bridge, they'll try and lock the door. Stop the door closing. They won't be able to shoot at you and the tug-of-war will distract them.'

'Roger, Keith,' replied Jessica and Tracey together.

'The Captain is starting to struggle, looks like he has lost a lot of blood and is going into shock. From what I can see through the companion way port, the Engineer is running out of hands. He can't make up his mind whether to deal with the prisoners first or the Captain.'

Keith continued his running commentary. 'He's pushed the prisoners to the deck, they can't get up taped together the way they are. He's rolling the Captain along the bulkhead and back through the door and onto the bridge. Looks like the Captain just fell though the bridge door.'

Three gun shots rang out, the bulkhead opposite the bridge door was suddenly splattered with blood, Jessica and Tracey rushed out of the conference room to see the Chief try and raise his right arm holding the gun, he looked up with surprise then resignation as the gun slipped out of his fingers and he collapsed on the deck.

Jodie and the General were rolling around the floor attempting to regain their feet, while hauling Brightly up between them. Jessica and Tracey pulled out their tasers and peeked round the door. The Captain had collapsed on the deck just inside the bridge, a smoking gun on his hip.

'There were only three rounds left, not fucking five,' commented Sara Jane, from her position behind the Captain's body.

Jessica looked at the Chief, the three shots had all hit him in the centre of his chest, 'You only needed one, SJ.'

'What did Dad always say, Jess, if you gunna do a job do it fucking properly.'

'I'm not sure he ever said that, and Mum would have kicked his arse if he dropped an F bomb.'

Joe walked over from the left side, where he had entered through the door to the bridge wing. He was slightly out of breath. 'She beat me up the ladder. Slammed through the wing door on that side as the Captain came back through, kung fu'd him to the ground, went down with him and came up firing. Shit, I hope I never get on your bad side, SJ.'

The General sheepishly peeled the last of the duct tape away from his wrists. Jessica and Tracey were untangling and untapping Jodie from Brightly who appeared to have fainted. Finally, they helped Jodie back onto her feet and the three them stepped over Brightly to join the others on the bridge.

Sara Jane smiled sweetly up at the General, 'Fucking good thing us non-combatants are around to save your soldierly-types' arses.'

'Shit,' yelled Jessica, 'Brightly was faking, he's doing a runner.'

CHAPTER 72

'Let him go, we need to regroup and recharge,' the General responded. 'SJ, thank you, you're a legend.'

Ha, thought Joe, *sign of a good leader, eating the humble pie before it's shoved in his face.* He suddenly realised how tired he was. He looked around at the rest of his companions; they all looked drained. The last of the adrenaline was draining from their systems.

'Right, it's midnight now, let's secure the top two decks and put a watch system in place.'

'Keith?'

'Yes, General,'

'How's the drone?'

'I have recharged one battery, the second is about half-charged and the one in the drone is down to about twenty-five per cent.'

'Jess and Joe, you two get some sleep, the four of us will secure the bridge and executive deck below. Two hours then we change around. Sorry Keith, you're gunna need to stay awake for the duration.'

'No worries, General, just to let you know the supply ship is still chasing the lifeboat. They are only a knot or two faster, which is making it slow going, being a stern chase.'

The radio squawked: 'Cargo ship *Shenandoah*, cargo ship Shenandoah please respond, this is Australian Warship HMAS *Hobart* responding to your EPIRB activation. Please state the nature of your emergency.'

'The EPIRB in the lifeboat, must have been activated when it launched. The emergency beacon would have been picked up in

Canberra and the *Hobart* must be the nearest vessel,' explained Jessica.

'HMAS *Hobart*, HMAS *Hobart*, this is the cargo vessel *Shenandoah*, over.' The General had snatched a radio microphone from the console above the helmsman's position.

'Reading you, *Shenandoah*,'

'Life raft accidently launched during a drill. Repeat accidental activation, no assistance required.'

'No worries, *Shenandoah*, Canberra have been trying to contact you on the emergency channel for the last couple of hours. We also notice you are dead in the water. We will be alongside around dawn.'

'Repeat not necessary, *Hobart*, situation in hand.'

'You are in the Australian economic zone. As such we are authorised to inspect your papers and your ship. Please hove to and await our arrival.'

'Looks like we will be having visitors. Keith any idea where the *Hobart* is?'

'Almost dead south of us, General. Estimated time of arrival 0530 hours, just after dawn.'

'It's 2230 hours now, so six hours, until we have company.'

'Hey, General,'

'Yes, Keith,'

'The supply ship in breaking off the chase. It's turning and heading north-west. Probably trying to avoid being seen by the *Hobart*'s radar.'

'Small vessel heading north-west, positioned one nautical mile east of the *Shenandoah*, please desist. Hove to beside the *Shenandoah* and await our arrival,' the command boomed from the bridge speakers.

'They are still running,' commented Keith.

Joe looked at the digital chart screen overlaying the radar on the binnacle in front of the helmsman's position. The *Hobart* was not in sight, only the supply ship could be seen crossing their bows, 'Looks like she's making a run for the coast.'

'Forget them, not our problem. Now, Jess and Joe find a cabin and get some rest. We'll take watches and bail out just before dawn. Let the *Hobart* take the credit.'

The movement of the ship changed. It was subtle at first but quickly became more apparent.

'*Shenandoah, Shenandoah*, this is HMAS *Hobart*. We see you are making way, hove to, repeat hove to,' commanded the speakers.

'What's happening?' asked Tracey.

'We're all fucked, head office has taken over the ship remotely. They'll head out of Australian waters and blow the bottom out of her.' Six sets of eyes swung round to see the Captain had pulled himself over to the bulkhead at the rear of the bridge. The movement had started his wound bleeding again, drenching the floor around him. 'They would have heard the *Hobart*'s hail, via the sat link. They won't want any trace of this ship found.'

'Where's the charge?' asked the General.

Gasped the Captain, 'My only regret is I'll be fucking dead before you lot die. Fuck you.'

The Captain sighed and stopped breathing.

No longer was the *Shenandoah* rising and falling gently from the stern as the waves came from behind; it was now rolling side to side. Joe looked at the digital compass. The ship was now heading east. He looked at the instruments and controls on the console in front of him. Standing in the helmsman's station, the lack of a wheel confounded him for a moment. Centred in the console was a small toggle or joystick, above it was a dial showing the rudder's angle. While he watched the toggle returned to its centre position and the arrow on the dial pointed straight to the zero position at the top of the dial. The throttles beside him clicked back another notch. 'They must be controlling the autopilot. If we disable the autopilot, we can regain control.'

'Joe, the charge is the priority. We must stop this ship sinking. There must be fifty to a hundred prisoners on board, living on or below the deck. Definitely no life rafts for them. Also, if we alter course or speed the head office will see it and maybe set off the charge immediately.'

Tracey and Sara Jane were pulling sheets of paper from the table behind the Engineer's station. 'Here's a diagram of the ship. Where would you put the charge?'

Everyone gathered around the bench looking at the diagram. It was a large scale. Joe spoke his thoughts aloud. 'It must be somewhere open, there's no point flooding a sealed compartment, so that excludes the fuel tanks.' Joe pointed out the two tanks running between the bottom of the cargo holds and the bottom of the ship. 'But see next to the keel, there is a passageway down each side of the bulkhead, running down the centre of the ship from the bow to the rudder post. The engine room's the heaviest part of the ship. I would blow a hole under there.' Joe pointed to a place on the keel directly under the stern castle.

'Jodie, you're the explosives expert, is Joe right?'

'Yes, General, most likely.' Jodie studied the map, 'How long do we have?'

Joe interrupted, he had returned to the helm's station and was studying the digital chart. 'My guess is they will try for international waters first, that's why we're heading east. If the *Hobart* catches us before then, they will detonate. But they could detonate any time if they believe we pose a threat. My guess is they are only receiving telemetry not video or audio, so we have a chance.' He scrolled out until he could see the east coast of Australia, then stared at the screen for a minute while completing some mental arithmetic. 'We should reach international waters in around seven hours. The *Hobart* won't catch us by then unless she speeds up, as we are travelling obliquely away from her.'

'Joe,'

'Yes, Keith,'

'The *Hobart* has sped up; she must have the *Shenandoah* on her radar and realises you are running.'

'Thanks, Keith. General, we need to assume the bad guys can see this,' Joe said, pointing at the helmsman's console, 'It may tempt them to cut their losses and sink us now. Keith, can we block communications to the ship. They must be using some sort of modem to communicate by satellite.'

'If it's wireless, look for a box with a light. It would have to be on the bridge or all the steel would distort the signal. If it's wired, look for ethernet cable, you know like in an office. Trace it to where it joins with other cables and that should be your router, which should be connected to the modem, if it's hardwired.'

Joe looked around. 'Most likely added after the ship was built, as part of the conversion.' In the rear right-hand corner of the bridge a box hung from the wall. 'That's a wireless booster for the bridge. It would be hardwired.' Joe pointed at the box, 'Follow it and we will find the router and modem.'

Standing on his toes, Joe pulled the device off the wall. A wire ran through the wall, disappearing into the next cabin. 'What's behind here?' he asked.

'Radio room,' answered Tracey, her finger on the schematic. 'You gain access through a door in the back of the bridge. Must be behind the curtain.'

'Makes sense, a black-out curtain, so the watch don't lose their night vision.' Joe pulled the curtains aside. Two doors appeared, one marked radio room, the other chart room. Joe opened the door and switched on the light. It was no longer a radio room, more a computer room. Racks, cables, flashing LED lights. There was no desk, no chair and no old vacuum valve radio.

'Don't touch anything,' yelled Jodie.

Joe stumbled back out of the radio room. 'What?'

'The charges could have a dead man's switch, as soon as they lose signal it may go off.'

'So, what should we do?'

Tracey was looking at the schematics, 'Close the watertight doors, that way if a compartment floods the ship may still float as the air in the other compartments keeps her afloat.'

In two steps the General was by her side. 'Start at the engine room, as we agree it's the most likely target. Work your way outwards. There are two hatches on the fantail, port and starboard, left and right, see them here, they will also need to be closed. Then work up and forward. Hopefully, even if the explosion breaks the ship's back, the front section will stay afloat long enough for the *Hobart* to arrive. Teams of two. Radios are probably going to be useless so try and keep in line of sight of each other so you can relay messages. If anyone sees the charge leave it, we'll deal with it later.'

Sara Jane was rooting round in the engineer's station. Pulling out a drawer she found a bundle of LED, strap-on headlights. 'Here take these in case you can't find the lights.'

'Remember, Brightly's still out there. Assume he is armed,' cautioned the General.

'Shoot first, ask questions later,' confirmed Jessica, 'I can live with that.'

Tracey rolled up the schematic and clamped it under her arm, 'Let's go, we need to get down to the main deck.'

Four companionways and four ladders later, they assembled on the main deck, just inside the doorway leading to the fantail from the rear of the stern castle. Tracey unrolled the schematic on the deck. 'The rear engine room access must be in those shed-like structures in the rear corners.'

Joe and Jessica stepped over to each structure. They were both unlocked. They stepped inside and dogged down two hatches set in the deck. They jogged back to the group.

'There should be an accessway at the front of the companionway, through the stern castle, taking us down to the next level.'

The group turned, re-entered the stern castle and walked forward. At the front of the companionway on the left, a hatchway was set in the bulkhead. Joe opened the door to a steep flight of stairs that led down to the next level.

'What's down here?' he asked.

Tracey studied the chart. 'Just some utility rooms it seems, then down another level to the watertight doors shutting off the engine room, then two more ladders down to a hatch which leads to a passage taking us along the keel. Along the passage are another five watertight doors, then another ladder leading to the foredeck.'

The General looked about quickly, 'Joe, Jessica, take the passage along the bilge. Once you shut the first hatch we will be out of touch until you reach the bow. Tracey and SJ, lock down the engine room. Jodie, where would you place the bomb if you wanted to kill this ship. I know I asked before but now we can see the structure of the ship.'

The group separated to perform their tasks. Jodie studied the schematic. 'In front of this bulkhead, the engine room's behind, so most chance of not only splitting the hull but also breaking the back of the ship, possibly splitting her open; she would sink in minutes.'

'Go search. Don't touch anything, if you find it, until we can disable the comms room.'

'Found it,' Jodie called over the radio. The General had placed Tracey at the top of the gantries and ladders connecting the front of the stern castle to the bilge in front of the engine room compartment. Radio signals couldn't pass through the steel of the ship, so communications needed to be organised by line of sight. Tracey relayed the message to Sara Jane on the fantail who in turn passed it on to the General, who was standing on the port bridge wing.

'OK, Jodie, can you disarm it?' asked the General.

'It looks like an old limpet mine, with a control box welded onto it. The control box is connected to an ethernet cable. Bottom line is no, as I can't disconnect the mine from the control box, and I do not know what booby traps have been built into it.'

Jodie's message was passed to Tracey who passed it to Sara Jane who passed it on to the General. 'Keith, did you copy? Your thoughts? If we can't disarm the mine, can we gain control of the operating program?'

'Yes, General, as it has been activated by a command received electronically, logically it is controlled by a program. Is there a computer connected to the ship's network you can access ?'

The General pondered this for a moment, before issuing his next orders, 'Meanwhile, Jodie, return to the top of the stairs, lock down all the watertight doors you pass. Sara Jane run to the bow, see if you can contact Joe and Jess, get them back on deck as soon as possible, but they need to lock down all the watertight hatches they pass. Then regather on the bridge as soon as possible.'

Jodie climbed back out of the bilge. She closed the hatch in the lower deck, shutting off the bilge compartment. She repeated the process on all four levels, not sure how many compartments would be damaged when the mine blew.

*

It was dark, deep within the hull. The passageway was crossed every twenty metres by the ship's ribs, each rib had a water-tight door built into it. These doors were currently open. Jessica and Joe stopped and clamped each one closed as they made their way to the bow. Dim overhead lights provided illumination. The doors had not been closed in a long time, each pair of hinges was slightly seized. Each door had a large wheel mounted in the centre operating the clamps which held it closed and made the waterproof seal. Each of the four wheels was stiff.

It took forty-five minutes. 'Where the fuck have you two been?' Sara Jane greeted them as they emerged through a hatch in the forecastle. 'Geez, you look rough,' she said a moment later taking in the sweat and grease-streaked faces and clothes. 'We need to return to the bridge pronto.'

She lifted her radio, 'General, SJ here, have the bilge rats, returning to the bridge.'

'Copy, SJ, clear,' the General's voice could be heard crackling over the radio in response.

Joe and Jessica followed Sara Jane back along the port gunwale. Brightly watched them leave from his position behind the anchor winch. He had been tempted to tackle Sara Jane while she was alone and throw her overboard but delayed too long. He cursed his cowardice.

Joe and Jessica spent the return to the stern castle catching their breath. They were going to need it climbing back up to the bridge.

'Remember the movie *Titanic?* Where they spent the whole time running up, down and around. This feels like a cheap remake,' Joe quipped.

'Least we ain't fucking sinking yet,' added Sara Jane.

'Yet!' repeated Jessica.

Dirty, greasy, sweaty and exhausted, they entered the bridge. 'Joe and Jessica, swap with Keith, we will need him on the computer, here, to disarm the program controlling the mine. Keith, you read?'

'Yes, General.'

'Bring the *Gazelle* alongside, you are our best hope of disarming this mine, swap with Jessica and Joe.'

'General,' interrupted Joe, 'I can be his eyes and ears and I can use one of the mobiles as a mobile hotspot so he can clone the screen here to the one on the *Gazelle*. By the time we climb back down, make the transfer, and Keith climbs back up here, you'll lose another thirty minutes we don't have.'

'Keith, will Joe's idea work?'

'Yes, General,' Keith replied, 'I'll come alongside, just off the bridge, so the signal doesn't have to travel far.'

Three minutes passed in silence. Joe opened the computer sitting on the Engineer's console. The login screen popped up. Joe began to search the desk, looking under the keyboard, then pulling out the drawers down the left-hand side like an ordinary office desk. No one could remember all their passwords, hopefully the Engineer was like most people and kept a list near his PC. He couldn't see anything in any of the drawers, so he knelt down and ran his hand across the underneath of the desktop. An envelope was taped to the underside of the desktop. Joe pulled it out. Inside was a list.

Joe unclipped his radio from his belt. 'Hey, Keith, I think I have found his passwords.'

'Great, I can actually see the wi-fi from here. Do you have a wi-fi login? I would think the Engineer would be in charge of the IT.'

'There's just a list, he hasn't identified which password is which,' replied Joe. Sitting at the Chief Engineer's console, Joe tried the first password on the list. It did not open the computer. 'Hey, Keith, try this one. It didn't work on the PC, "Shenandoah.2003". A bit basic but there is no one out here to steal your wi-fi.'

'Great, I'm in, but can you access the PC?'

'Got it, it was the second password. What now, Keith?'

'Joe, we need to find the program controlling the mine. Until we do, we can't risk deactivating it, as we don't know what booby traps are in the software. We trip one we could set off the mine prematurely. We'll assume the Engineer was the network controller, so his PC should access and control the server. Start with the task master, let's see what programs are running. Press CTRL-ALT-DELETE; a menu will come up and press Task Master. It should be the last option on the list.'

'Got it, Keith, two applications are running. One I think is the autopilot, and the second appears to be proprietary, not purchased, judging by the name, just some letters and a number.'

'Open the second program, let's see if we can read what it's doing. OK, I can see it now on my screen. Let's see if we can work out what it's controlling.'

A few minutes of silence, Keith could be heard over the radio tapping away at a keyboard.

'Fuck, not good.'

'What is it, Keith?'

'The program is redundant. It is definitely the controller for the mine, but once the instructions are passed down to the mine, they can't be reversed. The mine's timer can only be turned off at the mine. The mine is set for six hours and it will blow if it loses magnetic contact with the ship, so it can't be accessed. The course setting is controlled by the Auto-Helm software, and as long as we use the Auto-Helm program to steer the ship it will be OK to change direction. You will need to steer the ship through that computer and the Auto-Helm software.'

Joe realised the digital chart was calibrated in nautical miles, he factored this into his mental arithmetic, 'We are about a hundred nautical miles from the nearest point of the Australian coast, directly behind us. We are doing about fifteen knots. We need to run for the coast, no other way we can evacuate these people.'

'I believe you are right, Joe, and every second counts while we are heading the opposite direction.'

'Keith, begin the turn,' ordered the General.

Everyone held their breath, the *Shenandoah* began to turn, Joe watched the computer; the Auto-Helm was responding to Keith's commands while the program controlling the mine remained dormant.

'It's working, Keith.' They could all feel the movement of the ship change.

'It's the wind and sea,' Jessica observed. 'It's hitting us from the port rear quarter. We are getting a push from it, not bashing into it. Should be worth an extra knot or two until we get close to the coast.'

'*Shenandoah, Shenandoah*, this is HMAS *Hobart*, hove to and wait for us to board you, repeat, hove to and wait for us to board you.'

The General took a breath, picked up the microphone and pressed the talk button. 'HMAS *Hobart*, HMAS *Hobart*, this is General Anderson currently in command of the *Shenandoah*. Please contact NAVCOMM and have them contact Chief of the Defence Force, CDF. The *Shenandoah* is carrying human cargo and is booby trapped, we are running for the coast.'

'Understood *Shenandoah*. Understand we will be pursuing at flank speed, we will make contact with NAVCOMM and confirm your story. Stand by for a reply.'

'Understood and over. *Shenandoah* clear.'

The General clipped the microphone back to the helmsman's

console. 'Just after midnight, it will take a while for the chain-of-command to pass the message through to CDF. Then we will see what Marty has to say.'

'Marty'?

'Yes Joe, General Marty Jones, Chief of the Australian Defence Forces, my Commanding Officer. It should be an interesting conversation. Technically, I'm a Lieutenant General, he is the only full General in the Australian military. I'm also currently on leave, not officially on duty.'

'So, the question is not whether we are in the shit or not, but how deep we are in it?' asked Joe, a smile creeping onto the side of his mouth.

'I suggest you keep your chin up, son, so the shit stays out of your mouth,' replied the General. 'You might want to find a snorkel for when the Navy discovers we have stolen one of their newest toys.'

'Oh,' said Joe.

'Heading dead west, the following swell and wind have given us another two knots. The GPS is estimating about sixteen to eighteen knots, depends on whether we are on the face or back of a wave.' Jessica examined the digital chart and clicked on the coast of New South Wales. 'Five and a half hours to landfall, six hours until the *Hobart* catches us if she can hold thirty knots. But they will have time to organise a reception party for us.'

'We'll need to be gone by then,' added the General. 'What will happen when the mine blows. Any idea, Jodie?'

'Well, mines are designed to focus their ballast inwards, to not only pierce the hull, but damage internal bulkheads, so any closed watertight compartments adjacent to the blast will fail, thus increasing the pressure on the next bullhead and hopefully causing a chain reaction. This one is on the inside of the hull, and the ballast force is focused outward. All the watertight compartments are closed, so we will have a chance of containing the inflow of water. On the downside the structural integrity of the ship will be compromised, and especially at this speed she will quickly begin to break up. When that happens, we need a beach under the keel. Good news is the mine is remote from the fuel tanks so the oil spill should be minor.'

'Well, I can't see an alternative. Hopefully with six hours they can have the resources in place to clean up our mess,' reflected the General. 'But, I'm not going to leave these captives to die.' He paused for a minute. 'We'll need to assemble all the prisoners on the deck. No one can be below decks when the mine goes off. Any ideas on the numbers?'

'At least fifty, mostly women and children. That's my guess from our passes with the drone during daylight,' replied Keith.

'Right, Joe, keep watch on our course. Liaise with Keith. Keith, isolate the local network, deny the bad guys access. Everyone else start searching. We need to find as many lifejackets, or stuff we can use as buoyancy aides as possible. My guess is we are going to be woefully short. Stack it on the main deck level behind the door accessing the space where we saw the prisoners. At 4 am we'll need to muster the prisoners onto the main deck and work out a way to keep them alive if she blows before we make the coast.'

'Holy fuck, you need to see this?' Sara Jane's voice echoed round the bridge.

'Where are you, SJ?'

'On the fantail. You know the flat deck at the back. We just found this operating theatre, it's one deck below the main deck, in those rooms labelled "Utility Space" on the schematics. It gets worse, we found this fucking quack, he's an alco or a druggie, we couldn't wake the fuckwit up. He removes the organs for the black market.'

'Lock him in one of the cabins on the main deck and throw away the key. The recovery team can deal with him. Don't risk putting him with the others, they might try something when you open the door.'

'Oh fuck, oh fuck.'

'What's happened, SJ?'

'He's just made a run for it and dived over the back.'

Joe looked up from his position at the Engineer's console. 'Problem solved,' he muttered. He realised he was a changed man. Once he would have been shocked by such an attitude. Now, he understood, the Syndicate and its minions were dragging him down to their level.

'General, this is Keith.'

'Yes Keith.'

'Commander of the Defence Forces has requested contact with you. He is on the secure channel on the *Gazelle*. Would you like him patched through?'

'Thanks, Keith.'

A new voice boomed out of the bridge speakers.

'Lieutenant General Anderson,'

'Yes, General, sir.'

'Fuck Jon, you do have all the fun. NAVCOM's just woken me up, apparently you stole one of his top-secret toys and became a pirate? I suppose Fi's involved and Dr Teflon?'

'Yeah, you know how it is. One thing leads to another. Bad news is Fi was hurt, she's out at the facility by Bungendore, the last Attorney-General as well. It's to do with the Task Force I briefed you on last month,' replied the General.

'I'll drive out today and say g'day. I take it she'll be able to brief me?'

'Not on this last bit, but as soon as we are back, I will give you a full debrief.'

'You know this one's probably going to be a career killer?'

'Yeah, knew that all along, it's just one of those things. These arseholes cannot be dealt with in a civilised manner. They are just beyond it.'

'OK, Jon, take care, and watch out for your kids. I have the Prime Minister on the landline, I'll cover for you as long as I can.'

Joe, contemplated the General, 'Wow, always good to know your boss has your back!'

'He'll support us off the books as long as he can. But eventually there will be a reckoning. Marty's a good man. We went through a lot together. It was him, Fi and Fred a.k.a. Dr Teflon and myself for years, we were quite a team. Now I need a pint-size journo to rescue me from my own incompetence.'

'So now, he's the top dog, head of the Australian military?'

'Yes, he's the General, I'm a Lieutenant General, his second in command. I wouldn't want his job, it's all politics. Not that mine's much better. I only do this sort of thing during my annual leave. You know, a holiday from the paperwork. Though this little adventure will end my career, Fi's, plus Jodie's and Keith's,' chuckled the General. 'Even if we win, I'll never get away with flaunting the chain-of-command like this. Bit of a shit for Jodie and Keith. The rest of us will be taking "early retirement" or maybe a bit of "gardening leave", as we're all over the hill anyway.

'Shit.'

'What, General?'

'Fire, right up the bow. It's only small but we need to deal with it.'

Joe watched as the General walked out to the bridge wing. 'Everyone to the fantail,' he called over the radio.

Returning inside, 'Brightly, and most likely an ambush. Joe, come down, we split in two groups: one, to attack the fire, the other to defend the fantail. We don't want him accessing the stern castle.'

Joe was glad to leave the Engineer's console. There was nothing he could do, especially as Keith was remoted in from the *Gazelle*. Joe and General took the internal stairways, all four of them, down to the fantail where the rest of the team were waiting.

'Jodie, Tracey and myself will go forward. Hopefully we can flush Brightly out. Jessica, SJ and Joe, stay here and make sure he does not get past into the stern castle. All radios good? Check your battery charges. Also check your tasers and stun guns are still operational.'

Everyone checked their equipment. The General led the way round the left side of the stern castle, along the passageway and across the port gunwale to the bow. Looking over the stern, Joe was mesmerised by the phosphorescence lighting their wake behind them, like a spill of milk across a black sheet. Standing there he realised how tired he was. So tired he was seeing shadows move. Had someone or something moved by the lifeboat on the right-hand side?

Joe shook himself awake. He dared not say anything. He dared not move suddenly. But as he scanned slowly past the lifeboat's stanchions with his eyes, the only part of his being he dared move, he was sure there was more structure there than there should have been.

He thought for a minute. He wanted all three of them out of the sight line from the lifeboat.

'Let's go inside out of this breeze,' he said. As soon as he had backed towards the door and was passing the threshold, Jessica and Sara Jane followed.

Instead of crossing completely inside, Joe turned and flattened himself against the structure of the stern castle. He was out of any sight line from the starboard lifeboat.

'Don't look, but Brightly is hiding just around the corner by the starboard lifeboat,' Joe quietly told Jessica and Sara Jane.

'There's a good chance he is armed. He knew where the armoury was. He could have easily ducked into the conference room when he got away,' Jessica whispered.

Joe walked to the left side of the ship. He clicked on his radio's microphone, 'Hey, General, Brightly is hiding by the starboard lifeboat.'

'Received and understood. We'll deal with the fire then return down the starboard side, blocking his exit. I'll double click the radio when we have him trapped.'

'Understood.'

'Put the radio on the deck and turn around slowly.'

Joe dropped the radio on the deck and turned around slowly. Brightly was standing behind Jessica his arm crooked around her throat and a gun jammed up against her temple. It took Joe a moment to comprehend. Jessica and Sara Jane had been trying to follow his conversation with the General, and Brightly had used the moment to pounce, taking Jessica hostage.

'Where are you going to go, mate?' Joe asked quietly. 'Surrender and do a deal is your only chance.' Joe kept his voice down advancing slowly as he spoke.

'Fuck you,' Brightly responded, his voice nearly hysterical. 'We're heading west, I'll take this bitch and a lifeboat when we are near the coast. I'll be ashore and disappeared before your mates arrive.'

Brightly walked backwards towards the starboard rail, using Jessica as a shield. Joe and Sara Jane kept step with him. Brightly reversed up to the side rail of the ship, then started to slide forward along it towards the lifeboat station. Brightly was a tall man, so the rail pressed against the top of his thighs.

'We already have a reception committee waiting. This ship is being tracked by military radar. You'll walk right into an ambush. You have two options: surrender and live or run and die.' Joe spoke quietly so Brightly had to strain to hear him. As he spoke, he stepped towards the rear of the fantail. Brightly twisted, keeping Jessica between himself and Joe.

Joe kept his eyes focused on Brightly's eyes. From experience he knew stress could cause a person to focus on the problem. Joe wanted to be Brightly's problem.

'A smart guy like you, you'll be able to talk your way out of this. Kill a cop and they'll kill you.'

'You're fucking right I'll kill her. Stay where you are.'

Sara Jane was sliding along the rear wall of the stern castle, Joe had stepped further to the rear of the ship, Brightly had twisted further to the stern, centred on Joe.

Jessica started convulsing, Joe could see the twin lines joining her to Sara Jane's taser. Sara Jane was tasering her sister. The shuddering and convulsing caused Brightly to lose his grip and Jessica collapsed to the ground. Brightly waved his gun at Joe, as he took up tension on the trigger. He took the shot, and a second, both flying wide as he had not taken time to aim.

Sara Jane fired the second and third round from her taser, both sets of darts embedding themselves in Brightly, the gun flew from his hands and clattered along the deck as he fought to remain standing. Joe rushed in with his stun gun drawn, pushing the prod into Brightly's chest and pulling the trigger. Brightly staggered back against the rail, his upper body swaying overboard. The momentum of his head and shoulders pivoted his body further overboard; his arms juddering and unable to grip the rail, he tumbled silently over the side into the black sea rushing past below.

Joe rushed to Jessica's side, ripping out the darts from Sara Jane's taser as he did so. Jessica was paralysed on the deck for a couple of moments before struggling up into a sitting position. 'You fucking little bitch, you shot me with your taser. You missed Brightly completely.'

'I was aiming for you,' replied Sara Jane as a grin crossed her face. 'It was too tempting, I couldn't resist.'

Joe kept his mouth shut. Brightly shooting at him was nothing compared to intervening when Sara Jane and Jessica were having a disagreement.

'You fucking little bitch,' Jessica repeated, then paused. Quieter now she continued, 'You saved my life. You figured that if you zapped Brightly his muscles would contract firing the gun, which, wedged into my head, would have probably blown my brains across the deck.

'Now can someone help me up off this fucking deck?'

Joe took two strides and pushed his arms in under her arms, lifting her onto her feet. He turned Jessica around once she was standing and hugged her.

Boots could be heard thumping down the starboard accessway. Even their rubber soles couldn't hide the urgency as the General, Tracey and Jodie burst onto the scene.

'Where is he?' gasped the General.

Joe pointed over the side. The General glanced over, there was nothing to see.

The General picked up his radio microphone.

'Keith, search our wake, see if you can find any trace of Brightly. He went over the side, about two minutes ago.'

'Understood, will do. Keith clear.'

'I saw the splash. The cunt's gone,' explained Sara Jane.

The General paused for a minute, taking stock of the situation. 'Everyone up to the bridge.' He could see Jessica was beginning to shake. 'I saw the makings of coffee up there, and hopefully some cookies or something for a bit of a sugar hit. Then, you can take us through it.'

'Aye, aye, General.'

'Wrong service, Joe.'

The four flights of stairs to the bridge hurt. Joe had run out of adrenaline. He had run out of energy. Only the thought of caffeine and sugar drove him onwards and upwards. His companions were no better. Jessica needed some help as her strength slowly returned.

They entered the bridge. 'Lock the doors, the horse has probably bolted. I doubt there are any more bad guys roaming round, but lock them anyway.' He led the way to rear of the bridge where there was a kettle, a jar of instant coffee and a tin of cookies.

'Fuel up and hydrate, everyone, find a seat if you can, and catch your breath. Joe, is there any water in that fridge, we are probably all dehydrated. We still have three hours to go, and then we need an exit plan.'

'General, General, Keith,' sounded the speaker.

'Yes, Keith?'

'No sign of Brightly. Sonar did pick up a disturbance below the surface. Sharks follow this ship.'

'Understood, thanks Keith.'

The General clipped the microphone back to the console. No one spoke. They sipped their coffees, drank some water and nibbled on some chocolate chip cookies.

'We have to warn the prisoners. They all need to be on deck when the mine explodes. We don't want anyone trapped down below if it all goes wrong.'

'Joe, what if this tub starts sinking?'

'SJ, if we are still in deep water, we're up shit creek without a paddle.'

'Yeah, in a barbed wire canoe,' added Jessica.

'We found a dozen life jackets, we only have one lifeboat left, we have the *Gazelle* but that can only take a couple more once we are all on board,' Joe pondered, 'Yep the maths suck. We need to run this clusterfuck aground in case she breaks up when the mine goes off.'

The General thought for a moment. 'Have a look at the chart, it's all digitalised. We should be able to do a bit of time-on-distance calculation. How short are we going to be?'

'Line ball,' replied Joe, looking at the screen. 'The sea and wind are giving us a push. If they continue to the shore, we should just make it. If not, we could be short.'

'Whereabouts will we hit the coast?'

'Looking at the chart, our current course made good and projecting it forward, about halfway between Port Macquarie and Coffs Harbour. Around South West Rocks.'

Jessica looked at Sara Jane, 'We used to holiday there. If we can round the corner where the old jail is, there's a long sandy beach facing north. A heap of ships have ended up shipwrecked on it.'

Joe adjusted the screen on the digital chart. 'That works. We can't abandon the ship on the rocks, too many could die. But that beach looks perfect. We just have to adjust our course slightly to the north. The wind and waves will be more to our stern and should help push us up onto the beach.'

'Do it,' ordered the General. 'I'll call CDF and have him organise emergency services. The *Hobart* is still too far away to assist?'

'Even if we turned towards them, we would still be short, and we would need to transfer all the prisoners at sea. I don't see how we have a choice.'

'Thanks, Joe, looks like we'll make a sailor of you yet!'

'I can do the maths. It's keeping my lunch down, General, that's the issue.'

Another ten minutes passed in exhausted silence.

'Trace, you'll have to lead the muster. You're the only multilingual person we have.'

'OK, General, surely there's a PA system we can access from up here?'

'Good point. I have only been using the VHF to talk to Keith. Let's have a look at the helm station, see what we can find.'

Looking out from the well-lit bridge, it was impossible to penetrate the darkness outside. Examining the console, working outwards from the helm station, Joe and the General attempted to identify each switch.

'Here we are, over on the side, must be the Captain's station,' Tracey yelled from the left side of the bridge. She was holding a microphone attached to the ceiling console above what appeared to be an upmarket office chair fixed to the deck. Tracey climbed in the chair and pumped the height-adjustment lever. 'Even a short arse like me can see over the deck!' She clicked the mic open, 'Testing, testing. One, two, three.'

They all heard her voice booming across the deck below.

'Well done. So, Trace, have them all muster on the main deck in the quadrangle they have made with the containers.'

Tracey's voice boomed out across the deck again, 'Everyone on deck, repeat everyone on deck.' Then she repeated the message in three other languages.

'Any deck lights?' Joe asked her, assuming such controls would be near the controls for the PA system. Tracey started toggling some switches on and off. 'Not so fast, they may take a bit of time to light up.' Tracey flicked the switches to the on position and left them. One by one, floodlights popped on, the deck below emerging from the dark.

Joe stared down as the deck appeared from the darkness of the night. 'Look, people are coming out through those hatches cut into the tops of the containers. There must be some sort of living quarters below deck. Fuck, there are even more than we thought.'

'Joe, Jess and SJ, go down there, see if you can find some leaders or trustees. Last thing we want is a panicked mob on our hands.'

'No worries, General.'

'Jodie, keep watch from up here, advise Joe if you see any problems. First sign of trouble radio them, and Joe, Jess and SJ, you retreat through the hatch back into the stern castle. I'll come down and control the hatch. Remember, these people will probably think we are ship's crew, their tormentors. They may try and overwhelm us. Tracey, keep talking to them. They need to understand we are on their side.'

The General glanced at his watch. 'OK, just over two hours to go. Joe, go over the numbers again before we go downstairs.'

Joe moved the toggle on the plotter. 'Still touch and go but moving more to our favour. I think I have figured out how to put a waypoint off the beach so we can set the ship to turn automatically and run ashore.'

'Good work, Joe. Everyone, when the ship finishes its turn, we leave. The gangplank the supply ship used is still in place, we will board the *Gazelle* using it. By then, with dawn approaching, we should have a bit more light but not enough anyone from the shore will see the *Gazelle*.'

'They must drug the food or water,' Joe commented, 'They are so docile.'

Joe, Jessica and Sara Jane were assisting people forward and sitting them on the deck in rows facing the stern castle. The smell was overpowering. Joe shuddered to think of how these people would ever be rehabilitated. Most were of an Asian background, some looked like they originated from the Middle East or India. But most were so dirty and destitute their ethnicity could not be determined. A man approached Joe. He was pulling a woman along with him.

'Hey, mate,' the man slurred, 'help us. We were sailing between Sydney and New Zealand when they raided and sunk our yacht. Must have only been a couple of days ago'. Joe realised he was talking to an Australian. 'Most of these people were tricked by people smugglers into believing they were buying a ticket to Australia or New Zealand. Others, like us, they grab when the opportunity appears. But we can't find our daughters. They are only eight and ten. We woke up one morning and they were gone. We saw other men come aboard last night and fear they have been taken off the ship.' The man's wife raised her eyes, tears leaked out. 'They drug us, but I am bigger and it's only been a couple of days, so the dose hasn't affected me as much yet. Looking round there must be twenty kids missing.'

Joe looked around, he realised there were not many children. 'Shit,' he swore aloud, 'The supply ship. General, the supply ship, the kids'.

'On it. Thanks, Joe. I'll contact CDF, he'll make sure they are caught.'

'They may try to throw the kids overboard.'

'Shit, you're right. I'll use the secure channel through the *Gazelle*, and have them divert the *Hobart*.'

Joe turned to the couple, 'We'll do everything we can. Sorry if sounds inadequate, but they'll throw everything they have into saving those kids. But first we need your help, can you please gather everyone on deck.'

'It's like a hive below. They have joined all the containers together making bunk rooms. There are dunnies at the end. It's a fucking hell hole. We all have to be on deck as it's too hot below once the sun hits the deck.'

'Can you help us search?'

'I'll come with you, but leave my wife up on deck.'

'General, we are doing a sweep below deck.' Joe took his finger off the mic, 'What's your name?'

'Ben Stracham.'

'Mr Stracham will guide us.'

'Be careful, Joe. Radio's not going to work below deck.'

Joe, turned back to Mr Stracham, 'After you, mate.'

They clambered down a ladder. Joe, Jessica and Sara Jane switched on their torches. 'Fucking hell,'

Jessica gasped. 'The smell, the heat the dark. This must be worse than hell. Fuck me.'

'As the drugs wear you down you stop caring, you can't think for yourself, so you become worse than an animal. As the last onboard we are the most sentient but another day or two I would be like the rest.'

Joe staggered to one of the steel walls of the labyrinth; he lost his coffee and cookies. 'Fuck, shit, fuck,' he gasped.

They stumbled through, searching the ragged bedding for bodies. The ones they found, they forced up to the deck, where they would collapse.

Re-emerging into the night through another hatch, Joe turned to Stracham, 'You think that's everyone?'

'I think so.'

Joe thumbed his mic, 'We think we have them all, looks like a fucking hundred plus the missing kids.'

Tracey interrupted. 'I think I know why they have taken the kids off, we heard rumours of a slave auction coming up.'

'How would they get them there?'

'We couldn't nail down the details Joe. But the supply ship must be the first stage.'

'Everyone back to the bridge,' ordered the General.

'Not those fucking stairs again,' Jessica muttered under her breath.

The General held the door open for them as they re-entered the stern castle from the deck.

CHAPTER 76

They reconvened on the bridge.

The General immediately went to the radio, 'Keith, patch me through to CDF'. He took a deep breath while he waited.

'Lieutenant General Anderson, CDF here, proceed.'

'The small ship running from the *Hobart*, we believe she is carrying children as prisoners. Repeat carrying children as prisoners.'

'Thanks, Jon, we'll have the *Hobart* intercept her. Understand should you have a problem, she will not be available to help you.'

'Understood, Marty.'

'Also, there is a Ben Stracham on board. He said his family was snatched off their yacht a couple of days ago. His story will give us some hard evidence.'

'Copy that. Good luck, Jon. I'll go now and organise intercepting the supply ship. We'll use our RHIBS.'

'Thank you and clear.'

'What the fuck's a RHIB?'

'A Rigid Hulled Inflatable Boat. Basically, a fast interceptor. The *Hobart* will launch them while at full speed. They'll chase down the supply ship at forty knots, about eighty k's an hour. Looking at the radar they will be on board in ten minutes.'

Joe had followed the exchange, collapsed at the Engineer's station, sipping a bottle of water he had found in the bar fridge at the rear of the bridge. Jessica walked over to him. 'Feeling better?'

'That's the worst thing I have ever seen, smelt, heard or felt. It assaulted every fucking sense. Those missing kids are a worry.'

Tracey explained. 'I bet the crew of the supply ship don't even know. They were up in the conference room while we were hiding round the back. So *Shenandoah*'s crew must have moved them. The kids are worth a lot more if they are untouched, if you know what I mean. So, they wouldn't risk the supply ship's crew knowing about them.'

'Fuck,' replied Joe. He couldn't think of anything more articulate to say. He wandered over to the navigation plotter. They had been on deck for longer than he thought. 'The waypoint's coming up in twenty minutes or so. And we should have thirty-five minutes on the mine.'

The General looked at his watch. 'Joe, give us a warning every five minutes, then every minute for the last five. Keith, stand by, be prepared to come alongside once the turn is completed.'

They sat in silence; the throb of the engine could be felt relentlessly driving the ship to its doom. The freed captives were all seated on the deck, gently swaying with the movement of the ship, one or two having fallen over and returned to their slumbers on the hard deck.

'Fifteen minutes to waypoint,' Joe called from the plotter.

Silence again descended on the bridge.

Joe looked forward; the lights of a coastal town could be seen appearing slightly to the left of their course. It was as though a curtain was being drawn. Joe realised the headland was blocking the view of the town from the ship, but as they progressed north-west more of the headland slipped back, opening up the bay.

'Ten minutes to waypoint. The town's in view.'

He could now see the silhouette of the headland. He realised dawn was creeping up behind them.

Five minutes to waypoint.

'Keith, we are under five minutes to the turn.'

'On station, General.'

'Four minutes to waypoint.'

'*Shenandoah, Shenandoah*, this is *Hobart*, copy.'

'Copy,'

'General, our RHIBS have secured the supply ship and her cargo, will proceed to Port Macquarie. Cargo is intact repeat cargo is intact. *Hobart* clear.'

'Those kids are safe.'

'Fucking excellent.'

'Up and be ready to move people.'

'Three minutes,' intoned Joe.

'Unlock the door, Trace.'

'Two minutes.'

A pause.

'One minute'

They gathered round the plotter, alternately staring at it and the glimmer of the sandy beaches ahead and to their left. The steering toggle leaned to the left, the bow began to turn.

A hammer blow slammed the ship. They were bounced off their feet. Immediately a second blow landed.

'Fuck, fuck, fuck, there were two mines,' yelled Jodie. 'The second must have been in the bilge under the engines.'

'We're still moving forward. But we're still turning.'

The radio crackled. 'General, this is Keith. Two waterspouts erupted: one just in front of the stern castle, the second from under the stern.'

Groans and shudders could be felt traversing the length of the ship. Sirens, bells and flashing lights were erupting from the Engineer's station.

Joe watched the plotter and the beach ahead. 'She's not straightening up, the rudder must be locked over, we're going to keep turning and run up the inside of the headland instead of into the bay.' Joe looked out the left side bridge window. 'It's still a sandy beach but there's a bit of a wave.'

'General,' the speakers boomed, 'The gangway's gone, the explosion dislodged it.'

'Thanks, Keith. Get out of here. Start heading to Sydney. Bring the *Gazelle* in, after midnight. We'll rendezvous back at the base. Any ideas, people?'

'The lifeboat, the right side one, it will be on the side away from the breaking waves.'

The ship groaned and shuddered again. Joe raced over to the engineer's station. LEDs were flashing on a schematic of the ship built into the console. Some were green, others were flashing red. He studied for a moment or two relating the lights to the site of the explosion.

'The watertight doors are going one by one.'

Then there was silence. Joe looked again. The engine room was now showing a red light. 'I think the engines have flooded.' He turned to the bridge. The bow was still swinging to the turn. Now, to his left, walls of white water could be seen marching towards the ship. 'We're losing way. But we have entered the point break. It'll push the ship towards shore.' The lights flickered and went out, the instruments died one by one as the LED lights lost power.

They were all thrown forward.

'That's it, people. We are on the bottom. Time to leave.'

The General led the way out of the bridge and down the four flights of stairs for the last time, out onto the fantail and to the right side of the ship.

The bulk of the ship protected the lifeboat. They launched and the General steered them across the beach front, around a breakwater and into the mouth of a river. The town of South West Rocks faced the surf beach, the river flowed behind it. As the town awoke and stared at the ship beached across the bay, the General piloted the lifeboat into a berth at a small marina on the river behind the town.

Joe secured the lines and the six of them followed the pier to the shore. A late model people-mover pulled up. It had Army plates. A private soldier exited the vehicle and approached the group. He saluted Joe, 'Lieutenant General Anderson, your vehicle, sir.'

He handed Joe the keys. They watched the private walk away into town. 'Maybe I've been undercover for too long, even my own guys can't recognise me,' quipped the General. 'Let's get the fuck out of here before anyone askes any questions.'

'I wonder how the debrief's going?' Joe asked the room.

No one answered, everyone assumed it was a rhetorical question.

They had returned to their base. Jessica and the General had arranged a debrief with the Federal Attorney-General and the committee guiding the Task Force. It had been two days with no word. The team were staying off the grid until they heard.

Keith was watching the security monitor. 'There's a vehicle approaching. I believe it's them.'

'I'll go open the gate.' Joe jogged out to the back door where he had left the quad bike, fully charged, awaiting the return of their emissaries.

Tyres were heard crunching over gravel and then the door opened. Four people entered.

'Mum!' Jodie and Keith exclaimed, rushing to greet the extra person.

'How'd it go?'

'Hang on a sec, Trace, just gotta use the loo and grab a beer. Five minutes,' replied the General.

Joe busied himself retrieving some cold beers from the refrigerator. The others were standing round, too eager to hear the news to sit and relax. Minutes later the General reappeared, followed shortly by Jessica. Joe handed them each a beer.

The General took up position behind the counter.

'The bad guys: Brightly's dead. We had the sonar examined from the *Gazelle* and there is no doubt, if the fall didn't kill him the sharks did. The rest of the crew that survived, and the supply ship crew, have been taken to a secure facility. The three trustees from the facility will join them. The psychologists are trying to rehabilitate them but don't see much hope. The other prisoners from the facility are recovering well and are expected to be able to return to their normal lives. As you know the children were all recovered from the supply ship. The rest of the prisoners from the *Shenandoah* are still being processed. It will take a while for some of them as they are undocumented. The committee feels we have pushed the Syndicate out of Australia at this time. When they will be back is unknown. The Attorney-General is going to push for greater transparency and accountability. The Syndicate needs a corrupt environment to thrive. The Attorney-General has committed to denying it that environment.'

'For us, Fi is back.'

Everyone stood and cheered.

'But,' the General continued, 'The four of us are no longer officially with the Defence Forces. The whole borrowing of the *Gazelle*, and asking afterwards, was apparently against government policy. I am too old for this shit anyway, but it is a blow to Jodie and Keith.'

Joe stood and walked to the counter. 'Thanks, General, we also have some news. I'll have Trace explain.'

Tracey took Joe's place. 'Joe and I have been in discussion with my boss. Joe has transferred all the funds we stole from the Syndicate to the organisation I work for. The bitcoin drain he organised is also still working, though the Syndicate is slowly regaining control over it. This has two huge bonuses. We are now independent of the UN to a greater degree and the Syndicate's investigations will lead to my organisation not Joe. Something both my boss and Joe are very happy about! They have also agreed to base themselves on this property. What else, Joe?'

'Thanks Trace. I kept some funds for us. I'll divide it up evenly between us. If you don't want it feel free to donate the money to a charity of your choice. Also, seeing the evil that corruption lets in the door, I have used some of the funds to set up a corporation, overtly as Forensic Accountants, covertly as a means to chase down shitheads flying under the radar like Brightly and his mates. Jess will be a partner and SJ a consultant. The rest of you are welcome to join should you wish. Now my eyes have been opened to the crap that's out there I can't just walk away.'

'So, where the fuck do you start?'

'Well, to start with SJ, your sister's going to teach me how to sail a boat.'

*

'Keep her on the wind, Joe.'

'Aye, aye, Jess.'

'Better. But tell me, why did you buy Brightly's yacht?'

'It looked like fun, and I'm pretty sure he won't be using it any time soon. Some nice wine he had hidden in the bilge as well. And, playing with his toys, drinking his fine wine, while he rots in hell, was the best "fuck you" I could think of.'

'I didn't know you believed in the afterlife?'

'Yeah, maybe wishful thinking.'

Joe was learning to sail; Jessica was revisiting her previous career as a sailing instructor.

'Trace is pregnant from when they raped her; her and SJ are going to marry, and they are going to bring up the kid together. Mum's over the moon and Dad's confused.'

'Wow, that makes two weddings. Fred rang and invited us to his daughter and Keith's wedding.'

'Aren't the bride and groom supposed to do the inviting?'

'Yeah, Fred got a bit over enthusiastic.'

They rounded the point; Joe rounded the yacht up into the wind and they dropped the sails. The sea breeze made the water glisten as they turned into the late afternoon sun and motored towards the marina.

A small group was standing at the head of the berth: a man, a woman and two young girls. The man took their lines. The woman glowed with happiness, while the two girls appeared tentative and shy. Joe thought he knew them but couldn't place them. They were out of context somehow.

'You two are hard to find. We met Lieutenant General Anderson at the inquiry, and his wife gave you two up. You obviously don't recognise us all cleaned up, but I'm Ben Stracham and we cannot begin to thank you for what you did.'